DEATH BENEFITS

DEATH

BENEFITS

A NOVEL

Thomas Perry

RANDOM HOUSE
NEW YORK

Copyright © 2001 by Thomas Perry

All rights reserved under International and Pan-American Copyright Conventions. Published in the United States by Random House, Inc., New York, and simultaneously in Canada by Random House of Canada Limited, Toronto.

RANDOM HOUSE and colophon are registered trademarks of Random House, Inc.

Library of Congress Cataloging-in-Publication Data
Perry, Thomas.
Death benefits / Thomas Perry.
p.   cm.
ISBN 0-679-45305-9
1. Insurance investigators—Fiction. 2. San Francisco (Calif.)—Fiction.
3. New Hampshire—Fiction. I. Title.
PS3566.E718 D43 2001
813'.54—dc21   00-041476

Printed in the United States of America on acid-free paper
Random House website address: www.atrandom.com

2 4 6 8 9 7 5 3
First Edition

Book design by Caroline Cunningham

To Jo, Alix, and Isabel

DEATH BENEFITS

I

Ellen leaned forward over the sink and took a last, critical look at her makeup in the bathroom mirror. She could see that the eyes were good. The way to look trustworthy was to look trusting, and her eyes seemed big and blue and wide-open. The color on the cheeks was good, too: she could tell it was clear, smooth, and natural, even though the mirror was pocked with black spots, and the light in here was harsh and yellow. But she intended to be there early enough to slip into the ladies' room, do a recheck, and make any necessary revisions before she was seen. She had been training herself not to take anything for granted since she was nine years old, and she was twenty-four now. Not to anticipate problems was to invite them.

She went back into her kitchen, picked her purse off the table, and slung it over her shoulder, then opened her thin leather briefcase to be sure she had everything. She always carried a small kit consisting of the brochures and forms necessary to commit a customer to one of the common policies: term life, whole life, health, home owner's, auto. Before she had left the office last night, she had added some of the more exotic ones to cover art, jewelry, planes, and boats. The application forms she carried always had her name typed in as agent, with her telephone extension and office and e-mail addresses in the other boxes, and her signature already in the space at the bottom. She never left the home office in doubt about who should get the commission.

Clipped to the inside of her briefcase she carried a slim gold pen that felt good in a customer's hand when he signed his name, and she kept an identical one, never used, out of sight below it so there could never be a moment when she was ready to close on a customer and couldn't. Taking a few simple, habitual precautions was usually enough to keep her from lying in bed at night worrying about lost opportunity, failure, and humiliation.

She reached into the other side of the divider in her briefcase, pulled out the claim forms she had prepared, and examined them. She was not proofreading the entries. She knew there were no mistakes. She had been up late, studying the files, filling in the blank spaces on the forms with a typewriter, so there would be no real paperwork left to do. This morning she used the forms to test her memory of family names, addresses, dates.

She had no illusion that she was engaged in anything but an act of dissimulation. It was conscious, studied, and practiced, and anything less than a flawless performance would be a disaster. When she had all the personal details by heart it made her listener feel as though she cared about him. Having them wrong was to be caught out as a hypocrite and a fraud. If she convinced her listener that she cared—really had his interests at heart—then she was not halfway there, she was all the way.

Ellen made sure the coffee was unplugged and the lights were all off before she went out the door and locked it. As she turned, she heard a sudden noise over her shoulder and jumped. She stared in the direction of the sound, and decided it was nothing—just an orange falling from the tree in the corner of the yard. But it was still an hour before the sun would be up, and even Pasadena could be a bit creepy in the darkness and silence.

She knew that if she screamed, she couldn't expect the other four girls who lived in the small apartments in this building to come to her rescue, but they would at least wake up and look out their windows to see what was going on. If somebody grabbed her, she must not rely on her neighbors' altruism. She must yell "Fire!" while she fought. She had read that this was what the experts advised, and so that was what she would try to do.

She wished she weren't feeling so jumpy. For the past two days she had been increasingly anxious, and the discomfort seemed to have gotten more vivid this morning. She had to remind herself that this was not something to be afraid of. It was an opportunity. If she used it well, it was a step toward getting everything she wanted.

She looked down the empty driveway at the street, then stepped toward the open garage where her car was parked, and took the time to check and be sure the car was locked. This compulsion to check everything made her a bit ashamed. She had not just been worrying about accomplishing what she had to do this morning. She had been having feelings that something was wrong. At times, she had detected the sensation that someone was watching her. Yesterday she had been walking down the street in Old Town, looking in shops not far from the office, and had sensed eyes on her. She had stopped abruptly, pretending to look in a store window, and studied the sidewalk behind her in the reflection. She had waited until the other pedestrians had walked past her and had determined that they all appeared harmless before she moved on. She had told herself that she had just sensed some man staring at her. They did that, after all, and they meant no harm. But she had not convinced herself: when they meant no harm, they were always easy to catch. They wanted to be caught.

She made her way down the driveway to wait for the cab to arrive. She glanced at her watch. It was still not even five A.M. There was no reason to feel impatient. The cab wasn't late; she was early. Probably she had been spending too much time alone lately.

She defended herself from her own accusation. The isolation had not really been her fault. Even after a year here, the people in the Pasadena office were still the only people she knew in southern California. She had seen at the beginning that none of them were likely to become close friends. At best they were allies, and at worst they were obstacles, fixed objects she would have to work her way around. To get what she needed, she would have to deceive them about her feelings, keep certain information she picked up away from them, and use it to her advantage, all the while smiling and evading. She had done that. No wonder she was nervous.

She stared up the dark street, searching for headlights. In the heavy stillness of the residential neighborhood, she could hear distant engine sounds at the far end of the next block, where the street met Colorado Boulevard. Every few seconds, a car or truck would swish past the intersection, but none of them made the turn. The faintness of the sounds reminded her of how alone she was.

She had read an article in a women's magazine that said if a person had a feeling—an uneasy intuition that something was wrong, that a man she was with made her uncomfortable, that a place made her feel vulnerable—she should not ignore it. Her eyes had probably seen something, her ears had probably heard something, but her mind was trying to brush it aside and explain it away because denial was easier than facing the danger.

Ellen caught herself forming a clear mental image of John Walker. She could see his dark brown hair, his calm, wise eyes. She was sure it was the uneasiness that had brought him back. When she had been with him, she had always felt safe. It was not just because he was tall and broad-shouldered and physically fit. He had a quiet, thoughtful manner, and he was reliable. She felt a sharp pang that surprised her. She could have been with him—maybe not married him, because that would have ruined everything, but at least had him nearby. Driving over here before dawn to pick her up was exactly the sort of thing he would have done, and she would have known—positively known—that he would be here on time. She made an effort to push him out of her mind and obscure his image in her memory. The worst thing for a person to worry about was some decision she had made in the past.

She saw a pair of headlights turn off Colorado, took in a deep breath, and waited. The car passed under the first street lamp so she could see the white bar on the roof. It was the taxi. She let the breath out in relief. The cab began to make its way up the quiet street slowly. The driver must be searching for her house number, but he wasn't even on the right block yet. She stepped down to the street and waved her arm in the air. He didn't seem to be able to see her yet. He was still crawling along. How could he not see her? It was as though he were looking at every house, every stretch of sidewalk, to reach her by the process of elimination.

The cab crept to a stop at the end of the driveway. From here she could not see the driver's face, only a pair of big hands on the wheel in the soft glow from the dashboard. She hesitated. She reminded herself that she was being childish. She had called for a cab and here it was—she glanced at her watch—and it was actually early. The rest was just her overheated imagination.

She stepped toward the back seat of the cab, but the man didn't get out to open the door for her. He only waved his hand in a "get on with it" gesture. She pulled open the door, got in, and pulled it shut.

"I'd like to go to the airport, please."

"I know," he muttered irritably.

She began to regret calling a cab. It was a decision she had reached two days ago. She had made the call right away to reserve the cab, then repeated it this morning in case they forgot. She had meant to keep herself free and unencumbered this morning, but she could have driven her own car down there. A cab meant relinquishing control, and this driver was not very pleasant. At least the traffic would be light at this hour, so it wouldn't take very long. She could collect her thoughts before she had to start being convincing.

The cab pulled away from the curb and moved down the street. A few seconds later, she noticed that the back of the driver's head was easier to see, and then the mirror threw a bright reflection across his eyes. She saw him squint for a moment before he flipped the mirror up so the reflected glare was cast on the ceiling. Another car was behind them. She was surprised. She had not seen any car come off Colorado since the taxi had arrived, and she was almost sure she would have noticed if any of her neighbors had slammed a car door or started an engine in the silence.

The glow from behind did not go away, and ugly possibilities began to float into the front of her mind. She had heard that cab drivers who worked in the hours of darkness often got robbed. She had always imagined them being robbed because they were alone. But why wouldn't a robber strike when there was a passenger in the car? Certainly he would get more money, and she couldn't stop him. She looked at the back of the driver's head. He must know that he was a potential victim, but he didn't seem to be concerned. He did glance in the side mirror now and then, as though to verify that nothing had changed.

She waited for the driver to make the first turn, then another to head back toward Colorado, and looked behind. The car was still there. It had fallen back a bit, but it had not gone away. The driver turned again, and she waited. She counted to ten slowly, then extended it to twenty. The lights were visible again. Then it occurred to her that there was a reason why this might be happening, and she felt foolish for not thinking of it before. She worked for a big company in a competitive business. For over a year, she had been polite but aloof with her supervisors and colleagues. She had worked alone, developed her own leads, and pursued them. She had been earning commissions that were multiples of the ones other salespeople made. She had told her boss two days in advance that she would not be in today, because she was meeting a client. She had told him too much. She was amazed at herself for being surprised. Big companies spied on their employees all the time. Would it be so strange if the company had her followed?

She looked back. The car followed them onto the freeway entrance. "That car has been behind us a long time."

The driver said, "Really? I didn't notice." He looked into the side mirror again and shrugged. "Probably a cop."

"No," she said. "I don't think so. It's a compact car."

He was silent for a few seconds. "A lot of times, people who aren't sure where the airport is see a cab and follow. This time of day, you take a cab, that's probably where you're going."

It made no sense to her. He seemed to think she was a fool, and that made her panicky. "I know it's probably nothing, but it gives me the creeps. Can you please lose him?"

"How? We're on a freeway!"

"I don't know. Take an exit, then get back on, I guess. Nothing illegal or dangerous. I'll give you an extra twenty."

He looked behind, then pulled off the freeway at the next exit, went down the street a half block, and headed up the entrance ramp and back onto the freeway.

Ellen looked ahead for the car, then looked behind, and watched the ramp until the freeway curved and she could not see it anymore. No other car seemed to follow. She sat back and relaxed. "I think it worked."

The car radio crackled and buzzed, and she could hear a man's voice under the static. "Larry, where you at now?"

The driver lifted his microphone and held it so close to his mouth that Ellen could hear the amplified sound of his lips brushing it while he murmured, "Still on the One-ten south, heading for LAX." He fiddled with a dial on the radio. There was a lot of squawking and crackling, so that Ellen couldn't hear the dispatcher's next words, but she heard the driver say, "Okay."

She looked at the cars going nearly the same speed in the lane beside her, held there where she could study them. She was trying to see inside and speculate about who the passengers might be and where they were going. But in a moment the one she was staring at was slipping ahead, and the next two simply glided past. She looked over the driver's shoulder. He was slowing, pulling onto a freeway exit.

"Where are we going?"

"Got to pick somebody else up on the way. One of our cars broke down, and the guy's going to the airport too."

She looked at the dim, ugly, unfamiliar street that had replaced the freeway. They were passing through an area that seemed to be nothing but small stores with iron grating across the doors and windows, and a few larger buildings that were old and seemed to have some industrial purpose. She knew that the car breaking down was a lie. Mechanical breakdowns were a code, a vague, almost tactful thing that people in the transportation business said to silence people they felt were not entitled to an explanation. "You know," she began, "I'm sorry, but I don't feel comfortable with this. I don't want to share the cab. Please take me to the airport, and come back for him."

"No, I'm sorry," said the man, mimicking her tone exactly. His voice turned sharp and angry. "I'm within a couple blocks of his place. This is a good customer. I can't just stiff a regular customer for somebody I never saw before."

She felt as though she had been slapped. She tried to think of a tactic that would work. If she said "Let me out," it would mean marooning herself in this deserted industrial area alone before dawn. Probably the reason the regular customer had to be served was that few cabs ever came down here—might not even be willing to come. She was also a bit embarrassed because she had asked the driver to lose the car that had followed. She was aware that he already thought she was a stupid, hysterical woman. She sat in silence, trying to decide what to say, her eyes beginning to water.

The driver pulled to a stop at a red light where the street crossed a major thoroughfare. She looked out the window and craned her neck, trying to find a street sign that might tell her where she was. She could not see one, but she did see something else. It was a dull yellow cab, stopped at the curb on the cross street, where there was a lighted doorway of a tiny doughnut shop. As she watched, a pudgy middle-aged man came out the door, already eating a doughnut and drinking a cup of coffee he must have bought in the shop. He stepped around the front of the cab to the driver's side and set his cup on the hood.

She decided. She swung the door open, slipped out of the cab, and slammed it shut. The driver's reaction was to make a tardy grab for her arm. That made his cab lurch forward a couple of feet, then stop with a screech so that it rocked on its squeaky shock absorbers. "Hey!" His voice was muffled, but he pushed a button to open the passenger window. "What the hell are you trying to do?"

She pushed three twenty-dollar bills through the open window onto the passenger seat. "I'm taking another cab."

He yelled, "You can't do that!"

She said, "I'm not cheating you, I'm just leaving," turned, and stepped toward the other cab. She walked with her head up, feeling pleased with herself for speaking quietly and not relinquishing her dignity. She could see the pudgy cab driver chewing and watching her, so she made sure her performance was good. When she was near enough, she said, "Would you be able to take me to the airport?" It was only after she had said it that it occurred to her he might say no.

He nodded and swallowed. "Sure."

There was a loud blare of a horn, and Ellen looked back to see the cab she had just left still in the intersection. The driver twisted in his seat to look out the rear window. The light had changed, and there was a truck behind him. Reluctantly, he glared in Ellen's direction, then accelerated ahead to get out of the way and disappeared behind the building on the corner.

The new driver said, "Have a problem with the other cab?"

"Sort of."

"If you have his number, you can report him."

"It's nothing like that," she said. "I need to get to the airport, and he was taking me out of the way to pick up another person. I didn't get his number anyway."

He got in and started the engine. "Don't worry. We'll get you there." He carefully set his coffee into the drink holder beside him, and stuffed the rest of his doughnut into his mouth.

Ellen slipped into the back seat, and they were on the 105 freeway in a few minutes. Her heart began to beat hard. It was the same sensation she had felt the only time she had been in a car accident. Her heart had begun thumping like this, not during, but after the accident, when the danger was already past, and she had time to think about how suddenly and unexpectedly it had come. She consciously relaxed her body, closed her eyes, and breathed deeply until she felt better. When she opened them again, the driver had brought them onto the San Diego Freeway, and she recognized the stretch ahead.

When the driver came off the freeway on the long, straight ramp at Century Boulevard, he said, "What airline?"

"Just drop me at the Hilton Hotel," she said. "It's up ahead. On the right."

The driver was mildly surprised, and a bit confused, but it was not the sort of confusion that required him to ask the young woman any questions. He knew where it was. He knew all the major hotels. He pulled up into the circular drive, got out to open her door and accept his payment and tip. He got in again, recorded the fare in his log, then picked up his radio mike to call in, and let his eyes follow the young woman through the glass doors of the lobby. He watched her until she disappeared. Then he drove out onto Century Boulevard and maneuvered into the Arrivals lane of the airport entrance. At this hour, he was probably going to spend a lot of time in the taxi staging area, waiting for his turn to drive up and take on a fare. After he got there, he was still wondering.

She had been angry, and maybe just a little bit afraid of the other cab driver. He knew she was not the sort of person to argue about the cost, because she had given him an unusually generous tip, so she had probably told him the truth about the driver trying to double up on her and make her late.

On the other hand, everything else had been a lie. She had said the airport, but really wanted to go to a hotel. When he had heard where she was really going, he'd decided she had to be some kind of businesswoman on the way to a breakfast meeting, with that briefcase and all. Everything about her implied that she was meeting some big executive who had flown in from somewhere, and she was here to sell him something before he flew out again. That impression had only lasted a minute. When she had gone into the lobby, she had not gone to the front desk. She hadn't gone to the concierge's table to pick up the phone and tell somebody she was here. She hadn't gone to the dining room. She had walked straight to the elevators to head upstairs.

Nobody wore a suit like that to go to a hotel for an affair, and he had never seen anybody arrive for that purpose at five-thirty A.M., either. That convinced him. This young woman had done everything possible to make this look like business, so it wasn't business. After all, what else was upstairs but people's hotel rooms? And changing cabs on impulse was a pretty good way to be sure you had not been followed by some private detective trying to prove you were fooling around.

He thought the incident through one more time, to be sure he had not misinterpreted any of the evidence, and was satisfied, but not glad. He had instinctively liked that young woman from the moment when he had seen her jump out of the other cab and walk up to him, trying to look sure of herself. He hoped she had not gotten herself into something that she would regret when she was a little older, but he supposed she probably had. Everybody seemed to make a few mistakes after they looked grown up, and then really grew up while they were trying to make up for them. He pronounced a silent benediction on her and turned his attention to the airport dispatcher, who was already waving him forward. After that he was busy, and the young woman left his thoughts and then his memory. It was as though she had stepped into that elevator, and it had carried her out of the world.

2

"He's asking people questions," Maureen Cardarelli announced. She sat still, her eyes wide and expectant, waiting for Walker's reaction.

"Like what—'Can Cardarelli be trusted?' "

Her eyes took on a half-closed, suspicious look that still managed to be oddly seductive, her face lowered so a curtain of coal-black hair would fall to place it in half-shadow. "He hasn't talked to you?"

"No," said Walker. "Maybe he can tell I'm busy." He let his eyes move significantly in the direction of the pile of papers on his desk, then back to meet hers.

She said with slow malice, "Odd that he hasn't said anything to you, of all people."

"Why me?" Walker pretended that her uncharacteristic lack of subtlety had not made his mind stall for an instant while he searched his memory for guilty secrets.

She shrugged and stood up, then said, "It's a big building. Lots of departments, lots of places to camp out, but he seems to like it near you." She smiled indulgently to imply that it had been a playful slap and he was still one of her closest confidants. "Well, I'd better let you go back to sleep."

Walker watched her walk to the opening of his cubicle and spin around the corner to take her first few steps in that special way she had. It was at once too graceful to be conscious and too efficient and purposeful to be anything else. As she walked toward the elevators, everything from the set of her shoulders to the *pock-pock-pock* of her high heels on the terrazzo floor insisted that she was on a mission of importance.

Walker tried to force himself to return to his work. He looked down at the stack of handwritten papers on his desk, then surveyed the figures on his computer screen, but he could not keep his eyes from moving warily over the top of the monitor. There was Max Stillman again, just to the left of the opening in Walker's cubicle, sitting at a desk in the open office everyone called "the bay," surrounded by young typists and phone reps. Several times Walker had noticed, always with surprise, that Stillman was not an exceptionally large man. What he had was the curious quality of conveying mass and solidity, as though he were something very large that had been compressed into a dense, volatile object.

Stillman appeared to be about fifty, with more gray at his temples than brown, and a hint of gleaming cranium under thin wisps of hair on top. He hunched over the desk with his thick forearms resting on either side of an open file, his eyes fixed on it with cold concentration. He would sometimes glare at a page for five seconds, then set it aside and move to another one, and at other times he would sit, unmoving, for fifteen minutes. When he reached the end of a file, he would always close the folder, place it neatly on the stack at the right corner of the desk, and replace it with a file from the pile on the left.

Stillman had materialized nearly a week ago like something that had been conjured, already standing halfway down the center aisle of the bay just at noon, when the first shift of specialists and clerks and receptionists was streaming past him toward lunch. He seemed not to watch for anyone or even to pay much attention to them. He looked, Walker had thought, like a man standing in a room by himself, preoccupied with trying to remember something.

Walker still considered himself the first person to have noticed Stillman, although he knew that was nearly impossible. It would be very difficult for a stranger to make his way past the guards in the lobby, all the way to the seventh floor of the San Francisco office of McClaren Life and Casualty, without being asked some questions. This was headquarters, the spot where the firm had originated nearly a hundred and fifty years ago, and not a field agency: nobody sold insurance here. Walker had stepped out of his cubicle, smiled reassuringly, and said, "Can I help you, or give you directions, or something?"

Stillman's eyes had darted to Walker's face with an abrupt movement that had the alertness of a bird of prey, but his body had not stirred. An expression that was not quite friendly, but that Walker had interpreted as unthreatening, had come over his face. "Name's Stillman. Did McClaren tell you to expect me?"

Walker had grinned. "McClaren?" He had to remind himself that it was not a ridiculous idea. He sometimes forgot that there actually was a Mr. McClaren, and rumor had it that he spent most days in an office five floors above them.

Stillman nodded. "Right."

Walker had said, "He may have had someone call my supervisor. I'll take you there."

Stillman had followed Walker to the corner office. Joyce Hazelton had been standing at her window, staring out at the array of tall buildings across Van Ness Avenue, when Walker knocked. She had spun around, a distracted expression in her eyes.

Walker had not seen that she was on the telephone, because the receiver had been hidden by her dark hair, and the cord had been in front of her. "Sorry," he'd said from the doorway, but he'd heard her say, "I think he's here now . . . Mr. Stillman?"

Stillman had nodded. "Yes, ma'am."

She had said, "Mr. McClaren wondered if you had a minute to talk to him." She had handed Stillman the phone, then put her arm around Walker's shoulder to propel him out of the office with her, and closed the door behind them. She'd stood outside her own office for a few seconds, and the novelty of it had made Walker consider asking her who Max Stillman was, but the impulse had lasted only a moment, because her manicured hand had made a little sweeping motion to shoo him toward his desk.

He had turned and gone back. The day's figures for payouts in the casualty end of the business made a difference, but the unannounced arrival of some old rich buddy of the current McClaren was like a cloud passing a mile above him. There had been a shadow for a few seconds while it was overhead, but it had moved on.

When Walker had returned from lunch, Stillman had been planted at the unoccupied desk in the open bay that was usually reserved for temporary workers, and Joyce Hazelton had been scurrying around gathering piles of reports and policy files. Walker had taken a couple of steps closer to offer help, but she had acknowledged him with a perfunctory smile and given her head a little shake.

Late that afternoon, Bill Kennedy had slipped into Walker's cubicle to deliver the morning's figures from the field. "He's still out there, I see."

Walker had brought himself back from the structured, silent, logical world of statistics. "Who?"

Kennedy's voice had gone lower. " 'What bear?' huh? Good strategy, John. That's why possums rule the earth."

Walker had glanced over his computer monitor into the vast, open office. Stillman was glaring down at another file. "He's just some friend of Mr. McClaren's."

"He's a spy."

"On what?"

"On whom. On us. It's got to be. Accounting just cut a check for him. It's a hundred thousand, listed on the system as 'Security Expense.' "

Walker had shrugged. "Maybe he's going to overhaul the computer system so your twelve-year-old nephew can't break in and peruse the physical exams of actresses anymore."

Kennedy had shaken his head in pity. "Take a look. Is that a computer geek? No. That's what repressive governments send out if the general's daughter doesn't come home from the prom."

Walker had looked at Kennedy wearily. "And why do you suppose this stranger showed up in our peaceful village? Could it be that they hired him to find out who the village idiot is, and watch him rushing from hut to hut raving and talking wild?"

"Good point." Kennedy had smiled as he stepped off, then called back, "Sorry, got to get these figures delivered."

During the next few days, Walker had found that he was receiving more frequent visits from acquaintances in other departments. The men tended to step into his cubicle and move uncomfortably close to Walker's shoulder, where they could pretend to look down at something he was showing them on his desk or computer screen, then raise their eyes slightly to stare at Stillman without being caught. The women were more subtle. They would sit in the only visitor's chair, in the corner where Stillman couldn't see them, and simply watch Walker's eyes to see if Stillman did anything unusual while they fished for information.

Walker didn't have any. "If he's a security consultant, I assume he's here to make us more secure, right? So feel secure."

Marcy Wang stood and stared into his eyes as she drifted toward the door of his cubicle. "He's here to make whoever paid him feel secure. I didn't pay him, and neither did you."

This time, as Walker's eyes returned to his work, they passed across Stillman. He was alarmed to see that this time Stillman was not in profile, bent over the desk he had commandeered. He was half-turned in his swivel chair, staring frankly at Walker. Their eyes met for a heartbeat before Walker was able to nod nonchalantly and force his gaze down to the safety of his papers.

Each morning for the next three days, when Walker sat in the tiny kitchen of his apartment waiting for the coffee to drip through the machine, he remembered Stillman and felt uneasy. He thought about him as he dressed and drove to work, hoping he would be gone. Then he took the elevator to the seventh floor, discovered that Stillman was there again, hung his coat on the single hanger on the wall of his cubicle, and tried to obliterate him by concentrating on his work until nightfall.

Walker had worked for McClaren's for only two years, beginning the summer after he had graduated from college. When he was a junior, he had entertained a vague notion of working a year and then going to law school, but as his senior year went on, the idea of more school had receded in his mind, and the prospect of going to work had taken all his attention. When a man from McClaren's had come to the University of Pennsylvania campus near the end of Walker's senior year, he had signed up for an interview. The corporate mystique had intrigued him.

McClaren's was the company that had insured clipper ships making tea runs to China, and had covered gold shipments coming down from the mountains to San Francisco banks. The original head-quarters had been replaced by this modern steel-and-glass building, but the furniture in it was Victorian, made of heavy, close-grained wood that appeared to be relics of agents who had written policies on shiploads of elephant tusks brought here to make billiard balls and piano keys. There was a lingering hint of huge risks and huge oppor-tunities. Even now McClaren's kept a reputation for promotion from within that was rivaled only by the Jesuits.

When graduation had approached, he had still not received any offers that piqued his interest as much as the offer to work for McClaren's. He had always imagined he would work in Ohio within a few hours of home, but on the day before commencement, he had talked to his father and discovered that his parents had never given the idea much consideration. He had quietly set the plan aside and signed a contract with McClaren's. He had completed the training period of six months and been assigned to this cubicle on the seventh floor of the home office.

He had been placed under the distant but sane supervision of Joyce Hazelton. She had explained to him what an analyst did: "They give us raw data. We cook and serve." Information about all company op-erations was brought in, and he would screen the numbers for mean-ing and write reports that revealed trends and anomalies. She had said, "If we suddenly have seven percent of our clients dying on a full moon, I want that in block letters. If it's fifteen percent, I want it underlined too." Since then she had left him alone except to smile cor-dially at him once a day and meet with him every six months to show him that his performance ratings were all excellent.

He had found an unexpected pleasure in his work. The analysts all

made jokes about the job, but it was intoxicating. Examining the figures was like being a cabalist searching for messages about the future
encoded in the Talmud. Some of the messages were reassuring. At certain ages people had children and bought term life. By consulting actuarial tables, he knew how many of the policies sold this year would
come back for payoff at what future dates, and how many premiums
the company would receive in the meantime. He could consult the
company's tables on historical profit on invested premiums to produce
an estimate of total return. Because of the large number of policies and
the long stretch of time, the individual deviations from the norm disappeared to produce reliable predictions.

The work of the analysts was solitary because it demanded uninterrupted concentration, so they tended to savor encounters with
their colleagues, and they greeted each other with manic friendliness.
That made his time in the office pleasant enough, but he had not detected much improvement in the part of his life that took place between seven P.M. and seven A.M., and that had worried and depressed
him. He thought about it most often on the trips to and from work,
when he passed groups of people about his age who were walking together, because they seemed to have found some solution that he had
missed.

Each time he caught himself silently phrasing it that way, he
quickly corrected himself: it was all right to pretend confusion and be-
fuddlement to amuse people, but it was a pose, not an excuse he was
allowed to use to quiet his own mind. He sometimes presented himself as though he were new to this planet, a rational observer who
simply couldn't understand the mysteries of human behavior. The
truth was much more painful: he understood. He had been given his
chance at love soon after he had arrived in San Francisco—maybe the
only time in his life that it would come—and had wasted it. For a year
and a half he had been trying to get over his loss of her, and his disappointment in himself for having somehow failed to keep her. It
helped to immerse himself in the morass of details that the insurance
business generated. And now and then there were distractions—like
Stillman.

On the seventh day of Stillman, as Walker put his analysis of the quarter's performance bond figures into the drawer, out of sight, and took a step toward the coat hanging on the single hanger in his cubicle, Max Stillman's body suddenly filled the opening. "Time for lunch?" asked Stillman.

"I was thinking about it," said Walker. "But if you need help or something, I can go later. My schedule's pretty flexible."

"No," said Stillman. "Come on. I'll buy." He had turned and started off down the side aisle of the bay, toward the elevators, before Walker had managed to snag his coat.

Stillman's body seemed to project around it a zone of silence. It took Walker a few seconds in the seventh-floor hallway to see that it was because whenever he was in a crowd, the people who worked at McClaren's were acutely conscious of him, and the strain of thinking of small talk that was small enough to be said in his hearing made talk vanish altogether. During the ride down in the elevator, Walker became aware of sounds he had never noticed before: the distant groan of the electric winch that unwound the cable to let the elevator down, the sixty-cycle hum of the overhead lights. Everyone in the elevator assumed the same strange pose, facing the doors with the head tilted slightly upward to gaze at some distant, invisible point. People he had observed a dozen times chattering in the elevator as they left for lunch together appeared never to have seen one another before. He began to be aware that the people around him had taken note that he was with Stillman, and while he was wondering what they were thinking, he began to sweat.

It was almost a relief to follow Stillman across the lobby to the garage. He was going to find out what this man wanted. Stillman's car was a big Chevrolet that looked like the same model the police used, but when Walker got in, he saw the keys Stillman turned to start it had a tag from a rental company.

The day was bright and clear, and Walker tried to feel pleased about the novelty of sitting in a passenger seat while someone else maneuvered through the crowded and frustrating San Francisco streets. He watched the route Stillman took, from Telegraph Hill to Lombard, down Stockton across to Sacramento, but then he somehow made it to Sutter and Grant above the mess at Market Street and below the place where Grant became one-way in the opposite direction. The car stopped in front of a hotel where loud reggae music blared from the lobby, and Stillman got out of the car to make room for a parking attendant to get in and take it away in a flash of metal and squealing tires.

Walker looked toward the hotel, but Stillman was walking up the incline between the two stone lions that guarded the entrance to Chinatown. When Walker caught up, Stillman explained, "I have deals with a lot of parking attendants. This way, the kid gets a few extra bucks, and you get back to work on time."

"What about you?" asked Walker. He regretted the clumsiness of it, but he pressed forward. "You have to be back too, don't you?"

Stillman shook his head. "I'm working now."

Walker silently turned that statement around and around to study it, but Stillman said, "That's the good part of being in business for yourself. You get to start and stop when you feel like it."

"What's the bad part?"

"Your boss is an asshole, and he knows that you feel nothing for him but contempt. Of course, I wouldn't enjoy those compartments they put you in. It's not that I can't sit still or something."

"I noticed."

Stillman glanced at him. "Yeah, I guess you would have. But those little cubbyhole things . . ." He shook his head sympathetically. "The problem with them is that they're insulting. You're locked up, but there's no door to close, so people can look in on you." He paused. "Ever been in prison?"

Walker's head turned toward Stillman, but Stillman's expression had not changed. This was just part of the breezy conversation. "No. Have you?"

"It's like that, sort of. It's about who has the options. Prisons are set up so there's no question in the prisoner's mind that he's not going anyplace, but so he knows he can be watched—not that he is, but that he can be."

Walker had not missed the fact that Stillman had not answered his question. He said, "The cubicles aren't quite that bad. The wall cuts the noise and helps you keep your mind on what you're doing. On a good day I look down, then look up again and it's time for lunch. I come back, same thing. When it's time to go home, I print a hard copy of what I've done, and the amount I've done surprises me."

Stillman didn't seem convinced. "How long have you been at it?"

"Almost two years; a year and a half in my cubicle." It was almost reassuring that the questions were so transparent and simple. If Stillman were investigating Walker, he would already know all of this.

"Oh, yeah," said Stillman. "That's right. You were in the training class with Kennedy and Cardarelli and Snyder and Wang and those people."

Walker nodded, then stared ahead as they walked farther into Chinatown, past shops that were as big inside as department stores had been when he was a child in Ohio, but filled with a jumble of cast-resin imitations of carved smiling Buddhas, T-shirts that said GREET- INGS FROM ALCATRAZ, genuine antiques, and cases of jewelry that looked as though it might be spectacularly expensive. Stillman took him past restaurants on both sides of the street with oversized double bronze doors, but showed no interest in them. Walker decided that it was time to face the difficult part. He said, as casually as he could, "What are you doing at McClaren's?"

Stillman showed no surprise. "Once in a while they call me in when something's bothering them. I'm doing some investigating."

Walker felt his heart begin to pump harder. The job at McClaren's that he had liked shrunk and withered in his imagination. Enough, he thought. "Are you here to investigate me?"

"Hell no," said Stillman. "I'm here to eat lunch." He walked on more quickly, then turned a corner.

Walker followed him a few steps, then stopped abruptly.

Stillman turned in surprise, cocked his head, and waited.

Walker said, "I want to know whether I'm some kind of suspect."

Stillman took two steps toward him, and Walker remembered that he didn't know this man at all. From the beginning, Walker had noticed an air of barely suppressed violence about him, a permanent tension. Walker felt instinctively that if Stillman wanted to attack him physically, his best chance would not be to remain immobile and hope to fend him off. Stillman's face was only two feet from his own now, and he looked enormous. Walker got ready, his eyes on Stillman's and his arms tightening to strike first if he saw a sudden movement.

"Mr. Walker. John," Stillman amended. "I hereby swear, what I'm investigating is not you. If you've done something, it might be me that catches you at it, but I give you my solemn oath that I don't know about it now, didn't come to your office for that purpose, and don't give a shit about it. Now let's eat lunch." He remained motionless, like a wall across the sidewalk, his eyes holding Walker in place.

Walker stared back into his sharp, brown eyes. "If you were investigating me, would you tell me the truth?"

Stillman's face tightened into a happy grin. "Fuck no," he said, then turned and hurried into a doorway.

Walker followed Stillman into a dim alcove, then up a long flight of stairs lit only by a chartreuse and magenta neon sign in Chinese characters. When Walker reached the top and carefully pushed the door inward, he found Stillman in a bright yellow room where waiters bustled back and forth under sunlit skylights carrying large zinc-colored trays loaded with covered dishes. There were about thirty fashionably dressed customers sitting at black metal tables, eating and talking. A restaurant, thought Walker, and it was only then that he realized he had been convinced it would be something else.

They sat at a table near a window, and Stillman unabashedly amused himself by staring down at the pedestrians on the sidewalk below. When the waiter appeared with menus, Stillman said distractedly, "Just bring us whatever Mr. Fo had today."

The waiter said, "Very good, Mr. Stillman," and scurried off.

Walker said, "How do you know the owner didn't have seagull brains sautéed in rancid yak butter?"

Stillman shook his head. "Fo's not the owner. He's just a friend of mine who comes here on Tuesdays and Thursdays. It took him twenty-eight thousand meals to learn to pick out the best Chinese food, but

I'm hungry today, so I don't have time for experiments." He leaned forward on his elbows. "Life is too short to screw around trying to rediscover what somebody else knows already, so don't waste your time with it. On the small stuff, find somebody who knows, and then give him the courtesy of humbly admitting it. That way you'll avoid fifty years of heartburn and bad hangovers and stall-outs on free-ways."

He slipped into another topic. "So, do you hang out much with the people at work?"

"Not really," Walker said. "Once in a while one of us will invite another to dinner or have a small party. But most of the time, to tell you the truth, we bore each other. I mean, we all smile and talk at the coffee room, but we all know the same things." What he had just said was true, but saying it aloud made it worse.

Stillman nodded. "How about women? You're not queer." It was a statement, not a question.

Walker kept himself from looking around to see if anyone had heard. Stillman caught the expression and said, "Hey, it's San Francisco. Anybody here look shocked? A lot of people from Ohio come here just to sign up for the parade. You didn't. So why aren't you married?"

"I haven't met any woman I want to live with until I die," said Walker. "Unless I could be sure of dying in a month or so." He congratulated himself on saying the lie so fluently. He had met somebody, and he had let her slip away, but his life was none of Stillman's business.

Stillman nodded. "Yeah. I saw you gaping at Cardarelli when she left your cage the other day. Don't just ogle and wonder. Make a move on her. You might find that you wouldn't want the month to end."

Walker shook his head. "She's nice to look at, all right . . ." Walker stopped himself, shocked. He had almost been lulled into telling this stranger something that might harm her.

"But?" Stillman prodded.

Walker said carefully. "I guess sometimes relationships go that way, and sometimes they don't."

Stillman sighed happily. "Not with me. They always go that way.

I've had three really poisonous marriages, and I still hope to have one that lasts long enough to be fatal. Since you're young enough to learn, that's another thing I can give you a shortcut on. So far, the only thing I can think of that's worth any unpleasantness at all is a woman who's amenable to your favorite pastimes, and whose voice doesn't set your teeth on edge. Would I trade everything I've got for it? Sure. I've done it about four times."

"I thought it was three."

"I'm counting one who didn't let it get that far. I loved her. I even learned to make martinis for her—spent several evenings watching the bartender at the Mark Hopkins and asking him questions. It cost more than medical school on a per diem basis, and nearly ruined my liver. One night she was at my place, and I went to the kitchen to make some drinks. When I came back, she had bolted. The door was open, swinging on its hinges. Later, I asked her why she didn't want to marry me. She said, 'The martinis weren't strong enough for that.' I always count her."

He stared at the table for a moment in a reverie, then seemed to remember Walker. "Never judge people by what they have. That's mostly luck. Judge them by what they want." He waved his hand. "Do they want to mind their own business and be somebody decent, or do they never quite feel right unless they take what they get from somebody else and leave them bleeding so they can savor the contrast?" He lifted his eyes. "Ah, David," he said. "What have you brought for us?"

The waiter happily rattled off a group of unfamiliar Chinese phrases as he set plates on the table and proudly whisked the tops off. Walker could see dumplings, pieces of chicken and meat that he suspected was pork but could conceivably have been duck, and vegetables that he had seen before. None of it looked particularly unusual.

"Wonderful, David," said Stillman. "Thank you very much." He heaped various things from the serving dishes onto Walker's plate, and they began to eat.

Walker spent most of the meal wondering what Stillman was up to.

If he had invited Walker here in order to get him to incriminate himself or someone else, he was doing a poor job of it. He continued to do two-thirds of the talking, and showed far less interest in McClaren Life and Casualty than in women, weather, the behavior of passersby on the street below them, or food.

Walker had been deceived by the appearance of the food. He took two bites and decided it was the best food he had tasted in two years in San Francisco, and he felt bereft at the thought that he would never come to this restaurant again. If he tried, he would probably run into Stillman. Even if that didn't happen, he couldn't imagine ordering whatever Mr. Fo had ordered. It occurred to him that he had no idea what the place was called. He assumed it was on the menu, but he had not seen a menu.

On his way out, he made one last try. He pointed to the neon sign and said to Stillman, "What does that say?"

"Good luck," Stillman said. "They always say 'Good luck.' "

On the eighth day of Stillman, at five minutes to twelve, as Walker was trying to compose the concluding paragraph of his interpretation of sea-loss figures for the quarter ending June 30 in time to go to lunch, he caught a shadow in his peripheral vision, and looked up to see Stillman in his doorway.

"Come on, kid. Time to go."

"One second," said Walker. He decided to skip some of the preliminaries and rapidly typed the words "Recommmend no action at this time," then saved the report and let the terminal return to the main menu. He looked up again, but Stillman was gone. He supposed "Time to go" had been Stillman's way of saying he wanted to go to lunch again. Walker took his coat from the hanger and stepped out in time to catch a quick almost-glimpse of Stillman turning the corner into the hallway near the elevators, just a vague impression that a charcoal-gray coat had been there an instant ago.

When he reached the hallway, Stillman was standing in an elevator holding the door open for him. The rest of the McClaren people were streaming into elevator number three, possibly too impatient to wait, but probably relieved at the excuse for staying far from Stillman. He released the door as soon as Walker was in, and the elevator began to descend.

Walker said, "Where do you want to eat today?"

Stillman looked up at the strip of black above the door, where the floor numbers were lighting up, one by one. "If the traffic's moving, we might have time to pick something up at the airport."

3

Walker's head spun to look at Stillman. "Why would you want to go to the airport for lunch?"

Stillman said, "I said we'll try to get lunch. We may not have time. Our plane leaves in a little over an hour."

"Wait. Hold it," said Walker. "Our plane? I can't get on a plane." His thoughts unexpectedly clarified. "I don't even want to. What's this about?"

"If you need somebody to feed your goldfish or something, I can make a call." He added, "And don't worry about not leaving your key. The people I'll call are used to that kind of thing. They've evolved beyond the need for keys."

"I don't have a goldfish. I do have a job. I have—"

"You do," said Stillman. "And this is it." He glared at Walker for a moment, then sighed. "All right. I guess we'll have to make time for this." The elevator door opened, but Stillman pressed the button for the twelfth floor. The door closed, and the elevator began to ascend.

Walker gaped at him for a moment. He remembered Joyce Hazelton handing Stillman the phone and asking him obsequiously whether he had time to talk to Mr. McClaren. Walker had never even seen McClaren. He tried to determine whether Stillman was bluffing. They were already passing the tenth floor. If it was some kind of joke, he would have to stop the elevator in a second or two.

The doors opened and Stillman stepped out. Walker hesitated, followed him, then stopped just outside the doors. When they hummed shut he felt as though his retreat had been cut off. There was a woman in her thirties with perfectly arranged honey-colored hair and a cashmere dress walking toward the elevator as though she were a hostess going to answer the door. Walker had never seen her before. She met his eyes, a look of puzzlement appearing on her face. It stayed there just long enough to make Walker's heart stop beating: if she asked what he was doing here, he wouldn't know the answer. She gracefully turned on her high heels, opened a big oak door at the end of the room, and disappeared.

Walker looked toward Stillman, but he wasn't where Walker had expected him to be. He had moved off across the floor, and he was settling into a big wing chair under a painting of a clipper ship. Walker was distracted by the room. It was different from the rest of the building. It was like a men's club in an old movie about London. The chairs and tables were antique, and even the walls up here had somehow been contrived to have the solidity of things made by hand a long time ago.

The door opened silently, and seemed to open only a crack, but the woman miraculously slipped out and quietly closed it again. "He's just wrapping something up," she said. "He asked if you could give him a minute." Stillman nodded.

She turned and glided past Walker, and he had a chance to look at her without getting caught. He was comparing her to a fashion model in a magazine, then changed his mind. Her movements were designed to convey efficiency and polish rather than allure, as though her job was to warn people that everything up here was different, more professional, better.

A phone rang quietly as she was passing a desk in an alcove that looked like the set for the television news. She paused without diverting her course and snagged it from the front of the desk. "Mr. McClaren's office." Even her voice was beautiful, but it was perfection rather than warmth, like a voice broadcast from a great height. "I'm very sorry, sir, but he's just going into a very important meeting. We'll get back to you in about fifteen minutes." She replaced the receiver, and her eyes passed across Walker without a hint of a smile.

Suddenly the big oak door opened, and Walker realized that the flash of gray beyond it was his first glimpse of the man who ran the company where he had worked for two years. Rex McClaren was as tall as Walker, dressed in a gray suit. Walker could see wrinkles around the pale blue-gray eyes as he looked at Stillman and smiled. His hair looked as though it had turned gray early, because his face was not old enough to go with it. His voice was a deep, quiet one with a slight accent that Walker associated with prep schools in New England. "Max," he said. "Sorry to hold you up. I hope I didn't break your stride."

"It's okay," said Stillman. He looked at Walker and began to raise his hand toward him, as though to begin an introduction.

McClaren was too quick. "Ah," he interrupted. "John Walker." He stepped forward and gave Walker's hand a firm, hard shake. Walker saw that the smile made the wrinkles around the eyes return.

"Pleased to meet you," Walker mumbled.

McClaren looked puzzled, and in his confusion he reminded Walker of one of his professors at the University of Pennsylvania, mildly embarrassed at his mistake but comfortable in his admission: his position proved that any mistake of his was caused by the press of great matters, not by mere stupidity. "Oh, I guess that's right. We haven't met. I've seen you around, but I don't ever seem to get down to analysis lately." The word "lately" clearly meant during Walker's short career. "Joyce likes to run the place without any intrusion from on high. Good to meet you."

Walker nodded, but said nothing because his mind was stumbling over new impressions. He had never seen McClaren before, and he wondered how McClaren had seen him. He obviously had a long-standing relationship with Joyce Hazelton, but Walker couldn't remember anything she'd said to him that would have revealed that she had met McClaren. But even more mystifying was the oddly familiar tone between McClaren and Stillman.

McClaren looked at Stillman, his eyebrows rising as though they had something to do with listening. Stillman was up. "We just stopped by to get your blessing, Rex. We won't hold you up."

McClaren half-grinned, but there was a question behind it. "You've got it," he said. "But don't worry about holding me up. I thought you guys had a plane to catch."

Stillman glanced at his watch. "Oh, thanks. Yeah, we'd better do it." He raised his eyes to Walker. "You have any questions while we're here?"

Walker shook his head. "Thanks for taking the time to see us," he said to McClaren. He retreated, with as much dignity as he could manufacture, toward the elevators.

The car was out of the garage, a mile away, and accelerating onto the 101 before Walker said, "What's going on?"

"I'm afraid our hope of lunch is fading. We'll concentrate on making the plane."

"I didn't mean that."

"My investigation just turned something up," said Stillman. "Somebody from McClaren Life and Casualty has to go with me to check it out. That's you."

"Why me?"

Stillman slipped into the left lane and flashed past a line of cars, then veered to the right and shot through an opening into a clear space ahead. "I need someone who really works for the company, who knows a little about what goes on in all parts of it, and who can disappear from his cubicle for a while without having the company fall apart. I also need somebody who knows Snyder."

"Ellen Snyder?" said Walker. "This is about her?" He was shocked, pained.

"There. You do know her."

"She was in my training class," said Walker. "There were sixty of us, and I don't know her any better than the others do." He heard himself say it, and was surprised that his first, almost automatic response was a lie.

"I interviewed a few candidates, and I had to settle for you."

"Why?"

"Because you're not a psychological mess."

"Who is?"

Stillman looked at him in irritation. "The rest of them. They're hiding behind layers and layers of bullshit. I ask them where they were born, and they say, 'I'll check and get back to you.' I ask them if they filled out some stupid form in a file, and they tell me who they told to do it for them. They're so ambitious for the next promotion that they can hardly think about what they're doing for the next ten minutes."

Walker began to compose a defense for them, but he realized that all he would be able to come up with was "Being ambitious doesn't make somebody a psychological mess." This was not exactly true, or not always true, so he was silent.

Stillman said, "I'm afraid for people like that. And if they're on my side, I've got to be afraid for me, too. I'm going to have to teach my partner a few things as we go, and I don't have time to go back to the beginning."

"Partner?" Walker protested.

"Did I say 'partner'? It's a figure of speech," Stillman said.

Walker assembled his arguments and began to touch them off, one by one. "I am a data analyst. I was hired to work in the insurance business, not in security, or whatever you call it."

"Then maybe you ought to know more about insurance," said Stillman. "The problem with insuring against theft is that you can't always cover yourself against loss by raising premiums. Once in a great while, you have to leave your cubicle and go convince some actual thieves that you won't put up with it."

"You're joking." Having detected no change in Stillman's expression, Walker began to worry that he wasn't. He found himself remembering woolly tidbits of propaganda from his training class: the agent on the Malaysian ship who had held a sawed-off shotgun to the captain's head to keep him from surrendering to the pirates. What Stillman was saying made a certain surreal sense. "What, exactly, would you want me to do?"

"Most likely, not a thing," said Stillman. "I think it's a case of fraud. We verify that I'm right, collect some leads, and turn everything over to the police. It's a terrific deal for you."

"Why is that?"

"McClaren's is an old-fashioned company," said Stillman. "You've been around for a couple of years, so you must have noticed that much."

Walker said, "It's the only insurance company I've ever worked for."

"The company is what Wall Street calls 'closely held.' That means that the forty percent of the stock that isn't owned outright by people named McClaren is in blocks held by spindly-looking horse-faced daughters with different married names, their heirs, and their descendants."

"That much I know," said Walker.

"Well, every twenty years or so, they all get together for a picnic in the back yard of the old house on Nob Hill and decide who in the next generation ought to be president. They thank the last one and send him off to spend the rest of his life shooting clay pigeons, sailing boats, or raising grapes on a vineyard in Napa."

"How do you know all this?"

"Rex, the one you just met, is the third generation of the family that's hired me to do odd jobs, and he's probably the last I'll see, because he's younger than I am. It doesn't matter. He's so much like his grandfather and his uncle that I know what he'll say before he does. The point is, the company doesn't change, and they do pretty much what they want."

"I'm not clear on what this has to do with me."

"You like your job. The pay is decent. If you're at a cocktail party and some girl asks you what you do, you can say 'I work at McClaren's' and she will have heard of it and think you must be pretty respectable. And while I was in the building, I noticed your bosses don't pay much attention to you, so you probably are. If you want to, the McClarens will probably let you stay in that cubicle until you're seventy, and pay you a little more each year. You'll get promoted to Joyce Hazelton's job when she retires."

"Is that the terrific deal you're talking about? That I don't get fired from my job if I go with you?"

"Well, it's not so bad, is it?" said Stillman. "But there's a fast track, and while you were stumbling around, you blindly stepped on the low

end of it. A company like McClaren's will always need a lot of workers, but they're always looking for a small, steady supply of players."

"Players?"

"Gamblers," said Stillman. "Insurance is just gambling, with the
bets in writing. They're the guys the rest of us see when we think of
McClaren's, the steely-eyed bastards in the dark suits you talk to
if you want to insure your fireworks display or your oil-drilling rig.
McClaren's doesn't recruit them from outside. They just hire a bunch
of young people to do jobs like yours, and wait to see which ones grow
into the suit."

"And going with you is going to prove I'm a steely-eyed bastard
and get me promoted?"

"Hell no," said Stillman. "You get to spend a couple of days out of
your box telling me what the little numbers on an insurance policy
mean, and you get credit with McClaren's for showing promise."

Walker nodded sagely. "What I get is points with McClaren for
being a risk taker without taking any risks." He paused. "Of course,
if I don't go, then I'm already marked: I'm not promising."

Stillman shrugged. "Don't look at me like that. I didn't pick the
business you're in."

Walker glared at him. "But you did pick me, and told the president
of the company that you had picked me, without asking me if I even
wanted this golden opportunity."

Stillman grinned and slapped Walker's shoulder, making the car
take a dangerous wobble on the freeway. "There we go. That's what
got you into this. You cut right through the smoke and figured out
who did what, and you're not afraid to shove it up my nose. I don't
know if you're a promising insurance executive or not, and I certainly
don't care. You're good enough for this."

Walker's jaw muscles worked compulsively as he stared at the entrance to the airport parking area. "I know. I remind you of yourself
at this age," he muttered.

Stillman's head swiveled so he could stare at Walker in surprise.
"Not even remotely. Whatever mistakes your parents made, that
much they did right."

He pulled into a space too quickly, stopped the car with a jolt so it rocked forward, then went around to the trunk. He snatched a small suitcase, slammed the lid, and set off toward the terminal.

Walker got out of the passenger seat, closed the door, put his hands in his pockets, and stared at the pavement for a moment. The choices seemed to have narrowed in a very short time: either he could walk to the terminal, take a cab back to town, and start looking for a job, or he could start running to catch up with Stillman.

Walker began to saunter slowly across the broad parking lot. He thought about Stillman, and he savored his suspicion and resentment, but he recognized that he was only thinking about Stillman so he would not think of Ellen. For the past eighteen months, when he was tired or off-guard, anything might remind him: a woman's laugh he heard coming from a half-closed door in a corridor of the McClaren building, the sight of a couple about his age who were in love but were still nervous with each other because they didn't seem quite to trust the feeling yet. He could bring back the sight of Ellen without closing his eyes. Stillman had said this involved her. What could Stillman possibly be investigating that involved Ellen?

After a few paces, he noticed that something was wrong with his feet. They were moving faster than he had intended, and after a few more paces he had to take his hands out of his pockets to keep his balance, and then he was jogging, pumping his arms to bring up his speed.

4

There were no assigned seats on the plane, and when the passengers boarded, Walker realized his pass was in a different "zone" from Stillman's. Stillman sat near the front, and Walker found the only empty seat, beside a young curly-haired woman who seemed to view his arrival with disappointment. She had placed her purse, a shopping bag, and a couple of magazines on his seat, and now she sighed and slowly gathered them onto her lap.

"Sorry," he said.

She said nothing, just occupied herself with stuffing the magazines into the seat pocket in front of her, then tried to jam the shopping bag and the purse under the seat in front with her backpack, all the time eyeing Walker's feet resentfully.

Walker could not see Stillman from where he sat, but he was aware of him up ahead, and he felt an impatience that he could not find out what he was thinking. Why would he need somebody who knew Ellen Snyder?

The question shifted Walker's attention from Stillman and held it on Ellen. As always, she returned in short, meaningless fragments of memory, never still, but in motion: a few strands of blond hair straying across her left eye while she was talking, and then her hand would flit up to push them away. He wasn't always sure that he had seen precisely what he was remembering, that it had been chemically fixed in

his brain on some occasion, because sometimes the memory couldn't
be identified with a specific time and place. Other times, the memory
was clear and certain. He could see her on Market Street. It was after
class in the late afternoon. She had seen the cable car coming. "There
it is. We can catch it!" She had kept her eyes on it, tapped his chest
with her small hand, and he could feel it again, fluttering insistently
against him six times in a second before her first steps had taken it
away, and she had broken into a run toward the stop. He had followed
more slowly, because he had wanted to watch her. He remembered
that exactly—the blue sweater she had been wearing, the tight skirt
and flat shoes—because that had been the day after the first time they
had kissed. He had watched her all day, expecting her to be different
somehow: maybe softer and more affectionate, or in a nightmare version, strange and distant because she had regretted it afterward. He
had not detected any change at all. She had been exactly the same, ex-
uding happy energy, intense interest in what she saw around her, but
neither uncomfortable with him nor detectably more interested.

Walker banished the memory and tried to discern what Stillman
was doing. What if Stillman suspected her of something, some kind of
malfeasance? He had mentioned her, and said they were going to L.A.
to collect evidence about fraud. The idea that Walker would participate in an expedition to harm Ellen was insane. The simplest thing to
do would be to get off the plane, tell Stillman that he'd once had a personal relationship with Ellen and was not the right choice for this
assignment, then get on the next flight home.

Instantly he knew that he couldn't bring himself to do that. Stillman was an unknown. If Walker simply left, then Ellen would find
herself alone in the middle of his surprise investigation, with no advocate, and probably no witnesses. And what were Stillman's limits, his
rules? He wasn't a cop or something. He was just some kind of private
security expert. The company could hardly be relied on to keep him
under control: Stillman seemed to have a lifelong social connection
with the president's family.

The flight to Los Angeles was short, so Walker sat still and waited
it out, fighting images that intruded themselves on his consciousness.

He imagined himself walking into Ellen's office with Stillman, and looking into her eyes. The friendly, happy manner she'd had when he'd last seen her would vanish. She would detest him. He was going to come into her office looking like some kind of informer. She might even think that after she had dropped him, he had developed some weird scheme to get revenge by destroying her career.

Once again he considered simply getting himself out of this before she knew he had been involved. Seeing him with Stillman would destroy any respect that she had for him. Then he reminded himself of the facts. She had dumped him over a year and a half ago, well before the training period had ended. She had not changed her mind before she had left for her first post. She had not called him after that, or sent him a note. It was over.

Going along to make sure she was safe was a neutral, disinterested act that had nothing to do with any present or future relationship. It was simply necessary because in the course of their past relationship he had come to understand her well enough to know she was not dishonest. She wasn't a lover, and she never would be again. It didn't matter what she thought of him now. If it turned out that she needed an advocate, he would be there. Just as he was succumbing to a fantasy in which he cleared her name, she learned of it afterward, and appeared unexpectedly in San Francisco with gratitude that knew no bounds, his ears popped.

The plane was descending threateningly, moving in toward the runway. In a moment it bounced once and rattled to a stop. Walker overcame his impulse to hurry to keep up with Stillman.

Stillman was waiting for him near the end of the boarding tunnel, but while they walked, he did not speak. Walker noticed that at the car-rental counter downstairs, Stillman merely claimed a car that he had somehow reserved. He had been behaving as though he had received a telephone call at McClaren's and run for the airport. Maybe he had, and he had called ahead from the plane. But Walker determined to remember these small discrepancies until he could perceive a pattern that was unambiguous.

Stillman sat behind the wheel and drove out onto Century Boulevard. Twice Walker caught Stillman staring at him. Finally, Stillman said, "What the hell is the matter with you?"

Walker said, "Nothing. Nothing new, anyway. What are we doing?"

"I told you. Investigating."

Walker reviewed his question and admitted to himself that asking questions was a bad strategy. No matter what the answer had been, it would not have changed what he was doing, which was sitting in the passenger seat letting Stillman drag him wherever he pleased until he was sure Ellen was not in trouble.

Stillman's voice struck him as a distraction. "I'll tell you what I know so far, so you recognize names. A guy named Andrew Werfel bought a life insurance policy from McClaren's in 1959. It was one of those policies that rich guys buy to pay the inheritance tax so the government doesn't take everything when they die. The payoff was twelve million. Okay so far?"

"Sure," said Walker. "It's pretty common."

"He died a month ago. The beneficiary was his only begotten son, Alan Werfel. Everything cut-and-dried. A couple of weeks later, Alan Werfel showed up at the Pasadena office with a certified copy of the death certificate. After a few preliminary faxes and calls to the home office, he was given the usual forms to sign off on, and then a check for the twelve million. Still okay?"

"This doesn't sound like anything but a dull day at the Pasadena office. I assume there was something wrong with Alan Werfel?"

"That's the way it looks. The agent who handled the Werfel thing was the assistant manager of the Pasadena office, a young lady named Ellen Snyder. She's the one who verified the death certificate, checked Alan Werfel's ID, requested the payout, and handed over the check." Walker could feel Stillman's eyes on him.

"Is this where I come in?" asked Walker. "Do I think Ellen Snyder did something dishonest? No. Can I prove it? No. I just have no reason to think she would, and quite a few to think she wouldn't."

"I got that far on my own," said Stillman. "She has a good record, and when she was hired, nothing got into her personnel file that was faked . . . unlike a few other people."

"You're saying there's something wrong in my file?"

"I'm not investigating you. I didn't check everything in your file."

"You want to give me a lie detector test?"

Stillman rolled his eyes and then blew out a breath in displeasure. "You are not the problem. You are helping me analyze the problem. And by the way, don't ever volunteer to take a lie detector test."

"Why not—because people will just think I beat the machine?"

"You hear about that more than it happens. Most of the people who can do it are nuts, and you don't need a machine to know that you met one. What you don't hear about is—HAH!" His shout was sudden and deafening. "How's your pulse, kid?"

It took Walker a second to settle back into his seat. His shirt collar suddenly felt tight. The arteries in his neck were pounding, and a faint film of moisture had materialized on his forehead. He fought down the anger. "That wasn't funny."

"It wasn't supposed to be funny," said Stillman. "It was instructive. Your heartbeat, blood pressure, and breathing just took a big jump all at the same time. You're lying."

"You're saying the lie detector people are going to scream in my ear?"

"They don't have to. Any six-year-old on a playground knows how to piss off the kid beside him enough to get a reading."

"Then I'll stay away from playgrounds, too."

"Good. Now, back to Ellen. You fucked her, right?"

Walker sucked in a deep breath. "Are you still trying to be irritating?"

"No, it's a natural by-product of the search for knowledge," said Stillman. "Didn't you?"

"No. I didn't." He tried to detect whether the tone of his voice had betrayed him, and judged that the genuine anger in it had masked the lie. He tested a suspicion. "Did somebody tell you I did?"

"I don't remember who told me. Cardarelli, maybe. Or it could have been Marcy Wang."

Walker smoldered. The idea that they would express outrage to him that Stillman was spying on employees, and then tell Stillman all the personal information he wanted on other people, was incredible.

How had they even known? The revelation that any of them had known enough about what had passed between him and Ellen to make any conjecture was a shock. It had begun and ended in training, when they had all been almost strangers. "I can't believe it," he muttered.

"Then don't. Maybe I made it up and forgot. I heard you took her out during training. You didn't?"

Walker was tense and angry. What right did this guy have to ask these prying questions? This had nothing to do with his job or Ellen's. He said with feigned patience, "I asked her out to dinner once. Then I asked her to go someplace with me another time, and she said no. A concert. That was it. She wasn't interested, so I dropped it."

"What do you mean she wasn't interested?"

Walker sighed to convey his weariness of the topic. "She went out with me once. It was a nice place. We were both pleasant and smiled a lot. I liked her, and I wanted her to like me. A couple of days later, I got tickets to a concert, because she'd said she played the piano when she was a kid and still loved music. But when I asked, she gave me one of those excuses they have that tells you to forget it."

"Like what?"

"Like they have to wash their hair. It was better than that, but it was still—I remember—she had to study for an exam we were having the day after the concert." He glared. "Satisfied?"

"You were twenty-two, and so was she, and neither of you was married," said Stillman. "Jesus, I don't know about people in your generation. You look the same as people used to, except for the hair, but you're not."

Walker said, "What's the complaint?"

"It would seem to me," Stillman said, "that the natural thing would be to make friends, have foolish sexual relationships, blow your paycheck, feel remorse. But you don't. All of you are so serious, so interested in making the leap from third assistant manager to second assistant manager. What is it? Are you all crazy for money?"

Walker stared out the window, pretending not to listen.

"Tell me this. Are men and women still attracted to each other?"

"I was attracted, she wasn't."

"That reassures me about you, anyway. A twenty-four-year-old who can't wait to be sixty and move into the corner office has got a problem."

Stillman stopped the car in front of a convenience store, but he didn't go in. Instead, he walked down the sidewalk and turned the corner onto a residential street. Walker got out and caught up, but Stillman still seemed to be marveling over the degeneration of civilization.

"Mind if I ask where we're going?" asked Walker.

Stillman seemed pleased. "Not at all. In that house up there to the right is Ellen Snyder's apartment. Bottom floor, rear entry."

"Wouldn't she be at work? It's barely three o'clock."

"She would be, if she were doing that sort of thing these days, but she isn't."

"They fired her for paying off a policy?"

Stillman shook his head. "They didn't fire her, and she didn't quit, either. She just seems to have gotten scarce." Stillman was up the driveway now, and he approached the door.

An uneasiness came over Walker. "Then why are we here?"

Stillman reached into his coat pocket and pulled out a pair of thin leather gloves.

"You aren't . . ." said Walker.

Stillman knocked on the door, then put his ear to the door and listened. He knocked again. He shrugged at Walker. "See? What can I do?" He took out a pocketknife, wiggled the blade around between the door and the jamb for a couple of seconds, held it there, and pushed the door open. Walker backed a few paces away, but Stillman muttered, "Sitting in the car doesn't make you less guilty than I am, it just makes you easier to find."

Walker stopped backing away. He was almost relieved that Stillman had misinterpreted his reluctance. He was horrified at this man making this kind of intrusion on Ellen, but the mention of guilt made him realize that it was better this way. If Stillman was honest, he would see that there was nothing but evidence of Ellen's innocence, and leave her alone. If he was trying to frame her, then he had just made a mistake.

Stillman stepped in and held the door. "Come on in."

Walker had just crossed the threshold into a small, dark kitchen when Stillman edged past him and held his arm. "Don't touch anything."

Walker followed Stillman's eyes. He was looking at a window on the far side of the kitchen above the sink. The curtain swayed a little, then blew inward slightly as Stillman stepped toward it. He pulled the curtain aside to reveal electrical tape in an X shape from corner to corner of the upper pane, and a network of cracks. A couple of large triangles were missing.

"I guess she isn't very good at fixing broken windows," said Walker. "If I'd known, I might have tried telling her I was handy around the house."

"It's gotten lesser men where they wanted to go," said Stillman. "But that's not a repair job, it's a B and E. If you whack a window it goes crash, tinkle. If you tape it, it just goes thump. You reach in and unlock it."

Walker quickly moved through the doorway to the living room, his eyes scanning.

Stillman was instantly at his side. "What are you doing?"

"What if she was here when they broke in? She could be lying somewhere bleeding to death."

Stillman held his arm again. "Not for four days. If she's here, believe me, she can wait." He stepped ahead of Walker. "I don't think she is, of course."

"At least let me look." He jerked his arm away.

"I'll do it," said Stillman.

"Why you?"

Stillman sighed. "Because in your fit of chivalry you'll tromp all over everything that might tell me what happened here. Besides, I'm beginning to like you. A four-day stiff starts to get ripe. That means if she's here, somebody chopped her up and put her in a Coleman ice chest. You would find that looking at her would spoil the word 'picnic' for you forever."

Stillman moved rapidly across the living room, stepping in a straight path along the wall with his eyes on the floor. He opened a closet, then entered a doorway to the left that Walker judged must be the bedroom. In a moment he emerged, moved into another room, then returned to the kitchen. He stepped past Walker to the refrigerator, knocked on the front, opened it, then opened the freezer door. "Nobody's home in there," he announced. "Sit down and relax for a while, and I'll call you if I need you."

Walker hesitated for a moment. Why wasn't she here? He reluctantly admitted to himself that maybe if he left Stillman alone, he would find out. He sat at the kitchen table and watched Stillman through the doorway. He walked in a spiral motion around the living room, staring at the floor until he reached the center. He stepped to the bookshelf and moved books around. He examined the back of the television set, did something to the radio, studied the pictures on the wall, the empty mantel above the fireplace. He looked at the windowsills and latches, the light fixtures.

As Stillman completed each operation, Walker had to resist asking, "What's that? What are you looking at? What does it mean?" At six o'clock, he heard a car in the driveway, and then there were footsteps above the ceiling. They were light and quick—a woman, probably. In the silence he heard water running, faint music that he recognized as the theme of a commercial for dog food. Stillman kept at it.

Finally, when the sun was down and the kitchen was almost completely black, Stillman came in and took off his gloves. Walker said, "Did you come to tell me something?"

"Yeah. I'm hungry." Stillman walked to the door, opened it, and left. He was walking down the driveway when Walker came out. Walker hesitated, then pushed in the lock button with his fist, grasped the knob with his coat, and closed the door. He caught up with Stillman on the sidewalk.

After they had walked a short distance, Stillman reached into his jacket and pulled out a folded sheaf of papers. "I'd like you to look at this."

Walker took the papers. "What is it?"

"It's six sheets of paper. Look them over."

Walker scanned the sheets as he walked, but that didn't diminish his confusion. "It's a lot of addresses and phone numbers. Restaurants, hotels, car-rental agencies . . . hospitals. Why do you suppose she had them?"

Stillman took the sheets back. "She didn't. Whenever I go anywhere, I take a few addresses with me." He folded the sheets and returned them to his pocket.

"Hospitals?"

"You want to start looking for them after you need one?"

"Oh," said Walker. "Why did you want me to look at it?"

"Because I didn't find anything in the apartment," he said. "If somebody is watching the place, we want them to think we did."

"We do?"

"Yep," said Stillman. "If they broke in to look for something, they'll think we found it. If they broke in to clean up, they'll think they forgot something."

"What if they broke in because they're burglars who do that for a living?"

Stillman turned up a long, narrow alley that ran along the backs of the stores on the street where they had parked. "It's tough to get anywhere as a burglar if you leave all the stuff you can sell. The TV set is there. The radios are there. You can't get by stealing women's clothes and personal papers . . . and for Christ's sake, stop looking over your shoulder."

"Sorry, I—"

A weight collided with Walker and spun him around. His back and head hit a brick wall hard, and he felt a wave of nausea. When his eyes tried to focus again they couldn't seem to find a reference point, because there was a face too close to his in the dark, and a forearm across his chest, a big man leaning against him so that he could barely breathe. The face was full of anger and hatred. The emotion was so unwarranted that the face was a monstrosity more frightening than the pain in his chest.

"Don't move, you son of a bitch. LAPD."

The instinctive notion that his survival might depend on his doing something melted away. His survival depended on not doing anything. He was going to jail for burglary. He tried to turn his eyes to see what was happening to Stillman, but the man gave his chest a push that felt as though it was cracking his sternum. "Don't move!" snarled the face. Reports of people being killed struggling with the police floated on the edge of Walker's consciousness.

Then his ears were assaulted by a terrible sound. It was a loud, angry shout from Stillman, but the shout was almost instantly augmented by another voice, this one in pain. Both Walker and his captor turned in alarm.

Stillman's leg was on its way down from delivering a kick to the other policeman's groin, and he seemed to have punched him at least twice. The injured man bent over and appeared ready to topple.

Walker's eyes shot back to his captor's face in time to see that the fist was already on its way. Walker was unable to stifle the reflex to flinch. His right forearm jerked up to sweep the cop's arm away from his chest, while his body turned and his head moved to the side to avoid the punch. The cop's hand clutched Walker's coat, so Walker's sudden dodge kept the cop with him. The blow glanced off the back of Walker's head, and Walker saw bright red and green blotches explode into his field of vision and then float to the periphery.

Walker scrambled a few feet on the ground, then turned. Stillman had left his own opponent, and now he was advancing on Walker's. Walker was at once terrified and amazed. He expected the cop to do what cops did, which was to pull out his gun and kill Stillman.

Each instant that he didn't made Walker more frightened, because it meant it was certain to happen in the next. But the cop on the ground stirred, pushing himself to his feet. Maybe he would be the one.

Walker panicked. He had to stop him from firing. He picked up a fist-sized rock from the ground beside him and hurled it at the cop, then reached for another, sprang to his feet, and threw it at the one who had tried to arrest him.

Nothing seemed to have the effect he had expected. The two cops ran in different directions, then disappeared into the black spaces between buildings.

Stillman took Walker's arm and pulled him down the alley. "No time to hang around here," he muttered.

Walker stumbled along with him, slowly regaining his breath and letting his heartbeat slow. He felt a swelling of anger at Stillman. "Why would you do that?" He walked a few paces, faster, then turned. "We're going to jail." Then he added, "We're lucky we're not dead."

"Were you under the impression that those were police officers?" Stillman asked calmly.

Walker took in a breath to shout "Yes!" but he stopped. There was absolutely nothing about what they had done that any police officer he'd ever heard of would do. He changed his next words to "They scared the hell out of me."

Stillman nodded. "You knew you were guilty, so you figured, 'Sure. Of course they're cops. I deserve it, so they must be.' That's why they pulled that on us." He looked ahead up the alley. "Now you can compare."

"What?"

The squad car seemed to fill the alley like a train in a tunnel, leaving little space on either side. Its lights shot up into the sky as it bumped over the incline at the end of the alley, then settled firmly and steadily, growing brighter as the vehicle accelerated toward Stillman and Walker. The car stopped a few feet from them, then eased forward slowly until the window was beside them. The cop in the passenger seat was a young black man. He said, "Good evening, sirs."

The construction struck Walker as odd, mildly sarcastic. He said, "Good evening."

"We got a call that there was a disturbance in this alley," said the cop. "Know anything about that?"

Stillman said, "We did happen to run into two men a few minutes ago. They seemed to be interested in robbing us, but we managed to frighten them off, I guess."

The policeman opened his door and got out, sliding his billy club into a rung on his belt. Walker noticed that his hand lingered there, between the club and the gun. He stood close to them. "Someone said there was a fight. Shouting and so on."

"That's kind of an exaggeration," said Stillman. "It was just two guys about six feet tall, about thirty years old. They were getting ready to jump us, but when we got close, I think we were bigger than they expected, so they ran."

"May I ask what you're doing in the alley?"

He was staring at Walker, but Stillman spoke. "We're visitors in town, and we parked over there on the street"—he turned to point in roughly the right direction—"and we figured this was a good short-cut."

The cop kept his eyes on Walker. "And two men just came along at the same time?"

Walker knew he had to be the one to answer. "They seemed to be waiting here for whoever showed up."

The policeman nodded. "Would you mind showing me some iden-tification?"

Stillman pulled out his wallet and handed the cop his driver's li-cense, so Walker did the same. The cop handed the two licenses to his partner in the car, and the partner punched some numbers into the computer terminal mounted beside him. The cop returned his atten-tion to Walker and Stillman. "What brings you to Pasadena?"

Stillman was supremely calm and friendly. "We work for McClar-en's, the insurance company. There's a girl—a lady my friend here knew from his training school days, and he asked me if we could stop by and see her. No luck. We missed her at the office, and now she's not at home, either."

"I see." His partner muttered something and the cop leaned into the window to confer with him. He came back with the licenses. "Here you go." He looked up and down the alley, then said, "We'll make a report of this, but I'm not sure what good it's going to do you. They're long gone by now."

Stillman nodded. "I understand. They didn't get any money from us, so I guess there's not much harm done."

The policeman sat in the car seat again, but before he pulled his leg in, he said, "Even in San Francisco, walking down dark alleys proba-bly isn't the best idea."

"I've had better," Stillman said.

"Take care," said the cop. He shut the door and the car drifted down the alley. Now and then the bright beam of the spotlight shot out to the side and played about a row of garbage cans, a narrow space between buildings. Then the police car turned and disappeared.

Stillman stepped into the nearest passage toward the street. "Well, now that was a rotten piece of timing," he said. "I had hoped to get a couple of names out of their wallets, not give mine to a cop." He stopped and let Walker catch up. "What we need is dinner."

"It is?"

"Otherwise we'll have to drink on an empty stomach."

5

The Coast of Borneo was a relic of a period that Walker had missed, and he calculated that even Stillman had to be too young to have seen anything but strange little outposts cut off and isolated by flanking movements of change. The big bare-beamed dining room had out-rigger canoes hanging from the ceiling, and drinks served in ceramic mugs that were effigies of somebody's gods. As he followed Stillman deeper into the place, he gazed at a man in a chef's hat behind glass prodding a huge slab of sizzling meat over flames that threatened to flare up and engulf them both, then waited while an Oriental waiter in a tuxedo tucked two gigantic menus under his arm and conducted them across an unused dance floor and up onto the tiered gallery of tables.

Stillman sat down and squinted up at the waiter for a few seconds as though the two of them were in a poker game and the waiter had just raised. The waiter held a tiny pad in the palm of his hand with a pen poised over it. Stillman said, "Can your bartender make a real mai tai?"

"Old-fashioned kind?" asked the waiter, now assessing Stillman with veiled interest.

"That's right," said Stillman. "The old-fashioned kind."

"Two mai tai old-fashioned kind," the waiter announced, and put a strike mark on his pad that could not have been a Chinese character, then spun on his heel and went off. It seemed to Walker that the pad must be for appraising the customers, and Stillman had scored high.

"What's changed about mai tais?"

Stillman shrugged. "Beats me. It's pretty clear they've gone to hell like everything else."

The waiter returned with two large glasses filled with liquid the color of liver. Stillman sipped his, then said, "Perfect."

Walker tasted his, and guessed that "old-fashioned kind" must mean that the quantity of rum was up to the standard in force when driving drunk was still legal in Los Angeles. He tasted it again, and decided those days would be missed.

A few minutes later the waiter reappeared, his tiny pad in his hand and his eyebrow raised expectantly. Stillman nodded to Walker.

Walker replied, "Should we have what Mr. Fo ordered in 1949?"

Stillman shook his head. "Fo wasn't in this time zone then. We'll have to settle for prime rib, medium rare. And bring us more of these." When the waiter was gone, he said, "That's what everybody had before words like 'cholesterol' crept into the language. They're all going to be surprised after a lifetime of deprivation when they die of nothing."

Walker said, "They should spend time with you, and they wouldn't have that to worry about."

"So buy yourself some insurance. I need to hear about Ellen."

Walker had intended to sip his drink, but he noticed that the ice at the bottom already clinked against his front teeth. The drink was like a black hole that sucked everything around it into the glass and disappeared with it. He said warily, "I don't know a lot. You've seen pictures of her, right?"

"One in her file, and one copy of her company ID card. An escapee from cheerleader detention camp."

"She looks that way," Walker agreed. "Mildly athletic-looking, but not tiresome about it. I don't even know if she did anything to stay that way. She was alert and serious about the training classes. I remember she had a few interests that didn't have anything to do with work. I told you about the music."

"By the way, that was a reasonable try, kid." Stillman raised his glass in a mock toast. "They like evidence that you're listening when they move their lips. I wonder why it didn't fly. Is there a boyfriend?"

"The word I got was no." He stared into space for a moment. "Cardarelli. That's who told me. Now that I know Cardarelli better, I guess that didn't mean it was true. But Ellen didn't say anything about a boyfriend when she went out with me, and that would have been the time."

"No, before that would have been the time. What did she talk about?"

Walker was thinking about her again, searching for a sign that he had missed. No, there was nothing, even at the end, that showed she was thinking about another man. Stillman was staring at him, waiting.

"The one time you took her out," prompted Stillman. "What did she tell you?"

He needed an answer, and he was stuck with the lie that he had only taken her out once. He settled on the first time, at the Italian restaurant. He would answer questions about that. "As I remember, I guess she talked mostly about the future."

"That's what I wanted to hear," said Stillman. "We seem to be in it, so I'd like to know what the hell it is."

Walker tried to bring it back. "She had a kind of overall strategy. She was convinced that a woman in a big company like McClaren's had to make things happen, or they wouldn't."

"Are we talking about endearing ourselves to upper management? Dirty old men my age?"

"If we were, I didn't get it. What she said was that she had to be patient. Getting herself into the San Francisco office would put her into competition she couldn't beat."

"Like who?"

Walker shrugged. "Men, I guess. I think she mentioned Kennedy as an example. People who went to better colleges, and were just as bright and worked just as hard as she did."

"Who else?"

"Well . . . me," he said uncomfortably. "But it was just because if she hadn't said that, she probably thought I would have been uncomfortable. She wanted to be in one of the branch offices, but a particular kind. She said she didn't want to insure ship's cargoes or satellite launches or something, because the customers are the sort of men who wouldn't take her seriously. She said cute and perky weren't qualities they looked for."

"It sounds like something that might be true. But what about the tone? When she said it, what was her voice like? Bitter? Angry?"

"Not really. She figured that things were improving for women, but the time wasn't right yet. She said if there were layoffs at McClaren's, she'd be safer in an office with four people than in one with four hundred. She would concentrate on family stuff: life insurance gets bought by men, but the survivors are widows, and the minute there's a payoff, they're women with more money than their husbands had the day they died. There's no tax on it, either. But the tax kicks in hard for the next generation, so she would sell them life insurance to pay that for the kids, and probably long-term-care insurance because they were alone now, and if the money was big enough, she'd convince them to let the company manage it." He shrugged. "She figured that who she was and the way she looked would give her an edge."

"What did you think?"

"The numbers add up the way she thought they did—actuarial tables on male-female longevity, and so on. I don't know if the rest of it does. There are too many intangibles. It seemed smart at the time— she *is* cute and perky, and maybe that's the audience for it. Almost any plan seems smart to you if you don't have a plan."

"So she ended up in Pasadena. Did she plan that too?"

"She said that was one of her choices. There was Pasadena, some place in Orange County, Scottsdale in Arizona, Palm Beach in Florida, a couple of others. The idea was to be in a place where the demographics work out—income level, age of population, and so on." He let his drink swirl around, listening to the ice on the glass.

Stillman looked at him speculatively. "She must have sold a lot of insurance to make assistant manager in a year and a half. That's a rank above the rest of you, right?"

Walker nodded. "She said that would happen—that promotions come more quickly on the front lines. And she must have made something on commissions. If she made a dollar, it's more than an analyst gets."

"But what was the point of it—the end?"

Walker smiled. "I got the impression that in twenty years, when the rest of us have become permanent drudges in our cubicles, and some have killed each other off in main-office politics, she expects to come back. If present trends play out, in those twenty years the status of women can only be better. At that time she could be well up the ranks, maybe vice president and regional manager of a big chunk of the country. Then, if there's a certain combination of circumstances, she could end up running the company. She didn't say what the circumstances were."

"It would help if she changed her name to McClaren."

Walker shrugged. "You'll have to suggest it to her."

Stillman studied Walker as he said, "Actually, I think I know what she has in mind. Dynasties have a life span. She probably thinks that at some point, either there won't be enough McClarens, or there won't be the right McClaren. There could even be too many, so the stock is spread too thin among people who don't know each other. A competitor could start buying up those shares. It doesn't matter what it is. Each year brings the end closer."

"Really?" said Walker. "No more McClarens at McClaren's? Then what?"

"Hard times," said Stillman. His eyes drifted around the room as he spoke. "The company loses money. This happens to insurance companies on a fairly regular schedule. Then you've got a bunch of people in the San Francisco office who are associated with the discredited practices or decisions that failed. And you have a woman—she's only forty-four at this point—who has twenty-two years with the company and runs operations in some big, successful region. Because she's been out of sight, nobody knows anything negative about her. She gets a phone call from the board of directors." He suddenly returned his eyes to Walker. "How would you feel about that?"

"Me?" Walker looked surprised. "You mean would I be jealous or something? I don't think so. And I could think of worse people to work for."

"Really? Who?"

"It's just an expression," said Walker. "I meant she was good, not that anybody else was bad."

"It doesn't matter," said Stillman. "Now I understand why she wasn't interested in you. You're a nagging boil that appeared on her ass after she bought a nonrefundable plane ticket."

"It's nice to make an impression on people."

Stillman held up his hands. "Don't get me wrong. I'm sure you're a young woman's fantasy. A delightful, spiritual companion on life's highway who's hung like a horse. But that's all beside the point, isn't it?"

"It wouldn't be to me."

"She's whoring after strange gods."

"She's what?"

"It's just a line from a book nobody reads anymore. What it means this time is that it wasn't you she turned down. It's men. And women: she can't be a lesbian because that would be even harder to fit into the vision. If you've got a plan that's sure to fail unless absolutely everything happens in a certain way, then you have to make it all happen that way. A boyfriend in the San Francisco office would be a deviation."

"I'm not sure if I'm supposed to feel better about this or worse."

Stillman raised his eyebrows, took a long draft of his mai tai, and stared contemplatively at the hull of the outrigger canoe hanging above the table. "I'd say that our humanity requires us to feel . . . bad. Which we will tomorrow while these drinks claw their way out of our systems." He looked at Walker again. "You're in the clear, ego-wise. You could have been the aforementioned paragon of virtues, and she would have skipped the concert."

"Then what are we sad about, precisely?"

"Her. No matter how misguided the goal, we can't help rooting for the determined little human animal who wants it. That's why we watch people doing things like climbing Mount Everest—which, on the well-known one-to-ten Stanford-Binet stupidity scale weighs in at about a thirty—and actually, with shame and horror, admit to ourselves that we hope the little boogers make it."

"We don't know that she won't."

"The broken window tells us somebody broke into her apartment. The two guys show us that somebody was watching her apartment—somebody from out of town, or they would have known enough to impersonate Pasadena cops instead of L.A. cops. They may have been interested in getting their hands on her, or keeping our hands off her. But I'd say the idea that she's irrelevant to the little problem at McClaren's is about shot."

"So what can we do?"

"We find her." Stillman's eyes met the waiter's across the room, and he pointed at his empty mai tai glass. The waiter scurried off.

Walker stared at his glass while the waiter snatched it up and replaced it with a full one. It was beginning to take on a strange brightness, but then he realized that it was all right. It just looked bright because the breadth of his vision was now so narrow that the periphery was gone, and the glass was about all that was left. He felt a sudden regret so deep that he gave in to the need to draw in a quick breath. Maybe he was being stupid. What was he defending—her reputation? Her life could be in danger. He should tell Stillman the part he had not said. But as he contemplated it, he could not think of a single disparity between the truth and the lie that made any difference to anyone but John Walker.

6

Walker sensed that he was in a large, empty space. His ears told him that the sounds were coming from a distance, but it was some debased offshoot of human reason that told him he could not be alone. Spaces this size were public. Bits of memory rose into his consciousness. Had he passed out in the restaurant? He sat up quickly. It was a hotel room. He was still dressed, lying on top of a bed. He remembered walking in here and lying down, but he also remembered telling himself he was just going to test the bed for a moment to see if it was comfortable. He had planned to get up.

Stillman was sitting in a wing chair across the room, and the rustling noises had been the newspaper he was reading. He looked over the top of his paper at Walker, then turned a page.

"What time is it?" asked Walker. His voice didn't sound as though it belonged to him. He cleared his throat.

"About nine. Don't hurt yourself trying to roll the stone away from the tomb, though. We've got plenty of time."

Walker crawled off the bed and walked into the bathroom. He found a paper bag on the sink. Inside were a toothbrush, toothpaste, razor, shaving cream, mouthwash, comb, and a receipt that said Hilton Gift Shop. There were bars of soap in packages in the soap trays, so he decided he was adequately equipped for the moment.

Walker brushed his teeth and stood under the hot shower for a few minutes before he was ready to face considerations that had to do with the future. He began with the immediate future, because that didn't challenge his mind too much. He had come to Los Angeles with only the clothes on his back, so he didn't have to decide what to wear. As his mind began to forage beyond the moment, it collided with Stillman, and he felt the urge to stay right where he was, letting the water pound his scalp and run warm down his body to his toes until Stillman went away. He had heard him say, "We've got plenty of time." It was innocuous and undemanding, but it implied that there was something coming. He reminded himself that last night Stillman had said they were going to search for Ellen.

Moments later, Walker came out of the bathroom and put on his clothes. Stillman stood, refolded his newspaper, dropped it into the wastebasket, then stepped to the door. "Come on." It was only then that Walker noticed Stillman was wearing a freshly pressed gray suit that made him look like a senator.

Walker quickly surveyed the room, then realized he had been checking to make sure he had not left anything behind. He had nothing except his wallet and keys, and he could feel them in his pants pockets. He followed Stillman along the hall without having the slightest memory of the velvet-flocked blue-and-white wallpaper, then rode down with him in an elevator. The elevator stopped every second or third floor to pick up groups of middle-aged women who seemed to know one another, some of them pulling suitcases on wheels, so that by the time it had descended ten floors, Walker was occupying himself by estimating the weight of each passenger and her burdens, adding them up and comparing the total to the elevator's capacity printed on the little card beside the door.

When they got out in the lobby, Stillman turned to him. "How close did we come?"

"One more stop might have done it. We had about four hundred more pounds."

"It's kind of nice, isn't it?" asked Stillman. "Not dying by yourself, but with all those women hugging you and screaming all the way down, so our bodies would be all smeared together like a big, runny omelette." He stopped. "Hungry?"

Walker was defiant. "Sure. Do we have time?"

"Let me worry about that."

They ate breakfast in the hotel restaurant, and Walker felt pleased with his decision. The food seemed to give his body energy, and the coffee cleared his mind. He watched Stillman paying the bill, then followed him out the front door.

Stillman turned his head to stare at Walker critically, then waved off the valet parking attendant. "We'll have to stop and get you some clothes and stuff." He turned and walked west on Wilshire Boulevard.

Stillman stopped to look into the Neiman Marcus window, and Walker pointedly kept moving. Stillman called, "Hold it," and Walker came back. "I know you can't afford this, but don't worry about it. We're on an expense account."

"You may be," said Walker. "But I doubt that it includes me, and I'm sure it doesn't include clothes."

Stillman glanced at his watch and said affably, "It includes anything I say it includes. I don't itemize."

Walker cocked his head and raised an eyebrow.

"My clients know I'm not wasting their time on that sort of thing. If they want my services, they pay what I cost and don't get on my nerves. I don't bid, I don't give estimates, and I don't account for things."

"They go for that?" asked Walker. "McClaren's goes for that?"

"If they didn't want to, they wouldn't have to. They have a telephone book. Now, we're about to go meet some people. I want them to look at you once and make some unfounded assumptions. What that's going to require is that you go in there and buy yourself a good shirt, a suit off the rack that fits you, and a tie in a tasteful color and subdued pattern that does not include any stripes."

"So it's a disguise for a meeting?"

"Jesus, I hope it's not a disguise. I've been giving you the benefit of the doubt. We're going to see some people who need to assume that you're very high up on the food chain. We may see them more than once in the next few days. So while you're at it, start at the skin and work outward. Buy three or four suits, some jackets and pairs of pants, shirts, shoes and so on. I'll go buy you a suitcase to hold them in, then be back in time to sign the slip."

Walker frowned.

"What are you waiting for?"

"I'm wondering . . . why no stripes?"

"Because that's what British regimental ties have, and if you ended up with the colors of the Queen's Own Thirty-sixth Welsh Bushwhackers or the Eton All-Castrato Choir you wouldn't know it."

"I guess that's true," said Walker. "But would whoever we're going to see?"

"One of them might," said Stillman. "Just go."

Walker stepped inside the glass doors, but he watched for a moment. Stillman looked up the street, then trotted across and disappeared into another store. As Walker looked at suits, he tried to decide what was bothering him. It was the rapidity of the things that had happened, and were still happening. Time seemed to speed up around Stillman. It seemed to Walker that one moment he had been in the office, and the next he was rattling along on rails at eighty miles an hour. He might very well be heading in the right direction, but maybe moving at high speed was sufficient reason to drag his feet.

When the clerk had managed to work his way down the hay bale of clothes he had laid on the counter for Walker, add up the numbers on the price tags, and pack them all into four huge shopping bags, Stillman arrived, toting a suitcase. He handed the clerk a card, signed the slip, and helped Walker carry his bags to the street. Walker recognized the car Stillman had rented at the airport. Stillman opened the door and tossed his purchases into the back seat.

Walker said carefully, "Thank you for the clothes."

Stillman nodded. "Get in the back with them."

As they drove off, Stillman said over his shoulder, "You can get your clothes changed while we're on the way."

"In the car?"

"If you don't change your shorts at a red light, you should be okay. Just have your tie knotted and your coat on before we get to Pasadena."

Walker opened boxes until he had a complete outfit laid out on the seat beside him and the tags removed, then waited for Stillman to reach the freeway before he began to change. When he had finished, Stillman took the Colorado Boulevard exit and drove another fifteen minutes along tree-lined side streets before he stopped the car at the curb. "This is it," he said.

Walker looked at the two-story stone building and recognized a brass plaque that appeared to be a replica of the one on the main-office building in San Francisco. It said, in bold letters, MCCLAREN and, in smaller ones below, LIFE AND CASUALTY. He got out and stood on the sidewalk. When Stillman came around the car he studied Walker. "Good. You look about right."

Stillman pretended to be searching for something in his coat pockets. "Keep your eyes open. This isn't a cordial visit to a field office, it's an investigation. Watch everybody you can see all the time. People are going to smile and shake your hand, but they're no friends of yours."

He stepped off, opened the door to let Walker go in ahead of him, then lingered for a moment. There was a young woman at the front desk who wore a thin wire telephone microphone that came from a spot above her right ear across her cheek to a place just to the right of her lips. She was looking at them while she spoke, but Walker couldn't tell at first whether she was speaking to them. Then she repeated, "May I help you?" more pointedly.

"This is Mr. Walker, and I'm Stillman," said Stillman. Walker noticed that Stillman's manner seemed to have changed subtly. He was putting Walker ahead of him.

The girl's eyes focused ahead as she pressed a button and said, "The gentlemen are here for your meeting." Then she pressed the button again, took off her headset, and stood up. "I'll show you the way," she said, and left the telephone buttons to blink soundlessly.

Walker waited for Stillman to lead, but a steady pressure of Stillman's hand on his back made him move ahead. He had not been imagining it: Stillman was keeping everyone's attention on Walker. He stepped off smartly, looking around him at the office with frank curiosity. There were three people at desks that would have been like his if they had been in cubicles—a man in his thirties, a woman in her sixties, and a girl who looked like she was barely out of high school. He could tell from the forms on their desks and in their trays that they must be a sales support staff, processing new policies.

Then there was a hallway with doors on the right side. The first room they passed held a couple of fax machines, a copying machine, and the cache where the policy forms had come from. The second was a tiny office. At the corner of the building was a conference room.

As he entered, Walker could see there were three people already sitting around the long rectangular table. He sensed that he was supposed to take their minds off Stillman, so he became uncharacteristically aggressive. He smiled and said, "Hello. I'm John Walker, from the San Francisco office." Almost as an afterthought, he added, "And this is Mr. Stillman."

A tall, beefy man about Stillman's age in a dark gray suit and a white shirt that was too tight around his neck returned his smile and wrapped his sausagelike fingers around Walker's hand to give it an enthusiastic shake. "Dale Winters," he said. "I manage the Pasadena office. This is Daphne Pool, my assistant."

A thin woman about forty-five years old with sharp gray eyes and silver glasses chained around her neck over a slate-gray suit moved a silver pen to her left hand, gave Walker's hand a quick squeeze, and released it.

The third man was in his early thirties, three inches shorter than Winters, with blond hair that was just a bit too long and too expensively sculpted to belong to someone who worked in the insurance business. He jumped up with an abrupt energy and leaned across the table to shake Walker's hand, his coat open and his tie a little loose, but he didn't smile. He sat down again with exactly the same energy. Walker heard Winters saying, "And this is Mr. Werfel."

Walker's eyes shot to Stillman, whose face had assumed the remote, peaceful calm of a statue of Buddha presiding silently in the dim recesses of an empty temple. Walker forced his face into an achingly false smile and said, "Pleased to meet you, Mr. Werfel."

He took a seat across the table from Werfel and watched Daphne Pool's thin hand slide a red binder onto the table under his chest. He nodded to her and opened the cover. There was a photocopy of an in-

surance policy. He saw the name Andrew Werfel and turned past it to
the next divider. There was the death certificate of Andrew Werfel,
then a series of copies: a birth certificate that said Alan Weems Werfel,
and a driver's license that said the same and had a picture of the man
across from him looking with half-lidded eyes and disarranged hair at
the camera. Then there was a copy of the first page of a passport with
a much better picture of Alan Werfel. The final section contained
copies of the standard forms for settling an insurance claim, all signed
Alan Werfel and *Ellen Snyder.*

He closed the notebook and glanced at Stillman, who was now
leaning back beside him with his fingers knitted across his solar plexus
and his eyes opaque. Walker tried to imagine what an important person from the home office would say, but he wasn't even certain that he
knew what such a person would be doing here. He turned to Winters.
"Dale, can you bring me up to speed? Where do we stand now?"

Winters looked uncomfortable. His eyes flicked up nervously
toward Werfel, then he said, "That little binder tells you just about
everything. There was a policy. Mr. Werfel senior passed away. A
gentleman purporting to be Mr. Werfel junior called the office to find
out how to submit a claim. He was referred to our assistant manager,
Ellen Snyder, who explained the procedures and set up an appointment. Meanwhile she researched the policy, got the necessary information, requested a settlement check, and so on. When she met with
him, he had the proper identification . . ." He glanced at Werfel again,
this time in a way that seemed to be apologetic but wasn't quite. "Or
what seemed to be proper. Miss Snyder certified the claim, and dis-
bursed the death benefit."

Walker wished Winters had just said "money." "Is Miss Snyder
going to be joining us?"

This made Winters so embarrassed that Walker regretted the question. "She's not in today," Winters said numbly.

Walker pretended that had been an answer. He smiled again.
"And, Mr. Werfel, I assume you showed up the same way later, to submit your claim?"

Werfel nodded sullenly.

Walker wondered what Werfel was doing here. It occurred to him that maybe he had been waiting for Walker. The thought made a chill start in the back of his neck and move down his spine. Stillman had given these people the idea that Walker was a high-level executive, brought him in here dressed like one, and duped him into acting like one. There seemed to be no way out except forward. "I'm sorry for any inconvenience this may have caused you, Mr. Werfel."

Werfel's face seemed to harden. "You know goddamned well it has."

Walker turned to Winters for help. Winters said hastily, "It's a complicated matter. Lots of gray area. You see, the license and passport and so on that the man submitted were genuine. The check was made out to Alan Werfel. It was endorsed in the name 'Alan Werfel.' "

"I don't think I understand," said Walker. "I had understood that we'd paid the money to the wrong man—an impostor?"

"It seems we did," said Winters. "But the question that remains to be settled is, was this the fault of the company, or does Mr. Werfel also, through negligence, share in the fault? That is, we are responsible for recognizing false pieces of identification. If the identification presented is genuine identification, and the genuine owner has taken no steps to report its loss or theft, is McClaren Life and Casualty the one at fault? The only one? If not, is the company liable for a second payment of the full amount, or should some middle ground be reached?"

"So we're here to discuss his claim," said Walker. He tried to hide his fascination.

Winters looked at him evenly. "If Mr. Werfel was the victim of a theft of identity, then McClaren's certainly has to deplore that. But if, for instance, the impostor had executed a bank instrument in Mr. Werfel's name, and appropriated his bank account, who would take the loss? The financial institution? Of course not. Mr. Werfel would. The principle has been tested in California courts. If the impostor had used Mr. Werfel's identification to secure a loan, who would be responsible? Mr. Werfel."

Walker looked at Stillman, who was still immobile. His hands had not stirred from their position clasped across his belly. He did not blink, look at Walker, or show any sign that he had heard. Walker didn't take his eyes off Stillman as he said, "Are you saying the company won't pay the death benefit twice?"

Winters responded, "Certainly not the entire amount? Not twelve million dollars."

Walker saw a slight twitch at the corners of Stillman's lips. It could easily have been a tiny disturbance in the course of his dream.

Werfel could remain silent no longer. He spoke in a tight, quiet voice. "You can't say that you paid money to me when I never saw it, never touched it, never knew about it. I didn't think I had to bring my lawyers with me today, but—"

Walker surprised himself. He held up his hand quickly to forestall the threat. "Wait, Mr. Werfel." He glared at Stillman, but Stillman looked as though he could be dead. "Mr. Winters, can I talk with you for a minute?"

"All right," said Winters resentfully. He stood up and said curtly to the wall across from him, "Excuse us."

Winters was twice Walker's age, a head taller, and so broad that he seemed to fill the narrow hallway outside the conference room. He glowered down at Walker and waited.

Walker said, "I don't think this compromise thing is working. I don't think he's going to let us hold back what his father paid for."

Winters leaned forward a little, his face knowing and superior. "I can tell you that San Francisco is not going to let us pay out twelve million dollars on a clerical error."

Walker could barely keep his eyes on the face. It was almost a snarl, the face of a cornered criminal—angry and full of hatred, but frightened, too. Walker felt sorry for him. He had probably been selling insurance from this office since before Walker was born, and he was afraid of being fired. Walker guessed from his first glance at Werfel that he was the sort of rich that would have made working a ludicrous activity. His suit was a breathtakingly expensive example of the latest cut, but he wore it with a kind of carelessness, as though if he passed a rugby match on his way to his car, he might join it without giving his clothes a thought. Walker said, "This isn't your fault."

Winters looked only slightly less hostile: now he was suspicious.

Walker tried to soothe him. "The arguments you were making were right. Your office had a guy come in who must have looked like Werfel and had Werfel's identification. Your assistant manager had him sign the releases and quitclaims before she paid him. She followed the company's procedures. The position you're taking is correct: everything was done right. But the place for that conversation is inside the company, not with the beneficiary."

Winters shook his head as though to clear it of Walker's nonsense. "It's twelve million. Suppose it was you. Suppose you could get a smaller amount—say five million, or six—today. Or, you could go to court for years, waiting and paying legal fees, and maybe never get a dime. Would you take the offer?"

"Yes," said Walker. "I would. But the reason I would is that I don't have five million, and never expect to. If I were Alan Werfel, I think I would sue for it."

Winter smiled and raised his eyebrows. "Let him."

Walker tried again. "The company will get its money back when this fake Werfel is caught. Maybe all of it, maybe just a big part of it. The company has a really good record of recovery in simple fraud cases. Seventy-six point eight percent last year." He wished he had not said that. He was sounding like an analyst; high-level executives probably didn't have statistics spilling from their memories into their conversations.

"That could be the compromise," said Winters triumphantly. "McClaren's will pay Werfel some portion—say, four million—and if we recover the first twelve million, Werfel will get his other eight."

"We keep his eight million because he lost his driver's license?" asked Walker. "It's not fair."

Winters leaned close to Walker and his voice dropped to an urgent whisper. "We've got to get something."

"What?"

"You and me. Here and now. It's our chance to cut this loss. If we don't, we'll lose our jobs."

Walker thought for a moment. "Did somebody tell you that?"

"They don't have to."

As Walker stared at the face filled with despair, he considered. He said, with a confidence that he didn't feel, "I'll take the blame. We'll say I made the decision. You'll be in the clear, and I'll take my chances. Okay?"

Winters was angry and desperate, his eyes bulging. "No. It's not okay. Twelve million is too much blame for one person to take. The excess spills over on everyone. We have to get some of it back."

"By holding back eight million from the legitimate beneficiary?"

"By negotiating!"

"It's not right, and it won't even work."

"We'll see," said Winters. He stepped toward the conference room and reached for the door handle, while Walker took a deep breath.

"No," he said sharply. "We won't."

Winters turned toward him. "What did you say?"

"Excuse me," said Walker. He opened the conference room door. "Mr. Stillman?"

Stillman's eyes rose from the spot on his belly that he seemed to be looking at. He silently pointed at his chest: Me? Then he stood and joined them in the hallway.

Walker kept his eyes on Winters. "Mr. Stillman, can you get Mr. McClaren on the phone for me, please?"

Winters's face began to turn pale, but he let his features show no sign of surprise.

Stillman said, "Sure. I'll get him." He took his cell phone out of his coat pocket, turned it on, and listened for a dial tone, then punched in the numbers. His face showed no emotion. He kept the phone at his ear. "Hello. This is Stillman. Yes. Could you get Mr. McClaren for me, please?"

Winters made a grab for the telephone, but Stillman seemed to know it was coming. He half-turned his body quickly so that Winters's involuntary lunge was stopped when it hit Stillman's shoulder. Winters's breath came out in a huff, and he stood gasping, clutching the space under his ribs.

Stillman's voice was even and affable. "Wait, I think you'd better cancel that. I'm on a cell phone, and I seem to be getting interference. Tell him I may call later." He switched off the telephone and turned to face Winters.

Winters's own action had shocked him. His eyes were on Walker, but they seemed to be looking inward.

Walker said quietly, "Can you get somebody here to cut him a check?"

"All right," said Winters.

"I'll wait here." He watched Winters walking toward the rear office, then noticed that Stillman had already moved off to the front of the building, where the support staff was working.

When Winters returned, Walker opened the conference room door. Walker sat down beside Daphne Pool and waited for Winters to speak. Werfel was up, staring out the window with his hands in his pockets, but Walker could see from the way the beautiful suit hung that the hands must be clenched fists.

Winters said, "Mr. Werfel, we apologize for the delay, and we thank you for your patience while we worked our way through the bureaucratic difficulties. We've received permission to let you have your full payment today."

Werfel spun around, stared at Walker, and grinned. Walker didn't smile back.

7

Stillman walked out to the car carrying an armload of papers in files and binders, put them into the trunk, and got into the driver's seat. He had already started the car before Walker could slip in beside him. Then Stillman drove, maintaining his mysterious, peaceful expression.

"Aren't you going to say anything about it?" Walker demanded.

Stillman seemed to consider the question for a few seconds, as though he were deciding not how to answer it, but whether it had been addressed to him.

Walker persisted. "Did you know about that—that Werfel was going to be there? Did you set me up to take a fall?"

Stillman's eyes were cold when he turned toward Walker. "I don't see anything wrong with having you all together in one room. You're the insurance company, and he's your client. If you end up taking a fall, it's your fall."

Walker was silent for ten minutes while Stillman drove along surface streets, accelerating at the start of each block, then coasting to a stop to wait for each interminable red light. His mind vacillated between hating Stillman and wondering why what he had said seemed perfectly true.

After a long time, Stillman said, "Don't be so gloomy. What you got was worth the tuition."

"It was?" said Walker bitterly.

"Sure. One day out in the real world and you got your freedom."

"Oh, yeah," said Walker. "They used to call it 'at liberty,' didn't they?"

"Look at the dark side, then," Stillman said. "Say in ten minutes McClaren calls. He's got my cell phone number. He just heard you bluffed Winters into giving Werfel twelve million, and you're fired. No, let's make it good. You're fired, he's already having his secretary call other companies to make sure you never work in that business again, and he's going to sue your ass to recover the twelve. You don't have it, of course, but the story will be in the papers and you'll never work anywhere again."

"Seriously?"

"Seriously."

Walker thought for a few seconds. "Let's see. I guess I'd lose the lawsuit, and go bankrupt. Then I'd learn to live without credit cards and try to start over someplace where all that doesn't matter. Maybe I'd learn to do something—I know—I could go back to college for a year or two to pick up a credential, and try to teach. By then nobody in schools would remember I got sued, and they wouldn't care whether I lost twelve million or twelve cents." He paused for a moment, then said, "I wouldn't make as much money, but at the end of my life I'd probably feel better than I do right now."

"I doubt it," said Stillman. "At the end of your life you're dying. Probably feels like shit."

"In the larger sense."

"Not scared of it, are you?" asked Stillman.

Walker hesitated. "Not that I can detect, other than the dying part."

"That's freedom," Stillman said. "You've set yourself free. If you're doubting the value of that, go back and take a look at Winters—heart pumping, cold sweat, the taste of metal in his mouth. You should celebrate."

"I don't think I can afford it," said Walker. He was quiet for a moment. "But I think you're right. Maybe I'll quit before they fire me."

"Don't be too hasty," Stillman mumbled uncomfortably.

"I went to work at McClaren's because it had a famous name and they wanted me. I went along doing my reports, and after a while, I thought I knew more than I did. McClaren's is a fraud."

Stillman frowned at him for a second, then said reluctantly, "Well, not entirely." He looked at him again, then said, "I didn't want to tell you this right away, because it might cloud the issue and deprive you of your full measure of freedom. But you aren't going to get fired for what you did in there."

"I'm not?" He felt the unmistakable jolt of a parachute opening and jerking him to a near stop. He floated down in amazement.

"No," said Stillman. "They may even add five inches to your pen back in the stable."

"How do you know?"

"McClaren's is a peculiar operation. There are lots of bigger companies. They're probably more efficient and their rates are cheaper. What gets people to do business with McClaren's is the same thing that got you to work for them. It's the name. If McClaren's refused to pay that Werfel character on his father's insurance policy—for any reason, legal or illegal—it would be the beginning of the end."

"If enough people heard about it, maybe, but—"

"Of course they would. Rich people know other rich people. They go to the same two hundred private schools, then the same twenty-five colleges. They take vacations—more of them than other people do—in the same seventy-five spots on the earth, where they stay at the same seventy-five hotels. I'll bet it's sometimes hard for them to believe that the world contains six billion people, because they spend their whole lives bumping into the same six thousand. They won't talk to anybody but each other. And they file lawsuits. If *Werfel v. McClaren* got filed, McClaren's would have to settle quick and throw in a few million extra to soothe Werfel's ego and reassure everybody else."

"I saved them money?"

"Lots. Also probably Winters's ass. They wouldn't fire him for being fooled; they might for being dishonest."

Walker scowled. "Why the hell didn't you tell me that?"

Stillman shrugged. "It wouldn't count if you had known the right thing was also the smart thing. You had to say to yourself, 'If this job means I have to stiff this guy, then they can stick the job in their ear.' Now you'll never have to wonder."

"What if I'd made the wrong decision?"

"The wrong decision?"

"What if I had looked at those two and said to myself, 'Alan Werfel is just a rich asshole who is going to get richer, and Winters is probably a decent, hard-working man who started with nothing and isn't all that much better off now, and will probably lose his job. He's fighting for his life, and I should let him take his shot at it?' "

"You wouldn't be much of an analyst if you couldn't figure out that much."

"That doesn't answer my question. What would you have done?"

"Nothing," said Stillman. "I'm not in the insurance business."

Stillman was gliding along Colorado Boulevard when, without warning, he braked and swung quickly into a driveway. Walker made a grab for the dashboard, but his seat belt tightened across his chest and held him, his hands grasping nothing. "What?" he gasped. "What's wrong?" He held the door handle, not knowing whether to get out or clutch it in case Stillman accelerated out again. Walker was vaguely aware that they were in a large parking lot.

"Not a thing," said Stillman. "I just happened to see a vacancy sign, and we ought to get a place. There aren't many of them in this part of town."

Walker's breathing slowed to normal while Stillman eased the car into a parking space near the entrance to the lobby. "What happened to the other place on Wilshire?"

"Why? Did you leave something in your room?"

"No," said Walker. "I just—"

"It's not smart to get too attached to hotels on a case like this," said Stillman. "You get too predictable, you're liable to get popped."

"Popped?" repeated Walker. "You mean those two guys would kill us?"

Stillman said, "Unfortunately, Pasadena's finest showed up before I could ask them about that. But somebody stole twelve million bucks. You shouldn't let that slip your mind."

"That doesn't mean they'd kill us."

Stillman sighed. "There's no reason to get all sentimental about it. There are people within a block of here who would kill you for the change in your pockets. I'm pretty sure I'm one of them." He got out of the car and waited while Walker joined him.

"Then what's the difference between you and them?"

Stillman smiled peacefully. "If I have enough to stay alive you're safe from me. No matter how much a thief has, he still wants yours."

8

Walker found his room and unlocked the door, then realized that Stillman was following him inside. Stillman tossed his pile of files on the bed, sat down, and opened one. He looked up. "You weren't planning an afternoon nap, were you?"

"No . . ."

"Good. Then let's get started."

Walker set his suitcase down and stood still. "Doing what?"

"Figuring," Stillman said. "It's been three weeks since Andrew Werfel died. He was in New Mexico, and the cause of death was congestive heart failure." He looked up. "I suppose you read that on the death certificate."

"Yes," said Walker. "They always say that. Or pneumonia."

"Yep. It's always heart or lungs. I checked with an acquaintance in Santa Fe, who checked with the coroner's office. The cause was verified. No foul play, as they're fond of saying. Then, after about a week, when the certificate was issued, the bogus Alan Werfel showed up in Pasadena with a copy. He also had Alan Werfel's real ID, and collected a check. Your friend Ellen seems to have handled everything."

"I saw that too," said Walker. "Her signature is on every piece of paper."

"Another week passes, and who calls the Pasadena office but the real Alan Werfel? He wants to know the procedure for collecting on his father's insurance policy."

"Did he talk to Ellen too?"

"No, Winters. He asked for the manager, so that's who he got. Winters thought it was somebody trying to pull a scam, so he told him what he would need to bring, set up an appointment, and called the cops."

"What happened?"

"There were two plainclothes cops sitting at those desks out front when he got there. They waited until he had presented his claim, signed some papers, then showed their badges and dragged him downtown. After a couple of hours they managed to get his prints run and realized an apology was in order. They issued a bulletin for a guy who looks just like Werfel and uses Werfel's name." Stillman smiled. "I wonder how long it's going to take for Werfel to realize what they've done to him."

"Is that when McClaren's called you in?"

"Not yet," said Stillman. "The company traces the check it issued to the first Alan Werfel a week earlier. It was drawn on Wells Fargo in San Francisco. It was endorsed by the artistic but fake Alan Werfel and deposited in an account at Bank of America." He nodded to himself. "This is, not surprisingly, a new account. But it's a different branch of the same bank that Alan Werfel uses, and the check is to Alan Werfel from McClaren's, so it won't bounce. This keeps them calm, and they only put a hold on the three million they can't cover with his other accounts."

"Where is the money now?"

"It traveled. On day two, the fake Alan Werfel starts moving it fast. He gets a check to a real estate company for a new house. This is one of those certified, guaranteed, immediate-pay cashier's checks for closing escrow. This one is for seven million, six hundred thousand. He gets another check to an insurance company on the same basis: who wants to accept ownership of a seven-million-dollar house with no fire insurance? It's expensive. A hundred grand. Another hundred for earthquake. He also pays two hundred to a contractor as an initial payment for remodeling, four hundred to an interior decorator for antique furniture and shipping, two-forty to a landscape architect. On day five, he pays a million six to an art dealer for paintings. In fact, this guy manages to move ten million, two hundred and forty thousand before noon on day five. Then he takes a one-year lease on another house to live in while his is being fixed up: ten thousand a month for a total of one hundred twenty. He pays a probate lawyer three hundred thousand for settling his father's estate. He even pays for the funeral—twenty grand, plus twenty-five for the caterer."

"For a funeral?"

"An imaginary one, sure. Why be cheap? That must be the going rate, because it didn't raise any flags. That left the account with a million two ninety-five. He transferred a million two to an account at Union Bank with a notation on the check that it was for the rest of the remodeling, and closed the B. of A. account with ninety-five grand in cash. Presumably for tips."

"That's it, isn't it?"

"That's it. All before McClaren's knew enough to stop payment on the first check. Of course, each of the imaginary companies had its own account at a different bank. That bought them more time to move it before it could be tracked down." He paused. "What I'm interested in is this money at Union Bank."

"Why?"

"For one thing, it hasn't been pulled out as checks to businesses that don't exist. It's set up as a checking account owned by a woman named Lydia King."

"So?"

"The original amount was twelve million. The account was a million, two hundred thousand. It's ten percent." He glanced at Walker. "The account was set up after all the other money had been successfully moved, as though they were waiting for that to happen before they paid Lydia King."

"Are you saying it was a bribe to Ellen Snyder? That she's off somewhere living as Lydia King?"

"I'm not ready to make any bald pronouncements just yet," said Stillman. He opened another folder and paged through it. "She didn't go into the bank and get herself on the security tapes, so I can't tell you who Lydia King is. She just wrote checks and converted them all over creation. She wrote small checks to other women, who took the money in cash, and she used checks to buy things that can be converted: gold coins, some good jewelry, traveler's checks, money orders, foreign currency."

"So what makes this money different? They made up businesses, and they made up a person."

"The person paid for things I think are overhead: Hermès luggage at fifteen hundred dollars a bag, human-hair wigs, women's clothes, a few plane tickets to other cities where she was converting the money. It goes on and on, in a dozen different names."

"How do you even know it's one woman?"

"I don't. I'm guessing. The theory is, it doesn't matter if she calls herself Lydia King or Georgia Fatwood or Helen Highwater, if the money comes from one account, chances are it's one woman wearing those wigs and new clothes."

"It's still just moving stolen money around. Is the reason you think this account is different just that you know it was a woman who laundered it?"

"It's got a different feel to it, a different smell. A lot of the other money, the ten point eight, goes into some of the same stuff: cash, traveler's checks, gold, money orders, foreign currency, and so on. But none of it goes to overhead. Not a dime so far. What it feels like is that this is her money, and she's got the problem of washing it separately. She has to buy clothes, luggage, makeup, travel. That's all stuff that gives us leads, so it's dangerous. The other person—or persons, since this is a hell of a lot of work to do this quickly—are buying zero that isn't some substitute for cash."

"So you think that they were set up with whatever they needed ahead of time, before they got the insurance money, but Lydia King wasn't."

"Right." Stillman added, "What she looks like is a person who did some service, then got a ten percent payoff and a good-bye."

"When did McClaren's hire you?"

"Right about at that point," said Stillman. "They got nervous when the second Alan Werfel showed up. They looked at their canceled check, saw it had been deposited at B. of A. They called and found out the account was drained. They tried to get in touch with Ellen Snyder, learned she was gone, and went from nervous to agitated."

"And you did all this tracing?"

"Me?" asked Stillman in surprise. "Not personally. I just kind of diverted some of the people at McClaren's, and when they got in over their heads, I hired some subcontractors. I hate chasing paper around."

"What else have you got?"

"I'd say that it comes down to the disappearance of Ellen Snyder."

"You think she got her ten percent and ran off with a suitcase full of wigs."

"Do you?"

"Absolutely not."

"Why—instinct?"

Walker began to pace. "More than that."

Stillman spoke patiently. "You said you liked her. Haven't you ever noticed that on the TV news, every time a con artist gets arrested, they interview five or six old ladies who say, 'She was such a nice, sweet girl. I would never have believed it.' That's why they call them that. They get your confidence."

Walker said, "I know. I've been trying to pretend I don't know her. I just say, 'Okay, these people exist, and you have to use another way to figure out whether you've met one.' She spent two years with the company, six months of it with me in training. What did she make?"

Stillman searched through his pile of folders until he found one that had a stamp that said PERSONNEL—CONFIDENTIAL on it. He scanned a few pages, then looked up. "Are you sure you want to know?"

Walker waved the question away impatiently. "I won't be jealous. I haven't missed any meals."

"The first six months after training, she had a salary of thirty-seven thousand, so she actually got eighteen-five. She also got commissions adding up to sixty-two thousand."

"In six months?"

Stillman said, "She probably sold a dozen policies to relatives."

Walker smiled and nodded. "How about the next full year, after she ran out of relatives?"

"She got promoted to assistant manager at fifty thousand, and made a hundred and forty-four thousand in commissions."

Walker sat down on the bed, took the folder, and looked at the figures for himself. "Jesus," he muttered. Then he slapped the folder shut and collected himself, stood, and returned to pacing. "That makes it even clearer. She was young, single, and had hardly any expenses. Her apartment is even smaller and crummier than mine. She was following a plan, and it's hard to imagine how it could be going any better. Onto those figures you have to add the value of the company health insurance, the retirement plan, the—"

"What's your point?"

"The money isn't enough."

"A million, two hundred thousand?" asked Stillman. "At age twenty-four?"

"Right," said Walker. "She made nearly two hundred last year, plus, say, twenty-five percent in benefits. That's two-fifty. The money she would have gotten for stealing, if she invested it at eight percent, would bring her ninety-six thousand a year. She'd be living on less than half her former income. She would also have to give up everything she already had—her savings, past retirement contributions, free health insurance, whatever possessions she couldn't carry. If you forget everything except that she's bright enough to do these calculations in her head, then it's a deal she would never consider." He stopped pacing, turned to Stillman, and held out both hands, as though waiting for applause.

"Does the term 'immediate gratification' mean anything to you?" asked Stillman.

"To me, yes. If it meant anything to her, I might have had more luck with her. She's a person with a plan that's going to pay off over a twenty-year period, remember?"

"Suppose she had an immediate need," said Stillman. "She could have a gambling problem, a drug problem, some vulnerability to blackmail. Hell, they could have walked in with those papers and said, 'Sign off on this or your kitty-cat dies.' "

"You've been investigating—or duping other people into investigating. Do you believe any of that?"

"I don't know what to believe," said Stillman. "It doesn't feel like blackmail: nobody who blackmails you wants to get paid off in women's clothes and wigs." He frowned. "But Ellen Snyder has no history of knowing the sort of people who do this kind of crime, so it's hard to just fall into it. There's also the fact that she had visitors in her apartment before we got there. Friends don't usually come in through your locked kitchen window. But it's possible she could have been young and naive enough to make the mistake of becoming an unprotected, unarmed woman with over a million in her suitcase." He lay back on Walker's bed and stared at the ceiling. "She's the one part of this that bothers me."

"The rest of it doesn't? Werfel conveniently losing his license and passport and everything just after his father died and not reporting it?"

Stillman shook his head. "I told you I looked into the old man's death. Then I thought of Werfel the Younger. It could work: Alan Werfel files his claim with Ellen Snyder, and cashes his check. Then he kidnaps or otherwise gets rid of Ellen Snyder. He comes back to the office and says to Winters, 'Here I am. I'd like my check, please.' Then nobody fools around with false identities, forges any signatures, and so on. Very neat."

"That didn't happen?"

"No. Werfel senior was in Santa Fe, but Werfel junior was in Italy. He got a call, used a credit card to buy a plane ticket and the passport to get off the plane in New York. He then used the credit card again to buy a ticket from New York to Santa Fe. He got off the plane in Santa Fe, got whisked away to the father's house by relatives, then cared for by servants for the next five days while he's moping around the place. Then there's the funeral, and a lot more grieving friends and relatives, some of whom stayed on for four days. That puts him in Santa Fe when the other Alan Werfel was in Pasadena. He stays there, in fact, until the family attorney shows up to go over his father's papers with him. The lawyer tells him the various things he's got to get done—among them, filing an insurance claim. The call to Winters was from Santa Fe. It's on the phone bill."

"And all that time, he didn't miss his ID?"

"You don't need a passport to visit New Mexico, and you don't need a wallet if you don't leave the house. He seems to have figured the servants who unpacked his bags left his stuff in some drawer. He had them searching the house for it for a day before he called the credit card companies and the DMV and the police. These calls didn't exactly result in a manhunt. There hadn't been any charges on his cards since the plane ticket to New Mexico, so everybody figured it was a simple loss, not a theft."

"But how in the world did it happen? Where did it happen?"

"My guess is Kennedy Airport. He's at the ticket counter. He just got off an eight-hour flight, and he's waiting to buy a ticket for a five-hour flight. He's slow and dull and tired. He's also distracted, because his father just kicked. You saw how he dresses. He's probably got a six-hundred-dollar flight bag on the floor by his feet. He pulls out a soft leather wallet containing the passport, credit cards, and money. He hands the airline clerk his plutonium card, gets it back, and now he's got tickets, the wallet, and so on in his hands while he's trying to move away from the counter. He screws up. Maybe he slips the wallet into his bag and turns his back, or puts it in a pocket that a thief can reach—which is any pocket—and the thief sees which one it is. Or maybe later he sets the bag on a conveyor belt at the metal detectors and loses sight of it while some guy has to go through over and over again. It doesn't matter. You can't be in a major airport without being watched by pros, and he would have been Victim Number One in just about any crowd of ten thousand. It could have happened anywhere, but my guess is Kennedy."

"Okay," said Walker. "He's rich, he looks rich, he's exhausted and distraught, so he's the one who gets robbed. But how did they know about his father's life insurance policy? They didn't get that by picking his pocket in an airport."

Stillman shook his head. "No help there. If you steal the wallet of a guy like Alan Werfel, you run a credit check to see what else he's got that you can steal. If you try it on Alan Werfel, you'll see that his lists trust funds with his father as trustee. The address on his entry is his father's house in Santa Fe."

"But it certainly doesn't list his father's life insurance."

"It doesn't have to. Everybody knows rich people have insurance, and if you want to know the specifics, they're easy to find out. Andrew Werfel was an old, rich guy. Every time he filled out a loan application, a disclosure form to be on the board of directors of some company, or got sued in the last twenty years, that cash-value insurance got included. It found its way into the databases of a lot of companies that sell lists of desirable customers. He also got a divorce from Alan's mother a few years ago. The insurance policy was listed in the material the lawyers filed for division of assets. That means anybody who has an Internet account can call up the case and read it."

"Really?"

"Yeah," said Stillman. "There are other reasons to avoid getting a divorce too, in case you were considering one. I'll go into that another time if I think you need it."

"I can wait," said Walker.

"What I'm saying is, it took me about fifteen minutes to get from the social security card in Werfel's wallet to the life insurance policy," said Stillman. "But keep thinking that way. You may hit something."

"What does all this leave to investigate?"

"Ellen Snyder."

"I've told you everything I know about her."

"No you haven't."

Walker stared at him with narrowed eyes, his arms and shoulders tensed. Then he let out a deep breath. "No," he said. "I haven't. She was more important to me than I said. There was a bit more to it."

Stillman shrugged. "I know."

"How?"

"I heard it too many times from too many people around your office, in too many versions, to ignore it."

Walker's brow furrowed. "What did they say?"

"It doesn't make any difference," said Stillman. "What's the truth?"

Walker sat down on the bed. "I came to San Francisco just before the training class started. I was in a new city, in a part of the country where I'd never been before. I remember when I started college, everybody was alone in the same way, and people were desperate. There was a kind of hysteria in the first week to meet everybody you could. People walked the campus sending out smiles in all directions like SOS signals. By the end of the second week, they had met people, combined into cliques, and the emergency was over. I don't know what I expected when I came to San Francisco: I knew I could handle it, whatever it was. But cities aren't like campuses, and being a grown-up isn't the same as being a student. I arrived, and everybody was already settled, had jobs, families, friends, houses. I thought, 'Sure. Of course.' I rented a cheap apartment, showed up at McClaren's, and got put in the training class."

"And you met Ellen Snyder."

"Yeah," said Walker. "She attracted my attention for no particular reason except that she was pretty. You saw her picture. But when I talked to her I kind of felt at home, and that was better than pretty. When she smiled, it looked as though she was glad to see me, and I think she was. I don't know how to say this, exactly, but she wasn't just an instant friend, a person you meet that you find you can talk to. She was like a relative who already knows all about you, and was just waiting for you to drop by. We talked for hours, the way people do, but there was never any need to start at zero and explain what it was like where I came from, or any of that. She knew. Maybe it was because she came from a place that wasn't very different. When she talked to you, it wasn't like talking to a strange girl. She was like somebody's sister: she knew you well enough not to be especially impressed, but she understood what she knew well enough to realize you weren't so bad, either. After I'd talked to her a couple of times, somebody or other mentioned that she wasn't attached to anybody, so I asked her out."

"You told me that."

"I told you she shot me down after the first time. She didn't. It went on for a while. When you start training they give you all these loose-leaf notebooks full of manuals about business procedures, company policies, computer systems, sample forms, and so on. There are tests. We spent evenings together studying, went out a few times, went to lunch a lot, things like that. You asked before if we had sex. We did. It went on for almost two months. Then she stopped seeing me."

"How does this change what you said before?"

Walker squinted in frustration. "I didn't just start thinking about this. I've been thinking about it for over a year, and it's hard to slice out the parts you want. While it was going on, I noticed that it was different from anything I'd felt before. I don't mean I was happy to be with her. I couldn't get her out of my mind when I wasn't with her. I was up nights, then I'd be ready to go to the class at five-thirty just on the off chance that she'd be there early too. If I thought of something funny, I would save it, not tell anybody so she could be the one I told. I wasn't ready for all this—it came so soon after I arrived, so easily. I let what I knew make me stop trusting what I felt."

"What do you mean?"

"It was like a textbook case. You're in a strange city, alone and lost, doing a job you're not that happy about. You meet this girl who is in the same position, and you seem to hit it off and miraculously become closer than you've ever been with anyone. Miraculously—that's the problem. It's exactly what people warn you about: people in situations like that are vulnerable, lonely, eager to connect with anybody. They jump into big decisions, and then later regret them. Maybe they hurt somebody in a way they can't fix." He could see Stillman wasn't especially respectful of his thinking, but he at least understood. "It wasn't until she stopped seeing me that I admitted to myself that I was in love."

Stillman sighed. "Back up. The breakup is what I've got to know about. How did it happen?"

"She just stopped. There wasn't one of those talks where she said we weren't right for each other, or that nonsense they always give you about being friends. There was no argument about anything. I've gone over and over what I said and did, and what she said and did, and there was nothing. She just stopped. No real explanation. I would ask her out, and she was happy to talk to me, but she wouldn't go. I would go to where we used to eat lunch alone together, and she would still show up to eat with me, but bring five or six other people with her to the table. She would treat us all the same."

"Are you sure you didn't miss something?"

"I'm sure. I tried ignoring her and staying out of her way, and she would come and talk to me. But it was as though she had amnesia, and forgot everything that had gone on between us. It was the way it had been before we got together. She was this nice, friendly girl who was in my training class."

"Another guy?"

Walker shook his head. "There was still a month or two of classes left. I saw her every day, couldn't keep my eyes off her. There was never any guy around her. And she was always available at night for dinners or parties the whole group went to, even if somebody thought of it at the last minute. She always arrived alone and went home alone."

Stillman mused, "I suppose you've got to be right. A few of those people would have been falling all over each other to be the first to tell you, if there had been somebody. Didn't you press her to find out what was bothering her?"

Walker looked down, uncomfortable. "Sure. It's funny. At the time, what she said struck me as a lie—not exactly untrue, but as beside the point, an evasion. She said that she had come to San Francisco to take the training class, and do as well as she could so she could go off to her job at a field office and be successful at it. She said she had loved the time we spent alone together—her words—and would always remember it, but she was leaving for Pasadena soon, and had to concentrate on the future."

"I don't think it was a lie either," said Stillman. "I think she said what she meant." He glanced at Walker. "I'll bet it killed you."

Walker nodded, then focused on Stillman. "But that was a while ago, and I'm over it."

"Why did you tell me now?"

"It's why I decided to come with you," said Walker. "I know her. I thought it might be easier to convince you she was innocent if you didn't know that I was once in love with her. I also believe in privacy.

I think that telling any stranger who asks that you had sex with somebody is a betrayal."

"You thought I might be down here trying to frame her," said Stillman.

"It had crossed my mind," said Walker. "It's the only way that a person like Ellen could get in trouble. I decided tonight that what you've been trying to do was figure out what really happened. So I'm telling you everything. I didn't just meet Ellen in class and take her out to dinner once. I got to be very close to her, spent a couple of months watching her and listening to everything she said and turning it over and over in my mind. Then I spent a year afterward double-checking to figure out what went wrong. You're investigating her? Well, I already did: she's not somebody who commits insurance fraud."

Stillman sighed. "Maybe. Do you at least agree with me that the next thing we ought to do is find her?"

"Yes," said Walker. "But I don't know how to do that."

"I've got somebody working on it. After it gets dark, we'll go to see him."

9

Stillman stopped the car on a dark street in the flat outer reaches of the Santa Clarita Valley, just under the wall of jagged mountains that rose up implausibly to the north. To the left, across the street, was a high school athletic field with wooden bleachers behind an eight-foot chain-link fence, and beyond it a blacktop parking lot the size of a staging area for an armored division. Walker squinted into the darkness and made out that it had a metal post with a basketball backboard every hundred feet. Along the right side of the street was a row of nearly identical one-story houses that were darkened as though they had been hastily evacuated in advance of some natural disaster. "Nobody seems to be home," said Walker.

"They're in there all right," said Stillman. "They just go to bed early."

"The whole neighborhood?"

"Most of them have to drive all the way back into town in the morning to work. The rest have to get out of here by seven, before the kids arrive. The road gets clogged with buses and car pools and jaywalking teenagers." Stillman got out of the car and waited for Walker, who lingered at the door and stared around him.

"What are you looking at?"

"Just trying to be sure you're not cleverly trying to attract the attention of somebody who wants to break my skull, the way you did last night."

"I explained about that," said Stillman. "I just wanted to verify a theory I had. What point would there be in doing it again? Come on."

Walker started up the sidewalk to the nearest house, but Stillman tapped his shoulder. "Not in there."

"Then which one is it?"

"You can't see it from here. It's down the end of the street and across the basketball courts."

"Why park so far away?"

"It's a nice night. Southern California is a lot better at night than San Francisco, don't you think? The air drifts in and stays put. It's around all day getting heated up and lived in, so you're kind of attached to it by nightfall. It's a friendly arrangement."

"Why do you always park in some screwy place and then walk?"

"I told you, it's a nice night," Stillman answered. Then he muttered, "Besides, it's a habit."

"Why does that not seem to be an adequate answer?" asked Walker.

"I didn't say there wasn't a reason for the habit," Stillman admitted. "I told you we're going to see a guy who works for me."

"That was what you said."

"Well," said Stillman, "he doesn't always work for me. That means that at other times he has to work for other people, right?"

"What other people?"

"Well, now, that is the sticky part, isn't it?" Stillman said. "If he went around telling me things like that, he would probably tell other people who I was and what he did for me."

Walker looked at Stillman uneasily, then turned his head to survey the deserted neighborhood. "You park far away from his house because his other customers are criminals. Is that it?"

"Not necessarily," Stillman said. "I'm just respecting the great void in information I have. It's always a good idea. Constantine Gochay is the guy we're going to see. I use him for skip-tracing and similar dull, sedentary occupations that clash with my temperament. I save myself aggravation by hiring the best."

"He's the best?"

"Right. If I hire Gochay, I save money on the plane tickets I would have bought to places where somebody was six weeks ago. The problem with hiring the best is that everybody wants the best. A word like 'everybody' takes in a lot of people with a wide range of behavior patterns. It could, as you no doubt astutely surmise, include corporate headhunters trying to get background information on some job candidate, or the regular kind of headhunters. It could also include some of the strange, tropical flowerings of certain federal agencies that have been known to retain employees with names like 'Black Luigi' or 'The Poison Dwarf.' Do we want to meet them? No. Do we want them to see our car? No."

They were across the dark blacktop forest of basketball hoops, walking up a road that seemed to have no sidewalks or street lamps. The houses on this road were new, most of them set back on sloping lawns and obscured by high fences and thick hedges. Stillman grasped Walker's arm and pulled him through a gate set into a vine-covered wall. Walker's feet detected a stone walkway up the front lawn. The house looked as dark as the others, but Stillman walked to the front door and rang the bell.

A moment later, a young woman with close-cropped red hair and very white skin appeared. She wore blue jeans and a gray sweater that hung to the middle of her thighs. Her glasses reflected the yellow bug light above the porch, so she seemed to Walker to be staring at him with the wide, disinterested eyes of a cat. "Go on in," she ordered. "He's expecting you." Her accent sounded foreign to Walker, but it was so faint that he could not identify it beyond the conjecture that the continent must be Europe, and her appearance argued for the north.

She held the door, so they had to sidestep in to get around her, and Walker was too hesitant to do anything but mistime it. There was a second when she leaned forward to check the street while he was still moving in and they came together, Walker's chest fleetingly brushed by her breasts. The woman's sharp green eyes flashed dangerously up at him in deep annoyance and then clouded not in exoneration but mere dismissal. He mumbled, "Excuse me," and followed Stillman's back as it disappeared into an open doorway at the other end of the big room.

He passed a huge projection television screen that held an image of a woman's face a foot and a half wide with enormous lips and teeth, smiling about something the stereo speakers said was "scandalizing Hollywood." He heard the young woman behind him, flopping down on a couch.

He stepped to the doorway to find Stillman and another man already staring expectantly at him. The other man was taller and thinner than Stillman, with black curly hair in ringlets that made him look like the bust of a Roman emperor. He nodded at Walker, then turned away, his eyes focusing on Stillman for a half-second before they moved to his work table.

The room was like a disordered and confused repair shop, the floor tangled with bundles of power cords and surge suppressors, the tables around the walls crowded with computers and screens, most of them with no keyboards. Printed papers were on the floor and laid in overlapping stacks, with some tossed in the empty boxes the paper had come in.

"Ellen Snyder . . . Ellen Snyder," Gochay muttered as he looked at various pieces of paper, then put them back. He turned and squinted, then stepped to a table, tossed several sheets off the top of a pile, and snatched up a few more that had been on the bottom. Then he led Stillman and Walker through another open doorway into a narrow, dim hall that seemed to encircle the work room. He opened a door on the other side of the hall and led them inside.

The room appeared to have been transported here from somewhere in the Middle East. There were two big couches on either side of a large, low, copper-clad table that sat on an Oriental rug. Strewn around the room on the floor were oversized pillows upholstered with materials that seemed too complex—snippets of tapestries, Oriental weavings in patterns that weren't the same as the rug, and one that was iridescent like bird feathers. There were no windows in the room, and nothing hung on the walls. Walker looked more closely at the walls and saw that what had looked like panels of plasterboard cov-

ered with high-gloss paint was sheet metal: the room was insulated—
against sound? Electronic signals leaking out? He noticed a bank of
computer components that seemed to be connected in some tandem
arrangement humming quietly, with red and green lights no bigger
than beads glowing steadily, and decided that must be what was being
protected.

Stillman said, "What have we got?"

Constantine Gochay scanned the sheets. "I should have had Serena
add this up for you before. I don't know what the hell this is going to
cost." He reached the bottom of the last page. "Ah. I see. It's thirty-
five hundred."

Stillman's brows knitted. It was the first time Walker had seen him
react to any expense.

Gochay nodded in sympathy. "I know. It's not high enough, is it?
She isn't that hard to trace."

"No," said Stillman. "Is she even using fake names?"

"That much she's doing," said Gochay. "But it's not complicated.
She switches to a new one in each town, but then she'll buy something
with a card in the old name while she's there. Or she'll use it to buy a
plane ticket to the next place." He put the sheets in Stillman's hands,
then stood over his shoulder and pointed at the entries in order. "See?"
He paused, and looked at Stillman again. "Maybe you should be careful, eh?"

"I haven't thought of a reason yet why this one would want us to
find her," said Stillman. "I have to hope she's just not too good at
this."

Gochay shrugged. "Then you'll get what you get."

"Hard to argue with that." Stillman reached into his coat pocket,
but Gochay stopped him.

"No, no. Please pay the lady on your way out."

Walker followed Stillman into the hallway, through the work room,
into the long space that Walker now realized was a false living room,
placed between the outer walls and the rooms where everything illegal
went on, to fool eavesdropping devices. The girl was lying on the
couch staring disgustedly at a commercial with a red pickup truck
bouncing unpleasantly up a steep dirt road in some mountains.

She looked up at Walker. "Did you and Constantine bring each other to a mutually satisfying completion?" Her accent was gone.

Walker answered, "Actually, you're more my type." He silently cursed himself. Why had he said that? This wasn't somebody joking with him at the office. These people were criminals. She could even be Gochay's wife. He could feel the hairs on his arms standing up.

But she smiled back, her eyes half-lidded in a way that made her look even more like a cat. "I don't think so. I like girls."

Walker said uncomfortably, "We have something in common."

She brought her knees up and bobbed to her feet. "Good. We'll go out some night and cruise the bars for pussy. Money, please."

Stillman held out a handful of hundred-dollar bills. She snatched the money, folded the bills without counting them, then lifted her long sweater so she could stuff them into the pocket of her jeans. "Oh, Max. You shouldn't have."

"Good night, Serena," said Stillman. "Always nice to see you."

She opened the door. "Likewise, Max. Never darken my door again." Stillman stepped out into the night. Walker tried to follow, but the girl moved in front of him, stood on tiptoes, and kissed his cheek. Then she pushed him toward the door. "Now go out and play with Max. Shoo!"

Walker found himself on the darkened porch. He couldn't see Stillman, but he heard the voice. "She likes you."

"Serena?" He stepped uneasily off the porch, relieved when his foot touched a surface that felt like a stepping-stone.

"Yep, God help you." Stillman walked toward the street. "And whatever her name is, it's not Serena. That's just a six-letter computer password."

10

As they moved to the end of the dark street and came around the corner toward the high school, the silhouettes of three men materialized out of the shadows. Walker's muscles tensed, his mind first identifying them as the nameless, dangerous people he had been half-expecting to meet at Gochay's, then transforming them into the two men who had appeared the same way in the alley last night. But they weren't even looking in his direction. He reminded himself that he was near a high school. They were probably just boys hanging around after practice, the way he had at that age. They stepped apart to the edges of the sidewalk, so that Walker and Stillman could only pass between them. Stillman's pace never slowed. "Evening," he said. Walker had no choice but to fall a step behind, since there wasn't room to pass except single file.

There was no answer. As Stillman came abreast of the men, Walker could see their shapes were bigger, wider than high school boys. He detected a sudden movement in the dim light. The man nearest to Stillman brought his hand up, but Stillman was in motion too. His left hand batted the arm down, and held it while he spun the man around and brought his right elbow into the man's throat. The man instinctively backed up as fast as he could, trying to avoid the crushing force on his throat, until his head bounced against the face of the man in the middle with a hollow bone-sound.

Walker ducked low and hurled himself into the thickest shadows, where the two men's bodies seemed to overlap. He knew his shoulder hit someone's midsection when he felt the belly give inward and he heard a huff that came from somewhere above. He stayed low and punched wildly, his fists hammering at the two men as quickly as his arms would move. He leaned into them and kept advancing with his knees high, digging hard like a football lineman to keep the two men off balance.

His head rang and stung with glancing blows, and he endured two heavy hammer-thumps on his back. He kept moving, but suddenly ducked his left shoulder and swung his right arm higher toward the faces. In the darkness, the sudden hook upward caught someone by surprise and landed between an eye and nose.

There was a cry, and the resistance gave way abruptly. As he lunged forward into empty air, one of them landed a kick on the right side of his stomach. The sudden impact made his lungs refuse to breathe, and that induced a panic in him. He felt like a man in deep water struggling toward the surface. His legs pumped harder to get clear, and as they did, he realized his foot was pushing off the torso of a man who was down.

He felt his foot tangle in the arm of the fallen man, and then he knew the pavement was coming. His arms instantly pushed out in front of him in a reflex to break the fall, but they skidded on concrete and the burning sensation shot up to his elbows. He rolled and kicked out, and heard a wet *thwock* sound that told him his heel had made contact with an open mouth. He scrambled to his feet and felt a strong pressure around his shoulders that pulled him forward. The voice of Stillman was close to his ear: *"Run."*

He dug in and ran a few steps with Stillman before he heard the noise. It was not as loud as it should have been, just a pop like a firecracker. His lungs expanded with alarm and sucked in a breath over the hurt, overruling whatever cramp it was that had squeezed his chest for the past fifteen seconds. He was running harder now, dashing along the street with each leg straining to put another footstep between him and a gun. He was aware of the quick, rhythmic tapping of Stillman's shoes on the pavement to his right. He heard *pop-*

pop-pop and spun his head to look, but Stillman was still up, and Walker's awkward movement had given Stillman a chance to get a step ahead.

According to some rule that was too basic to put into words, that meant Walker was free to run as fast as he pleased. He stretched his legs, pumped his arms, and dashed onto the broad asphalt surface. He veered away from Stillman to keep from bumping him, and the next shot hit the pavement between them, splashing bright sparks and bits of powdered asphalt ahead like skipped stones.

Walker weaved in and out of the tall poles that held basketball backboards, then realized that would make his next move predictable. He let his next sidestep take him off at an angle away from the poles. He heard a bullet ring a pole and ricochet into the darkness, then determined to stop trying to be clever.

He heard Stillman's voice. "Something's wrong," he rasped.

"No shit," said Walker, annoyed.

"They're not running after us."

"Good!"

They reached the end of the pavement and Walker felt faster running across the grass, but the light from the street lamps seemed inordinately bright. He ran still harder, but in a minute he began to slow down to keep from jarring his feet on the sidewalk. He heard Stillman behind him, and then the heavy footsteps slowed too. "The car," Stillman gasped, winded.

Walker stopped. It was true. He had been running away from the gun, not running toward anything. But they had reached the street where Stillman had parked the car, and he should have been able to see it, but he didn't. He looked around to check his bearings. It should have been right across the street. He looked at Stillman and said uselessly, "It's gone."

Walker tried to sort out the possible implications. Stillman had parked in a place where cars got stolen, Stillman had left the keys in it, Stillman had made some other reckless mistake. His eyes settled on the end of the road. There was a major thoroughfare up there. Headlights were passing by—one, then two in opposite directions, then a big truck—as though nothing were happening down this quiet side street, and Walker wasn't about to die. He started toward the lights.

"Wait!" said Stillman. "Don't go that way."

Walker looked back. "Why not?"

"I think that's why the car's gone. They want us on the street." He crossed the road and started up the front lawn of the nearest house. When he reached the front steps he turned to beckon to Walker.

Walker lowered his eyes to take the first step, and his shoe seemed to glow. He lifted his foot, and it threw a dark, clear shadow on the whitening sidewalk. Then he heard the engine. The trajectory of the car was wrong. The lights were supposed to be illuminating the road, with a slight bias to the right side, not shining up here on the sidewalk. Walker's hands and then his shirt brightened, and then the lights were in his eyes. The car was coming toward him.

He began to back up onto the school lawn, shading his eyes to make out the shape of the car. As soon as he was out of the glow of the headlights, he could see the side of the car. A window slid down. There was a head in the window, and beside it a gun barrel. As the barrel came out the window and began to level on him, he turned and ran hard. He heard the engine coast, then heard brakes, and he dived to the grass, waiting for the report of the rifle.

The sound was not the one he expected: a loud impact and then glass shattering and tinkling onto the street. He raised his head a little.

Stillman was at the corner of the house. He hurled a second big stone from the rock garden at the car, pivoted, and ran before it smashed into the side window. He disappeared between two houses. The car wheeled around and rocked to a stop, the headlights aimed in the direction where Stillman had gone. Walker could see that the windshield was cratered from Stillman's first rock, the center milky and opaque, with spiderweb cracks extending to the roof and side struts. Stillman was gone, and a couple of lights went on in houses up the block.

The car turned again and the headlights swept across Walker, then disappeared as the car sped off up the street. Walker stood and began to trot toward the place where he had last seen Stillman. By the time Walker reached the sidewalk, Stillman had emerged again a hundred feet up the street, walking toward the lighted thoroughfare. Walker ran until he caught up.

Stillman said, "Time to get a roof over our heads." They walked on for a time, and he began again. "I think it's also time for you to be getting back to San Francisco. Glad you put it off until now, though. Otherwise, I'd be lying back there while those three guys went through my pockets."

"Just a common courtesy," said Walker. "As if I had a choice."

"It's not a common courtesy," Stillman said. "Not common at all." He walked on a few steps. "The human instinct if you're not brain-dead is to turn your back and run. Nine people out of ten are brain-dead, so what they do is stand there wringing their hands, not knowing whether to shit or go blind. They don't run, they don't fight, they just watch. I'll be sorry to see you go."

"Save it," said Walker. "I'm not leaving yet."

"I think you ought to give it some time, and tell me in the morning. Our little inquiry hasn't gone the way I predicted."

"It's reassuring to know that you weren't planning to get beat up every time you went outside."

Stillman's eye moved to the corner toward Walker for a moment, then stared ahead. "Yeah. I thought the case was going to be about the details of the insurance business, but it kind of moved beyond that."

Walker kept striding along beside Stillman. His heartbeat was beginning to slow, but he kept turning his head to look behind them, then to the sides, then ahead. The fear and anger and excitement had subsided a bit now, leaving him with nerves seared and tender, muscles strained by the sudden exertion. He began to notice the dull throb of injuries left by punches he had noticed at the time only as bright, momentary explosions of pain that he had somehow transmuted into rage. As he walked, he decided it was as though his body had been temporarily occupied by a deranged, destructive tenant who had abruptly departed, leaving it scraped, battered, and strained. The most remarkable sensation was exhaustion. When he lifted his right hand to investigate a tender swelling above his eyebrow, the weight of his arm surprised him.

Stillman was watching. "You've been in a few fights, haven't you?"

Walker was nettled. "Not like that. Not until I met you."

"Then it's good that we got into a fight in the dark, with that kind of guy. I figured you'd be okay."

Walker was amazed. "You did?"

"Sure. The way they were standing on the sidewalk waiting for us, trying to look big and hairy, I wasn't worried."

"What does it take to make you worry?"

Stillman pondered the question for a few paces, then stopped. "You know a fight is about to start, and then you notice that one guy is standing like this." Stillman faced Walker with his knees very slightly bent and his arms out from his sides in what looked like a welcoming gesture, with the hands open. Stillman straightened and walked on. "If you see one of those, drop everything and run."

"What the hell would that tell you?"

"He's a ninja."

"Like in the movies? You're kidding."

"No, not like in the movies," said Stillman. "Not one tiny bit. Ninjutsu has made a comeback, sort of like karate. Only what this guy has been training himself to do isn't just to block your punch and put you on the ground. He doesn't think fighting is fun. He's not in a sport, he wants to kill you quick. If you're going to stay in California, you're going to see a lot of strange stuff. Those guys tonight were within our capability."

"They had guns."

"One of them did. Even he didn't start out to shoot us. He just realized they'd been overconfident, and tried to make up for it. I was watching for it. A guy who uses his right hand to reach behind his belt in the middle of a fight probably isn't tucking his shirttail in. The only things he could want back there are a knife that's too big to fit in a pocket, or a gun." He looked at Walker. "That's something else to remember."

Walker said, "I think maybe I'll just stay out of fights."

"The best way is to keep away from people who get you into fights," said Stillman. He led the way and got them both inside a doughnut shop just as the first three police cars sped past on their way to the scene of the shooting. Walker turned to stare out the big window at the fast-moving metal and flashing lights. A second later, Stillman's reflection in the window caught Walker's eye. Stillman tugged his sleeve back to see his watch, nodded noncommittally, then stepped forward to survey the glass case where pastries were arrayed seductively in ranks.

Walker whispered, "How'd they do?"

"Just fair. About six minutes." Stillman turned to the young Hispanic boy behind the counter. "Evening, barkeep. Two cups of coffee, two of these cream-filled beauties with the chocolate on top, two glazed, and two of this crumb kind."

"Old-fashioned," the boy corrected him.

"I admit it," Stillman said, "but give me the doughnuts anyway."

"The doughnuts. That's what they're called."

Stillman accepted the bag of doughnuts. As the boy handed him his change, Stillman handed the coins to Walker. "Here. Call us a cab while I escort these fellows to a table."

"Where should I say we're going?"

"Burbank airport. We'll rent a car there." He paused. "Maybe you could buy a plane ticket."

Walker made the call, then sat down at a tiny table across from Stillman. There were three doughnuts sitting on a napkin in front of him. "Go ahead," said Stillman. "They're very soothing, which is why the Red Cross is always forcing them on people. Nothing burns energy faster than disaster . . . except sex, of course. And whatever deity was in charge of printing up our agenda tonight seems to have slipped up and left that one out."

Walker took a bite of the big cream-filled doughnut with gooey chocolate on top. It was strange, but he reluctantly and silently acknowledged that it tasted better than anything he had ever eaten. He was overcome with the need to eat all of it. Then he picked up the next one.

Stillman said, "We'll have to get another half dozen to take with us before the cab gets here. I don't want to have to go out in the middle of the night for more. The streets around here don't seem to be safe."

II

Stillman drove the new rental car past the hotel, then around the block, looking intently at the windows, the parking lot, the doors of the lobby. Then he drove into the parking lot and up a couple of rows before he parked.

Walker asked, "Is there something else I should be expecting?"

"Not at all," Stillman assured him. "But it's always important to have good health habits when you travel." He got out of the car, ceremoniously locked it, and walked into the lobby. He stopped at the little shop and began to scrutinize the shelves. "You don't have to wait for me."

Walker held up the bag. "I've got your doughnuts."

"I'll catch up with you."

Walker went upstairs to his room. He unlocked the door with vague trepidation, then stepped away from it and listened, prepared to sprint back down the hall if he heard a noise. There was silence. He pushed open the door, leaned in to fumble with the light switch, then stepped back again. The door swung shut, but before it did, he had a glimpse of the room that included no intruders. He unlocked the door again, slipped inside, and let it close behind him.

Everything was in its place, the bed was made, and he was alone in the quiet and order. He walked to the folding stand and opened the lid of the suitcase Stillman had bought him. The new clothes were undisturbed, the coats folded, the shirts in their packages, the creases in the pants still in straight lines. He took off the coat and tie he had been wearing and examined them. The coat needed dry-cleaning, but he detected no tears. He looked down. His pants had dirt on the right knee, but nothing that appeared fatal. He was tired of having nothing but clothes he couldn't afford. They had been bought as a disguise, but they had settled into his mind as a fiduciary responsibility.

He moved to the bathroom and looked in the mirror. His face was smudged and sweaty, and there were a couple of angry red scrapes—one above the right eye and another on the left cheek. He touched the side of his head and involuntarily sucked in a breath: the pain was insistent now. There was a hard lump, and the hair was stiff from blood that had dried there. He touched two other places above the hairline, and the nerves there sent dispatches of alarm.

There was a knock on the door. He stepped close to it and said, "Who is it?" then slipped to the side, not knowing whether he was getting out of the way in case the door flew off its hinges or because he feared bullet holes would appear simultaneously in the door and his chest.

"It's me," said Stillman's voice.

Walker opened the door and let Stillman push inside and close it. Stillman fixed the chain and turned the deadbolt, then noticed Walker's expression. "Always lock everything that locks," he said. "It doesn't cost a cent."

"The doughnuts are on the bed," said Walker.

Stillman said, "I just called the airport for you. There was some fog earlier, so the flights were delayed and they're still catching up. I got you on the United shuttle for tomorrow at eight."

It took an effort for Walker to force out the words. "Thanks, but I told you I'd like to keep at this until we find Ellen." He was tired and dirty, and he didn't want to argue. He didn't want to be here, and fighting for the privilege was more than he was willing to do.

Stillman was putting things in Walker's bathroom. "Well, sleep on it. Here's some antiseptic and stuff," he said. "Don't let any scrapes get infected, especially the ones you got on somebody's teeth. I know a guy who did that one time, and his finger swelled until it was as big as his dick—or at least that's what he said. I didn't compare." He picked up the bag of doughnuts and placed two of them on a napkin atop the little refrigerator beside the television set. "Here's your share of the doughnuts. You want something to drink with that?" He opened the refrigerator. "There are lots of little liquor bottles left by the pygmies."

Stillman poured a tiny bottle of scotch into a glass and took a sip, then winced. "We made some progress in a day and a half."

"We got beat up twice."

"Beat up? Hell, this isn't beat up. There hasn't been a winner of a title fight that looked better than us since the young Muhammad Ali—and he looked better to start with. I'm talking winners now. The losers, they looked—well, like losers."

Walker nodded. "Good thing for us the Japanese assassins didn't show up."

"Probably couldn't get a flight into L.A., what with the fog and all," said Stillman, staring interestedly at his drink. He brought it to his lips, took a big gulp, and squinted. "Have you noticed we're getting contradictory signals?"

"I'm not getting any signals."

"Tonight was the second time we had guys trying to get whatever pieces of paper we had. I guess they want to know what we know. But tonight they seemed to think the second choice was to kill us."

"If that's a signal, I got that."

"Well, it doesn't go with this." He pulled some folded pieces of paper out of his coat pocket. As he unfolded them Walker recognized them as the ones Constantine Gochay had given him. "See, Constantine traced Ellen Snyder for us. She made five blips on his screen since she disappeared. She was here in Los Angeles for a night or two, at the Holiday Inn near the airport. That was two weeks ago. She used the name Jo Anne Steele."

Walker's brows knitted. "How does Gochay know she was Ellen Snyder?"

"It's the name of a woman who's a customer of the Pasadena office of McClaren Life and Casualty. All of Jo Anne Steele's personal information was in the office files. Somebody used it to apply for credit cards and licenses. They're great for ID, and if you don't actually use them to pay, you're in the clear. She—somebody—used them to register, then paid in cash so there would be no credit card record. Very sensible."

"How did Gochay know that?" Walker persisted. "Any of it? If she didn't pay with the card to avoid a record, why is there a record?"

Stillman took another sip of his drink. "He didn't pick up anything interesting by checking credit reports, so he broke into some hotel reservation systems and started to pick things up."

"But how did he know enough to look for the names of women customers from McClaren's files?"

"I told him."

Walker's irritation was beginning to come into his voice. "But how did you know?"

"It was the way she opened bank accounts and bought stuff when the million two disappeared. I had him run the twenty-five or so in the files who were the best matches: about the right age and sex." He paused. "You know, if you carry life insurance, auto, and home owner's with one company, you get a big break on the rates, so—"

"I know that," Walker interrupted. "The company knows everything about you—birthday, family, jobs, social security number, credit records, physical exams, driving records. That's what I do for a living, remember? I use that information."

Stillman shrugged. "So did she."

"And so did Gochay?"

Stillman smiled. "Now you're catching up."

"That's illegal," said Walker. "All of it is illegal."

Stillman sighed. "That's why he doesn't come cheap. You can't pay pocket change and expect people to commit felonies for you." He finished his drink and stared at the glass regretfully before he set it down. "She's not alone."

"What?"

"She's not traveling alone," said Stillman. "I thought you might like to know that."

Walker shrugged in irritation. "If you're trying to say I wasn't good enough for her, I knew that before you showed up."

"Nobody would be. It's two guys." He stared at his papers again. "Or I think it is. Constantine looked to see if there was anybody whose reservations corresponded exactly with hers—same check-in and check-out in more than one city. To his surprise, there were two. Every place she went, there were two men checked into an adjoining room."

"I'm amazed," said Walker.

"Of course, the other possibility when you have two guys is that they're keeping an eye on her. She could be doing this against her will." He picked up the doughnut bag. "Well, got to go. I've got to get us both to the airport early tomorrow." He headed for the door, and Walker expected him to stop and say something else. But he stepped out and closed the door behind him. A few seconds later, Walker heard another door down the hall close.

Walker sat in the silence of the strange room and stared at the wall. He thought about Ellen. He brought back the quiet, friendly way she talked. She was pretty, but that had only been what had made him notice her, and it seemed irrelevant now. His memory couldn't hold her in stasis so he could study her features. She was moving, talking, and he supposed it was her direct, pleasant manner that had attracted him. It had somehow also given him the notion that an invitation of some kind would not be scorned. If she didn't want to go, she would simply say so. He had asked her to dinner at Scarlitti's and thought his guess was confirmed. She had said, "I'd like that. I don't know anybody up here, and it will give us a chance to talk."

Kennedy had said something to him after training class one day that had puzzled him. He had said, "What do you make of Ellen Snyder?"

Walker had answered, "Make of her? I like her. She's always pleasant and friendly. Great smile, too."

Kennedy had smirked and cupped his hand beside his mouth to call, "Hello? She's in sales."

"What do you mean?"

"She's been training herself to sell insurance policies. Am I getting through to anybody in there?"

"So she's not going to kill somebody to get a desk in the main office. This means she's insincere when she says 'Hi'?"

"It means she knows she's good at making people like her and making them think she likes them just as much. If they believe that, then they'll like her even more, and pretty soon they're writing a check. She's using us to sharpen her skills: we're her tackling dummies."

The dinner had been full of things to think about. The evening had begun with a certain promise. He had been pleased when he had smelled a hint of perfume and seen that her makeup was different—the lips redder, a little blush on the cheeks, and eye shadow. He had interpreted those changes as having been intended for him, as indications that she liked him and wanted to show him. No, he remembered, he had made more of it than that. He had decided that she was declaring a change in their relationship. He had seen that she wore flat heels and sweaters for business, so how could the dress, high heels, and perfume not be messages?

The conversation had been full of moments when he had thought he sensed something unusual happening. They had both talked about themselves more openly than he would have expected, because when one of them stopped, the other would ask another question that prompted the next set of revelations. It was as though each of them were a series of doors leading inward. Each question was a knock on the next door. The one inside would hesitate for a moment, then decide to make an exception and let the visitor in one more door—just one more.

Her revelations about the past were as unmemorable as his: a family far away that was more remarkable to her than to anyone else, a childhood and adolescence that had been embarrassingly free of serious obstacles. There were big differences in their thoughts about the next twenty years of their lives, but he had noted them without alarm. She had grand strategies. He didn't believe in the efficacy of grand strategies, but he was interested in them, and enjoyed hearing about hers.

When he had left her at her apartment she had lingered at the security gate at the front entrance and thanked him simply and warmly. He had wondered if she was waiting for a kiss, or if it was the furthest idea from her mind and she would think he was sophomoric to do the sort of thing that high school kids did instead of what grown-up business colleagues did . . . whatever that was. By the time he had reached the conclusion that since he wanted to kiss her, the only sane and logical course was to try, the opportunity had expired. She was chirping an energetic "Good night" and closing the gate behind her. He had replied, "Night," turned on his heel, and taken himself off.

A couple of days later, he really had asked her to the concert, and she really had refused, just as he had told Stillman. When she had refused, he had looked back on their first date differently. The makeup and perfume and the little dress and shoes had been brought out because it was evening, not because she was interested in seducing him. Her conversation had not been intimate, just open: free of paranoia or guile. She had asked questions about his life because she was interested in life, not because she was interested in John Walker. He decided he had been foolish, but only mildly foolish. He had offered his company in a polite and friendly way, and she had just as politely declined. Maybe she had given him a hint in her conversation that he had missed. The twenty-year plan she had described had not included any time or space that John Walker could imagine he might occupy.

But after the exam she had made a special effort to corner him and talk to him. He remembered it exactly. They had come out of the exam at six, and he had taken the elevator to the lobby alone and found her waiting at the door. "That was so easy," she moaned. He had shrugged and said carefully, "I guess we shouldn't complain." But she had persisted, staying with him as he walked into the lower level of the parking garage, making no attempt to veer off to where her car was parked. "But I spent half the night studying when I could have been listening to the Third Horn Concerto. What a dope. Next time remind me."

He had pondered that conversation for two days, hearing over and over the words "next time." She had not been telling him to leave her alone: she really had wanted to study. He decided that he might have just received a lesson about communicating with women. Maybe sometimes when they said something they weren't delivering an encoded subtext. The words meant to them exactly what they meant to him. On the third day, while he was still formulating theories and comparing them to her behavior, she settled the issue. She walked up to him before class and said she had bought two tickets to the next concert in the series.

After that he had studied her with an intensity that he had never applied to anything in his life. She was different. She seemed to read him accurately, know what he was thinking without spending time at it, and never be surprised at what she knew. They had been thrown together more and more by the odd circumstance that they were doing exactly the same things at the same times each day—even having the same thoughts, as they listened to the instructors in the training classes and committed to memory the various aspects of the business. But when they were alone together, they seldom needed to talk about the work. They saw each other as relief, a corrective to the insurance business. Before long, they were together nearly every night.

Their only argument had been about sex. One night, after about a month, they had walked back to her apartment after a movie, and he had kissed her as usual and started to leave. She had looked at her watch and said, "It's not that late, and tomorrow's Saturday. Come in." She had not looked to see whether he was coming, just unlocked the gate and closed it after him, then led him to her apartment, closed the door, and kissed him again without turning on the light. They had stayed there for a long time, in deep leisurely kisses as his hands moved, beginning to trace the shape of her body. Then, a sudden concern held him back. He had paused because he could not see her face, and he had begun to worry that maybe he was moving faster than she wanted to.

He tried to formulate the difficult, uncomfortable question he knew he was supposed to ask. "Do you want to—"

"Cut it out," she said sharply.

He had released her and stepped back.

Her voice had been annoyed. "Not that." He had tentatively reached for her, but she backed away too. "Too late. Now we have to go through it. I know how that got started. It's those stupid student codes. I'm always amazed that it got to be hammered into all of our brains at every high school and college in the country, until everybody's afraid."

"Sorry," he said. "I didn't think you'd be offended if I asked before . . ." He wasn't sure how he wanted to phrase the rest of it, so he left it unsaid.

She let out a breath in frustration. "I'm not offended, I'm resentful. You've been warned that if you don't stop right at this point and make me give my clear and affirmative declaration, then you're going to be a criminal. You must know I'm in a situation where I'm trying to fight a lot of shyness and nervousness anyway—I'm afraid you're going to think I'm fat or ugly or something—and this makes it worse. It forces me to go through a conversation that's much more embarrassing than letting you see me naked could possibly be."

"I'm sorry," Walker said. "I thought you expected it, or I wouldn't have said it." He put his arm around her.

She pulled away and said, "Expecting it isn't the term. I was waiting in dread for it."

"I don't like it either," he said. "But I'm not sure that I disagree with the idea that people should have a chance to think and decide whether they want to do something important."

She shook her head. "That's so insulting. This issue didn't just get invented and sprung on us out of the blue, did it? We've been together practically every minute for a month. What did you think I was doing all this time? I was getting used to you, and making that decision. You decided on the day I asked you to go to the concert."

His brow furrowed. "You knew that?"

"Of course I knew," she said. "You really wanted to before, but you were being cautious and responsible. You knew this was not a smart thing for either of us to do, but at that point you decided it wouldn't do any lasting harm to either of us. It just took me longer to be sure you were right. You've been patient and thoughtful and all that, and I appreciate it. That's part of why everybody immediately sees that you're the real thing."

He stepped closer. "Is that good or bad?"

"It's great," she said. "Stop trying so hard. Your impulses are good: we're allowed to want sex."

He had held her close and started to kiss her again, but once more she pulled back. "Not yet."

"I thought—"

"That was advice for your future," she said. "This time it's too late. So here goes: I am a mentally competent person, over twenty-one years old. I am not under duress, have received no threat of violence or loss of income. Although John Walker and I are employed by one company, to wit McClaren Life and Casualty, neither of us serves in a supervisory capacity over the other, or expects to do so in the future— or even to be assigned to the same city. I have not consumed any alcoholic beverages or mind-altering substances. Having given it due consideration, I have decided to accede to John Walker's stated wish— which I liked better implied rather than stated—that I have sexual intercourse with him. I give him permission to get on with it, and let me go back to being a little more passive, which is the way I will feel most comfortable tonight. In so doing, I do not give up any vested rights, including the right to revoke permission at my sole discretion and without notice."

She put her arms around his neck, raised her face to look into his eyes and asked, "Now do you feel better?" He had hesitated, and she had brought her lips up to his. "In a minute you will."

He had thought he'd forgotten the exact words, remembering only that they had been a sexual-conduct code rephrased in the legal jargon of a McClaren's document. Now certain parts of it came back with a new meaning. She had warned him that it was not going to be permanent, said that they weren't ever going to work in the same office. He had allowed all kinds of plans to develop for a future together that she had told him at the beginning was out of the question. She had been honest with him from the first night at the restaurant until the end. She had been honest with everyone. He was convinced that the last thing Ellen Snyder would do was commit fraud.

Over the next year and a half, Ellen Snyder had been vividly present to him, a problem. Tonight, he realized that the problem had been imperceptibly changing since he had left San Francisco. He had begun with the feeling that the relationship had just begun, then been cut off abruptly. He had searched his memory for the mistake he had made, scrutinized himself for some inadequacy that she had overlooked at the beginning but had finally found repulsive. But it was not that way at all. It was a story that had a natural beginning and a natural end. The end had arrived on schedule over a year ago. The girl was gone, but that had not changed who she was.

Stillman had said it was time for Walker to go home. Walker had already made his best arguments for Ellen Snyder's innocence, and repeating them would not make them stronger. But the problem had changed again. He wasn't worried that some accusation might stick to her. He was afraid she was in danger. As long as that remained a possibility, giving up was out of the question.

He heard another knock on the door, and sighed. Stillman hadn't suddenly changed after all. As Walker went to the door he began to compose a greeting: "Did you hear a heartbeat and decide to finish me?"

He swung the door open while he said, "Did—"

"Did not." It was the girl with the red hair. Serena. Her green eyes held him from behind the glittering glasses with an unabashed, unapologetic gaze. It was an expression that some people would have called curiosity, but seemed to Walker to be its opposite—the quality of having taken in everything she was interested in instantly. She just had not bothered to look away yet.

Walker leaned out of the doorway and pointed toward Stillman's door. "He's right down—"

"Good for him." She ducked past Walker into his room.

He hesitated for a moment, then followed her inside and closed the door. "Did the cops come to Gochay's? Are you hiding?"

"Don't be ridiculous. I just heard shots and didn't find your bodies, so I knew you would be here."

"How?" he asked.

"How what?"

"How did you know that we would be here?"

She smirked. "I asked my crystal ball what Stillman's credit card was doing tonight, and up came this place." She pointed to the scratches on his face. "Got anything to put on those?"

He involuntarily reached up and touched his face. "Stillman picked up some things, but I haven't had time for that yet."

She took off her oversized jacket and tossed it on the bed. "What were you waiting for, gangrene?" She grabbed his hand and examined the knuckles, then released it and went into the bathroom.

He heard her going through the paper bag Stillman had left, then heard water running in the bathtub. She appeared at the door. "Get in the bathtub and scrub any breaks in the skin."

He stood there. It was exactly what he had planned to do before she had arrived, but he couldn't think of a reason to tell her that. She came out past him and said, "Go on."

He went in and closed the door. He caught sight of himself in the mirror, and the angry red marks made him want to do something about them, so he took off his clothes, stepped into the bathtub, and gingerly settled into the steamy water. He unwrapped the soap and began to scrub his body with lather. He found the shampoo and worked on his hair, but the shampoo stung his open wounds. He leaned back, ducked his head under the water, and stayed there with his eyes closed, listening to the sound of pipes and water while the pain subsided.

The sounds changed. He opened his eyes to see Serena standing over him beside the tub. He sat up quickly, covering his groin with his hands.

"Don't be stupid," she scolded.

"Oh, yeah," he said. "I forgot. You only like girls, so I shouldn't be uncomfortable, right?"

"I'm also an RN." She knelt beside the tub and began to part his hair gently with her fingers, looking at the cuts.

"You're a registered nurse?"

"Why wouldn't I be?" she asked combatively. "Okay. You can get out and dry off now. I'll tend to the medical part." She stood and waited.

He sat in the tub. "I'd rather do this myself."

She rolled her eyes and turned around, then put her hands over her eyes. "Dry off and wrap the areas you're so ashamed of in a towel so we can finish up."

He stood and said, "I am not ashamed."

"Oh," she said, unconvinced. She walked out to the bedroom.

He closed the door, dried himself, and tucked the towel around his waist, then came out.

She said, "Sit." He sat on the bed while she applied antiseptic to his wounds, one after the other, then placed bandages on the cuts and scrapes. When she had finished she said, "There. You'll be fine."

"Thanks," he said. He got up and walked to his suitcase to find some clothes. "Now that I'm cured, we can get to what was on your mind. Did you bring something for Stillman, or what?"

She smiled mischievously and looked at him over the tops of her lenses. "I came to pick you up so we could go out cruising for chicks together, like we said." She reached into her jeans and held up a small package of condoms. "I picked these up for you in the shop downstairs."

Walker gaped at her in amazement. "That . . . that was very thoughtful."

She shrugged. "But it's already so late that the only chick I could find on the way over was me."

"Oh well," said Walker. "Some nights are like that, I guess."

She shrugged again. "So we'll have to make do with what we've got." She grasped her sweater and pulled it up over her head, then tossed it aside. Her skin was almost as white as her bra, so she seemed to Walker more than naturally naked. She unbuckled her belt and unzipped her jeans, then paused, looking at him again. "Unless you don't want to?"

Walker's arms seemed to move to her waist without his volition. As she snuggled against his chest, her face lifted and they were kissing. They moved to the bed without seeming to have gone there. A few minutes later, or maybe much later, she whispered in his ear, "I lied about being a nurse," and he whispered, "You look much better without the uniform." And some time after that, she said in a breathless gasp, "I'm not really a lesbian either." He managed to say, "Evidently."

For the rest of the night when he heard her voice it was not meant to be broken into words. They communicated by touch. Later, there were periods of lazy quiescence, when they lay together with eyes closed and barely touching, sometimes only the edge of a hand held gently beside a thigh as though to maintain an electrical contact.

But then, through the contact came a silent message, at first only a faint stirring, maybe only a pulse that very gradually quickened, answered by a slight rise in the temperature of the skin that could have been a blush. They turned to each other and the warmth became heat and motion again.

Walker caught sight of the hotel's clock radio on the stand beside the bed, and it made no sense. It seemed to say 4:30. He sat up to face it, then lay back down.

"What time is it?" she asked.

"It seems to be four-thirty."

"Kiss me."

He turned and they kissed, holding each other tightly and lying so they could touch their foreheads together, their chests, bellies, thighs, feet. They stayed that way for a long time, and then she wriggled away and stood up.

"Now look at me."

He raised himself on one elbow and looked. She slowly turned her back, looking over her shoulder at him, and kept going until she faced him again. "You're beautiful," he said.

She nodded. "I want to be sure you remember."

He gave a puzzled smile. "I'm not likely to forget."

She made no move, no effort to cover herself or to avoid his gaze. "My name is Mary Catherine Casey. Do you like it?"

"It's a good name. Mine is still John Walker."

"Very pleased to meet you." She looked into his eyes for a moment, searching until she found something that satisfied her. Then she sat down on the bed beside him and looked around, picking up pieces of clothing. "When you're through with Stillman, you can get in touch."

"I don't have to go with Stillman," he said. "What are you doing tonight?"

She shook her head. "Finish with Stillman first."

"I told you I don't need . . . Do you know what Stillman and I are up to?"

She looked at him as though she were disappointed with his intelligence. "I did your trace." She put on her panties. "If she's yours, get her out of your system. If she's your enemy, you can't let her get away with it. If she's in trouble and you abandon her without trying, you're no use to anybody." She looked at him closely. "Figure out which it is, and get it over with." She stood up to fasten her jeans and walked around the room looking for something. The sudden transformation into a composed, businesslike person was so dramatic that he felt a sense of loss.

She slipped the big sweater over her head, then stared around her again. She focused her eyes on the floor. "Oh, here they are." She picked up her glasses and put them on. She threw her coat over her shoulder and walked to the door. "Bye."

She was out the door and gone.

12

While Walker was in the shower, letting the hot water wake him up and soothe his sore muscles, he thought about Mary Catherine Casey. He directed his mind to the question of what was in her mind. He knew that the term "charming eccentric" was an oxymoron. Whenever he had met girls who had said and done things for effect, he had instinctively known that they were trouble. Some lobe of their brains had been pinched by forceps during birth, or had been atrophied by a chemical put in women's food as a substitute for fat or sugar. He had imagined that one night he would wake up in bed and hear the sound of one of these women firing up a power drill to run it into his forehead and let the demons out. Mary Catherine Casey had not made him uneasy: she just seemed to have decided that she liked him and wanted to play with him. Serena made him very uneasy.

He turned off the shower, dried himself off, and walked to the bedroom. There was a man standing there, looking down at his bed. The man turned: Stillman. "I knocked, but apparently you didn't hear me, so I let myself in. You alone in there?"

"Of course I'm alone in here."

Stillman glanced at the wildly disarranged bed again, then back at Walker. "Better get a move on if you're going to make it back to San Francisco before they start storing golf clubs in your cubicle."

"I'll take the chance," said Walker. "I'm not going back."

"If you're going with me, you'd still better get a move on. We just have a different flight to catch."

Walker dressed quickly in a suit like Stillman's and began to collect his belongings. He noticed the condom wrappers on the floor, hastily torn apart and flung there. As he picked them up, he looked at Stillman, who was staring intently out the window at the parking lot. Finally, Walker latched his suitcase. "Let's get out of here."

When he was sitting in the car beside Stillman, he squinted out the window at the glaring world. Los Angeles had always struck his Ohio eyes as shades of tan and light gray, with a few sickly pastels, but this morning it was patches of deep green grass and towering eucalyptus and palms, with scarlet roses and tangles of bougainvillea vines with impossible magenta flowers, and jacaranda trees that snowed purple petals on the ground. The sky was a blue so clear that it had never occurred to him that it was a condition that ever happened: it was a theoretical sky, without the hint of a cloud. "I see the fog lifted," he said.

"Yep," said Stillman. "I guess you didn't have a chance to watch the weather on TV, but they said the clouds were 'low night and early morning.' When that high pressure kicks in around here, it'll dry your eyeballs."

"Okay, so you know about her."

"It wasn't my toughest case," Stillman admitted. "I've never seen her find anybody tolerable before."

"What about Gochay?"

"They live on different planets," said Stillman. "No, the field is a wasteland. She leaves nothing alive within pistol range . . . until now, anyway." He looked at Walker contemplatively. "I'd be willing to pass on some wisdom if you're in the mood to listen."

"Why not?"

"You might think twice before you get too involved with a woman with her technical skills. She can hunt you down like a mad dog without leaving her computer. It would take her a minute or two to destroy your credit, delete your driver's license, and transfer somebody else's arrest warrant to your name."

"I wouldn't have done it if I'd planned to piss her off."

Stillman smiled wistfully. "We never plan to piss them off. It just happens. In my short and uneventful life, I've had a woman go after me with a claw hammer, attempt to dust me with a twenty-two target pistol, and aim parts of her china collection at my cranium from a fourth-story window."

"The same woman?"

"Of course not. She'd have to be an idiot."

"So would you."

"I suppose so, but I have a forgiving nature. Women don't. At some point you might want to give her a call just to see if you ought to rest easy or make a run for the border. I wouldn't trifle with Serena's affections, as they say."

"Her name's not Serena."

"Did she tell you to call her something else?"

"Yes."

"First and last name?"

"Middle, too."

"Flowers, then," said Stillman. "Definitely flowers. Big red roses. They like to be ambiguous, but they don't like you to be."

"I'm supposed to take advice from a man that women chase with a claw hammer?"

"One way or another, I get under their skin," said Stillman. "It doesn't matter. I trust you'll know what's appropriate."

"Thank you," said Walker.

"And she's intriguing. If I weren't old enough to be her father, I'd have been interested myself."

"I would never have suspected that Max Stillman would let mere propriety enter into that kind of decision."

Stillman turned to look at him in surprise, then returned to his driving. "Age isn't a matter of propriety. It's a whole series of inexorable changes that have already happened before you notice them. The ones you can't see are bigger than the ones you can. One day you just discover that you can't watch this movie or read this book or have this conversation anymore. Sometimes you've had it too many times already, but at others, it's not even that. It's just that nothing in it is anything that you're interested in anymore."

"You mean you know too much."

"Not exactly. There's nothing wrong with the conversation, and maybe it's a set of thoughts everybody ought to have pass through his brain at a certain time of his life. Everybody has a right to be young. It's a crime to be the one who's there when a young woman is having some kind of exciting revelation and not be in it with her: to be just kind of watching from a distance and knowing everything she's going to figure out in the next five steps. Because you're there, she can't be with somebody who will be surprised with her. It denigrates and devalues the experience she's having, makes her suspect that she's naive and foolish, and destroys it for her. She sees there's no uniqueness in it, and she knows it's not even her thought or experience, because plenty of people have had it first." He frowned at Walker. "You can kill somebody that way."

Stillman brightened. "If they're at least thirty-five or forty, and there's anything they still haven't found out, been taught, felt, or experienced, then it's high time and Max Stillman's their man."

Stillman swung onto the divided drive into the airport. "If you'd like to go to San Francisco, you've got a ticket waiting. That's your terminal coming up. I'll pop the trunk, you can get your suitcase out, and be on your way. Last chance."

Walker said, "I told you before, I'm not going to San Francisco. I'm not going to bail out until we find her."

"Good. Then you can make yourself useful," said Stillman, with no surprise or hesitation. He swerved suddenly to the white curb. "Go in there while I return this car. Go to the American Airlines desk. They have your name."

Walker stopped at the counter and the airline woman produced two tickets, one in Stillman's name and the other in Walker's. They were for Chicago. He looked at the date of purchase. It was yesterday. Again he tried to retrace Stillman's movements, and again Stillman had left tracks in all directions. Had he really made a reservation for Walker to fly to San Francisco on United this morning? If he didn't want Walker to go to Chicago with him, he would not have reserved a ticket to Chicago for him. He had said "Good" when Walker had told him he was not going home. So he had wanted Walker to go to Chicago with him. Maybe at the last minute, Stillman had been planning to offer him some inducement that had not been necessary. And maybe he had sent Serena to provide the inducement.

When Stillman came into the terminal with his little suitcase, Walker fell into step with him. Walker said, "How did she know we were staying at that hotel?"

"That's what she does for a living. She traces people."

"Did you call her and ask her to come?"

Stillman raised an eyebrow. "Did you get the impression that if I had, she would have done it?"

"No," he admitted.

"Then what made you think I called her?"

"She told me if I wanted to see her again I had to go with you and find Ellen first."

Stillman stared ahead as he walked on. "Interesting."

They waited to get through the metal detectors, then walked to their gate and waited some more. When they were in the plane at last, Walker leaned back and closed his eyes. The noise and vibration of the plane's engines relaxed his muscles and put him into a dreamless sleep.

He did not wake until the plane jolted his spine and rattled down the runway to a stop. As the plane turned ponderously, and then bumped along toward the terminal, he slowly came to full awareness and looked out at a huge field striped with runways. O'Hare Airport, he reminded himself: Chicago.

"You okay?" asked Stillman.

Walker said, "I guess so." He came to himself. "What are we doing here?"

"I'll tell you on the way."

Walker was getting used to Stillman's routine now. He stayed at Stillman's shoulder while they shuffled down the long, narrow aisle, then walked with him along the concourse to the escalators and down to the rental counters. He knew that the process would take fifteen minutes, and when the time had elapsed, they were on the road again.

Walker said, "Are we in a hurry?"

"Not really," Stillman answered.

"Can we stop at this plaza up here?"

Stillman swung the car into the parking lot and stopped in front of a florist's shop. He reached into his pocket, pulled out his wallet, and produced a business card. "Here," he said. "You'll need the address."

Walker accepted the card. He walked into the shop and ordered a dozen long-stemmed roses to be sent to Mary Catherine Casey. When the girl at the counter handed him the form to fill in the address, he looked at the business card. It was Stillman's, not Gochay's. He flipped it over and saw that Stillman had used the back as a scratch pad. Walker copied the handwritten address onto the form, then put the card back in his pocket and handed the girl his credit card.

When he was back in the car he said, "Thanks," and held the business card out.

"Keep it. It's worth the printing cost to know I've salvaged your disordered personal life."

Walker looked at the card again. "Who are the associates?"

"What associates?"

"It says, 'Max Stillman and Associates, Security.' "

Stillman started the car and backed out of the parking space. "That's just so new clients don't get the erroneous impression that when they hire me, all they get is a middle-aged, balding man with rubber-soled shoes."

"So it's a lie."

Stillman shook his head. "No. Stillman and Company would be a lie. Stillman, Fozzengraf, Pinckney and Wong would be a lie. Stillman and Associates is the truth."

"Except that the associates are imaginary."

Stillman turned out of the lot and accelerated onto a freeway ramp. "No, you're not."

13

Walker stared at the facade of the big hotel as Stillman drove past it. There were doormen wearing green comic-opera general's uniforms with gold braid and shiny-brimmed hats. Cars were pulling up and letting off passengers, then being driven away by other men wearing different, short-coated green uniforms that seemed to be patterned after some kind of cavalry. Stillman turned onto a side street and into a parking ramp. "If you're sure this person is in there, and you know the name she used to register, why not just call the police?" He hoped Stillman had noticed he had not conceded it was Ellen Snyder.

"I have," said Stillman. "In their infinite wisdom, they have determined that we don't have enough evidence to give them the right to raid a hotel room and roust the guests."

"Just using a false credit card would seem to me to be enough," said Walker. "What's the problem?"

Stillman shook his head. "It's how we know it's a false credit card. They've sniffed our story, and smelled the fine hand of someone like Constantine Gochay. This makes them nervous. They can't be told exactly who he is, because that would force them to pursue the issue of what felonies he's committed to find out what he knows."

"Are you kidding?"

"You can't blame them. All this has zip to do with the public safety of the citizens of Chicago. Ellen Snyder—guilty or innocent—is the problem of an insurance company in San Francisco, and the abuse of computer security systems is the problem of a well-known but distant government in Washington."

Stillman found a parking space with the car's nose against the wall in the first level of the garage, and turned off the engine. They got out of the car, but Stillman said, "So now we investigate. Get in the driver's seat."

Walker moved around the back of the car to the driver's side and got in.

"Adjust the mirrors so you can see the doors of the elevator."

"Okay," said Walker. "Now what?"

"Now I go upstairs to the lobby. I call the room of Mrs. Daniel Bourgosian. If I get her on the phone, I tell her I'm waiting for her downstairs, ready to help her. If she's innocent, she'll come see me. If she's a thief, she'll come out that elevator on this level and head for her car, or come out on a lower level and drive right past you to get to the exit."

"What if she's being held against her will?"

Stillman shrugged. "Then she won't be the one to answer the phone. They'll still have to come down that elevator to get out. They won't want to have to bullshit their way through the lobby, because I've just told them that's where I'll be."

"What if they come? What am I supposed to do about it?"

"See if it's Ellen Snyder and try not to get shot." Walker waited for something more specific, but his eye caught the rearview mirror and he could already see Stillman heading for the elevator. Walker reached for the door handle, then stopped.

He didn't believe that Ellen Snyder would come down in that elevator. In the first place, she was innocent. In the second, nobody could hold a grown woman—a smart grown woman, at that—in a fancy, crowded hotel without her screaming loud enough to pop their eardrums and shatter the wine glasses in the dining room. That left—what? It left nothing. The reason Stillman had posted him here was not so he'd accomplish anything. It was just to keep Walker out of the lobby, where Ellen might see him and recognize him. Stillman was preserving the remote possibility that he would corner her by surprise, then scare her into confessing. Walker sat back and relaxed, then readjusted the mirrors so he didn't have to crane his neck to keep an eye on the elevator.

It opened ten minutes later. Stillman emerged and returned to the car. "Come on," he said. "I guess we'll just have to lower ourselves and do this the easy way."

They emerged from the elevator in the lobby and Walker waited until Stillman was at the pay telephone beside the gift shop. Then he moved to the front desk. There was a clerk helping a couple check out at the far end of the counter, and a young woman shuffling some papers at the near end. She would be the one. The telephone just behind the counter rang. She picked it up and said, "Front desk." She listened, then said, "I'll ring for you."

Walker watched her consult her computer screen, then punch 3621 and hang up. She came toward him with her professional smile. He said, "I was wondering if there was a good Chinese restaurant within walking distance."

She whisked a small map from under the counter and held her pen like a magic wand to point to an intersection. "Right here is Won Dim Sum, which is my favorite." The pen seemed to rise higher into her hand by itself, and she made a quick circle at the spot, then quickly drew a line from the restaurant that extended into a circle around the hotel and handed him the map. Her mouth tightened into a closed-lipped smile to signal that the conversation was over.

"Thanks," he said, and walked across the lobby and followed Stillman around a corner to another hallway that led to a second set of elevators.

Stillman stepped inside with him. Walker said, "Thirty-six twenty-one," and Stillman pushed the 3 button.

When the elevator stopped, Stillman walked smartly up the hall. "This kind of thing is best done quickly," he said. "There's not a lot that's likely to happen as time passes that will make things better."

Walker turned to look behind him to see if there was anyone to hear. "How about silently? Isn't that best?"

"There are only so many precautions I'm willing to take," said Stillman. "Stand here." He pushed Walker into a position by the door with his back to the elevators, so he blocked the view. Then he leaned down to examine the lock. After a moment he produced a pick and a tension wrench from his wallet, fiddled with the lock, and pushed the door open.

Walker took a final look up and down the hallway, then stepped inside after him and closed the door quietly.

Stillman was standing in the middle of the room, turning and turning slowly. He stopped, facing Walker. "Don't touch anything."

"Don't worry," said Walker. "When I'm with you, I never touch anything. What's wrong?"

"The bed's messed up, the bathroom light is on, there are towels on the floor."

"I guess she's messy."

"No suitcase." He used a handkerchief to open the closet door. "No clothes. She hasn't checked out or they wouldn't have rung the room, but she's gone."

"Okay," said Walker. He stepped toward the door.

"Hold it."

"What?"

"We've got a lot of work to do. Look carefully at everything in this room."

Walker stared at the bed, the bathroom, the coffee table, the armoire that held a television set above and a bar below. "What am I looking for?"

Stillman said, "Any sign that Madeline Bourgosian is Ellen Snyder. Anything at all." He opened the upper section of the armoire to reveal the television set, then tested the bar cabinet to see if it had been opened. He moved toward the bathroom.

The bar had been the place that Walker had considered most promising, so he looked for something else. The bed. He stared closely at each of the pillows, trying to spot a blond hair, but found nothing. Maybe women didn't lose the occasional hair while they slept, the way men did. Probably if there were any, Stillman would find them in the bathroom sink in front of the mirror, where she had brushed her hair.

He pulled back the covers of the bed. If he were to leave something accidentally in a hotel room, that was where it would have been. He sometimes sat on the bed while he was dressing, and usually laid things out there when he was packing. The awful, complicated patterns on hotel bedspreads often made small objects hard to see in dim light. He saw nothing, so he ran his hand over it to be sure.

He moved to the telephone on the nightstand and looked from the side at the little notepad the hotel had left, but he could see no imprint from a sheet that had been torn off. He peered into the wastebasket beneath the little desk. He began to walk the room in a spiral pattern, scanning the floor.

"What are you doing?"

He saw that Stillman was staring at him. "I saw you doing this in Ellen's apartment."

"There's not enough room in here. You'll screw yourself into the floor. Just look." He returned to the bathroom.

Walker went to his knees and looked under the bed, opened all the drawers he could find, then returned to the telephone. He read all of the possibilities on the card for numbers to dial, but "redial" was not one of them. There must be some way of knowing what calls had been made; certainly the hotel knew.

He was turning toward Stillman to ask when his eye caught a glint from the darkness behind the nightstand. He bent closer. "Max. I found something."

"Don't touch it." Stillman appeared at his side, then knelt down and looked. He raised his head and stared along the top of the night-stand. "Hmmm." He took a pen from his pocket, carefully reached behind the nightstand, snagged the object, and pulled it out to the open floor. It was a gold woman's watch. "Is it hers?"

"I don't know," said Walker. "She had one sort of like that—an oval center with a round face in it, about that size, I think."

Stillman prodded the watch to turn it over. "Take a look on the back of the case."

Walker could see engraving. "E.S.S. 10/2/95." He felt his heart begin to thump, but it was as though it was pumping energy out of him. "That doesn't mean it's hers, or that she left it here."

Stillman hooked the band with his pen and dropped the watch be-hind the nightstand again. "It sure ain't Madeline Bourgosian's."

Then he went to the coffee table, where there were two magazines the hotel had left. One said, *Chicago—That Wonderful Town,* and the other said, *Guide to Amenities.* He began to leaf through them quickly.

"Why did you put it back? It's our evidence."

Stillman didn't look up. "If the cops find it, it's evidence. If we break in and find it, I'd say it's demoted to something less . . . a clue, maybe."

Stillman moved to the chest of drawers Walker had already opened. "What we want now is another one."

"What is it this time?"

"Something that tells us where she went from here."

"What's the likelihood of that?"

Stillman scowled as he stared around the room, then seemed to notice the second telephone on the desk. "Oh, I'd say the odds are nearing ten to one for." He opened a desk drawer and took out the telephone directory. He turned to the yellow pages and began leafing through them.

Walker stared over his shoulder in disbelief. "You're not even through the A's. Are you going to look at every page?"

"Nope." He stopped. "There it is. Airlines. Lo and behold. She's circled American Airlines, and written her flight reservation right on the page. No doubt she copied it over afterward. Flight 302, from New York to Zurich. Thursday the twelfth. That's tonight. Easy, isn't it?"

He used his pen to write it down on a business card, then closed the book and put it back. He stood up again and walked to the connecting door to the next room that people opened to turn the rooms into a suite. Then he walked across the floor to the door connecting with the room on the opposite side. "This one," he said.

"What?" said Walker.

"Don't you remember? We've been operating on the theory that she's traveling with two men. Maybe she got involved in this because she fell in love. That's what love is—cajoling a woman into actively participating in something she wouldn't have thought of doing by herself, right?"

"Ever the romantic," Walker muttered.

"Well?" Stillman said. "I've heard of women falling in love with two men at once, but I never heard of one who actually ran off with both of them. Even if she did, they would take two rooms. They're not traveling on a budget, you know. Even if their favorite means of expressing this affection were the time-honored Mongolian cluster fuck—"

"Is this necessary?" Walker interrupted.

"Sorry. I let it slip my mind that she was once the object of your infatuation. Even if she were insatiable and they had to go at it in shifts, person number three would need a bed to sleep on and regain his strength while the party of the first part and the party of the second part partied. He was in this room over here."

Walker's frustration and annoyance were growing. "How do you know it wasn't the room on this side?"

"That one hasn't been opened since the last time the woodwork was painted. There's a little bit of white enamel between the door and the jamb. It's not exactly painted shut, but the bellman might need to use one of these." He produced his pocketknife and opened a blade. He turned a little wing knob to open the door, then put his ear to the door behind it and listened. "Nobody's home."

"I thought we knew that already."

"Not necessarily," said Stillman. "See, whoever was in that room will have checked out when he left, to keep the world from seeing the connection. I'm hoping the hotel hasn't rented the room again." He used the knife to remove the screw holding the latch on the other side of the door, then poked the latch forward through the screwhole, and opened the door.

Walker could see the bed had been professionally made, and everything was in place. He said, "I guess we're out of luck. They already cleaned it." He turned to go, but Stillman held him.

"Look around anyway," he said. "Each chance you get only comes once." He went to work on the room, searching everywhere, then replacing things exactly. When he reached for the two magazines, Walker was fascinated. How could they be anything but identical to the ones in the first room?

"Now here's something the maid missed," Stillman said. "Page ninety-two is ripped out. Bring me hers."

Walker went back to the first room and returned with *Chicago—That Wonderful Town*. Stillman took it and found the page. "I thought so. The missing page is a map of the Chicago area for visitors—northwest quadrant."

He held up the page behind the missing one. It was a map with a larger scale that showed only downtown Chicago. He set the page on top of Ellen's map and held a spot with his finger. "There's a line," he said. "It would take you right out here onto this road west of Waukegan."

He put the magazine back on top of the other one, and handed Ellen's to Walker. "Let's get out of here. You leave through this room, and I'll leave through hers so we can latch both sides of these connecting doors. I'll meet you in the car."

Walker waited until Stillman had screwed the latch back in and closed the door. Walker latched his side, went to the door, and listened. He heard no sound, so he stepped into the hallway and closed the door behind him. The elevator opened and a middle-aged couple stepped out. He turned away from them and walked ahead in the same direction they were going. He made a turn, then another, and another, until he reached a dead end where the hallway stopped. He took the emergency stairway down to the next floor and found his way to the elevator.

He arrived at the basement level and stepped out to find Stillman sitting in the car. When he was inside, Stillman started the engine and drove toward the exit. "Look for a phone," he said.

As soon as they were out on the street, Walker saw a pay telephone beside a restaurant. "There." Stillman pulled to the curb, got out, and made a call. After a few minutes, he came back and drove off.

"I just called American Airlines," he said. "I checked on her flight from New York to Zurich to see if it fit what she wrote down."

"Does it?"

"Of course it does," said Stillman. "While I had them on the line, I thought I'd ask whether there was a direct flight to Zurich from here tonight. There is. One a day, in fact. And there are still seats available. Odd, isn't it?"

"I'm not sure what you're getting at," said Walker.

"The only reason I can think of to fly to Zurich is if you want to get to Zurich," Stillman said. "Am I getting through to you?"

"Yeah. We lost them," said Walker. "Can you call somebody in Zurich to meet their plane or something?"

"I would if I were a cop," said Stillman. "If I were a cop, I'd do a lot of things like that, because I could afford to stumble all over myself until the truth came out. In the morning, the hotel maids will open the room to clean, see she's gone, and the manager will call the cops. They'll find what we found. They'll see the watch and say, 'Aha! This isn't Mrs. Bourgosian.' They'll figure out E.S.S. is Ellen Sue Snyder. They'll find that somebody used the telephone book as a scratch pad, and they'll call Zurich. In a day or so, they'll admit they lost her. She slipped out of their cunning clutches. They'll assure the nearest reporter that they're turning Europe upside down to extradite her and bring her to justice."

"You mean they'll be lying?"

Stillman shrugged. "They may try to do it. If people start thinking they can escape a crime just by going to Europe, it'll be impossible to get a seat on a trans-Atlantic flight. They'll all be booked until doomsday by fleeing felons."

"I take it what you're saying is that Ellen didn't go to Zurich."

"Somebody using her name made a reservation from a hotel room in Chicago to take a flight out of New York. But I didn't see any note about a reservation on a flight to New York. Did you?"

"Maybe she didn't write it down. Besides, there must be a flight from O'Hare to Kennedy about twice an hour. She could show up and get one."

"True. Is that the way you would do it?"

"Probably not," admitted Walker. "Maybe she drove to New York."

"She would have to drive about a hundred and twenty to get there in time." He sighed. "Here's the way it looks to me. You have this young woman who pulls a very odd little crime that requires lots of elaborate moves: washing her cut of the money, using fake names and IDs and so on. Then she's in a hotel in Chicago. She's alert enough to know that we haven't lost her. She leaves without checking out of the hotel so anybody following her will think she's still there. This is not hard for a woman to do, because the clerks and cashiers always assume she's with some man who just paid, or will be along in a minute. Fine so far?"

"Fine," said Walker.

"She leaves in such a hurry that she forgets her watch, which is exactly what a person in a hurry would miss first. When you're trying to catch a plane, you look at your watch every minute or two. As it happens, this watch is not ordinary. It has her initials and a date engraved on it. The date is October second, which is Ellen Snyder's birthday."

"You know that for sure?"

"I haven't had time to check, but it will be."

"It is," Walker admitted. "But it could have been the anniversary of something: maybe the day she got her braces taken off, or the day her grandmother swam the Hellespont."

Stillman nodded. "Maybe. But look at it backwards. Suppose you wanted not only to be sure somebody knew you were in a particular place at a particular time, but to be sure that they didn't make a mistake and think you were somebody else. How would you do it?"

"I'd leave a signed note."

"How about renting a hotel room, which narrows the time down to twenty-four hours? Then leave something there that's yours. A watch with initials and a birthday isn't a bad choice. The only thing missing is her social security number. That watch is better than a birth certificate. A gold watch is too valuable to look like you left it on purpose, and this one looks like it has sentimental value. And, unlike a birth certificate, it doesn't even have to be genuine to fool an expert. You could go into a jewelry store and buy a watch and have anything you want engraved on it."

Walker said, "So you think it's another trick. Ellen is trying to throw us all off and make us think she's in Europe."

"I think somebody is," said Stillman. "The watch was left on purpose, and nobody who's running uses a phone book as a scratch pad to write down her next flight." He paused. "She wouldn't have had to do any of that herself."

He drove along the lake, then turned west, staring ahead at the dark road, then at the map he held on the steering wheel. Then he turned north onto a smaller road and set the map aside. From time to time he would slow markedly and look out the window at landmarks in the dim landscape: a construction site, a stand of trees that had at first looked like a woods but turned out to be only the narrow green windbreak beside a large condominium complex. He seemed to be evaluating places and rejecting them.

"What are you doing?" asked Walker.

"This is the road that was marked on the map they took with them."

"I thought you said everything we found was faked."

"I don't think leaving an impression on the page beneath the map was something they did to mislead us," said Stillman. "If it was, they would have left it in her room. Nobody was supposed to know the people in the next room had anything to do with Ellen Snyder. And it wouldn't be contradictory. You don't leave false trails leading in two different directions. You pick one and leave signs to it. I think they picked Zurich. So I'm trying to drive this route and look at the things I see from a different point of view." He sighed. "Now I've got to ask you to be quiet for a while and let me think."

Walker sat in silence while Stillman continued northward. Now and then he would slow the car down, look at a particular configuration of buildings or fields, then seem to reject it and speed up again.

After another fifteen minutes, he pulled the car onto the shoulder of the road beside a large field that had once been a farm but had no buildings left except a single bare-board barn with a caved-in roof. Through the empty front doorway, Walker could see stripes where the moonlight streamed in through gaps in the back wall.

Stillman flipped on his bright headlights and Walker could see the green reflective surface of a road sign at the edge of a narrow perpendicular line of pavement. It said LOCKSLEY RD. Stillman turned the lights off and cut the engine. Walker realized with growing uneasiness that this was the first place they had come to that was completely quiet and deserted, the first place where he could see no electric lights in any direction.

When Walker turned his head to look at Stillman, he could see the sober expression and the sad, watchful eyes. "I'm not asking you to do it," Stillman said. "If you want to wait here, you can."

Walker shook his head, not so much to deny the thought as to dispel the cold, prickly sensation that had settled on the back of his neck. "It doesn't have to be. It could be nothing. Somebody else could have marked that map and ripped it out of the magazine two weeks ago."

Stillman turned and stared out the window into the dark field. "It'll go faster with the two of us."

14

Stillman opened his suitcase and took out a small Maglite, then handed an identical one to Walker. "Save your batteries until we get out there." They closed the trunk of the car and stepped to the edge of the field. Stillman said, "We've got maybe six hours before farmers and commuters start coming up that road in force. You start down on that end, and I'll start up here. Walk the field in rows, as if you were plowing it."

Walker asked, "What will it look like?"

"I think if they were here at all, it was probably sometime today. The weeds will have been trampled down, and they won't have had time to stand back up."

Walker made his way up into the edge of the field, thinking about Ellen Snyder. Whenever he approached a spot that looked like a gap in the weeds, his breathing became shallow and his arms began to feel weak. He was expecting to see the white face appear in an open-eyed stare between two clumps of alfalfa. But as he walked to the end of the field and came back beside his own tracks, his thoughts became calmer.

Two years ago, if she could have imagined this night, what would she have felt? The one searching for you should be some close relative, not an old boyfriend you had left, expecting never to see him again.

There was something intrusive about this. He turned again and came up the next row.

As he walked, he began to believe that what he was doing was spending the night tromping around in an empty field, getting burrs and seeds stuck to a pair of pants that had cost about two days' pay, and scuffing a pair of shoes that cost more. Stillman had paid for them, he thought. He can decide how they get wrecked. Walker glanced to his right to watch Stillman's light sweeping back and forth ahead of him as he trudged on.

There was a quiet rhythm to the night sounds. Walker could hear unseen crickets chirping, the distant call of some invisible night bird, the swish of dry plants against his legs. He set his pace by the sound of his own footsteps, methodically marching the distance out and marching back.

He heard a sharp, shrill whistle, and turned his head. Stillman's light had stopped moving. It shone straight down into the weeds. Walker heard the whistle again. "No," he whispered. He began to walk through the weeds toward the light. "Let it be the money," he thought. "Let it be nothing at all."

He came near Stillman and looked down cautiously, letting his light slowly move toward Stillman's feet. He could see nothing. "What is it?"

Stillman moved his foot and a clump of weeds fell over. "That," he said. "Somebody did some digging here, and then replaced some of the plants. In a few days, they probably would have taken hold again."

Walker was silent, waiting.

Stillman sighed. "We're not going to do any digging, so you can forget about that. We're going to have to concoct a very convincing bullshit story and then locate the nearest cop so we can tell it to him."

It took a few minutes to reach the next town. As soon as they passed the sign that said WALLERTON, POP. 953, time seemed to stop. There were lights on in the tiny police station, but when they went inside they discovered that the man on duty at the desk was not the watch commander. He was just there to answer the telephone and then walk across the station to the radio desk and ask the woman who served as night dispatcher to put aside the book she was reading and summarize the call to the three patrol cars that were out on the major highways waiting for speeders.

It took Stillman only a couple of minutes to convince the desk officer to make the walk across the room, but it took nearly fifteen minutes for the patrol car to pull up outside.

The two patrol officers climbed the steps into the station, arranging their nightsticks and hitching their belts. The shorter one opened the glass door and went straight to Stillman and Walker. It took Walker a second to see that she was a woman. She had short, dark hair tied back tightly, and the body armor under her shirt gave her torso a square, plump look. The other cop was a tall, rangy man in his forties who had a weathered, sunburned face and crow's-foot wrinkles beside his eyes, as though he spent his days on a tractor. Walker read their name tags.

The female, whose tag said ORMOND, asked, "Are you the gentlemen who found something in a field?"

"That's right," said Stillman.

Walker waited for the next round of questions, but it didn't come. She said, "Why don't you show us where it is?" then turned and walked toward the door.

Walker didn't like getting into the back seat of the patrol car. There were no door handles, and there was a metal cage that separated the back from the front. But Stillman slid in and Walker joined him.

Stillman said, "It's the field on the corner of Locksley and Waterman Road."

"The old Buckland place," muttered the male policeman.

Walker closed his eyes. Things were dreamlike—not quick or startling enough to be a nightmare, just a dream with a slow, growing sense of familiarity as things got worse and worse. It would have to be called something like "the old Buckland place."

"How did you happen to be out there this time of night?" asked the woman.

"We're insurance investigators from McClaren Life and Casualty in San Francisco. We've been following a suspect in a fraud investigation," said Stillman. "We had a lead that she was in the Ritz-Carlton in Chicago, but when we got there she had just left. We looked at the routes she might have taken to get out, and this one seemed most promising."

"It did?" The surprise in her voice was what Walker felt. "Why is that?"

"A lot of reasons," Stillman said. "For one thing, in a couple of miles you're in Wisconsin. It's a new state, where she hasn't been seen before, with lots of rural roads all the way north to Duluth, Minnesota."

"You think she's going to Duluth?"

"No, I think she may be planning to keep going all the way to Canada," said Stillman. "Now, you and I know that going to Canada is one of the worst ways to stay hidden. Americans don't look any different from the locals, but the locals know the difference, and anybody looking for you has about a tenth of the faces to look at. But this is an inexperienced, first-offense white-collar suspect. If this turns out to be nothing, we'll probably take a plane and wait for her at International Falls."

The policewoman didn't assent or deny it. She just said, "What kind of vehicle description?"

"Blue Pontiac Grand Am was the last one she rented, but that was in Denver, and just because it hasn't been returned yet doesn't mean she's still got it. We thought maybe what she's been doing is avoiding the interstates and taking back roads."

"This used to be a main road," said the male cop. Walker thought he detected a little resentment. It was all part of the dream, and this place stood for all of the small towns that had been bypassed by the interstate highways and had slowly withered, leaving ruined barns and a few embittered loyalists.

Stillman seemed to Walker to have said too much already. He seemed to be giving them a thousand chances to catch him in a lie. Walker held his breath, hoping the policeman would fill in the time, tell Stillman all about the way the town once was, and the betrayal that the federal government and the politicians in Springfield and the Chicago business interests had pulled forty years ago.

The cop said no more. The car stopped, and Walker saw the sagging skeleton of the barn to his right. The female cop suddenly backed up and swerved to the side in reverse, then turned off the engine. The male cop took the microphone off the dash and said, "Unit One-two-eight. Show us Code Six at the junction of Locksley and Waterman, out."

Then Stillman was leading them back into the field with his flashlight, following the trampled weeds.

Suddenly Ormond's flashlight came on. It was a four-battery model that he had earlier mistaken for a club, and its beam was incredibly wide and bright. It flashed ahead for a moment, then swept across the field toward the area Walker had searched, and lingered there. "What were you doing over there?"

"That was me," said Walker.

She turned to study him as though she had not seen him before. "What were you doing?"

"We split the field up and started on both ends."

"What did you expect to find?"

Walker shrugged nervously. "Best case—maybe she buried the money out here. Worst case—" He realized he had probably made a mistake, so he changed his sentence. "I guess I don't know what that is."

She stared at him for a moment. "You don't, huh?" Her eyes bored into him long enough to determine that he had no answer, then she turned away and followed Stillman.

"I see it," called the male cop. "Somebody's been digging, all right."

Walker followed the others at a distance. He stayed on the periphery of the bright area cast by their flashlights. The beam of Officer Ormond's flashlight suddenly transfixed his chest. He knew its purpose was to illuminate his face without making him squint and turn away. She asked, "How much money was it?"

Walker answered, "Twelve million dollars, roughly. We think she was carrying about a million of it."

The light didn't move. "I'm still not clear on why you think she would pick the old Buckland place to bury it on."

Stillman intervened. "It was my hunch. We drove out of Chicago, and this was the first place we saw where you could be fairly sure of getting it done and not get noticed."

"You agree with that?" she asked Walker.

"Yes," he said.

"What made you think she'd bury it at all?"

Walker hesitated. "We . . . I think she knew we were close behind her. She wouldn't want to have it on her."

The two police officers looked at each other for a moment. It was the male who spoke. "It'll be first light in an hour or so."

Ormond squatted and touched the ground, then fiddled with the stem of a plant that wasn't rooted. "We'll have to get some people out here."

They drove back to the station in silence. Walker and Stillman sat on a long wooden bench, drank stale, acidic coffee, and watched the police officers make six or seven telephone calls from the desks on the far side of the counter. The sky outside the glass doors of the station achieved a pale, gray glow, and others began to arrive. There were two men in a pickup truck who wore blue jeans and baseball caps, then a couple of other cops, who went behind the counter to talk to Ormond and her partner with their backs to Stillman and Walker, then left again.

After Walker had finished his third cup of coffee, Ormond came around the counter and said, "They're already getting started out there. I imagine you'd like to be there." Walker could barely imagine anything he would like less, but she had set off for her car again, so he and Stillman followed and climbed into the back seat.

When they arrived, there was another police car pulled up at the side of the road. There was yellow POLICE LINE tape strung on fresh wooden stakes in a ring around the spot Stillman had found. A cop was taking Polaroid photographs of the ground while the two men in baseball caps leaned on shovels outside the ring. When he finished, they stepped over the tape and began to dig. Stillman, Walker, and the two police officers stood along the road and watched.

The policeman with the camera came out of the field and leaned on the door of Ormond's patrol car. Walker decided he must be at the beginning of his shift, because his uniform looked newly pressed, with the creases all sharp and clear. The cop said philosophically, "You never know on these things. Last year we got called out because a lady tipped us her neighbor had dug a big hole in his back yard. We went over, and sure enough—fresh dirt. We were in a real grim mood digging it up until somebody's shovel hit an antler."

He slapped his thigh and laughed. "He'd hit a buck on the highway, and figured the meat shouldn't go to waste. But then he got scared and figured, it being out of season and all, he better do something."

A half hour later, the sun was above the horizon beyond the field, and the low angle seemed to make it impossible for Walker to keep it out of his eyes. Ormond walked out of the field, opened her car door, and sat behind the wheel. She picked up the microphone and closed the door. As she spoke into the microphone, Walker could not see her lips, but her eyes never moved from his. After a minute she stepped out of the car.

"Have you got a picture of the suspect with you?"

"It's back in town in our car," said Stillman.

"Then one of you will have to come take a look."

15

"We've got ourselves a female Caucasian here."

Walker heard the words over and over in his memory. Ormond had held him in the corner of her eye as she had said it, and Walker could still see her making her way through the weeds, pretending to look down at her feet but contemplating him, even after they had stopped walking and it was time for him to look into the hole.

One of the other cops had gone to some trouble to wipe the dirt off the face, but there were still a few grains, like sand, at the corners of the eyes, and the hair was stringy and stuck to the head so it looked wet. The Ellen Snyder he had expected was gone—but only just gone, as though he had missed her by a few minutes, a few seconds, even. Her lips were pale and her face was cold and composed, the muscles smoothed and drawn back by something—death itself, or the circumstances of it, or maybe just lying on her back under the ground. He had no idea. She had made the odd transformation. It had amazed him since he was a child, when he had gone to funerals of relatives who lay in coffins somewhere between deep sleep and not being the same person at all. They seemed to be some not-quite-accurate statue made by an artist who had never met them and only reconstructed a likeness from a photograph. The part of her body he could see was naked, still covered with a thin film of dirt, but his reaction to that fact was indifference.

He had felt no impulse, for modesty's sake, to cover this girl that he'd cared about so deeply, and no competing urge to look, out of retroactive curiosity about her. In death, the body had lost its particularity and become a type, an example of a class of human bodies. The words that had always seemed to him to be stupid in their simplicity—female Caucasian, twenty to twenty-five, five feet six inches, blond hair—were actually wise and accurate. There was nothing specific, because whatever made people different from all of the others of their size, age, and sex went away with life.

"That's Ellen Snyder," he had said. They had driven him and Stillman back to the station and put them in different rooms.

After that, the questions got to be more insistent and less polite. The tall cop came in and brought Walker to still another room, where he took his fingerprints, then asked him to stand in front of a ruler painted on a bare wall, put his name on a black felt rectangle with white letters, and took his picture.

At noon, the police chief arrived. He was a big, wide man named Daniels who had a belly that hung over his belt when he sat. He cultivated one of Walker's least favorite poses, which was that he was a simple country boy who had trouble remembering things. He began with, "Ever find a stiff before?"

He needed to have the whole story from the beginning, with every nuance explained to him. Walker went through the long and delicate process: how Ellen had authorized payment to the wrong beneficiary and disappeared, how Stillman had brought him down to Pasadena to help with the investigation because he had known her, and how he had met with Alan Werfel. He explained how the canceled checks to clear the accounts had given the company a trail to follow: each had been written to a different person, and each new person had given the company another of Ellen's aliases and a location. He summarized the next part to leave out the felonies. He simply said, "By computer search, we picked up the last time she had used her most recent identity, and found she was still registered at the Ritz-Carlton in Chicago. When we got there, she had left." He repeated at each stage his belief that she was a victim. She had done nothing except under duress.

The chief interrupted every couple of sentences with questions timed to be devastating. Whenever Walker thought he was nearly to the end of the story, Daniels would ask something that would bring him back to the start. "If she was gone to begin with, how did you know that she was really the one who ordered the check to the wrong guy?" When Walker began again at that point and went all the way to the finish again, Daniels asked, "What made you think Ellen Snyder was the one to look for?"

Walker saw that the interrogation was a duel against an opponent who never got tired, could never make a mistake, and gave no quarter. Daniels would nod sagely while Walker breezed past some particularly dangerous part of the story, then jump back to make him repeat it twenty minutes later. "How did you know this Mrs. Bourgosian was gone if she hadn't checked out?" Walker made up a version that left out the felonies: "We called repeatedly, waited, knocked on her door." Then, when Walker actually got as far as the moment when he and Stillman had identified the body, the chief said, "How did you know the place to look was the old Buckland property?"

Walker had thought about this since the beginning, knowing it was going to be asked many times. He said, "We drove out of Chicago toward the north along a route Stillman thought someone like her might take—away from the major highways. When the road led to a place he thought was a good hiding spot, he stopped the car to take a look."

The truth was much more disturbing to Walker, and he couldn't say it, because this man was not his friend. When he had watched Stillman working, driving slowly through the night, staring out the side windows, he had detected a strange, unfamiliar expression on his face. It had been narrow-eyed, cold, and intense, but it had not been merely concentration. There was something more, almost a change of personality. Stillman had become somebody else. It was not until later, after the car had stopped, that Walker had understood who that must have been. This was what Stillman had meant by "looking at the things I see from a different point of view." Stillman had suspected from the moment he had seen the watch that Ellen was dead.

Daniels's eyebrows rose into an arc. "And you just went along with it, no questions asked?"

"I sit in the main office of an insurance company all day, writing reports," said Walker. "He's the security specialist the company hired to look into this case. What would you do?"

Daniels seemed satisfied with that, but a few minutes later, he jumped back. "What made you decide that Waterman Road was the way out of Chicago?"

The answer was the same. "You'll have to ask Stillman."

The interrogation seemed about to end at seven in the evening. Daniels stood up and said in a conspiratorial tone, "That Stillman, he's something, isn't he? Quite a reputation."

Walker said, "Really?"

Daniels looked down at Walker speculatively. "Maybe it's just in certain circles." His voice dropped and he leaned closer. "I'd get as far away as I could." Then he left.

It was nearly an hour later when the tall, thin cop came into the room and said to Walker, "You're free to go."

When Walker reached the street outside, it was dark. He walked down the sidewalk to the parked car, but he didn't see Stillman anywhere. It occurred to him that his own interrogation had probably been little more than a preparation for what they wanted to ask Stillman. Walker turned and entered the station again, picked up a pen and a form that was on the counter, and wrote on the back, "Went to look for a drink." Then he stuck it under the car's windshield wiper and walked down the quiet street.

He came to the front entrance of a hotel that seemed to have a lot of activity. He heard music drifting from the open doorway of the lobby, and lights spilled out onto the sidewalk at his feet. He stepped in past an elderly desk clerk who seemed surprised to see him, and followed the music to a large, dim room where there was a long mahogany bar. Behind it there were six rows of bottles full of colorful liquid that seemed to glow with the light from the wall-length mirror.

Three of the tables across the room were occupied by men drinking beer and ostensibly watching a football game on a television set on a shelf high above them. Walker claimed a stool at the bar and said to the bartender, "Scotch and water, please. Any kind."

The bartender was a bald man with a bushy mustache that looked as though he had grown it as a badge of his profession. He poured Walker a double shot, as though it were a relief to the bartender to serve something besides beer. Walker reached into his wallet and set a twenty-dollar bill on the bar, then sat staring at the mirror, watching the soundless football game in reverse.

He was on his second drink when Stillman came in and sat beside him. Stillman raised a hand to the bartender and pointed at Walker's drink, and the bartender brought another. Stillman tasted his and nodded at the bartender, then turned to Walker. "Don't worry, I won't drink too much. I'll still be able to drive you down to O'Hare airport tonight."

"Not unless we're going there anyway," said Walker.

"You wanted to stay with it until we found her, and we have. I thought you'd be anxious to leave," Stillman said. "Why aren't you?"

Walker considered for a moment. "Because they killed her, I guess."

Stillman looked at him thoughtfully. "I'm sorry I got you into this. When this started, I had the impression it was over—that you had both gone on to other things."

Walker nodded. "We had."

"But you were still in love with her, weren't you?"

Walker shook his head. "No. For a long time, I was: so long that I got attached to the idea, comfortable with it. I was always going to be this guy whose best shot at having a life was already over. I was so sure of it that I got out of the habit of checking to see if it was still true until you came along and forced me to think about every second that I had ever spent with her. Over the past few days, I did it. I slowly realized that I didn't feel the same about our time together anymore. When I remembered it, I still thought the same things about her. I just didn't feel them anymore. She was everything I ever imagined she was— smart, funny, brave, good—but now it had nothing to do with me." He frowned. "Do you understand?"

"I do," said Stillman. "You knew she was a decent person, and she was worth your effort to try to save her. So what's keeping you from quitting now?"

Walker took another sip of his drink. "I was just on the edge of figuring that out when you came in," said Walker, and looked at the glass. "The problem with this stuff is that just at the moment when it's managed to dissolve enough of the fog, whatever's left in your stomach hits your bloodstream and you get stupid. But I think it has something to do with what I've been doing for the last couple of years, and what she has."

"McClaren's?" Stillman looked suspicious. "You're suddenly interested in whether the company shows a profit on this year's annual report?"

"That's the funny part," said Walker. "I'm not interested at all. It hasn't crossed my mind since we were in Pasadena."

"Then what do you mean?"

"I meant how I was spending my life before that. I was trying to be the perfect employee. I had convinced myself that if I was going to be a solid, serious person, that was the way to do it. If I worked really hard to fit into the cubicle, then in time I would be the kind of man my family would be proud of. Steady, reliable. That meant something." He smiled. "I tried pretty hard. I went to work, came straight home—sometimes walked home to keep in shape, ate a frozen dinner, watched the news on TV, and went to bed so I could do it all over again."

"How does she come in?"

Walker answered, "She was making the same choice, only she was better at it. We were delayed-gratification pleasure seekers. The longer you put it off, the better it will be." He cocked his head and stared at Stillman for a second, then returned to his drink. He took a gulp, waited for the little explosion in his stomach to reverberate upward and warm his brain. "It didn't quite sink in until I saw her there with strangers brushing the dirt off her face."

"What was it that sank in?"

"That she and I might have read the instructions wrong."

"Her, anyway," Stillman agreed.

"Me too," said Walker. "There she was. And I asked myself what she could have done that would have avoided heading for that hole. And you know what?"

"What?"

"The answer wasn't spending more hours and more energy selling insurance."

Stillman sipped his drink. "What happened to her is not a bad argument for life insurance."

"True," said Walker. "But it's not such a good argument for trading anything important to get ahead." He frowned. "What was it you said? 'For twenty-four-year-olds who can't wait to be sixty so they can move into the corner office.' "

"What else did you figure out?" asked Stillman.

"Nothing. I unfigured. I found out that some things I'd already figured out needed some work."

"How about an example?"

"Murder. There's something about seeing the way it looks—turning a person into a secret, dropping her into a hole after dark and hiding even the hole. Her face looked calm, composed. Maybe she died gently. But I know that somehow, even if it was for a tenth of a second, even if she never got to say it, some remnant of her brain was thinking, 'Please. Not yet. Let me have another day, another few minutes.' They didn't." He took the last quarter inch of his drink. "I always thought people like that ought to be hunted down. It never occurred to me that the one who ought to do it might be me."

16

Walker awoke, showered, and dressed, then went to the next room to knock on Stillman's door. He found Stillman on the bed with file folders from the Pasadena office spread around him and the telephone in his hand. Walker went to the only chair in the room and sat down.

Stillman was saying, "Yeah, so get it to me. Hard is just another way of saying expensive, and I already threw myself on your mercy. Call me here at the hotel before you send anything."

He hung up, then dialed another number. "You might as well get some breakfast. This is going to take a while."

Walker found that the dining room was closed until dinner, so he wandered down the street past the police station until he got to a diner. When he returned to Stillman's room, Stillman was talking in the same tone. "What is it with everybody today? Here's how it works: you do what I ask, you send me the bill, and then *I* complain. You don't get to bill me and complain too. You think you're mentioned in my will and I'm depleting the estate? Good guess. I'll be waiting." He hung up.

"You finished?" asked Walker.

"Unless I can think of somebody who can do something else for us. I like to get people working on my problems early in the morning, when they're fresh."

"What are they doing for you?"

"That one's running hourly credit checks on these two guys—Albert Mayer and Richard Stone. They're the ones who kept turning up at the same hotels as Ellen Snyder."

"Won't they stop using those names now?"

"You never know," said Stillman. "They have no reason to assume that anyone was following them, just Ellen Snyder. If they're smart, they won't take the chance—or any other chance. I'm just trying to get something that will move us to the next set of names they use. I've got somebody else spreading the word that I'm paying for a man who looks like Alan Werfel."

"I don't think there is a man like that," said Walker.

Stillman looked intrigued. "You don't?"

"No. It came to me when I woke up. If they had one, then I don't think they would have done things this way."

"Why not?" asked Stillman.

"I accept what you said: that the first thing they did was steal Werfel's ID in the airport. I believe that they knew about the insurance policy in some other way—maybe just by learning what they could about him before they started using the credit cards. But I don't think they brought in a ringer and fooled Ellen Snyder into thinking he was Alan Werfel. It's never felt right to me. It's too hard to do quickly, and when you send him into the office, too many things could go wrong."

"That's right," said Stillman. He spoke gently. "That's the unpleasant part of this. It works best if somebody on the inside is handling everything, making sure nothing does go wrong."

"Ellen didn't do it," Walker insisted. "This could have been done a lot of other ways."

Stillman sighed. "You can't catch a thief by figuring out all the things he could have done. You have to think of things from his point of view. What did he want to have happen, and what did he think he needed to do to make it happen? The point is, the thief can't know what all the obstacles are going to be when he starts this. Only an insider knows. As soon as I heard a rough description of this, I started looking for somebody like her."

"But you didn't know her, and that's why this never made sense to me. Ellen Snyder wasn't in on it. She didn't want a quick million, she wanted a career. And if they really had found a guy who could convince a stranger he was Alan Werfel, they wouldn't have needed to pay Ellen. And if they could pay her, they wouldn't have needed to kill her."

"You think her only purpose was to take the blame."

"That's right."

"Because she's dead?"

"Not just dead, but dead that way, out here in the middle of nowhere, so it looked as though she got away with the money and disappeared. They couldn't just fax in a copy of Werfel's stolen driver's license and expect to get a check for twelve million in the mail. They needed the paperwork to come to the main office filled out by a real McClaren's agent who seemed to have seen the guy in person and gotten him to sign the affidavit and release forms."

"You think she didn't fill out the papers?" asked Stillman.

"I don't know if she did or not. I just know she didn't intend to participate in any fraud. If the fake Alan Werfel called her in advance and said, 'I'm coming in on Tuesday to sign the papers,' then she would probably have filled them out on Monday. She would never let a man like that sit in the office waiting while she was at a typewriter putting stuff into blanks on a form. Don't you see? He fits the profile of the kind of customer she was after. She described him to me the night I took her out to dinner."

"I thought she was after women?"

"She was after heirs, and he was an heir: a person who suddenly had a lot of money he didn't have before, and had to come to her office. She would have seen that as a giant chance to sell him something—maybe get him to let the company manage his money, maybe buy an annuity. Twelve million bucks at six percent is a slam-dunk, no-risk seven hundred and twenty thousand a year, tax-deferred until he starts drawing it. If nothing else, she would think he was a good prospect for insurance. He's just had the biggest reminder of mortality you can get, so she'd try whole life, or health. He's just inherited a couple of mansions, so she'd try home owner's." Walker threw up his hands. "You've got her file open. Look at her sales figures. That's what she did for a living. Ellen would have done everything she could to make him feel as though she was a comforting ally in his time of need. She was in sales, for Christ's sake."

Stillman said, "So she would fill out the papers ahead of time. I can buy that. Then what happened?"

"I don't know," said Walker. "Maybe they told her to meet Alan Werfel someplace outside the office with the papers. People do business at lunch all the time. She would have jumped at that. She would have wanted him alone and in a spot where the other people in her office, like Winters, couldn't snatch him away or screw up her pitch. A restaurant would give her a psychological advantage: no office furniture to remind him that she was just some stranger in a business. It would be special treatment to show him he was important, and so on. What he's dealing with is an insurance company, but what he's looking at is this pretty, soothing young woman going out of her way for him. And lunch takes time—maybe two hours—which gives her a hell of a long period to wear him down."

"Okay," said Stillman. "Let's grant that this is one possibility. Then why did somebody break into her apartment?"

"I didn't say I knew what happened, exactly. Maybe they set it up so she would have to take the papers home with her. They could have set it up as a breakfast meeting, so no sane person would go to the office first. That way they could break in the night before and grab her and the papers, send the forms to San Francisco overnight, and leave nobody in Pasadena who knew anything. Maybe they broke in later, after they'd kidnapped her, because they were afraid she had something written on her calendar that would prove she hadn't planned to leave." He shrugged. "That's why they jumped us on the way out of her apartment, right? Because we were flashing papers."

"Kidnapped her?" Stillman repeated.

"You think she took off her clothes and buried herself in a field in Illinois?"

"Of course I don't," said Stillman. "But she seems to have done things after she handed over the check. She seems to have boarded airplanes, rented hotel rooms."

"Then maybe that wasn't Ellen Snyder. Maybe they broke into her apartment just to kill her and take her keys."

"What keys?"

"To the office," said Walker. "She definitely had keys. You met Winters. Do you think he was the one who showed up every morning at seven to open up, when he had a twenty-four-year-old assistant manager to do it? They could have killed Ellen, used her keys to get into the office, filled out the forms, faxed them to the home office, then got what they needed from the files about the office's women clients."

"Then what?"

"Then they have another woman travel around using false names that came from Ellen's office files. Somebody made it look as though Ellen was on a plane to Zurich. That's not Ellen Snyder trying to make Ellen Snyder look innocent. It's them trying to make it look as though she and the money disappeared together. Then they buried her in a place where they thought she'd never be found."

Stillman's eyes were focused on the wall. "Not found," he said absently. "Identified."

"What?"

Stillman waved a hand. "Bodies almost always get found at some point. The trick is to make sure you leave one in the right place. Out here, the family farm doesn't look like it's making a comeback anytime soon. So you leave the body here, buried on an abandoned farm. You put plants over it so it won't look any different after a couple of weeks. It might be ten years before some developer buys up all this land and starts scraping it with bulldozers. They didn't take her clothes because they were perverts. They did it so when the body was found, there wouldn't be any chance of tracing it through the clothes. They were hoping there would be nothing left but bones by that time, but they knew they couldn't count on that. Rains and frosts sometimes bring a body to the surface. Hunting season's only a couple of months away, and there will probably be men and dogs tromping through that field—the dogs being the ones they'd have to worry about."

"What they wanted was a Jane Doe?"

"Right. That's why they didn't go even farther out, why they picked this place. If you want a Jane Doe to fade into a notation on a very long list, your best choices are in the vicinity of a big city."

Walker stared at Stillman for a few seconds. He was different today. Or maybe it was Walker who was different. "What do you think happened?"

Stillman shrugged. "If I were to guess, I'd go with your theory."

"Then why didn't you say so?"

"Because I don't have to guess just yet."

17

Walker stared across the desk at Daniels's gold badge. It was as huge as he remembered it. It looked more like a plaque the chamber of commerce had given him to nail to his office wall than like anything a man was supposed to pin to his shirt. It had CHIEF OF POLICE in quarter-inch enameled letters along the top and a wheel in the center with a blue "1" at the hub.

Daniels looked good behind a desk, because when he sat forward with his weight on his elbows, the bulging stomach was compressed against the top drawer, and all Walker could see were the big arms and the shoulders jutting outward from the thick neck, and the small brown eyes. He looked somber, and his expression was mirrored in miniature on the childlike face of Officer Ormond.

"The police in Pasadena, California, have dug out the report of your run-in with the two men near Ellen Snyder's house, and we gave them the description you gave us. Now they're wanted for questioning in connection with this murder here in Wallerton," said Daniels.

"Thank you, Chief," said Stillman.

"I honestly don't know what good it'll do," he said glumly. "I invited you two here to tell you we've about reached the end of our investigation. I'm going to give you what we've got now, before it gets kicked over to Springfield and disappears in somebody's filing cabinet."

Walker glanced at Stillman, but there was no answering glance. It was exactly as Stillman had predicted, but he did not seem to notice. Instead, his face was as somber as the chief's. Walker could see that Ormond was sitting with a couple of file folders on her knees, her face now taking on an expression of distaste.

Stillman said, "We appreciate it, Chief."

"Sandy?" said Daniels.

Officer Ormond took a deep breath, her mouth in a pout as though she were contemplating some drastic action.

"Sandy, give him the damned file," said the chief wearily. She leaned forward quickly and set the file on Walker's lap, like a woman reaching into a cage at the zoo, then retreated back into her chair. Daniels said, "Officer Ormond has objected to sharing this information with private persons," he said. "Ordinarily I would agree with her, of course. She's an excellent officer."

Walker wondered what had made Daniels overrule her. He could see from her stony expression that the compliment had not mollified her, but Daniels seemed to have accepted that in advance. He said, "There are no tracks around the scene that haven't been connected with your shoes or ours. There are no bits of physical evidence conveniently left around for us to bag and analyze. We've interviewed everybody along Locksley Road, and everybody on Waterman, but nobody saw or heard anything. So all we've got is a corpse. What we know so far is that she was dead at least twelve hours before you found her, probably buried between nightfall and dawn the night before."

"Any cause of death yet?" asked Stillman.

"Well now, I'm not sure yet. The autopsy is being done in Chicago. They haven't filled in that line yet, but they've given us some hints. Her blood tested positive for heroin. That wouldn't be unheard of for a young lady on her way from Chicago, but nothing you fellows have given us would indicate she would have taken it voluntarily. That right?"

"Absolutely," said Walker as firmly as he could.

"So my money is on heroin overdose as cause of death. She also had morphine in her blood, which strikes me as an odd combination. Probably that was what kept her under until they were ready to give her the overdose. She has . . ." He turned to Ormond. "How many needle marks, Sandy?"

"Sixteen that they've found so far," said Ormond.

"No abrasions around the wrists or ankles?" Stillman asked her.

"Nothing obvious," Ormond answered. "There's a bruise on her right arm." She raised her own to point to a spot on the inside below the biceps, and Walker could tell she was acutely aware of the similarity between her body and Ellen Snyder's. It was both inevitable and strange that she used herself as a visual aid. "That could be an indication of force. There's also a scrape here on the left hip, but both could have been caused by the strain of moving a half-conscious person in or out of a car."

Stillman kept his eyes on her. "So you think she was probably kept drugged for a long period, then killed and brought here?"

Ormond answered, "It's possible they just made the other needle marks to make a heroin overdose plausible. But that's what I think."

"Any evidence of sexual assault?"

She shook her head. "Not so far."

"So far?" Stillman raised an eyebrow.

"They haven't given us all the results of the autopsy. The smear was negative for semen, and there was no obvious abrasion of the vaginal area. But she's been missing for two weeks. We can't say the test shows what happened to her during about the first twelve of those days."

Walker looked at the chief, who was staring down at the blotter on his desk, as though he had noticed something there that demanded his full attention.

Stillman stood up with the file in his hand. "Chief, Officer Ormond, you've done us a big favor, and we appreciate it."

Walker caught his cue, stood up, and muttered, "Thank you."

Ormond said nothing, but the chief stood too, and said, "I sure wish we could have gotten somebody to take to trial on this one, but we're not really set up to go very far beyond what we can investigate locally."

"Nobody could have done any better," said Stillman. "This was just the place they happened to hide the body."

"Well, Officer Ormond will send on copies of whatever we get from Springfield." He waited, his eyes on Ormond.

Ormond was looking at him, angry and unblinking. "Yes, sir." Walker wondered what the conversation had been like that had brought her to that point.

He followed Stillman out of the police station. They walked along the quiet, sunny street toward their hotel. It was not until they were inside Walker's room that he spoke. "That's it?" he asked. "They collect all this information and put it in a file and send it to the state capital?"

Stillman's stare seemed to be an evaluation of Walker. His eyes were not without sympathy, but Walker could tell he was not in a pleasant mood. "They're not doing it for now," he said. "They handled the scene professionally, made records of everything, preserved the evidence, searched for witnesses while anything they saw would have been fresh in their minds and not picked up in a newspaper."

"What do you mean, 'not doing it for now'?"

Stillman sighed. "Frauds, embezzlements, things that we've been worrying about up until now, are passing events. If they don't get settled pretty quickly, not much is going to be accomplished later. Murder is different. The cops investigating a murder that doesn't seem likely to be solved work for the future. They hope that somebody, sometime will get an inspiration or an informant, or invent a new gadget that will make sense of the evidence they preserved."

Walker shook his head. "It's not good enough."

"It's not good at all," said Stillman. "It's just what there is." He stared at Walker for a moment. "Pack your suitcase. It's time for us both to go home."

18

Walker and Stillman emerged from the baggage claim at the San Francisco airport as the sun was going down. Walker could feel a steady breeze, and somewhere beneath the mixture of half-combusted fuel and grit that was the smell of big cities, he could pick up a cold fresh smell from the ocean. He had been far inland for several days, and he realized that what he was smelling now had become the smell of home.

He turned and found that Stillman was already on his way to the white curb. Stillman said, "You probably didn't have much cash on you when we left. Have you got enough for a cab?"

Walker nodded. "I guess so. I hardly spent anything."

"Fine," said Stillman. He raised his hand and a cab pulled out of the line and glided to the curb. "You take the first one."

Walker was suddenly flustered. He hadn't expected that the trip would end at the airport. He hadn't expected anything. "Max, I . . ."

"Yeah, I know. We did what we could, but now it's time to do something else. If I find anything out, I'll tell you. So get in."

Walker got into the cab with his single suitcase, and Stillman slammed the door. As the cab pulled away, Walker looked out the back window. Stillman was already on the curb, raising his hand to summon the next cab, betraying no inclination to watch Walker go.

When Walker climbed the steps, went into his apartment, and

closed the door, he found himself back in the morning four days ago. The air from that morning had been locked in the four small rooms all this time, and it still had a stale aroma of cooking, dust, and maybe old laundry. The dishes from his breakfast were soaking in a three-inch bath of cold water. The coffeemaker had a parchment-brittle coffee-stained paper filter with dry grounds in it. He looked into the refrigerator, and noted with relief that there was very little food that had to be thrown away.

As he stood in the middle of his small, sparsely furnished living room, he tried not to think about Ellen Snyder. Right now, her family would be together, immersed in misery of a sort that he had never felt. Where had she said she had come from? Oregon. Salem, Oregon. He went to the telephone and dialed long-distance information.

There were five Snyders, but he determined not to let that be his excuse for giving up. He picked the wrong number the first time, then chose wrong again, but the third time the man who answered said, "I'm her uncle."

Walker said, "I'm sorry to bother you. I was . . ." then realized that he was claiming more than he had a right to: that had been over a long time ago. "I knew Ellen. I was in her training class at McClaren's in San Francisco. I was just calling to say how sorry I am."

The man's voice was soft and tired. "Well, we all are. It's been a shock to everyone who knew her. You're the third one in the last hour. McClaren himself called, and a fellow named Spillman, or something like that. Nice of you to call." The uncle seemed to be restraining himself, trying to respond to Walker's gesture, but not feeling much like it. He wanted this to end.

"I'm sorry to ask," said Walker, "but would you happen to have her parents' number handy? I—"

"Parents?" Mr. Snyder repeated. "Her father's in Illinois. He went as soon as she was found. Her mother . . . we haven't heard from her in fifteen years. Don't even know how to get in touch to tell her, or if she's heard already."

"Oh, yeah," said Walker. "Of course. I . . . Well, I just wanted to say I'm sorry. I won't keep you on the phone."

"You didn't tell me your name."

"Oh. John Walker," he said. "Please give Ellen's father my regrets."

"I'll do that."

Walker stood by the phone for a moment, trying to get over the discomfort so he could remember. For now, the image of the dinner at Scarlitti's was before his eyes in absolute clarity—the red leather upholstery in the booth, the velvety texture of the dress Ellen had worn, the exact look in her eyes. He had listened to every word she had said, hearing more than the words because he had been trying to interpret the tone of her voice, weigh the emphases, and even search the pauses for messages. He remembered the heady feeling that they were revealing things as they spoke. It was not the dangerous revelations that had impressed him, the ones that had to do with ambition or tiptoed too near to sex. He remembered the others, that were dangerous in another way, because they were confessions that there was nothing remarkable or exotic about either of them.

Ellen had not exactly lied to him, but she had deftly kept his attention away from that particular door. She had covered the topic of mothers by saying that she looked like hers. Her mother had been gone at least since she was eight or nine. That must have been one of the central facts of her life, but she had never alluded to it. The uncle's tone had given Walker the impression that there was something shameful about the circumstances, and that knowledge would have been worse for Ellen. After that night, the topic had never come up—or been allowed to come up—again.

Walker had no doubt that he had discovered something that was of enormous importance to understanding Ellen Snyder, a fact that might reveal who she was and why she chose to do certain things and not others—maybe why she worked so hard, maybe why she had become so independent so early, maybe why she had developed a manner that was calculated to draw people to her, but not too close to her. He also knew that none of it mattered. His using it to analyze her character and behavior would be wasted effort. It wasn't part of reality anymore. It was as though she had never been born.

Somebody had studied the Pasadena office, learned which two people could approve a check, and decided that the one who would be easier to overpower and drag around the country would not be the six-foot-seven, overweight Dale Winters but the small, approachable assistant manager, Ellen Snyder.

Walker looked around the small apartment, searching for something to keep his mind occupied until he was tired enough to sleep. First he unpacked, hanging the beautiful suits and jackets in the closet at the end of the pole, separated from the rest of his clothes, and putting the folded shirts, as they were, in a drawer of their own. He drifted into the kitchen and opened the cupboard under the sink. He found rags and sponges and cleanser, and began to clean. When he next looked up at the clock on the wall, his laundry was washed and dried, his kitchen and bathroom scrubbed, his living room and bedroom dusted and vacuumed. He had stripped the bed to wash the sheets, but now as he looked at the freshly folded ones he felt no inclination to put them on. He flopped down on the bare mattress and fell asleep.

In the morning, he chose a sport coat, shirt, and shoes that he had owned before he had met Stillman. He rode a cab to work, had it leave him down the street from the McClaren building, and walked to the garage entrance to verify that his car was still there. He started it, drove around the block listening to the engine, then parked it again and walked to the lobby to take the elevator to the seventh floor.

He went to his cubicle as usual, turned on his computer terminal, and called up the report about quarterly sea loss in the maritime insurance division, then looked up from his screen to see Joyce Hazelton in the doorway, gazing down at him. She stepped inside and glanced at his screen.

"I already printed that out and sent it on," she said. "It was solid." That was Joyce's highest compliment, which meant that the data were complete and the conclusions perceptive and defensible.

"Oh," he said. "I had intended to hand it in that day, but then I was gone."

"I'm very sorry about Ellen Snyder," she said quietly.

"Thanks." Walker felt discomfort at her sympathy, and it remained an irritant until he had told the truth. "But I don't rate any condolences. We were close once, but we'd lost touch a long time ago."

Joyce accepted it, and said, "They want you upstairs at seven forty-five. Go up in the elevator. When you come out, turn right. There's a receptionist to let you in."

"McClaren's office?"

"Oh, that's right. I forgot you know the way." There was nothing in her eyes that Walker could interpret. She looked at her watch. "Better get going." She waited while he put on his coat, then watched him step into the open bay as though to be sure he was actually heading in the right direction.

The elevator rose to the twelfth floor without stopping. The morning rush into the building was still ahead, and the usual traffic from office to office would not begin until after that. The doors opened and he stepped out to find that the woman he had seen up here before was standing a few feet away with her hands clasped behind her, as though she had been waiting for him. This time the honey-colored hair was tied in a different, equally complex way, and she was wearing a beige suit that seemed to have come from a shop that no ordinary person was allowed to know about, which made clothes that could never wrinkle or stretch at a seam.

"Good morning, Mr. Walker." The way she said it gave him the impression that she had been here for hours, long before anybody else was awake.

"Good morning," he said. He had been right: she had been waiting for him. He was not used to having his arrival be something that was awaited, or even noted.

"Mr. McClaren is ready for you." She turned and led the way. She opened the big oak door and Walker waited for her to precede him, but she stood aside and nodded to show him she wasn't going in. He stepped inside and the door closed quietly behind him. The office was enormous, a suite rather than a room. The section where he stood had a big antique partners' desk with chairs on both sides. He sensed that it probably belonged in a museum, but the broad, shining surface was littered with papers, bound reports, telephone message slips, and yellow legal pads covered with notes in small, tight black script. There was a computer terminal on the far side, and it was the same model as Walker's.

The voice came from somewhere to his right, the deep, quiet accented sound that Walker remembered. "Come on in here."

Walker followed it under an arched opening into a larger space dominated by tall bookshelves lined with leather-bound volumes that had come in matched sets, so tightly and uniformly arranged that Walker could not conceive of them ever having been moved. McClaren was in a blue suit today, but it was cut in exactly the style of the gray one he had worn the last time. He leaned forward to shake Walker's hand. "Thanks for coming."

"No problem," Walker muttered.

McClaren sat down on the nearest couch, and Walker sat across a low coffee table from him. McClaren leaned forward. "It seems to me that I ought to apologize to you."

Walker's brow knitted. "What for?"

"When I told Stillman he could take you with him, I didn't know that it was going to be that sort of trip." He seemed to hear a false note in what he had just said, so he amended it. "I should have. In my own defense, I was sure that Ellen Snyder couldn't possibly be involved in anything dishonest. I was sure that you felt the same way."

"How?"

McClaren just raised an eyebrow, but Walker saw what he meant, and rephrased it. "How did you know about her, or about what I thought?"

McClaren looked more uncomfortable. "It's a fair question. I don't want you to think that we're spying on people in the company. We're not. But small bits of legitimate information come to us as a matter of course. Supervisors evaluate you periodically. And we've always held to the old-fashioned policy here that when you produce a piece of paper, you sign your name to it. Not every company does that. Over time, we get to know one another. What we learn sometimes borders on the personal—also for legitimate reasons. In the training program, the instructors don't just evaluate your memory and your mental capacity. They observe how well new people adjust to the work environment—whether they get along, make friends, and so on. You and Ellen Snyder became . . . close friends. People liked her, people liked you. When she got her transfer to Pasadena, those people were concerned that it might have an effect. It didn't, so the matter was set aside." He paused. "That doesn't mean it was forgotten. When we learned Ellen was the agent on the spot during a crime, and that she had disappeared, we remembered that you knew her well." He hesitated again, then went on. "I was a big fan of Ellen Snyder's, although I had never spoken to her face-to-face. So you were acting as my surrogate, the one who held my point of view. Again, I'm very sorry," he said. "It must have been very painful."

"Don't be sorry," said Walker. "In some ways it's better for me that I was there."

McClaren looked at him for a moment, as though he had not really seen him before and realized he had missed something. Then he seemed to incorporate it into his mind, and start on a new basis. "There's another reason why we needed to talk. I don't have to tell you we've got troubles. I need to find out . . . more: I wanted to say 'how bad they are,' but that's wrong, because having a kid like Ellen Snyder murdered is about as bad as things get. But I want to know if that's it—if we've lost a promising young person and now it's over—or if we've got to worry about other people."

Walker nodded.

"Don't just nod at me," McClaren said. "Give me your guess." He sounded exactly like a professor.

Walker said, "They got away with it. We didn't figure it out in time. I don't know much about criminals, but I don't know anything that would keep them from trying it again."

"Stillman thinks that the biggest danger is the possibility that we've got a traitor, an inside person. What do you think?"

Walker shrugged. "I think Stillman's the expert."

"Too easy," said McClaren. "You have an opinion."

"I don't disagree with him," said Walker. "That would be the worst case, and it's possible. It would be difficult to go into an insurance company and collect a death benefit that wasn't yours unless you knew the procedures in advance. But it must be even more difficult for a criminal to approach somebody inside a company and ask him to do something like this. Are there other ways for a thief to find out enough to be able to do it? Sure. I think—"

He saw that McClaren was distracted. The assistant had come in the door silently, and now she stood like a statue in front of the big desk. McClaren patted Walker's arm apologetically, muttered, "Sorry, excuse me," and got up to join her by the desk.

He stood very close to her and listened while she spoke to him just above a whisper. McClaren answered just as quietly, and she turned and disappeared. McClaren returned with a weary expression and sat down again. "Something else to think about. The National Weather Service has just upgraded Tropical Storm Theresa to a hurricane. It's just passed Guadeloupe. They don't know yet if it will make Florida, of course."

Walker said, "They usually don't."

McClaren stared down at the coffee table, then seemed to remember something. "That's right. Yours was one of the names on the vulnerability assessment for Florida last year. There's a copy on my desk right now."

"I didn't do much on it," said Walker. "Just checked the statistics and made sure the arithmetic supported the recommendations."

"But you know the problems," said McClaren. "We live on the business of wealthy individuals. If you won't insure their houses, they won't let you insure their lives, cars, jewelry, and art collections and sell them annuities. A bigger company will put together a package and sell it cheaper. You can lay off some of the biggest bets with reinsurers, raise deductibles. But disasters are a matter of time. Sooner or later, you have to pay off."

McClaren gazed at the table again for a moment, then straightened. "Well, let's do what we can about the problem we already have. I want you to hand off the routine stuff and stay on this Ellen Snyder business. Joyce knows you're occupied. Go back through dead files and records. See if there have been any other instances when we might have paid these people. I've got to know if this is the first time or the twenty-first."

"All right," said Walker.

"The second thing—and this could be harder—is that you've got to keep this project to yourself." He caught Walker's expression. "Stillman again."

"I recognized him."

"Stillman is . . . what he is. If you want his services, you have to make some attempt to do what he says. You can't get a modified version of Stillman." He paused. "His ways of thinking sometimes have a special utility in a place like this, where everybody is smart and everybody knows how to keep up a good appearance."

"I have no objection to keeping what I'm doing secret. If Joyce knows I'm occupied, it shouldn't be hard. We all generally work alone anyway."

McClaren stood and began to drift toward the outer office, so Walker knew he was about to be dismissed. "While this is going on, if you want to tell me anything, come directly up here. Now that Sarah knows you, there won't be any problem." They shook hands in the doorway, and Walker turned and heard the door close behind him.

As Walker made his way to the elevator, he passed the big desk in the reception area. He glanced at the woman, and tried to fit the name Sarah to her. She was now facing away and typing something at an incredible speed on a computer terminal while she spoke to someone on the speaker of her telephone. He knew she must be aware of him passing, but she took no notice of his departure.

When he got out of the elevator on the seventh floor, he heard the elevator beside it open, and people arriving for work spilled out toward the bay. He felt a small hand tighten on his biceps, and turned to see that it was Cardarelli, looking up at him happily.

"Walker," she said. "You're much cuter than I remembered you." She looked more closely, released him, and shrugged. "No, I guess you're not. My mistake. The light must have been in my eyes for a second."

"Hi, Cardarelli," he answered. "Thanks for not putting tacks on my chair while I was gone this time."

"The janitor must have seen them and put them in your desk. Where were you, by the way?"

"I was on my honeymoon."

She stopped and stared at him suspiciously, not quite positive that he wasn't telling the truth. She said, "You got married?"

"No. I just try to get to the good parts first, in case there's an earthquake or an act of war."

She nodded. "Reading actuarial tables can salvage even the most dismal life. It's a surprise to see you, though. Some of us thought Stillman had dragged you off to jail."

"Who?"

"Stillman. The security guy. One day you were gone, and so was he."

"Oh, him," said Walker. He took another step to the entrance of his cubicle. "That's a relief."

She hesitated for a moment, then said, "Well, welcome home. I've got to go warn the typists to wear longer skirts again," and stepped off down the aisle toward the corridor.

Walker began his new assignment as soon as the others were all safely occupied in their own cubicles and offices. He found a surprising array of fraudulent claims over the past ten years. There were faked injuries, fires that the investigators found were arson, people who caused car accidents intentionally and then got quack doctors to certify spinal damage. There were even a couple of clients who had been murdered by the beneficiaries of their life insurance policies. What surprised Walker most was that in about half of the cases, he found the tracks of Max Stillman. The signs were never obtrusive. Usually he didn't appear until the page summarizing the accounting for the case. There, among the legal fees, copying costs, and long-distance telephone bills, would be a notation that said simply, "Stillman and Associates."

He studied the cases, but found nothing about them that reminded him of Ellen Snyder. In even the most elaborate schemes, the culprits were stationary. They would submit a false claim and stay put, waiting for payment and hoping that nobody would learn what they had done or, in any event, would never find enough evidence to prove it.

Ellen Snyder's murder was not like that. The killers had known in advance that the fraud would be discovered, the checks traced, the trails followed. Their solution had exploited the weakness in the system, which was that these things took time. They were prepared to move faster. When the check came, they had it deposited within an hour in an account where it was sure to clear early, so it could be paid into the next set of accounts. And they had provided a prime suspect by making the McClaren's employee who had approved payment disappear.

That night, he went home and stared at the telephone for five minutes, then walked to a restaurant a mile away to eat a solitary dinner. When he came home, he found himself staring at the phone again. He took the card out of his wallet, turned it over, and dialed the number.

Serena's voice said, "Yeah?"

Walker paused for a moment at the sound. Now that he had heard it, this was real. "Hello," he said. "Serena?"

"Yeah."

"It's me," he said.

It became Mary Catherine Casey's voice, tight with suppressed laughter. "Which me is it? Am I supposed to guess?"

"John Walker."

"Oh, that me," she said. "Are you calling to tell me that you've been dreaming of me every night, or that you want your money back on the flowers?"

"I'm glad you got them," he said. "At least that went right. You like flowers? I never asked."

She said, "I liked that Constantine was stricken with fear and dismay when they came here. He's afraid I'll run off with you. Don't get excited: if I felt like running, I'd run. Flowers wouldn't have much to do with it."

"But I have been dreaming about you."

"How romantic. Did I have clothes on?"

"What kind of question is that?"

"It's a perfectly reasonable question," she said with a laugh. "I didn't, did I?"

"Well . . . not really."

"That's comforting," she said. "I was beginning to be afraid you were more complicated than that." She went silent for a moment. "I see you're calling from home. You must have found the girl."

"She's dead," said Walker. "They killed her in Illinois. I guess I thought Stillman told you, but . . ."

"I wondered why I hadn't picked her up again," she said. "Are you okay?"

Walker took a breath as he considered. "I'm not sad for me. I guess that's what you meant. I'm sad for her. She was just this girl, a nice person who did her job and didn't harm anybody."

She assumed her business voice, as though he had been talking to Mary Casey and had not heard the click when his call had been transferred to Serena. "If we can help, call us."

"Not 'us.' The one I was calling was you. I wondered if I could fly down on the weekend and see you."

"Uh-uh."

"If this weekend isn't a good time, I could—"

"Not interested," she interrupted.

"Oh," he said quietly.

"You haven't finished with her."

"She's dead."

"That's worse. She's not going to turn out to be a thief, or make any mistakes you can't forgive. I can't compete with her."

"Who asked you to? She's gone."

"I can hear her in your voice. Look, if she was this nice person, then thinking about her for a while is no more than she deserved from you. So do it. When you've let go of her, you can call me." The line went dead.

Walker spent the next two hours searching his mind for arguments that she had not given him a chance to use. He was over Ellen Snyder, and if he had not been, she was gone. He still thought about her sometimes, but the way he thought had changed. She was an assignment, a case that his boss had asked him to study and solve.

As he formulated the argument, he realized that it sounded false even to him. He was not in love with Ellen Snyder, but Ellen Snyder was not a case. She was a person who had been subjected to fear and probably pain, and worse, a nightmare feeling that nobody knew what was happening to her, and no help would come. And no help had come. It made him sick. The fact that he had once loved her had made her so familiar that he could see it happening in his imagination, know what she had been thinking. He did not love her anymore, but Serena was not wrong.

The whole next day, Walker worked on the fraud project. He moved forward in time to cases that were currently under investigation, but it was impossible to find anything that was suspicious in the same way as Ellen Snyder's case. It was nearly quitting time when he noticed a commotion in the bay. There were heavy footsteps, male voices, the sounds of furniture being moved.

He saw Joyce Hazelton pass by his doorway, so he stepped out. "What's going on?"

"Nothing, I hope," she said. "We're just getting the bay ready. If Hurricane Theresa keeps moving toward Florida overnight, we'll need to have a phone bank to handle the calls. Everybody sits in here and grabs whatever phone rings. After the L.A. quake in '94 we were at it for nearly two weeks."

"What should I be doing?" he said.

"Going home," she said. "Get lots of sleep. If you're smart, you'll pack an overnight bag and keep it ready, so if it happens you'll be able to brush your teeth and wear clean clothes. They've clocked winds up to a hundred and twenty and growing. If it doesn't lose steam, the phones will be ringing when you get here tomorrow."

The call came even earlier. It was three A.M. when Walker's telephone rang, and he was awake instantly. Joyce Hazelton's voice was quiet and clam. "John, it's what we talked about this afternoon. I just got the call myself. We've all got to get into the office right away. It's already morning in Florida." She hung up before he could ask any questions. As he dressed, he decided she had probably been wise. The questions that he could have asked were things he would find out when he got there.

Walker drove through the nearly empty streets, making good time. He listened to the radio, tapping the button from station to station, hearing the drone of voices on call-in talk shows, snatches of sports reports, blares of music. When he finally heard the word "hurricane," it was on some sort of listing that had to do with travel, and the next words were "and in Minneapolis, partly cloudy turning to fair."

He parked in the garage at three-forty, started toward his trunk to bring his suitcase with him, then thought better of it. The parking spaces around him were filling up quickly. If he arrived with a suitcase, some of those people would be amused. If there turned out to be a need for it later, they would be much less so. He entered the lobby and saw that night security was still in effect, so there was a short delay while he signed in at the desk, and then another delay while a security guard used his key to operate the elevators to the upper floors.

When Walker reached the seventh floor, he saw that the transformation was already complete. Twenty of the forty desks in the open bay were occupied. There were typists and receptionists beside actuaries and underwriters. There were even a few of the investment people in the spaces at the corner nearest their corridor. But his most vivid sensation was the sound of telephones ringing all over the room.

People were snatching up receivers, uttering a few acknowledgments as they took notes on message pads. Then they would tap in policy numbers on their computer terminals and stare at the screens while they tried to answer questions. Walker could see already that many of them were out of their depth. A few would look puzzled, then raise their hands in the air like schoolchildren.

Joyce Hazelton would stride up the aisle to answer the question or take over the call, but it was a Joyce Hazelton he had never seen. She had always been made up and combed like a minor official of the State Department, always wearing a ring, a pin, and small ear studs of some semiprecious stone that matched her suit. Today she was wearing faded blue jeans, a pair of bright white running shoes, and a gray sweatshirt that said PRINCETON 70 in blue letters. He moved closer to her as she took a telephone out of the hand of a man he recognized as a vice president who issued performance bonds on construction projects.

"Yes, sir," she said into the phone. "I'm a supervisor. My name is Joyce Hazelton." She was leaning down to read the computer screen. "Your premium was received on the twenty-third, which is plenty of time." She pointed to a line on the screen so the vice president could see where it was. "Your coverage is in full force." She listened. "What I would do in your place is make a videotape of the house. Just walk through every room with your belongings still in place, and then the outside too. That part I would do while I was getting into the car to drive away from the beach area." She paused and listened again. "No, sir. If there really are hundred-and-fifty-mile-an-hour winds, we'd rather pay off on your home owner's policy than your life insurance."

While she was talking, Walker saw that there were some other managers walking the aisles, some of them getting novices set up at desks with hurried instructions, and others handling questions. He moved toward one of the empty desks, but Joyce handed the telephone back to the vice president and caught up with him. She guided him away from the desks and up the aisle, talking rapidly.

"John, did you bring your suitcase?"

"Yeah," he said. "Thanks for the warning. Where do you want me to sit?"

"We don't know yet if the hurricane will make it to the mainland, but it just brushed the edge of the Dominican Republic. It tore roofs off brand-new buildings and caused floods that took roads with them. The Miami office doesn't have enough people, so we're trying to rush reinforcements in ahead of the storm."

"Me?" said Walker. He stared at the activity around them. There were already people with their hands up.

Joyce saw them too. "You were on the list from upstairs. Obviously you don't have to—"

"I'll go," he said. "What do I do?"

"Meet the others at the airport as soon as you can. Delta Air Lines." She took a step toward a confused-looking twenty-year-old typist. She stopped and looked back at Walker. "Keep your receipts."

Walker watched her turn her attention to the new problem, then hurried toward the elevators. When he arrived at the airport, Bill Kennedy came across the polished floor to meet him. Walker could see that Kennedy already had a ticket in his coat pocket.

"We can't fly to Miami," Kennedy said cheerfully. "They're afraid their planes will get stuck on the runway when the storm hits."

"What are your tickets for?"

"Atlanta."

"Atlanta? That's got to be five hundred miles away."

"Six hundred sixty-three," said Kennedy. "That's what they said, and they're an airline, so they must know."

"Can't we do better than that?"

Kennedy shrugged. "Better? From a rational perspective, Anchorage would be a lot better." He put his arm around Walker's shoulders and turned him toward the ticket counter. "Look who's here."

Walker recognized Marcy Wang, Maureen Cardarelli, and a few of the new people who had just completed training to be agents. "So?"

"We're all young and unmarried. It's a squadron of the unloved, the unwanted, and the cheaply dispensable. It's an insurance company, for Christ's sake—they're weighing risk against reward. They know they're liable to lose somebody. Atlanta is only an hour from Miami if planes are flying when we get there. If they're not . . ."

"What about Orlando?"

"Orlando? Don't know him. Let him die."

"Florida. That's only a couple of hundred miles from Miami, and there are huge numbers of flights. Has anybody checked to see if they're still on?"

"Beats me," he said. "The flight leaves for Atlanta in a few minutes, so if you want to go . . ."

Walker stepped to the counter, where a middle-aged man was waiting. "Are the flights to Orlando still scheduled?"

The man looked at him judiciously. "At this time, there haven't been any cancellations."

"Are there any leaving soon that I can still get on?"

The man clicked his computer keys, stared, then clicked some more. "There's one in twenty minutes." He turned his attention to Walker. "There are lots of passengers who haven't checked in yet. I don't know if you've heard, but they're expecting a hurricane in Florida. I could sell you a ticket. You'll probably get on, if it goes. I have to say that I think the no-shows are probably right. If the plane takes off, it may be diverted. If it lands in Orlando, you may regret it."

"I know," said Walker. "I have to try. It's an emergency."

The man seemed to be making an effort to say no more. His eyebrows slowly rose as he clicked in the reservation and started to print the ticket. At last he said quietly, "I happened to be working there when Andrew came in. You haven't seen an emergency until you're stuck in one of those things."

Walker took his ticket and returned to the waiting area to tell the others, but they were gone. He looked up at the schedule on the television screen, and saw the flight for Atlanta blinking. In a moment, the notation changed to DEPARTED.

Walker hurried through the airport to his gate, and got in line to board the flight for Orlando.

At one o'clock in the afternoon, Walker was making his way through the Orlando airport toward the baggage claim. As he reached the escalator to take him down to the lower level, he heard a sweet female voice announce, "All incoming flights have been canceled."

A few minutes later, Walker was in a rental car driving out of Orlando on the turnpike toward the southeast, staring across the flat country at a small, distant bank of puffy white clouds just above the horizon.

19

Walker found an all-news station on the rental car's radio and kept it on as he drove. The weather reports had been superseded by recitations of an official notice that said a hurricane watch had been declared for a stretch of Florida from the Keys up the Atlantic coast to Daytona Beach. It was followed by a long list of the communities that fell within those boundaries. Since Walker still had not reached the first of them, he began to feel increasingly uneasy, especially after he heard the revision that extended the watch all the way up to Jacksonville.

When he reached the coast, the sun was shining brightly on the road ahead, and the white surf stood out from the sea as it did in every picture of Florida he had ever seen, but the puffy white clouds in the distance had changed. They seemed to be piling on top of one another, growing into towers. Somewhere beyond them, something very big was happening, something that he had never seen before. It was as though he could see the night following the sun in from the east, slowly rolling in over the ocean and darkening it across the whole horizon.

The voice on the radio said, "The Weather Service has just upgraded the hurricane watch to a hurricane warning. Hurricane Theresa is now seventy miles east-southeast of the Florida coast, moving at approximately twenty miles an hour. It contains extremely heavy rains, and winds up to one hundred and sixty miles an hour. All residents are advised to take immediate precautions, and to expect that the storm will make landfall within the next four hours. I repeat. The hurricane watch has been changed to a hurricane warning . . ."

It was shortly afterward that Walker noticed that the lanes coming toward him were filling up rapidly. He noticed that some of the cars were heavily loaded with luggage. He supposed that most of these people probably were tourists who had decided that this might be a good time to move on to the next stops on their itineraries. But before long, traffic on Walker's side began to thin out and move faster, so the contrast was more and more clear. He kept remembering that these were people who had spent time in this part of the country. Many of them probably had been through hurricanes before. If they were leaving, driving in the other direction began to seem more and more like idiocy. He could be sitting in a hotel in Atlanta with the others, drinking mint juleps and watching weather reports on the television above the bar. He had been too clever for that.

The words of the radio announcements did not change much for the next half hour. It was the voices that changed. The announcers were sounding less slick and jovial, reading their scripts carefully now with a sober, measured enunciation. They began to add a short paragraph about the Emergency Broadcast System. A few minutes later, advice was inserted from some official agency that low-lying coastal areas could be subject to damaging waves, particularly during high tides. Then they read a list of cities that were precisely like that, all the names that evoked college spring vacations: the Keys from Key West to Key Biscayne, Coral Gables, Miami Beach, Fort Lauderdale, Pompano Beach, Boca Raton, Palm Beach, and sixty or seventy that he had never heard of, most of them with the words "beach," "island," or "shores" in them somewhere.

By the time Walker reached North Miami Beach, the announcers were reading addresses of buildings that had been designated as shelters for those who wished to leave their homes, and warning others that official evacuation orders might be issued. It was not the radio that undermined Walker's confidence. What bothered him most was being nearly the only one driving southward past the hundreds of cars moving steadily north, while the enormous, dark shape over the ocean to his left grew bigger and darker.

He had never been within a thousand miles of a hurricane, and had paid attention to them only in the most detached way while he was growing up. They were television pictures of palm trees bent in the wind. After he had gone to work at McClaren's, he had learned a bit from checking the facts in Kennedy's vulnerability assessment of south Florida, but it was becoming clear to him that his imagination had failed him.

The report had been about money—about dollar values of specific properties and projected replacement costs—and not about small clouds in the distance that grew into horizon-to-horizon black masses that rolled in and killed you. He sensed that he had better be indoors before the spectacle turned into an experience.

Walker had to stop at a telephone booth to look up the address of the McClaren regional office. He paged through the telephone book and found it, then pushed a couple of quarters into the phone and dialed. A recording came on of a soothing female voice: "You have reached McClaren Life and Casualty. We're sorry, but due to increased calling volume, all our lines are busy. Please hold and the next available representative—" He hung up. Of course their lines were busy. That's why he had been sent down here. He got back into the car and drove until he found a gas station.

He filled the tank and bought a good local road map, then asked the man at the cash register for directions. The man gave a nervous glance over Walker's shoulder. "Gee, I'm sorry, but there are five customers behind you, and more coming in every second. You can wait if you want, and I'll try."

Walker stepped aside to let the next person take his place, then moved down the line and stopped. The faces in the line bore that mixture of sullenness and eye-avoiding stolidity that seemed to come over people forced to wait. He held up his map. "Can anybody give me directions to Seventh?"

"Street or Avenue?" It was a man in late middle age with a Spanish accent who stood near the end of the line.

"Uh . . . Street." He added, "Seventy-five eleven Northwest Seventh."

The man raised his hand to point out the window with the package of flashlight batteries he had picked up while he was waiting. "Streets are east-west, avenues are north-south. And they get duplicated. There's a Southwest, Northwest, Southeast, Northeast. Northwest Seventh Street is down there about ten, fifteen blocks. What's your cross street?"

Walker looked at his map again. "I think . . . Southwest Tenth Avenue. Is that possible?"

"Sure it is," said the man. "Down there ten, fifteen blocks. Turn right and keep going about a mile."

"Thanks," said Walker. "Thanks a lot." He reached to shake the man's other hand, but there was a big package of cookies in it.

The man smiled. "Better get going, though. It could get here soon."

Walker stepped outside and felt a stirring in the air, not a gradual increase in the breeze, but a solid mass of air that hit him as it passed across the blacktop, then was gone. It startled him, a sudden slap from the hurricane, and not a playful pawing. It felt like a test, a first pass from something that wanted to eat him. He stepped to the car, and as he opened the door the wind arrived, this time like an invisible wall. His hair blew and fluttered, and the colored pennants strung on a wire overhead began to flap and make snapping noises, straining until the wire was as taut as a bowstring. There was a steady hissing sound that he knew was just air whistling across the openings of his ears.

He got in and slammed the door, and there was silence. He brushed the hair out of his eyes, then started the engine and drifted out onto the road. He followed the directions the man had given him, searching for each street sign with extreme care, straining to reach beyond the distance he could see in order to make out as early as possible that one sign had too many letters, the next too few. When he saw Northwest Seventh Street and managed to complete the right turn onto it, he felt his chest swell in gratitude. The man who had gotten him here had said there was only a mile to go, and now it was a straight line, with no possibility of a mistake.

The wind blew harder, the sudden onrush of air making the car rock slightly, and he overcompensated by gripping the steering wheel in surprise, then slowly, tentatively, loosened his grip. He could hear invisible specks of dust ticking against the window beside him as he searched for Tenth Avenue.

He saw it. The low brick building could have been anything—a store, a restaurant. But beside the door he could see a small brass plate like the one on the agency in Pasadena. He turned into the driveway and continued around the building to a parking lot that looked as though it would hold about twenty cars. There were only two in the lot.

He looked up at the sky, and decided he didn't have time to ponder why there weren't more cars. He could see the underbelly of the storm now, like a dark gray ceiling closing overhead. He opened the car door with surprising difficulty as the wind pushed against it, pounded down the button, let it shut, and leaned back against the wind to control his speed as he trotted to the door of the building.

He swung it open and slipped inside, then experienced the blessed quiet again. He straightened his collar and pushed back his hair as he looked around. The room had the same aged quality of all the McClaren's offices, as though a single decorator had gone around the country buying up the antique furniture in each city and placing it in the same patterns. His eye caught movement, and he turned to see a short, bald man in his early sixties standing at the window. He had half-turned to place a steady, appraising gaze on Walker. He wore a three-piece suit that must have been tailored for his slim, narrow-shouldered frame, so he looked like a wizened boy. "I see the wind is up." The accent was a soft, genteel southern elongation of vowels that Walker associated with Charleston.

"It certainly is," said Walker. He stepped closer. "My name is John Walker. I'm from the San Francisco office."

The small man stepped forward in a leisurely way and shook Walker's hand, then stood with his hands clasped behind him and rocked twice on his heels. "Ah, our reinforcements. I'd been led to believe that there was a bit more to you, numerically speaking. I'm Charles Evans, regional manager."

"The others flew into Atlanta," said Walker. "They should be on their way."

"I sincerely hope not," said Evans. "The storm would catch them out. Have you ever been in a hurricane?"

Walker glanced toward the window. He thought he heard the wind picking up. "Not yet."

Evans said, "Well, this one won't be as bad as it could be."

Walker brightened. "No?"

"That's the whole premise of our business, isn't it? It's never as bad as it could be. If it ever were . . ." He left Walker to complete his sentence. "You came at a calm moment. When the front rolled into sight, people stopped calling insurance companies and turned to conveying their concerns to the Almighty. I sent home everybody who lives close enough to get there. Miss Turley and I are the only ones left, so you may as well ride it out with us."

Walker said, "I'd be happy to have something to keep me occupied. Is there any paperwork I can get started on?"

Evans looked at him through the corner of his eye, amused. "McClaren's has had a presence here since the turn of the century. As soon as hurricane season begins, we prepare all the paperwork."

"You go to all that trouble just in case?"

"I can see you really haven't been in a hurricane. The first thing that happens is that the power goes off. You're returned to a more primitive era, without computers or copiers."

"Of course," said Walker. "I'm sorry. They called me in the middle of the night, and I guess it took most of my brainpower to get here."

"Well, you're here now, so all we've got to do is wait it out." The sound of the wind began to mount noticeably. Evans turned and stared out his window. "Here it comes."

Walker stepped closer and looked. He could see a line of rain like a curtain sweeping toward them across the parking lot, turning the pavement dark and shiny with a hissing sound, throwing a thousand little splashes on the hood and roof of his rental car, then exploding against the office window like the spray of a hose.

Evans reached to the side of the window and pressed a button, and a metal shutter slowly lowered to cover the glass. Then Evans went to the other windows on that side of the building and repeated the process. "That should do it for the present," he said. "The winds move clockwise, so it's possible that later on they'll hit the building from the other side."

The lights gave a small, sick flutter, and then went out. "Ahead of schedule," said Evans.

Walker went to the other side of the room, where there was a small unshuttered window, and stood looking out at what had replaced the late afternoon. The sky was an opaque dark gray, and below it a sourceless twilight, as though light had simply been trapped there when the sky closed up. Puddles seemed to Walker to rise up from the ground, with the wind sending wrinkly wavelets across it, then lifting spray off the surfaces to add it to the rain.

Somewhere, lost in the steady beat of rain and wind, Walker thought he heard a voice. It grew louder and louder. ". . . has reached the mainland with strong winds and extremely heavy rain. The possibility of flooding—" A middle-aged woman with silver hair appeared from the hallway, holding a flashlight and a portable radio. She turned off the radio. "The phones are dead too."

Evans said, "Miss Turley, this is John Walker from the San Francisco office, come to save us from the ravages of nature."

"Here. Have a flashlight," she said. "We've got plenty. If you run out of batteries, they're in the cabinet over there. If you would like some coffee, get it now or it will be cold."

Walker took the flashlight. "Thanks," he said.

"Well, I'm going to see if I can sleep with all this racket," she said. "All hell has to break loose and knock out the phones before a person can get some rest." She was still talking when she passed too far down the corridor to be heard.

Evans said to Walker, "I think I'll try to get a nap myself. As soon as the weather lets up, we're all going to be very busy." As he stepped away, he said over his shoulder, "There are couches in the offices."

Walker stayed at his window, watching as more of the hurricane came in. The wind was screaming along the eaves of the building now, and in the street Walker could see it lofting leaves and wet papers and bits of unidentifiable debris high into the air. He could still see an occasional car pass by on the street, crawling along with headlights on and windshield wipers flicking back and forth frantically, the tires already making rooster-tail wakes in the puddles. He watched each one as long as he could see it, hoping the person inside was very close to where he was going. After twenty minutes had passed, he saw no others. The people had given their city up to the hurricane.

An hour later, the volume of the wind seemed to increase again, and Walker's uneasiness increased with it. He found himself thinking, This is it. This is as high as it goes. Then it would seem to increase again. He began to see objects in motion that he had never expected to see. There was a blue sheet-metal rectangle that gave prices for Regular, Self-Serve, and Full-Serve. It flew through the air for fifty feet, then cartwheeled along the center of the street, fell flat, and lay there, but the next time he looked, it was gone. It was two hours later that he noticed the smaller pieces of debris, dark, flat rectangles fluttering in the air to scatter like leaves. It took more time before a group of them landed near enough for him to see them clearly. They were shingles. The storm had begun to tear off roofs.

Night did not fall. The darkness simply acquired depth until Walker conceded that he could not see anymore. He turned away from the window and realized the room was as dark as a closet. He felt for the flashlight Miss Turley had given him, then went down the hall until he found an office door that was open. He went to the couch and lay down on it with his jacket as a blanket. He listened to the roar of the wind, and the splashing of the water rushing out of the gutters to the ground outside. He tried to feel whether the force of the wind was having any effect on the structure of the building, but he could detect no movement. The storm had reached such an intensity that the sounds had lost their variation. They were just an unchanging roar with no startling rises or falls, and the sameness slowly put him to sleep.

At some point in the night, he awoke to the sound of small objects being hurled against the building in a sudden patter. He sat up for a moment and tried to gauge the strength of the wind, but he could not detect a change. He lay back and thought about the sudden noise that had disturbed him. He wondered if it had been more shingles. Leaves and trash and even signs blowing around meant nothing. Shingles were different. Shingles meant that somewhere not far from here, somebody's house was filling up with water.

20

Morning was just the sound of Miss Turley walking past his door in high heels. Walker got up and went to his window. There was a diffuse gray light that let him see. The street outside was a running stream from curb to curb carrying unidentifiable debris, mud, and leaves. Farther up the block he could see three tall palm trees that had fallen, and the water formed unmoving waves where it washed past them.

He heard the sound of a radio, so he followed it to find Evans's office. "The eye passed over south Florida at around four A.M. The governor has issued a statement that some search-and-rescue teams have been out during the night, and that disaster-relief personnel and equipment from all over the nation are already being assembled in command centers outside the hurricane's path, ready to move in as soon as conditions warrant."

Evans looked at Walker. "It's over. They're not ready to say that, but it is."

"What do we do?"

"These people have been paying us fat premiums for years in the fear that this was going to happen. Now we convince them it was worth it."

"How?"

"What we need is a policyholder who saw an agent from McClaren's show up like an angel without waiting to be called. And if they need it, we'll take care of them."

"Take care of them?" said Walker.

Evans nodded. "If the damage is small, we'll help board up a broken window or two, fill out a claim form, take some pictures, and move on to the next client. But judging from the radio, some of the houses are going to be uninhabitable. Clients will need food, clothes, lodging. We'll be there to cover it. Each policy file already has an envelope with five hundred dollars in cash and a blank, signed check. See what I'm getting at?"

Walker nodded. "You want friends for life."

"For generations. A little sympathy, a small advance on a payment we'll have to make later anyway, will make all the difference."

"When do we start?"

"Now. You'll take some policies and I'll take some. Pretty soon our own people will start making it in one by one, and Miss Turley will send them out." He pointed to a pile of folders with a camera on top. "Take that pile. They're all in one zip code."

Walker glanced at the first address, then at his road map. He checked two more, and he couldn't help noticing the sizes of the policies. "You've got some pretty expensive real estate on the books."

"We're starting with the big ones because they're easier to reach, and they're more likely than most to still be standing. You know the old insurance adage: the Lord hates a trailer park. As the cleanup gets going, we'll be able to reach the rest."

Walker took his pile of policies and forms and joined Evans at the door. Walker looked out at the gray sky and said, "You're sure that's it? Do they stop and start again?"

"This one's over," Evans said. He opened the door, then stopped Walker. "One last word. The reason these people deal with us is that for a hundred and fifty years, the company was run by gentlemen, and now by ladies and gentlemen. What we're doing is reminding them that ladies and gentlemen are better than their word. Conglomerates are not."

Walker looked carefully at his car and saw that there was mud up to the hubcaps, but nothing else seemed to be wrong. He tried the key, and the engine started and ran strong, so he opened his road map, drove out of the lot, and headed toward the ocean.

The next day and night merged into a continuous, exhausting blur. The first houses were huge and elaborate, some of them built in eccentric, grand rococo styles, some in art deco revival. A few looked like clubs, built above private quays with jetties extending outward, a couple of them only to serve as artificial shoals, where the caved-in carcasses of ruined yachts lolled absurdly.

Walker would arrive, show his identification, look at the damage, offer emergency help, fill out the form, and take photographs with the Polaroid camera Miss Turley had given him with the files, then move on to the next house.

Walker made it back to the office after dark. When he opened the door he was startled at the change. There were people at all of the desks, and wet, tired-looking men and women coming in, as he was, to drop off claim forms, get more film for their cameras, and pick up the next set of files for the next zip code. He saw Kennedy, Cardarelli, and a few other San Francisco people processing forms at desks, but there were many others he had never seen before.

There were genuine local appraisers, who had been reinforced by appraisers from other states. They were easy to spot, because they had come prepared with appropriate outdoor clothes, their own cameras, and things that novices like Walker didn't have, like tape measures clipped to their belts. A few of them even wore hard hats.

Walker went out again, this time to a new neighborhood. This one was situated above a lake that must once have been small, but it had grown to include quite a few lawns and gardens, and even the ground floor of one house. Walker worked in a kind of fog, taking on everything that presented itself. He drove a woman to a hospital, taped plastic over broken windows, started a wet electrical generator that ran a pump, opened a power garage door by disconnecting it from the screw mechanism, and helped to wrap up a painting that looked to him as though it might be a genuine Vermeer.

Walker slept on the floor of the office for a few hours, then went out again at dawn. This day was the same, a succession of houses with windows blown in, roofs denuded of some of their shingles. There was a note on one house that said the occupants had gone to an evacuation shelter, so he drove there in search of them, and found several other clients too. He filled out the forms with generalities: "Customer believes house is a total loss," or "Customer states that the flooding damaged the first floor but did not reach the second." When he returned from the last trip of the day, he handed his claim forms to Cardarelli.

She looked up from her desk. "Ah, Walker. Tell me, is it day or night out there?"

"Night."

"Good. I thought I was going blind." Her expression suddenly changed, and she was all business again. "Thank you," she said, and returned to her work.

Walker turned, and Evans was beside him. He led Walker aside. "Have you met Fred Teller?"

He correctly interpreted Walker's blank look. "Appraiser from New Orleans?" Evans prompted. "Tall, thin fellow with blond hair—wears a canvas jacket."

Walker looked at him in tentative agreement. "I think I've seen him, but I haven't talked to him. I've been out a lot." He detected something in Evans's expression. "Is there a problem?"

"Nobody remembers seeing him since last night."

"Do you know where he was working?"

"The last batch of policies he was checking were in Palm Beach."

"He could have car trouble or something. With the phones out, he'd be stuck. If you've got another copy of his list, I'll go out and take a look."

Walker drove out of the lot and looked at his watch. He had been working for sixteen hours straight, but he felt a quiet contentment. The weight of his depression over the search for Ellen Snyder had not disappeared, but it had been forgotten for a time. For the past two days, he had been able to forget about Ellen Snyder, and about himself, and concentrate on the simple, direct business of making claims. He reminded himself that now he should be thinking about Fred Teller.

He picked a house on the list of clients that Teller had been given, and drove to it. The owner had seen no appraiser, so Walker took the time to fill out a claim form, then checked his map and picked a second house that looked like the closest.

It was a big, rambling place on a slight rise in the land that looked artificial, with a tile roof that seemed to be intact and a two-car garage. He walked to the front door and knocked, but nobody came to answer, so he walked around the house to the back to see if they had not heard. There was a tennis court that looked shiny in the darkness. The net had provided the wind with a place to deposit broken branches and leaves and the ubiquitous bits of trash paper, so the pile in center court had grown into a barricade.

He knocked on the back door, but there was still no answer, so he walked toward the street, where he had left his car. He was preparing to go to the next house on the list when something caught his eye. There was a single set of muddy tire tracks on the driveway, leading from the garage door to the street.

He stared at it for a moment. If the car had been in the garage during the hurricane, and someone had driven it out, why would the tracks be muddy? If they had taken the car out after the hurricane and then driven it into the garage, there might be a single set of muddy tire tracks. But that would mean the car was still here, and the owners home.

He walked to the side of the garage and looked in the window. There was a boat on a trailer on one side of the garage. On the other was a four-wheel-drive vehicle with a toolbox showing under a tarp, and what looked like a briefcase. Walker went back to his car and got his flashlight, then shone it in the garage window. The reflection off the glass made it hard to see, so he manipulated the flashlight a bit, and the light passed across the license plate: Louisiana.

Walker went to the side of the house and shone the flashlight in the window. It was a dining room. Everything was in place, and he could see no broken windows. He tried to imagine what had happened to the appraiser. If he'd had engine trouble, and the client was gone, would he have put his car in the client's garage?

Walker looked up, but he was too close to the house to see into any of the upper windows. He went back to the tennis court to see if he could detect any sign that someone was awake upstairs and had not heard the door. He stood near the net and looked up, but he could see no glow of flashlights or candles. He tried using his own flashlight, shining it in the upper windows to cast a light on the ceiling, but he detected no shadow of a person looking out to see what he was doing.

As he lowered his light, it shone on the grass. He brought it back, then moved it from side to side. There was a long depression where the grass had been crushed. He moved his light a few feet to the right and picked up a second depression—tire tracks. He tried to fathom the sight. Someone had driven a car back here? Maybe the home owner had asked the appraiser to use the utility vehicle he drove to move or carry something for him. But then Walker remembered that here, too, there was only one set of tracks. Whatever had come this way had not come back.

He picked up the parallel tracks again on the far side of the tennis court, and followed them. They led down a broad gravel path through a garden, then to another rectangular expanse of pavement. He moved closer and directed his light over it. It wasn't pavement. It was the cover of a swimming pool.

He let his light move along the edge of the pool cover. It was the kind with an electric motor that turned a reel to pull it back into a wooden housing at the end of the pool, and wheeled guides on a track at the edges. But what caught his attention was that the cover was clean. He looked around. The pool was in a protected spot below the hill, but the cover should have been plastered with wet leaves and trash and mud like everything else. It must have been rolled up in its housing during the storm and rolled out afterward. There had been no electricity, so someone had pulled it out by hand. He stared at the pool cover for a moment.

He stepped to the end of the pool, dreading what he was going to find but not sure what it was. He knelt to grasp the bar that held the cover and managed to push it a couple of feet away from the deck. He picked up his flashlight and trained it down into the water.

The light played along the hood of a black Mercedes sedan. He went down on his elbows, aimed the light again, and sucked in a breath. There were two bodies. The man in the back seat had floated upward, and all Walker could see of him from this angle was a leg that had drifted out of the open window, the pant leg halfway up the calf, so his shoe and sock and a length of white skin were visible. The woman was held in the front passenger seat by her seat belt, sitting there with her dead eyes staring ahead.

Walker quickly stood and yanked the cover back. He turned to look around him, not because he expected to see something else but because he hoped he would not. He didn't know whether to keep the light on or turn it off, so he flicked it off and felt worse, then pushed the switch on again. He walked up the path quickly, his head swiveling from side to side in an attempt to see all around him at once. When he made it to the tennis court, he broke into a run.

He reached the street, got into the car, and drove a mile or more, searching for a police car, a fire truck, any vehicle that looked as though it belonged to someone in authority, but he saw nothing. This area had not been hit hard, and he knew the emergency vehicles must be in other neighborhoods. He drove on, feeling more and more desperate, but then to his left, down a long, straight avenue, he saw a faint glow on the pavement: electric lights. He turned and drove toward the glow.

It was a large building with a few lighted windows. As he came nearer, he saw that there was a big set of letters along the top of the building that were not illuminated. He picked out the word HOSPITAL. Of course that was what it would be. They all had emergency generators. He turned up the driveway and into a lot, then ran toward a lighted doorway.

The automatic doors didn't work, but he pushed one open and stepped into chaos. There were people on gurneys in the hallway with IV stands set up beside them, nurses and orderlies rushing back and forth, people who wore dirty clothes and fresh white bandages, children crying, old people sitting on floors because there were no chairs. Down the hall in the lobby, he saw what he had been looking for, the dark blue uniform of a policeman. Walker hurried toward him with such speed and determination that the cop's body went tense.

Walker said, "I just found two murder victims."

The cop looked into Walker's eyes for about two seconds, then picked his radio off his belt and began to talk.

It was four hours later when a police car finally dropped Walker off back at the hospital. He had taken one set of policemen to the pool and shown them what he had found, then waited while they broke into the house and told him that they had not found Fred Teller inside. After that it had been a long night of waiting in the back seat of a police car, then waiting in the station, then waiting for another police car to take him back.

While he was driving his rental car back to the McClaren agency, the lights began to come on. At first the streets were dark, and then there was a sudden flickering around him, and the street lamps came on, not all at once, but with a brightening that shot along the straight stretch of road ahead like a row of dominoes falling. A few seconds later, other circuits came on in random groups. Lights that had been on when the power died all came back—upper windows, neon signs and fluorescents in closed stores, alarm systems that now clanged and hooted along the empty streets. Traffic signals that had been dead for two days suddenly began to blink on and off.

He turned into the driveway at the McClaren's office, snatched Fred Teller's list off the seat, and ran into the building. People who looked as though they had been asleep were standing up and moving toward desks, a few of them looking around and picking up papers off the floor as though they had not noticed them before. Walker saw Evans come out of the hallway that led to his office, putting on his suit coat and looking pleased.

Walker hurried up and grasped his arm. "Are the phones working?"

Evans turned and led him back down the hall. "I'm not sure yet. Did you find him?"

Walker's mind had gone so far beyond the surprise of it that for a second the question struck him as insane. "I'm afraid I didn't. The police are looking now. I've got to try to make a call."

Evans stopped and looked back at Walker, but Walker dodged by him and hurried ahead. Walker stepped into Evans's office and reached for the telephone, but as he did, he heard a ringing in the main office, and then a half-ironic cheer from the people gathered there. He dialed the number of the McClaren's office in San Francisco. It rang twice, and then a pleasant female voice said, "You have reached the office of McClaren Life and Casualty. We're sorry, but all—" He hung up.

He sat at Evans's computer terminal, typed in Joyce Hazelton's e-mail address, and began to type.

"URGENT, URGENT, URGENT for anyone in the McClaren's office, from John Walker in Miami."

Walker moved his finger down Fred Teller's list until he found the address, then turned to the screen again.

To his surprise, the screen was not empty. It said, "John, this is Joyce. Go ahead." She was there.

His heart beat hard as he typed, "Have any payments been requested or authorized for policy number HO-6 135834, to Mr. and Mrs. Michael Cosgrove of Palm Beach?"

He waited, aware that Evans was reading the screen over his shoulder, then conscious that Evans was staring at him, waiting for an explanation that he didn't have the time or energy to give, because it would divert his concentration. There was motion on the screen again.

"Yes. Claim received by fax via Tampa for limit of policy. Authorized for payment by Frederick G. Teller, appraiser. Check cut and sent."

Walker typed his response. "Stop payment ASAP." He hesitated for a second, then typed, "Get Stillman."

21

"Walker. Get up."

Walker opened his eyes and looked around him. The office was a momentary surprise, but his memory came back. It was daylight, and there were phones ringing. Standing near the open door was Stillman.

Walker sat up on the couch and rubbed his eyes. "How did you get here so fast?"

Stillman said, "I didn't waste any time because I heard it was you that rubbed my lamp."

Walker stood. "Yeah. That was me." He said, "Here's what happened. I was out looking for—"

"I know what happened." Stillman looked at his watch. "It's nearly four o'clock. Time to go."

Walker put on his coat and pulled one end of his tie to bring it back up to his neck, then sat down on the couch to tie his shoes.

Stillman watched him impatiently for a moment. "That your suitcase?"

"Yeah," said Walker.

"Bring it with you. If we can't find a better place than this to sleep tonight, we deserve what happens to us."

They went out to a dark blue rental car, a big sedan like the ones Stillman always rented. Stillman snatched Walker's suitcase, tossed it into the trunk with his own, leaned farther into the trunk, plucked out a folder that had the home office logo on it, and handed it to Walker. "Here, take this."

They got into the car and Stillman drove toward the area Walker had explored the night before. The traffic looked to Walker to be almost normal—or at least, what it had been before the storm. The streets were clear and dry, but there were many buildings with boarded windows, roofs with bare patches that showed torn tar paper and plywood. They passed two buildings where water was being pumped out through long hoses to the gutters. He looked at the street signs going by. "Hey, wait. You're going the wrong way. The house is up this way."

Stillman shook his head. "No point in going there. The owners are still dead, and I don't want to waste time talking to cops."

"They might have learned something by now."

Stillman shook his head. "They're busy convincing themselves those two were killed in a robbery. They think Fred Teller may have arrived at an inopportune moment."

"Hard to argue with that."

"It wasn't just bad luck. This was all set up because they knew somebody like Teller would be along shortly," said Stillman. "Teller was sent out with cash, claim forms all ready to go, presigned blank checks, and a bunch of ID with his signature on it. One of the killers probably said he was Mr. Cosgrove, let Teller in the house, and grabbed him." He drove on for a minute. "The blank checks all got filled in and cashed yesterday."

"How? The power was off."

"Here it was. Not in Tampa, Tallahassee, or Mobile. There's no bank in the world that won't cash a check from McClaren Life and Casualty. These were like cashier's checks. Evans had them issued before the hurricane against verified accounts."

"Do you think they're the same people—the ones who killed Ellen Snyder?"

"Yeah, and so do you," said Stillman. "It's just a small variation on what they did to her: they send in a fraudulent claim approved by a real McClaren's employee, then make the employee disappear. If anybody suspects fraud, the employee is the suspect—at least long enough for the checks to clear. The only difference is that they heard there was going to be a hurricane, and came in ahead of it. They knew that the phones would go out, the power would be off, and the police would be busy pulling people out from under tree trunks. They also knew that the minute it stopped raining, there would be insurance claims adjusters brought in from everywhere swarming all over the place."

Walker was silent for a moment. "It's the same trick, but it seems too small. When they did this to Ellen, they got twelve million. The checks we were all carrying had a ten-thousand-dollar limit on them. Even if Teller had twenty-five like I did, and all of them cleared, it's still not enough."

"Who said that was all?"

"It's not?"

"It wasn't intended to be, anyway. You know the San Francisco office sent a check for the Cosgrove house. That was two point three million. Well, there are other claims with Fred Teller's name on them faxed in and processed at San Francisco. Pretty soon we're going to be getting into some real money."

"Hasn't the company stopped payment?"

"Sure," said Stillman. "I don't know whether it's in time, and more to the point, Fred Teller still hasn't turned up."

"If you're not driving to the Cosgrove house, where are you going?"

"We're going to take a look at the rest of the houses on Teller's route." He glanced at his road map, then handed it roughly to Walker. "Here. Find me the Dillard house. The address is 3124 Shaw Creek Road."

They drove from one huge house to the next. Some of the people who lived in them were at home. Two had even seen Fred Teller and signed claim forms that he had promised to submit.

It was night when they reached the ninth house. It lay on a cul-de-sac at the end of a new road that led out onto a filled-in artificial plateau in what must recently have been wetlands. In the distance they could see tall mangroves hung with Spanish moss, and the gleam of water between the weeds.

As they parked in front of the house, Stillman said, "Interesting."

"What is?"

"Well, the power is on around here, but this place is dark. It doesn't look as though there was much damage."

"Yeah," said Walker. "It does seem a little odd. Maybe when they heard the weather reports they turned everything off and hit the road. In town, when the power came on, whatever had been left on lit up."

Stillman said, "Who lives here?"

Walker looked inside the folder and read it by the map light. "Mr. Jeffrey Kopcinsky." He looked at the other sheets attached to the policy. "He's also got life insurance, with his brother in New York as beneficiary, and auto on a new BMW. One driver. I guess he lives alone out here."

Stillman shrugged. "I suppose I wouldn't have stayed alone in the middle of a damned swamp with a hurricane coming either. Let's go see if he just goes to bed early."

They walked up the driveway. Walker pushed the button for the doorbell and heard a faint chime somewhere in the house. "Power is on," he said quietly. He reached up to knock. Just as his knuckles hit the door for the first time, a small light went on above their heads. "And it looks like he's home."

Stillman pointed up at the fixture. "It's a security light. Noise turns it on." He pushed the doorbell again.

They waited for a minute, then another, but there were no sounds of footsteps. Just as Walker was preparing to ring again, the light above their heads went off. Walker said, "I want to take a look in the garage."

Stillman stared at him with interest, but said nothing. They moved toward the wide, three-car garage, then around it to the side. Walker put his hands beside his eyes and leaned close to the glass. "There are two cars in there."

"There's room for three, and a man can only flee for his life in one," said Stillman. He took a step toward the street, but Walker stopped him.

"He has an insurance policy on a BMW. That's in there. If he has two cars, or three, why wouldn't they all be on the same policy? It's a hell of a lot cheaper."

Stillman stood motionless for a moment. "Let's look around."

They walked past the garage to a small terrace made of flat slabs of stone, with four chairs and a table. An umbrella was folded and lying on the stone. Walker stopped. "Look," he whispered. "The furniture."

"What about it?"

"It's here. There were winds over a hundred and fifty miles an hour. The furniture should have blown into the swamp. It must have been stowed in the garage and brought out after. If he left before the storm, who did it?"

They kept walking across the terrace, then into a garden. Walker could see in the moonlight that the low plants had been severely undermined by the rain, pushed to one side and uprooted by the wind. There were four small trees in big wooden planters that had been knocked over.

Stillman walked slowly through the garden toward the lawn beyond. Walker stepped backward and studied the house as more of it became visible. The roof looked intact. There were more security lights under the eaves, then tall, narrow windows set deep into the stucco exterior in a vague evocation of the windows in a castle. None of them was boarded, but none seemed to be broken, either. He supposed the fake medieval architecture had saved them. At the corner of his eye he thought he caught movement in one of the narrow windows near the end of the house. He froze and stared at the window for a few seconds, but he couldn't induce his eyes to see it again.

He decided the movement must have been his own. He had been walking, and maybe as his angle had changed, it had simply brought some piece of furniture across his line of sight, or caught a bit of moonlight on the glass. He didn't blame himself for the alarm he had felt, but he had to control it. Just because he had found the scene of a murder, it didn't mean that every house in Florida was harboring something he had to be afraid of.

He turned and stepped more quickly to catch up with Stillman, who was walking along the edge of the lawn, staring out at the dim, ghostly trees in the swamp.

As he came up behind Stillman, he heard him mutter, "Shit." Stillman bent over and looked down. "Another one."

Beside the exposed, gnarled roots of a mangrove tree was the half-submerged body of a man. The face was under the murky water, but Walker could see an ear, the rim just breaking the surface, and the glint of a watchband on the left wrist.

Stillman straightened. "I would guess that's probably Mr. Kopcinsky, wouldn't you?"

"Or Fred Teller."

Stillman had his cell phone in his hand. He punched on the power button, studied the display, held the phone to his ear, looked again, then turned it off. "The relay stations still aren't up and running. We'll have to go bust a window to call the cops."

Walker stared back at the house. "I know this is stupid, but I thought I saw something behind a window up there before. Then I figured it was nothing. But now . . ."

Stillman looked at the house too as he considered. "If there is somebody in there, this wouldn't be a good place to get cornered. It seems to me we ought to walk back the way we came, as though we didn't notice anything. As soon as we get near the patio, make a turn and put the garage between us and the house."

They began to walk toward the garden. Walker kept scanning the tall, narrow windows.

"Slow down," Stillman whispered. "The only reason to hurry would be if we found the body."

Walker brought his pace down to match Stillman's. He said quietly, "It was probably my imagination."

"No, it wasn't," Stillman whispered. "Run!"

Walker took two quick steps, trying to push off hard. He flicked his eyes at the dark house to make out what Stillman had seen, but before he could, everything changed.

A shot clapped Walker's ears as he saw the muzzle flash in the corner of his eye, but the shot seemed not to end, because instantly the flash expanded into a brightness like daylight. The noise had triggered the security lights along the eaves of the house and the garage.

In place of the muzzle flash was a man crouching along the wall of the house holding a pistol in his right hand, caught in the unexpected glare, shocked and half-blinded. He raised his left hand to shade his eyes just as Stillman's body hit him at chest level and hurled him backward into one of the tall windows. There was a crack, then a crash and tinkle of glass.

The man's pistol had left his hand. It was still in the air, spinning to the right side, when Walker's left foot pushed off, changing the course of his sprint to intersect with its trajectory. It hit in the center of a big sandstone slab, bounced once, and slid as Walker bent to reach for it.

A second shot came from somewhere to Walker's left, and pieces of stucco exploded off the house into the air above his head. He lunged at the gun, got his right hand around it, and dipped his shoulder to let the lunge's momentum turn it into a roll. As his roll brought him to his belly, he saw the second man in silhouette beyond the lights.

He dimly understood that this man had been waiting for him beside the garage when the first man had seen Walker break into a run and fired. Walker's right arm was in front of him, holding the pistol on the man. He saw the man's right shoulder rise slightly as he lowered his arm to bring his aim down toward Walker. Walker's fingers jerked tight, and the noise of the gun in his hand startled him. The recoil kicked his forearm upward, but he forced it down, found the man's shape crouching lower, and pulled the trigger again, then again. The man fell and lay still.

Walker rolled onto his back and did a quick sit-up to find the man with Stillman, but the man was in the narrow alcove, the upper part of his body crammed through the broken window into the house and his legs sprawled on the terrace. Stillman was just stepping away from the window. He had his jacket sleeve pulled down over his right hand, and clutched there was a long, jagged shard of glass.

He slowly lifted the piece of glass above the height of his shoulder.

Walker could see blood running along it in two long streaks. Stillman brought the hand down and the long shard flew against the remaining sheet of glass in the upper part of the window, breaking it and bringing it down on the body in dozens of indistinguishable fragments.

Walker gaped as Stillman stood there, examining his sleeves carefully in a way that could only be to see whether he had gotten the man's blood on him. After a moment he met Walker's gaze evenly. "If there were others, they'd already be here."

Walker's heart was beating hard. There was a roaring in his ears that had something to do with the noise of the guns, but now in the silence, he could still hear it. His eyes were drawn to the man Stillman had pushed into the window. His legs seemed to be limp like a doll's legs, feet pointed unnaturally to the sides, knee joints bent inward in a way that must only be possible when all of the muscles had gone limp. He felt his stomach tighten in a retch, but fought it down.

Stillman was on the lawn squatting beside the other man now. "They're both dead?" said Walker.

"Yep."

Walker sat perfectly still, not thinking, just enduring the thoughts that swept through his mind. Walker knew that his life had been irrevocably altered, not just because this would change the future, but because it had already changed the past, going all the way back. He had not wanted ever to be the kind of person who did this. Everything he had thought and done while he was growing up in Ohio had been predicated on the empty faith that if he did what he had been taught— controlled his temper and appetites, struggled against the subtle diminishing effects of resentment and spite, spent his time working and learning things—he could expect something better than this.

The enormity of what he had done frightened him. He searched through his impressions, grasping for excuses: he had not intended to kill anyone; not made a decision; not been given a chance. But his mind could not hold on to the arguments. In the second when he had thrust his arm forward with the gun clutched in his hand, he had not felt anything but the urgent need to hold it steady on the man's chest and fire first.

Stillman's legs crossed Walker's line of vision, and he let his eyes follow them. Stillman stepped close to the man in the window, reached in, and turned the man's face. "Have you ever seen this guy before?"

Walker grimaced and shook his head. "No." He involuntarily turned to look at the man he had shot. "The other one either."

Stillman looked down at the man in the window. "We saw two guys in that alley in Pasadena, and three more out by Gochay's house. Now these two. It's starting to feel like a lot of people." He bent over to search the dead man's pockets. He found a wallet and looked inside. "Nothing but a license and one credit card, which means they're both fake," he muttered, and put it back.

"Doesn't it bother you?" asked Walker.

After a beat, Stillman seemed to notice him. "What?"

"They're . . . dead. We just killed two men."

Stillman took a deep breath, then let it out, and said in a voice that was tired but patient, "I'm not much troubled by ethical considerations, no. I made all my decisions on the subject a long, long time ago. If somebody tries to kill me, he'd better do it on the first try, because only one of us is going home." Walker was silent. After a moment, Stillman said, "I know what you're feeling. It's not going to do anybody any good. You don't get to go through life with clean hands. I'm sorry."

Walker involuntarily looked at his hand, and noticed the gun still in it.

"Leave the gun where you're sitting," Stillman said. "Don't wipe it off or anything." He watched while Walker gently placed the gun on the ground and stood up. "Go take a look in that guy's pockets." Walker hesitated, but Stillman said, "Go ahead."

Walker knelt by the body and felt inside the coat. There was a wallet, but it too had only one credit card, a driver's license, and some cash. He found a heavy metal rectangle he guessed was an ammunition clip for the pistol, took it out, verified the impression, and put it back. There was something else in the breast pocket that was long and hard, so he pulled that out too. It was a case for a pair of eyeglasses.

He opened it, and found a pair of sunglasses. He closed it again and was about to return it to the pocket.

"What's that?" asked Stillman.

"Sunglasses."

Stillman said, "Here." He took the case, then slipped it into his own jacket pocket.

"What are you—"

Stillman interrupted. "We don't have time. This is a story the police had better hear first from our point of view."

As they reached the car, Walker saw the security lights go off again, returning the house and the two dead men to the darkness. He closed his eyes and felt his heart once again begin to beat in a frantic rhythm. The security lights had timers, so all of it, from the first shot until now, must have taken five minutes. It seemed a very short time.

22

The lawyer's name was Diernholtz. He arrived an hour after Walker and Stillman had been brought into the police station, then said to Walker, "It's getting so you can't discharge a firearm into a living human being anymore without having people ask a lot of prying questions. I hope you didn't answer any of them yet."

Walker shook his head.

"Good for you," said Diernholtz. "The call I got from your company said you would know that much. Now, before you make your statement, I assume you did shoot that man?"

"Yes."

"Self-defense, then. I'll be with you when they interrogate you."

The interrogation took hours, but then it simply ended. Walker was left in a room by himself that had no bars. For a time he paced, and for a time he sat. Finally, after the sun was high, he laid his head on the table and slept, then awoke and paced again. It was late afternoon before the police captain came in.

"Sit down, Mr. Walker," he said. "Let me explain the situation to you. We've verified that Mr. Stillman was the one who called the police after the incident. The hands of the man you shot have the same powder residue on them that we found on yours, so we know he fired his weapon—presumably before you did, since the one who fires last is generally the one who's still with us. The second man's hands have also tested positive to show he had fired a pistol at some point. An assistant district attorney was listening while you gave your statement. Another was with the forensics people at the scene. They just confirmed that they're not going to file any charges."

Walker said, "Does that mean I can go?"

The captain paused. "Not just yet. They have recorded it as an instance of self-defense. I've been a cop for twenty-two years, and I never saw an armed assailant who died that way."

"What way?" asked Walker.

"He got thrown through a plate-glass window, managed to accidentally get a piece of glass across his throat, and bled to death. Isn't that what you saw?"

Walker hesitated. "Yes." He remembered Stillman raising the big shard of glass and hurling it into the window, so it would break into a shower of pieces mixed with the others. He had been destroying the weapon.

The captain seemed to sense what Walker was thinking. "You don't know Stillman very well, do you?"

"The company hired him to investigate a fraud case, and assigned me to help," said Walker. "That was only about a month ago. I don't know anything bad about him, if that's what you mean."

The captain stared into Walker's eyes for a moment, then seemed to soften. "You're a young guy. You have an education, a clean record, so I'll give you something for free." He leaned forward. "Cops talk to each other. We go to conventions, just like insurance salesmen, take training courses together. Other people probably wonder what we talk about. A couple of times what I've heard cops talk about is Stillman."

"Why Stillman?"

"Did you know he was a police officer?"

Walker returned his stare, and shook his head.

"About twenty years ago," said the captain. "In Los Angeles. There weren't any charges against him that were made public, so it's hard to know the reason he left. I have a few guesses. Since then he's been in business for himself."

"The security business," said Walker defensively.

The captain looked unimpressed with the term. "He's ready to do a little of everything. Does surveillance, executive protection for companies, handles some stalking cases, quite a bit of insurance work. There have even been a couple of times when somebody was kidnapped and he's the one who delivers the money and handles the exchange."

"I don't think I understand," said Walker. "Is that stuff illegal?"

"No," said the captain. "He's got all the licenses a man can have, and nothing he's done has stuck to him . . . so far. I can vouch for that, because I just checked." His eyes seemed to grow more intense. "A surprising number of these cases end up with somebody getting hurt bad. Or killed."

"Clients?"

"Not clients," said the captain. "Stillman is the guy you hire if you've got a problem you want solved, and you don't care what it costs and especially don't want to know how it's done. What you want is a big . . . vicious . . . dog. That's Stillman. Do you understand what I'm saying?"

Walker sat in silence for a moment. "I guess I do. I'm not sure why you're saying it to me."

"You just got into a mess, and had to kill somebody to get through it. And you're in the clear this time: self-defense. I would like to give you some expert advice on self-defense. If whatever it is you're doing for McClaren Life and Casualty puts you in a position where you have to spend time doing what Stillman does, you might want to look for another line of work." He stood up. "Pick up your personal belongings at the front desk."

"Miami police are still unable to identify two slain combatants in a late-night shootout at a Palm Beach residence. At around midnight last night, police responded to a nine-one-one call. When officers arrived just minutes later, they found that two damage appraisers for the McClaren insurance company had apparently foiled a robbery attempt by disarming one of a pair of gunmen. One suspect was shot in the chest, and the second suspect was fatally injured in the struggle for a second weapon. Both men were pronounced dead on arrival at West Palm Beach Hospital." The woman on the television set gave a practiced look of disapproval, moved the sheet of paper to the bottom of her pile, and said, "Next, a cable snaps on an amusement-park ride, with grisly consequences."

Walker stared at the woman on the television set as she faded and was replaced by a commercial for stomach medicine. There was an odd diction to television news, a special jargon. Nobody in a face-to-face conversation said "slain," or referred to anybody as a "gunman." There was a pitch to the descriptions that was edgy and tense, with no variation, like an unchanging song with the volume always turned up, but the news readers smiled through it, as though they were repeating words in a foreign language.

There was a knock on the door of his room, and Walker let Stillman in. Stillman said, "I just checked in with the cops. Still unidentified. They don't seem to be in this the way they need to be."

"You want to see if that lawyer—what's his name—Diernholtz can get anything? He seems to have a relationship with them, and he's already on the payroll."

"Good idea, wrong time. It's not that they won't give. They don't have. They've already run their fingerprints, and it seems they're not in the FBI's NCIC system. This is not normal."

"It's not?"

"No. It means they've never been arrested anywhere. People in businesses that involve shooting you tend to get printed at some point. The fact that they're not isn't good."

"I guess not."

"It means the cops have to use the hard ways—sending pictures around, and so on. They're a bit busy for that right now. They also seem to think somebody will be in any minute to claim the bodies and tell them who they were."

"Do you want to take turns hanging around the station to see who shows up?"

"It won't happen this time. If it did, it wouldn't happen fast. You can't just pull up to the back door with a station wagon and drive off with a body. There will be autopsies and so on. Then they have to get the bodies picked up by somebody who has a license to do it, like an undertaker. Waiting isn't going to do anything but waste more time."

"What choice do we have?"

Stillman reached into his jacket pocket and pulled out the eyeglass case that Walker had found on one of the men.

"You didn't give that to the police?" Walker was amazed.

"I wanted to take a closer look than I could in the dark, and the police erroneously assumed the glasses were mine," said Stillman. "I'd like to know what's printed on the case."

"So would I," said Walker.

"Then let's do it." Stillman went into the bathroom and snatched three tissues from the box on the counter. He pulled a tiny bottle with a black label out of his pocket. "I picked up some Wite-Out." He turned on the desk lamp, set the bottle on the desk, then took out the eyeglass case.

Stillman opened the bottle, then used the little brush in the cap to paint over the three lines of print that had been pressed into the side of the case. He used a tissue to wipe the white liquid off the case, then handed it to Walker.

Walker stared down at the case, where the letters were now in clear white. He read them aloud. "Foley Optical, 1219 Main Street, Keene, New Hampshire 03470."

23

Walker glanced at his watch. He had a few more minutes before boarding time. He took the card out of his wallet and dialed the number of Constantine Gochay.

"Hello?" It was Serena's voice, but she sounded as though her usual detached manner had been somehow forgotten for the moment.

"Hi," said Walker. "This is John Walker."

"I know that," she said. "Are you all right?"

He hesitated. "Yeah. I'm okay. How are you?"

"Don't. Don't do that." She was Mary Catherine Casey now. "I wasn't being mean last time, so don't punish me with that taciturn, manly thing now. You had a horrible experience, and I was worried."

"How did you know about that?"

"I've been reading the on-line *Miami Herald* since your credit card left for Florida." She paused, as though she were hearing something in the silence. Then her voice sounded amazed and affronted. "You weren't even going to tell me, were you?"

"I'm not sure what I want to say about it yet," he said. "It's . . . something happened, and I'm not really sure what it is—all of it, anyway. I think I need time."

He heard keys clicking. "Stillman just bought more plane tickets. Boston. Why aren't you coming home?"

"We found something on one of those guys. Glasses from Foley

Optical in Keene, New Hampshire. I guess we must be flying to Boston and then New Hampshire. Stillman wanted me to ask you to see what you could find out about Foley Optical."

She became Serena again. "Tell Stillman I'll find out what I can about Foley Optical and about Keene, New Hampshire. I'm surprised he didn't tell you to ask about that. He hates to go anywhere without a printout of hospitals and hotels and things. I'll have it ready if you call me from there."

"Sure. Look, I wasn't hiding anything from you. I just don't—"

"You don't know what happened? You hunted down the men who murdered Ellen Snyder and killed them. That's what happened," she snapped. "Don't you have a plane to catch?"

"Yeah. I—"

"Then do it." The line went dead.

Walker stared at the receiver for a second, but he heard the muffled female voice echoing above his head: "United Airlines Flight 922 to Boston is now boarding at Gate 52." He replaced the receiver and looked around for Stillman. He had not seen him for the past few minutes, and now he was gone. Walker picked up his pace, moving to the escalator and then climbing it as it rose. He rushed to the metal detectors, then trotted toward Gate 52.

When he arrived at the gate, he saw Stillman coming out of a bookstore carrying a flat white plastic bag. Stillman seemed not to look at Walker, but Walker knew he was aware of him. He strolled directly to the line of passengers and showed no interest when Walker joined him, only handed him a ticket.

Their seats were near the rear of the plane, so they had to stop in the aisle while dozens of passengers ahead of them stood to push oversized bags into overhead compartments, or danced back and forth searching other compartments for an extra inch of space.

After they had found their seats and the plane was taxiing down to the end of the runway, Stillman said, "How are things in southern California?"

"Variable, turning cool," Walker answered.

"Watch your step with her."

Stillman waited for a few seconds, then sat back in his seat while the plane reached the start of the runway and the engine noise rose to a roar. The plane began to move, acclerating quickly, and then it was nosing up into the sky. Stillman lifted his bag to his lap, took out a road atlas, and began to turn pages.

After a few minutes, the plane leveled, and Walker said, "What are you doing—figuring out how to get to Keene?"

"Partly," Stillman replied, his eyes still on the atlas. "Also why to get there." He noticed Walker's puzzled look. "A map is an interesting conceptual leap. Travelers spent thousands of years looking at everything from ground level before they thought of making a picture of it from above—long before anybody had ever been above. It's what places would look like to God."

"And He tells you why we're going?"

"He never returns my calls. But if you look at a map, sometimes you can figure out things you might miss if you were on the spot—designs and patterns that you wouldn't put together."

"What kind of patterns?"

"Like Keene, for instance . . ." He held up the atlas so Walker could see the full-page map of New Hampshire. "You have to ask yourself why a criminal would choose to spend time in Keene, New Hampshire. The obvious thing is that it's about as far from the San Francisco office as you can get without getting your feet wet."

"It's certainly not the first place I'd look."

"Right. It's small," said Stillman. "The chart says the population is under twenty-five thousand. That's a little puzzling, because a person in his line of work usually likes big cities, where he can come and go without attracting attention, there are lots of like-minded individuals, and lots of places to spend other people's money. But the map suggests some mitigating factors." He handed the atlas to Walker. "See that?"

"See what?"

"The roads. They're laid out in a pattern you seldom see—like the strands of a spiderweb—eight highways leaving town at the points of a compass rose: north, northeast, east, southeast, south, southwest, west, and northwest. If somebody left town just before you got there, you wouldn't have the faintest idea which direction he went. Then there are borders."

"What about them?"

"You drive west across the Connecticut River into Vermont, it's about twenty miles. Keep going another forty and you're already in New York. Go south twenty miles instead, and you're in Massachusetts. If you want to fly, there's a small airport south of the city. There are others in Manchester and Nashua, or Pittsfield, Massachusetts, or Albany."

"So he looks like he's in the middle of nowhere, but he can get anywhere," said Walker.

"Assuming we're right, and that's where he lived," Stillman said. He took back his atlas.

"It's a quite an assumption, isn't it?" said Walker. "He could have been there on a vacation five years ago and lost his sunglasses."

"It's thin, but not out of the question. It takes a while to get an appointment with an eye doctor, see him, get the prescription, go to an optometrist, get glasses made. It's not something you can do in a day in a strange town. But there's still something about it that doesn't feel right yet, some other attraction to the place that would make him go there. Maybe there's something I'm missing, that you can only see from a human's-eye view."

"Serena said she'd find out what she could about the place."

Stillman raised his eyebrows. "You ought to hold on to that girl."

"She hasn't made up her mind."

"Then it's up to you to convince her."

"I haven't made up my mind either."

Stillman glared at him. "If the world is turning too fast for you, then careful analysis will tell you that there are a limited number of things you can do about it."

During the next couple of hours, Walker found himself several times thinking about what Stillman had said. All of his life he had lived by observing in retrospect what had been going on around him for a period of time, discerning the trends and patterns, then deciding what to do about them. That had always seemed to him to be a rational, wise course of action.

But since the day when Stillman had arrived, everything seemed to happen too quickly; events came at him like punches. Looking at things in retrospect was not a good way to decide whether to duck, run, or hold your ground. It was a good way to figure out how you came to be lying on your back, gazing up at the sky in queasy regret.

24

The plane came in over Logan International at sunrise, so its circling to take its turn at the runway kept bringing the sun into Walker's eyes. He said, "Want me to rent the car this time?"

"I think we'd better wait on that," Stillman answered. "A place that small, I'd like to try to sneak up on it."

Stillman's description was accurate. They took a cab from Boston to Lowell, then a second cab across the New Hampshire border into Nashua, where Stillman had them dropped off at a car-rental agency beside an enormous shopping center. He rented a black Ford Explorer. He took a second look at the rental papers and said, "Pretty good. There's no sales tax here."

As they put their suitcases in the back, Stillman looked at his watch. "I've got to do some shopping. Let's drive over to that mall."

From then on, Walker seemed to spend most of his time going in and out of the mall entrance. Every time he returned from stowing Stillman's purchases in the back of the Explorer, Stillman had another load for him. Once he found Stillman in an electronics store, and later at a bookstore, then at a luggage store. Finally, he returned to find him at a large food court strolling from counter to counter surveying the menus.

They bought food and carried it on trays to a quiet table. Walker said, "I can see why the sales tax would be an issue for you."

Stillman smiled. "I'm just trying to make our stay in New Hampshire a safe and happy one, as my new guidebook says."

"So far it hasn't been bad," said Walker. "Kind of a roundabout way to get there, though."

"I suspect the number of men who come to a rural area on vacation wearing three-thousand-dollar suits is pitifully small. We've got to be reasonably inconspicuous. I also suspect that a car with New Hampshire plates draws a little less attention than one with out-of-state plates. The tinted windows might help keep our faces from becoming too familiar. And I picked up a few things that are easier to get here than in a small town."

"How much more do you have to do?"

"That's it. Now we eat. By the time we're done, people on the West Coast should be up and at their desks."

When they had eaten, they split up again to find pay telephones. Walker's was in a hallway that led to rest rooms. One of the phones was being used by a young woman in a paper cap and a maroon shirt that was the uniform of the Mexican-food stand where he had bought his lunch. She was talking in dramatically inflected Spanish, and it sounded to him as though she was giving a disparaging assessment of whoever was on the other end of the line.

He moved in beside her, picked up the unused telephone, and dialed Gochay's number.

"Yeah?" He would have been relieved that it was Serena's voice once again, but the tone was cold.

"It's me again," said Walker. "Right now I'm thinking about that little spot right in front of your ear, where the skin is unbelievably smooth and white. I wish I could put my lips there and tell you a secret."

The girl beside him spun her head, gave him an approving smile, then raised her free hand in a thumbs-up sign. Walker returned the smile uneasily and she turned away to continue her own conversation.

Serena said skeptically, "Did somebody tell you to say that?"

"Of course not. Who would tell me that?"

"I don't know. Maybe you read it in one of those magazines they give you on airplanes."

"No," he said. "This time it was about places I can't afford to go, and diseases I hope I don't have. I spent most of the time trying to figure out why I don't understand you."

"Who do you think you understand?" The question made Walker lapse into silence for a moment, but she was already on to another subject. "You were in the Miami papers again."

"Did it say whether the police had found out who those two guys were?"

"If they know, they aren't saying. I'll see what I can find out about that too," she said. "You're on a pay phone again, aren't you? My caller ID doesn't say anything. Are you in New Hampshire yet?"

"I'm in Nashua, in a mall. We'll be leaving for Keene when I hang up."

"I checked it out for you."

"Anything interesting?"

"Sure. The state amphibian is the spotted newt. The state motto is 'Live free or die,' and the song is 'Old New Hampshire.' I'd hum a few bars, but I've never heard it."

"I guess that's all I need to know."

"Keene has only twenty-two thousand people, but that makes it the largest city in that part of the state, so it's where people in the villages around there shop."

"Villages? We're talking villages?"

"They're all little places with a few hundred people. Think of a place that used to have a textile mill that closed fifty years ago. Now it's dairy cows and tourists. Figure a church with a steeple, the old mill, covered bridges, and a lot of antique shops. Tell Stillman not to shop around for hospitals. There's only one."

"He'll like that."

"He should. Go back to him and get this over with. Let me know where you are." The line went dead. He put the receiver back in its cradle and walked back along the mall.

He saw Stillman drinking a cup of coffee near the exit to the parking lot. He was staring out at the soft gray light beyond, apparently lost in thought. But when Walker was still a hundred feet away, Stillman stepped outside and walked toward the Explorer, paying attention to keeping his cup level.

When Walker caught up with him, Stillman handed him the car keys. "Do you mind driving?"

"No." Walker took the keys and climbed in, then watched Stillman step in beside him, guarding his coffee.

Stillman held out his cup. "Want a sip? I figured one of us had to drive, so I only got one."

"No, thanks. Where am I going?"

"North on 3, west on 101 to Keene. It's sixty-two miles."

Walker drove out on the highway, then began to watch for signs. When he had found 101 and was up to speed, he said, "Did you find out anything on the phone?"

"Our two unnamed assailants are still unnamed. Their photographs haven't rung any bells, their prints aren't on file anyplace, their guns were stolen from a store in California a couple of years ago. The FBI told Rex McClaren they're doing a lot of lab work."

"What kind of lab work?"

"Beats me," Stillman said. "They don't mind wasting money, but they don't seem to think they are. Rex got the impression that their interest was piqued by something they found that they're not talking about."

"What do you think?"

"I think that's what Rex wishes. Probably it's just that they're wondering why they don't already have fingerprints for two guys like that. You can't blame Rex for wishful thinking, though. He's aware that he has some responsibility to protect the people who work for him, but he's not sure how to go about it." Stillman fell into silence and sipped his coffee.

Walker drove to Keene past New England towns like the ones Serena had described: Wilton, West Wilton, Peterborough, West Peterborough, Dublin, Marlborough. Keene was the same sort of place, but bigger and livelier. Main Street was wide and pleasant, and led up to a circle with a town hall and an eighteenth-century church with a tall steeple. Here and there along the street were buildings that had probably been here since the Revolution, but as the numbers grew higher, the buildings seemed more modern and functional. There were restaurants, stores, a movie theater.

They drove around for ten minutes, looking. Finally, Stillman said, "Well? What do you think of it?"

"It's not all that different from little towns in Ohio," said Walker. "A lot older, I guess. But the people don't seem any different. It doesn't look like the sort of place where either of those guys in Florida would choose to live."

"True," said Stillman. "But does it look like a place you'd drive to from New York or Boston to get your optical work done?"

25

At one o'clock they registered at a Days Inn, and Walker began to unload the bags of purchases Stillman had made in Nashua and carry them into Stillman's room. Stillman was busy. Walker saw him open a box and take out a new video camera, remove the battery, put it into the charging unit and plug it in, then move to the next shopping bag.

Walker carried his suitcase into his own room, then returned to the Explorer. He carried Stillman's suitcase in and lifted it to Stillman's bed. "What's in here, anyway?" he asked. "Did you buy a set of weights?"

"Just some electronic gear I bring along sometimes on this kind of case."

"What kind of electronic gear?"

Stillman answered out of his distraction. "Tape recorder, voice-actuated. Listening equipment. Nightscope, an old scanner, that kind of thing."

"Old?"

"Yeah, pre-1994."

"Is that when everything went to hell in the electronics industry?"

"No. That's when it got to be illegal to manufacture them to tune to eight hundred megahertz. That's the frequency of cellular phones."

"You bought a video camera too?"

Stillman stopped perusing the instruction booklet and held up the little camera. "Nice, isn't it?" It was barely larger than the clenched hands that held it, and had a small screen on the back.

"What's it for?"

Stillman set it aside. "When you're my age, your memory goes."

"What now?"

"Go through those bags and take out the clothes that are your size. Pick out something to wear that looks like what the people we saw on the street are wearing." He reached into his suitcase and took out the dead man's sunglasses. "While you're at it, spend some time looking closely at these glasses. Memorize everything about them."

It was just after three when Stillman knocked on Walker's door. He was wearing a pair of jeans, a short-sleeved summer shirt, and a pair of Mephisto walking shoes. He was carrying a leather bag that was just a bit too small and thick to be a briefcase. Walker appraised him. "You look like a bank president on a trout-fishing trip."

Stillman raised his eyebrow and moved in past him. "Then we'll be very convincing."

"Who are we convincing?"

"Whoever is at Foley Optical. You ready?"

"I guess so." They stepped outside, and Walker began to move toward the parking lot.

"Leave the car," said Stillman, and began to walk toward Main Street. "When you want to be easy to find later, the best thing you can bring is a car. We don't."

"Since you always lose the damned things, it's probably just as well. What else do I need to know?"

Stillman said, "We're going into the store. You are the customer. Your name is David Holler. You live in Los Angeles, but you're on vacation. You forgot your sunglasses. Now, think back on what you saw when you were looking at the dead guy's sunglasses."

"Okay, I'm thinking."

"Order a pair just like them."

"I thought people don't order them on vacations. Besides, I don't need a prescription. My eyes are perfect."

"That's why you're the customer," he said as he reached into his pocket. "Pay for them with this." He held out a shiny plastic card.

Walker took it, glanced at it, and saw the name and the Visa logo. "A fake credit card? I know this is your field, not mine, but why do something illegal when you don't have to—for practice?"

"It's not a fake credit card," Stillman said patiently. "It's a real credit card. The bills go to a real address, and my accountant pays them on time. David Holler has been a treasured employee of Stillman Associates for upwards of ten years. He just doesn't happen to have a literal, biological existence. I use him now and then." He reached into his pocket again and held out another piece of plastic.

Walker accepted it with dread. When he looked at it, he put it away even more quickly. "A driver's license?"

"That's not legal either, in case you were wondering. All I can say for it is that it's not evil. Nobody's screwing Mr. Foley's optical store."

"How did you even get my picture?"

"From your personnel file. I figured we might need it."

Walker said wearily, "Who signed for our hotel room and rented the car?"

Stillman smiled. "Me: Bill Taylor." Then he turned serious. "It's important that you pay with the credit card. I want to see what he does with it when you do."

"Okay," said Walker.

They approached Foley Optical, and Stillman said, "Don't worry about this, and don't pay any attention to what I'm doing. Just buy yourself the right kind of sunglasses, and we'll get what we want."

They went inside, and Walker looked around. It seemed to be like every optician's that he had ever seen. There were frames of all shapes and sizes on special racks attached to the walls, and every inch that wasn't occupied by frames was a mirror. There was a low counter along the right side of the shop with seats in front of it, and the wall behind it was another big mirror. At the rear was a higher counter with a cash register and a computer, and beside that was a doorway into what seemed to be a small workshop. A tall man in late middle age with a bald head and hands that looked abnormally soft and clean came through the workshop door and smiled. "Hello. Can I help you?"

Walker said, "Yes, please. I'd like to pick out some sunglasses."

"Do you have a prescription?"

"No," said Walker. "I have twenty-twenty vision."

"You're lucky," the man said. "Even at your age, that's not as common as you'd think."

"I know," said Walker. "What I'd like is a good, sturdy set of frames. Metal with a gold tone."

"And the lenses?"

"Dark green, but really dark, so when you look at them from the front they look almost black."

"Let me get some frames and sample lenses to start narrowing things down." Mr. Foley sat at his seat behind the counter where he fitted glasses and reached up under the surface, then came back with a set of keys on a big brass ring. He used one to open the lock on the case.

Walker went through the surprisingly long and complex process of making choices. Each decision he made was based on the pair of glasses he had found in the dead man's pocket. When he had finally found the right shade of lens and the right frames, he said, "Perfect." He saw Stillman give a slight nod.

Mr. Foley was walking back toward the workshop. "Let me see, though. I'm not sure if I have this size in a plain tinted lens right now."

Walker looked toward Stillman, but Stillman ignored him. He had opened his leather bag, and was fiddling inside. Walker saw the distinctive titanium gleam of the new video camera. Stillman moved the bag about an inch, aiming it at the mirror behind the counter, then closed and zipped it.

Foley returned. "I'm sorry to say I don't have it. Are you gentlemen from the area?"

"No," said Walker. "California. We're here on vacation, and I forgot my sunglasses."

"If you're going to be here for a day or two, I can get the lens from my supplier as early as tomorrow morning," said Foley. "I could have them in for you by this time in the afternoon."

"How much are they?" asked Walker.

"One ninety-five for the frames. The lenses will be another fifty-five. Two fifty total." He looked apologetic. "But at least there's no sales tax here."

"I guess I'll take them," said Walker. "I can wait a day." He felt a certain vindication of his lifelong habit of buying cheap sunglasses.

"I'm afraid I'll have to ask for a deposit. Would half be okay?"

"Do you take credit cards?"

"Sure."

"Then you might as well charge it all now. It's easier to keep my records straight." Walker took out the David Holler credit card and rested his thumb on the fake driver's license, but Mr. Foley didn't ask for it, so he didn't offer. Foley typed some numbers on his cash register, swiped the card on a magnetic reader, then waited for a few seconds while Walker held his breath. The tape printer began to type, scrolling out a receipt. He tore it off, plucked the pen out of his breast pocket and handed it to Walker, then watched him sign.

Next he said, "Don't leave yet. I have to take a couple of measurements before you go." He ushered Walker to one of the seats at the counter and sat across from him. He put the frames on Walker's nose, held a small ruler across the top of them, made some notes on a pad, measured the distance to the top of Walker's ear, fiddled with the frames a little, then said, "Good. One more moment."

He went to the computer keyboard behind the counter, and Walker could hear keys clacking. "Name . . . David Holler . . . local address?"

"The Days Inn over on Key Road."

"Would you know the number there?"

"Sorry, I—"

"It's okay. I'll only need to reach you if my supplier doesn't have what we need or something, and if that happens, I'll look it up. Home address?"

Walker surreptitiously tipped his wallet under the counter so he could read his driver's license. He lived in Los Angeles.

"Phone?"

Walker made one up.

"Thanks," said Foley as he finished typing. "I don't know if we'll need any of that, but there's a two-year warranty on the glasses. If you break them, we'll replace them, no questions asked."

"Thanks," said Walker.

"I'll call this in to my supplier now, and see you tomorrow."

Walker looked up and saw Stillman's reflection in the mirror. Stillman's reflection gave a small nod. Walker said, "Good-bye."

When they reached the motel, Stillman opened the door of his room and said, "Come on in." He opened his leather case. "I set this up so the camera shoots out this end of the bag." He carefully extracted it, ejected the videocassette, and inserted it in a recorder that was on top of the television set.

Walker hadn't seen the recorder before. "Did you buy that in Nashua too?"

"Got a good deal on it." He turned on the television set, then pressed the recorder's PLAY button.

Walker could see the inside of the store, but it seemed reversed. Stillman had set the recorder on the counter, aimed at the mirror. Walker saw Mr. Foley walk into the back room. Then Walker saw the picture jerk from side to side, until Stillman achieved the angle he wanted. The camera was looking into the mirror behind the counter at the image of the mirror on the back wall behind the computer screen. Then the camera zoomed in so that the computer was all that was visible, and stayed there.

Walker heard the recorded voice of Mr. Foley, and then his own voice, sounding less deep and less pleasant than he had remembered it.

Stillman leaned over the cassette recorder. He pressed the FAST FORWARD button and rushed the tape until a pair of hands appeared, then let it slow. The optician pressed the space bar and the screen said PASSWORD: he typed RFOLEY. Then he typed SALES. The screen display changed to show a series of words with lines beside them: NAME, ADDRESS, PHONE, DESCRIPTION.

Walker watched him type in the information for David Holler.

"Okay," Walker said. "You got his password and the customer file name for only two hundred and fifty bucks. Now what? Do we go copy his files on a disk? I assume you bought a computer too."

"No," said Stillman. "I didn't know he had one. I was picturing something more like a card file. But we'll adjust."

26

At eight, Stillman and Walker left the motel and strolled to Main Street, watching people enjoying the warm summer evening. There were older couples just coming out of the restaurants on both sides of the street after early dinners, and a stream of sunburned families who had probably stopped for the night in preparation for climbing Mount Monadnock, or heading north to the White Mountains or the lake country.

Walker said, "Have you picked out a restaurant yet?"

"I'm afraid we won't be having dinner for an hour or so. If we see a good one, we'll stop on the way back."

Walker said warily, "I thought we were killing time until later. You want to break into a store on Main Street at eight o'clock? The streets are full of people."

Stillman answered, "It's the best time. Right now there are still plenty of businesses open, still lots of strangers out on foot. If we wait until after midnight, it will just be us. A light showing through a store window will bring everybody on the public payroll but the governor."

"But there's an alarm. There were electric eyes on the floor inside the door. Don't you remember the *bing-bing* noise when we went in today?"

Stillman sighed. "Not all alarm systems are the same. Businesses like banks have systems you don't want to think about, because what they deal in is money. What Foley's got to sell is eyeglasses. They're expensive enough so he doesn't handle much cash, and certainly doesn't leave it overnight. Stealing frames and lenses isn't practical, because there's no resale. Nobody who needs glasses is going to get them ground and fitted by a thief. Foley's got expensive tools and instruments, but they're no use to anybody but an optician."

"How do you know Foley sees it the way you do?"

"He's a sensible sort of man. He bought himself an Impler 2000, which cost him five hundred and ninety-five. It's got three settings: chime, so he knows when a customer comes in the door, off, and alarm. What happens when it's on alarm is the door opens and breaks that beam you saw. Then Mr. Foley has forty seconds to punch his code on the keypad and turn it off before a god-awful noise begins."

"Do you know his code?"

"I don't need to. There's a shutoff switch, located inside a locked metal box somewhere on the premises. A thief can't go in, find the box, open it, find the switch, and flip it in forty seconds."

"I take it you can."

"Fortunately I'm not a thief. If you get the right angle you can see the box in one of his mirrors. It's mounted on the wall in the little workshop in back."

"Are you sure you can get into it in forty seconds?"

Stillman looked at him for a moment. "You've got to learn to live with a little more risk, if you're going to get anywhere."

When they reached 1219 Main Street, Stillman took out his pick and tension wrench, leaned over the door lock, fiddled with it for a moment, then turned to Walker. "Check your watch and time this. Let me know when to go."

Walker waited as the second hand ticked. "Four, three, two, one, go."

Stillman opened the door and hurried to the back of the store while Walker stepped in and closed it. He heard Stillman mutter, "Damn."

Walker's eyes shot to Stillman. The door to the work room was closed. Stillman knelt beside the knob with his pick and tension wrench. "Sing out the time."

"Thirty-four seconds."

Stillman muttered, "Not working."

"What?"

"It's going to take too long. The lock is too good."

"Can't we break it down?"

"We can't break the man's door and expect him not to notice. We'll have to get out."

"Wait," said Walker. "There were keys. He had a big ring with keys on it when he opened the display case."

Walker swung his legs over the low counter where he had sat to be fitted, then dropped to all fours. He could see nothing, but he groped in the pitch-black enclosed space under the surface of the counter. His hand hit a heavy metal object, and he heard a jingle. He grasped it, scraping his finger on the head of the nail where it hung, then pulled it out and tossed it at Stillman. "Heads up."

He heard the heavy ring hit Stillman's chest, then fall to the carpet at his feet. He heard Stillman grab it. Walker lifted his wrist to his eyes so he could see the watch and called, "Fifteen seconds, fourteen . . ."

He heard Stillman jab a key into the lock, rattle it, then try another. The doorknob turned, and Walker could see a deepening of the darkness as the door swung inward.

He called, "Ten, nine . . ." and heard a metallic scraping as Stillman tried to insert a key into the metal box and the others dangled. "Eight . . . seven . . ." He heard another scrape, then jangling. "Six . . . five . . ." The door suddenly closed and a horizontal stripe of light appeared at the floor. He knew that Stillman had closed himself in and turned on the light in the windowless work room. Walker crouched and prepared himself for the sound of the alarm. "Three . . . two . . ." He stood and took a backward step toward the front of the store, his eyes still on the little strip of light.

The light went off and the door opened. "It's off," said Stillman. "In the future, if you know where the keys are, you might mention it to me before I go through the exercise of picking three locks in forty seconds."

"It didn't come to me until we were in here," said Walker. "I remembered thinking the key ring was too big and heavy to carry around in his pocket."

Stillman moved behind the counter to the computer. "Now, let's print out a copy of that file on paper and go get a drink."

Walker moved in beside him, switched on the computer and the screen, then looked around him. "No printer. Did you see a printer in the back room?"

"Let me look." He stepped off in the dark, closed the door again and turned on the light, then turned it off. "Nothing." He sighed. "This is getting harder than it has any right to be. Bring up the file."

Walker tapped the space bar as Foley had done, typed in RFOLEY and SALES, and the first entry appeared: Asheransky, Linda. Stillman took his video camera from his bag, propped it on the shelf behind the computer screen, and turned it on. "Now," he said, "give it about three seconds on each entry, then scroll down to the next. Get every one of them on tape." He stepped away. "And remember not to get in front of the camera."

Walker counted the seconds as he centered each entry on the screen. He wondered how long this was going to take. He would need a minute to get twenty names, an hour to get twelve hundred. But Foley had spent about twenty minutes with them today, and nobody else had come in. Maybe he didn't have twelve hundred customers. Walker tried to give himself hope as he scrolled from entry to entry. It was a small town, and people who needed glasses would need new ones now and then. That would be enough business for a shop this size. He looked up for Stillman, but he didn't see him at first glance, and he needed to return his eyes to the screen. When he tried again, Stillman was by the doorway, looking out at the street to keep watch.

The minutes passed slowly, but at last he reached Mona Ziegler and gave her the three seconds. He scrolled down, and saw the entry for David Holler. That was him. Foley had not ordered the computer to fit it into the alphabetical list yet. He held his breath and scrolled down again. The cursor stopped. "That's it," he whispered. "I've got them all."

"Good," said Stillman quietly. "I was just getting ready to tell you to turn it off."

Walker closed the file and switched off the monitor, then the computer. The room was in deep darkness again. His eyes were no longer used to the dark, so he couldn't read his watch.

Stillman's voice reached him from the vicinity of the front door. "There's a cop coming up the street rattling doorknobs."

Walker sat on the floor behind the counter, then remembered the video camera. He reached up and pulled it down into his lap. He heard Stillman moving beyond the counter along the side wall. Stillman's voice whispered, "Remember the mirrors."

A bright beam of light pierced the darkness above Walker's head. It flitted quickly across the room, and when it hit the mirror it seemed to split and come from everywhere. Walker froze, hoping his immobility would keep the police officer from recognizing the shape of his shadow on the carpet as human. The flashlight beam caromed here and there, flashed a couple of times, and disappeared. Stillman's whisper came through the dark again. "Don't move yet."

The light came on once more and moved slowly around the shop, then went out. Walker waited, but there was no more sound. After five minutes, Stillman said, "Let's bid a fond adieu to Foley Optical."

Stillman took the video camera out of Walker's hands, and put it into his bag.

"How do we get out of here without setting off the alarm?" asked Walker.

"Just the reverse of before. I'll go into the back, flip the switch, lock the box, come out, lock the work-room door. Then I'll hand off the keys to you. Put them where you got them, and head for the front door."

Walker waited behind the counter where he had found the keys. When Stillman hurried past, he snatched the keys, hung them on the nail under the counter, and hurried to the door. He was barely out when Stillman swung it shut behind him. He took a step, but he noticed Stillman wasn't coming. "What are you doing?"

Stillman took his pick out of the lock and stepped off. "Locking the door for Mr. Foley." He began to move more quickly. "It's a simple pin-tumbler model, so you just have to poke one of them out of line. Let's go get something to eat before everything closes down."

They walked up the street toward the center of town, and Walker saw that Stillman had been right. The first few restaurants they passed were dark. But then they found a small Italian restaurant, and stepped inside. It was dim and cool, with checkered tablecloths and shelves of old Chianti bottles that had basketwork around their lower halves. The side walls were made of bare red bricks decorated with long twining vines of artificial ivy.

They ordered eagerly and waited. Walker had the urge to talk, but the room was too quiet to risk it. After taking a breath for the fourth time to say something, he analyzed what he would have said. It was merely a nervous recitation of what they had done. He would have recounted each move to get over the tension. When he recognized that, he lost the need to speak. He sipped his wine and ate his food, then paid the bill magnanimously with the David Holler credit card.

It was not until they had walked back to Key Road and were on the last stretch outside the motel that he said, "When we set the alarm off, were you afraid?"

"Afraid?" said Stillman. "By the time you got the keys I had pretty much concluded that I had made a mistake. I figured we were going to have a tedious and unpleasant evening, one way or another. But sometimes things work out."

"But were you afraid?"

"It's a complicated question," said Stillman. "My heart starts beating fast, I sweat a little, get a dry mouth. But after that's happened enough times for enough unrelated reasons, you begin to get used to it. Fear isn't some kind of disease, you know. It's a survival mechanism. The purpose of that shot of adrenaline is to get your body ready to put out its maximum effort—greatest speed, greatest strength, greatest intake of oxygen. It makes your mind work better too, if you let it. You just have to keep it off the subject of how scared you are, and get it involved in what you're going to do about it—like when you remembered the keys. It's still fear, I guess. But it's not the same feeling that you used to have."

"I don't know," said Walker. "It still feels about the same to me."

"You're most of the way there already," said Stillman. "All that's left is to get to the point where you give yourself credit for it." He smiled. "Of course, when things get ugly, all I really care about is how you act. I don't give a shit how you feel."

They walked into his room and he popped the videotape out of the camera and put it into the VCR. While the television set buzzed and crackled on an empty channel, he handed Walker the pad and pen from the desk. "Make notes while we eliminate people." Then he started the videotape.

Walker watched the tape of Linda Asheransky's entry, then the next, and the next. Whenever they reached a male name, Stillman froze the tape and they examined it closely. More than half were women. Only about a third of the male customers had ever made an order that included tinted lenses, and only half were green-tinted. The rest were blue, brown, gray, or photosensitive.

When they reached David Holler, Walker counted the names he had written down. "I've still got fifty-six names."

Stillman began to rewind the tape. "What do you want to look at this time?"

"How about frames?"

"All right. Cross off everybody but the ones with gold frames."

The second time through, they eliminated all but thirty-two men. As Stillman rewound the tape again, he said, "We've got thirty-two males who bought gold frames and green-tinted lenses that aren't photosensitive. What else is there about them?"

Walker stared at the first entry again. "What's a diopter?"

"A unit of refraction. The more of them, the stronger the lens. Our guy didn't think he needed glasses to shoot us, so we have to assume he could see pretty well. But I don't know how many diopters that is. Let's stick to the easy stuff."

"The lenses are plastic, not glass."

This time they eliminated only five men. Stillman said, "Twenty-seven is still a lot of guys." He stared at the screen for a moment. "Let's take another look at the glasses." Walker went into his room and came back with them. Stillman held them up to the light and stared through the lenses.

"Okay," said Stillman. "The guy was just a bit nearsighted. He didn't need bifocals. This time, check the prescriptions. There will be two entries, one marked R and the other L. If there are two for each eye, it's bifocals."

When they had gone through the tape again, Stillman looked at Walker's list, then stood up and began to pace. "We're down to twenty-one. All of them have male names, green-tinted nonphoto-sensitive lenses in gold frames without bifocal prescriptions."

Walker stared at the entries as they began to go past again. He froze the tape and pointed. "What's this number: fifty-three by twenty, forty-six by twenty?"

"I don't know. My knowledge of optometry is starting to get used up." He stared at it for a few seconds. "It's by the frame order, so it must be a size."

"Then what's this—one hundred and fifteen?"

"That I understand. It's millimeters: the length of the arms that go from the lens to your ears. Probably the other is the size of the circular part that holds the lens."

Walker snatched up the dead man's sunglasses and studied the frames. "Fifty-nine by twenty. One forty-five." He went back up the list in reverse, writing down the numbers beside each name.

When they had gone back to Linda Asheransky, Stillman picked up the notepad and the pen, and began to cross off names. When he had finished, he said, "Our man could be Donald Ross, James Scully, Paul Stratton, or Michael Tyler." He began to speed through the tape again, stopped at Michael Tyler, and began to write.

"What did you find?" asked Walker.

"Phone numbers."

"You're just going to call them up?"

"It's probable I'm going to bother three harmless guys with a nuisance call in the middle of the night. The fourth is the only one I'd worry about making suspicious, but I don't have much chance of reaching him. He's dead."

27

"Listen to this." Stillman handed the telephone receiver to Walker.

"This is Jim. If you want to leave a message, wait until you hear the beep." Walker hung up, then looked up at Stillman. "That's him?"

Stillman shrugged. "He's the only one who wasn't home when I called."

His name was James Scully, and he lived in a town called Coulter, New Hampshire. Walker had not heard the voice before, because when he had shot the man, he had heard nothing but the sound of the gun. He had just finished listening to a ghost. Walker looked at his watch. "It's three-thirty A.M. We've got his name and his address. What do you think? Do we call the police or the FBI?"

Stillman frowned at the wall for a few seconds. "Not just yet."

Walker watched him. "What do you have against the police? You were a cop once."

Stillman slowly turned to face Walker. "Who told you about that?"

"The police captain in Miami. The one who asked all the questions," said Walker.

Stillman looked at the carpet for a moment, then raised his eyes again. "I don't have anything against the police. Or the FBI, for that matter. But they're in a slightly different business than we are."

"What do you mean? What's different?"

"They're in the business of arresting and convicting people."

Walker stood up and walked across the room. "Isn't that what we want? This isn't some isolated fraud that's going to be okay the minute we get the money back. They're not just stealing money from a company. They're doing it by taking ordinary people, one at a time, and killing them. Somebody's got to get arrested."

"I'm just not sure this is the time," said Stillman. "Suppose we call the FBI and bring them up here. They're at Scully's house by morning. They begin an investigation—go around methodically and thoroughly collecting all the evidence in little plastic bags. The investigation hits on all cylinders, they eventually ferret out every one of the people who were in on this, put them on trial, and convict them of everything they did."

"Yeah. Let's do it."

"The trouble is, an investigation like that takes at least two months with a strong wind behind it. If it succeeds, they make arrests. The trials begin six months after that, if the federal attorneys prepare their case with due speed and diligence. All that has got to happen, of course. And since they're already on the case, we couldn't get them off it if we wanted to."

"So what's the problem?"

"What I just said. The second we make that call and let them actually talk to us without McClaren's in between, we're out. The FBI is not going to let us keep poking into everything we have a theory about."

"Are they wrong?"

"No," said Stillman. "They're right. But right now we know who one of these guys was and where he lived. His buddies may or may not know that much. Maybe they know Scully's dead, but the last time they could have seen him was in Miami, where the police are telling reporters they don't know who he is. It's possible that James Scully's house is just the way he left it. By the time the FBI could get up to speed, it may not be."

Walker thought for a moment. "What if the Miami police have already figured out who Scully and the other one were? How do we find out at this time of night?"

Stillman shrugged. "The time of night isn't the problem. If they don't want to release information, they won't. If they do, it'll be in the papers."

"Serena," said Walker. "She was reading the *Miami Herald* today. Maybe it's late enough for the morning edition." He dialed the number, and Serena's voice came on instantly.

"Yes?"

"Hi," he said. "It's the usual me. I'm sorry to call you at this hour, but it's—"

"What hour?"

"It's three thirty-five here, so it's twelve thirty-five there, right?"

Her voice was amused. "You didn't know? This is when we do most of our work, sweetheart. The preteen geeks and stock traders are asleep, the phone lines and networks are clear, so things happen faster. Haven't you ever noticed that languid, sensuous look I have around the eyes in the daytime?"

"I've never seen you during the day," he said.

"Oh. Well, we'll have to go have a picnic beside the freeway, or whatever it is people do."

"I called to see if the Miami police had announced anything about who those two guys were."

"No," said Serena. "But they're still trying. The FBI has been doing tests on the two bodies."

"We know," said Walker. "The company has been talking with them."

"Do you know about the blood tests?"

"No. What about them?"

"The cops type the blood at a shooting scene right away to figure out whose blood got spattered where. These two both had O positive—not unusual, but inconvenient. So the FBI sent samples to a lab in Wisconsin that does DNA tests. That was in the Miami papers, so I hacked into the e-mail at Donnard Laboratories to see what they were saying to each other. Apparently there are at least two kinds of examinations. One takes a month or two, and tells you more than you wanted to know. But while they're doing it, they get preliminary results that can at least tell one person's blood from another's. They told the FBI that the two men were relatives. Not brothers, though, or father and son. Something more distant, like second cousins."

"Can they tell that?"

"They seemed to think they could, and I don't know why they'd say so to the FBI if they weren't sure. I mean, how many customers can a company like that have? And it makes theoretical sense. First cousins would share one-eighth of their genes, so these guys share less than that, but more than two random guys." She paused. "Are you even listening?"

"Yes," said Walker. "I'm trying to figure out what it means."

"I don't know," she answered. "It's not going to be a shock to the FBI that criminals sometimes have relatives who are also criminals. Do you have news for me?"

"I guess all I've got is questions. We've figured out that one of those two guys was named James Scully, and he lived at 117 Birch Street, Coulter, New Hampshire."

"C-O-L-T-E-R?"

"With a U. C-O-U-L—"

"Got it. Right here on the handy New Hampshire tourism Web page. What do you want to know?"

"Whatever you know."

"Population, four hundred and twenty-eight—or twenty-seven, now." She paused. "No pictures of it. Founded in 1753—no big deal. So was everything else around there. It's not too far from Keene. It's about an hour northeast of you, on Route 9. That's marked as a scenic route, so let me see if they say anything about that. Yes. It's called the Old Concord Road, because eventually it gets to the state capital. It says 'eventually' because it winds around a bit. That's all I can see. Coulter seems to be just one of a few dozen places just like it."

"Okay. We'll find it."

"You stopped using Stillman's credit card. Where are you calling from?"

"The Days Inn in Keene. The number is—"

"That much I just got, from caller ID. What room?"

"Stillman is 93, and I'm 95."

"Cozy. Are you going to Coulter now?"

"I guess so," he said.

"Be careful. Stay close to Stillman and do what he says." She corrected herself. "I guess staying close to Stillman isn't being careful. Just remember he's been doing stupid things a long time, and he's alive, so pay attention."

"He'd be flattered."

"I'm going to drop everything else and find out whatever I can about James Scully."

"Do you—" But the line was dead.

"I'd be flattered about what?" asked Stillman. Walker turned and saw that he was taking things out of his suitcase, putting some of them into his leather bag, and others into his pockets.

"She pointed out that you're alive."

"Smart as a whip, that girl. Presumes very little on your time, too."

"That hasn't escaped my attention," said Walker glumly. "I've talked to her about three times in the past two days, and she's hung up on me every time." He added, "The police don't know the names yet."

"Get your stuff. Wear jeans and hiking boots and a jacket. Try to look like a harmless, respectable guy on vacation. I'll meet you in the car."

Five minutes later, Walker found Stillman sitting in the passenger seat of the Explorer studying a map in the light from the open glove compartment. Walker got in and drove out West Street until he saw the sign for Route 9 he had remembered. He looked at the clock on the dashboard. "It's already almost four. She said it's about an hour away. Is four forty-five A.M. a good time to arrive in Coulter?"

Stillman said, "It'll do. We'll take a look around before they get to look at us."

"There are four hundred and twenty-eight people."

"I'll keep count when I see one," said Stillman. "What else did she tell you?"

"The FBI apparently hasn't identified Scully and his friend yet, but they know they were related."

"What do you mean, related? How?"

"Like second cousins, but not as close as first cousins. They had some company do DNA tests. Don't ask me to explain more than that. She stole it off some e-mail the company was sending to the FBI. Smart as a whip, as you said."

Stillman was staring ahead at the road, and his brow was furrowed.

"What?" asked Walker. "Does that mean something?"

"It's odd," Stillman mused. "Brothers, I can easily take in stride. Somebody comes up with a way of making big money, tells one of them, and asks if there's somebody else he can trust to bring in on it. The one he thinks of is his brother. Fine for us, because we can find a brother. But this business of second cousins twice removed or something, how do we use it? Most likely they'd have different last names, and nobody but them would even know they were related. That's no help."

"I suppose not," said Walker. He drove in silence for a while. Stillman's sharp eyes stared, unblinking, into the dark, until Walker said, "Is there something else wrong?"

"I was thinking about all of them: Ellen Snyder, Fred Teller, the two people who got killed in their swimming pool, the guy in that swamp in Florida."

"What about them?"

"I was thinking we're way behind. We still haven't figured out very much about the way these people are doing this, or what they'll do next. I'd say that all we can be sure of is that they always move a little faster than we can, and they don't mind killing people."

"We know a little more than that. We know about James Scully."

"Oh, yeah," said Stillman. "After all this time, we managed to get through all the intentional confusion just once. This time while we were flailing around, we reached in blind and got our hands on a throat. The fellow's dead, but all we can do is keep squeezing."

28

They drove along the Old Concord Road, following its meanderings around gentle hills that had been cleared two hundred years ago for sheep that would keep the woolen mills along the Ashuelot River spinning. There were no sheep now. As the mills had died a slow death, the land had been turned, acre by acre, into pasture for dairy cattle, but now another change had occurred. At short intervals, the pastures would be interrupted by stands of second-growth forest, the tall trees blocking the dim purple glow that had begun to tinge the horizon beyond the eastern hills, making it full night again.

There were few cars on the road, but as they drove on they began to see houses with dim lights glowing from windows near the back, and Walker decided somebody must be getting ready to make breakfast. Once when Walker coasted to a stop at a blinking traffic light, the silence let him hear birds chirping unseen in a big tree to his left.

A few minutes later Stillman said, "Wait a minute. What was the name of that last town?"

"South Haverley."

Stillman switched on the dome light and studied the map. "That was five or six miles ago, I think. Okay. We should be at Coulter, or almost."

"Could I have driven through it without seeing it?"

"I doubt it," said Stillman. "Keep going, but slowly."

After another mile, there was a crooked stretch of road that traced the bases of two identical hills, and then Walker saw a narrow secondary road that met the highway to the right. On the left was an old, sparse apple orchard with rows of low, gnarled trees that looked black in the dim light. At the shoulder was a small blue sign that said COULTER. He continued on the highway for a mile, but there seemed to be no buildings. "This can't be right."

"Go back," said Stillman.

Walker stopped and turned the Explorer around, then drove until he came to the sign. He decided it was safer to park on the secondary road, so he made the turn. A few yards down the road was a sign that said MAIN ST.

"Well, hell," said Stillman. "Here we are, right on Main Street." He glared at his map, then waved it at Walker. "See the dot that says 'Coulter'? It's on the right side of the road, but it never occurred to me that the whole town was off the highway. Go ahead. Let's see what it looks like."

Walker drove on slowly. The narrow road pierced the space between the two hills. At a narrow curve where the hills edged up to the road on both sides, the tires passed over a wide metal grate that gave a hollow, ringing noise.

"Wonder what that was for," Stillman said.

"Must be a cow stile," said Walker. "The cows won't walk over one of those, so it works like a fence. I guess that must be why it goes all the way across from hill to hill."

"Maybe," said Stillman.

As soon as it was out of the pass between the hills, the road widened. Curbs had been poured, and the pavement was new, black macadam.

"Looks like the Department of Public Works is on the job," said Walker.

"Right," said Stillman. "Odd that they didn't take it the last two hundred yards to the main highway."

"Summer isn't over yet," said Walker. "And cities here must be like everywhere else. They get people to vote for a bond issue, and by the time anything gets built, the price goes up."

"It's possible," said Stillman. The road passed into a wooded lot, then curved a bit and there was a sign that said BRIDGE 100 FEET. The road straightened, and before them was an old wooden covered bridge.

Walker slowed to five miles an hour as they came closer. "That's something, isn't it?" As he was about to drive under the roof, Stillman said, "Stop for a minute."

He got out of the Explorer, and Walker pulled over to the narrow shoulder and got out too. He found Stillman kneeling on the bridge, looking down between two of the thick planks. Walker bent down too. Between the boards he could see a black stream of water. He said, "You afraid it won't hold us?"

"No," said Stillman. "The roof and sides look really old, but the bed has been replaced. If you look down here, you can see they've left the old cross ties in, but they shored it up by putting concrete piles and steel beams between them. You drive to the end of it, and I'll join you."

Walker went back to the Explorer and drove it slowly across the bridge. In the middle, both sides were left open for a space of about four feet, where he could look out and see the course of the stream. He revised his assessment, and promoted it to a river. The current was flowing steadily, but the surface had the untroubled look that deep water had, and it was wider than he had expected. He stopped at the end of the bridge and watched Stillman walking to the open spot. Stillman looked out at the river, then went on.

When he climbed into the Explorer again, Walker asked, "Why are you so interested in the bridge?"

"I don't know what they're supposed to look like," Stillman answered. "I'm not about to drive all over New England looking at covered bridges to compare. If the bridge was out, it would be pretty hard to reach the town by road."

"That's probably why they shored up the beams with steel supports."

"Right," said Stillman. "Your tax dollars at work."

"Not mine," Walker said.

"Don't be too sure. Any city council that couldn't get federal money to preserve a landmark that also happened to be the bridge to the main highway wouldn't be worth a damn."

They drove on for another mile, past open fields that Walker judged must be pasture for cattle that were let out at dawn. There were a couple of old barns, but he didn't see any lights or any vehicles. "This should be about milking time," he said.

Stillman looked at him. "I'll have my secretary free up an appointment. Have you been reading the farmer's almanac, or what?"

"I grew up in Ohio. There's pasture, and there are barns." Walker added, "You said—or implied—that I should be mentioning things that I notice. This is when dairy farmers feed and water their cattle, and milk them. When that's done, they let them out to pasture and clean the barn. But I don't see any signs of life. No lights, no pickup trucks. If the barn's that far from the house, you drive there." He shrugged.

Stillman said, "That's a point. I suppose what it means is there are no cows. If you have to get up this early to shovel cow shit, they were probably murdered."

Beyond the next row of trees that had been left as a windbreak at the end of the field rose the gray roofs of buildings. The little river they had crossed at the covered bridge had looped ahead of them in its meandering. It ran along the edge of town in a stony bed, and the trees were just above the riverbank. There was a short, modern steel bridge with no sidewalks about fifteen feet above the water, and then they were in town.

Walker drove slowly along Main Street, turning his head to take in both sides in alternation. The buildings along Main looked old in the same way as the ones in other towns, the biggest faced with red brick and three stories high, with ornate struts holding the overhangs of the eaves. There were others in wood and clapboard that had pilasters flanking the doors and triangular cornices above the windows that gave them the look of the eighteenth century. Stillman said, "One more nice little town. Everything's squared away and shipshape. Look for Birch Street."

The town was too small for traffic signals, but there were stop signs at each corner. Walker would coast to a stop, look at the street sign on a post to his right, stare up and down the cross street, and then move on. The side streets all appeared to be about four blocks long, disappearing at either end into an empty field or a building or a stand of trees. The names in this part of town were the names he remembered from small towns in Ohio: Washington, Adams, Jefferson, Franklin, then jumping ahead to Grant. More recent heroes came too late, probably after the town had stopped growing.

They passed a two-story brick building, set back on a lawn, that proclaimed itself Coulter Library and looked like one of the thousands built in the era of Andrew Carnegie. Beyond it was a white clapboard church with a tall steeple that looked like all of the others he had seen in the past two days. Ahead he saw a lighted blue sign that said simply POLICE, so he turned off Main onto Grant and went up the parallel street to his left.

When he passed Sycamore, then Oak, he knew it was coming. There was Maple, then Birch. He paused at the corner, looking at house numbers. There were no lights in any of the windows on this block, but he could see that the dim purple luminescence in the east had begun to make colors distinguishable. He turned up the street. The houses were old, most of them Georgian or early Victorian, but there were modern touches—sidewalks and driveways poured within the past few years, porch lights and fixtures that were shiny and recent. When he braked as he approached 117, Stillman said, "Keep going and park around the corner."

Walker stopped in front of a low fence that separated the street from the beginning of a pasture. He got out and waited while Stillman went to the back of the Explorer and opened his leather bag. Walker could see him putting things into his jacket pockets, and then he appeared at Walker's side. "We'll have to do it efficiently," he said. "We've only got twenty minutes before the sun comes up."

"Maybe we should come back at night."

"No," said Stillman. "This is fine. It's not prime time for burglars, so if somebody sees us, we're not automatically in trouble."

He walked briskly up the block, turned in at 117, then kept going around to the back door, looking up at the eaves of the house, stopping to study windows. When they reached the back door of the house, Walker stood by and waited, but Stillman kept going. There was a sloped wooden cover for a basement entrance a few feet away with a door on it and a padlock.

Stillman knelt on it, put a thin metal object into the padlock, and opened it as though he'd had a key. He lifted the door and went down the narrow concrete steps. Walker came down after him, then pulled the door shut.

As he watched Stillman pull out his pick and tension wrench and insert them into the lower door to the basement, Walker said, "How did you open the padlock?"

"A shim pick. I'll get you enrolled in a class on locks sometime, and buy you a set of picks for graduation."

Walker didn't respond. He watched Stillman swing the door open and step inside.

Stillman said, "Or, if we get caught one of these times, we can spend a couple of years on it."

The basement was the sort of place he remembered from his grandparents' house in Ohio. In the summer it had been cool and damp, and had a faint musty smell. Stillman switched on a small flashlight and moved it slowly around the walls.

The walls were bare and the concrete was coarse and old. It seemed to have crumbled in places and been patched and painted over with whitewash. There was a hot-water heater in one corner, a work bench with a vise and tools in another, and in the middle an oil furnace with a big storage tank. There were a new washer and dryer along one wall beside a big metal sink.

Stillman switched off the light and quietly climbed the wooden stairs to the landing above. When Walker joined him, Stillman whispered in his ear, "Give me five minutes." He opened a door and disappeared into the first floor of the house.

Walker listened, looking out the back door at the lawn. The sun was beginning to rise, and he felt each second passing, taking away a little of the darkness. When Stillman opened the door again, he jerked in nervous surprise.

Stillman said in a normal voice, "He lived alone," then turned and walked across the kitchen. Walker could see a gleaming stove and marble counters, a big side-by-side refrigerator.

"Are you sure?" he whispered. "Look at this kitchen."

"I have. Look in the fridge and you'll see this is just where he came to open his next beer. Anyway, there's no women's stuff anywhere, and no toys or clothes for kids. He slept up there." Stillman pointed up the stairs to the second floor. "He had a sort of den down here. I'm going through that. You go up and do the bedroom." As Walker climbed the stairs, he added, "Remember, we're looking for things that will give us the names and locations of his buddies—address book, phone bill, photo album, birthday card."

Walker found the bedroom and did a quick survey, but found no photographs or papers in the open, so he looked for storage places. He had watched Stillman do this enough times that he could dispense with wasted motion. He searched the drawers of the dresser, pulled them out to see if anything was behind them, and looked under the bed and in the closet. He found nothing, so he looked for hiding places. He went into the small bathroom, lifted the tank cover of the toilet, searched the area under the sink, tested the baseboards and tiles to be sure none of them were loose. He moved quickly back to the bedroom, checked the mattress for slits in the fabric on the top and bottom, squeezed the pillows. He moved close to each light fixture to be sure nothing was in it. He tested the carpets to be sure no section had been lifted. Just as he was running out of places to look, he found the gun.

He had noticed that the headboard of the bed seemed thicker than most, so he tapped it in a few places to see if it was hollow. When he tapped the center just above the mattress, a small door opened outward. There was a squat, square-cornered SIG pistol sitting where James Scully could reach it in the night. He closed the little door and kept searching.

The walk-in closet was another proof of James Scully's neatness, but the clothes surprised him. Walker counted twenty-two suits and sport coats hanging neatly side by side, all facing to the left. His shirts were all, likewise, hanging with their fronts to the left on another pole.

His shoes were in a cupboard, four pairs to a row with the toes outward.

Walker stood on a chair to look at the top shelf. There were hats—mostly baseball caps with the bills facing forward and the logos of heavy-machinery companies on their crowns, and a short-barreled shotgun with a box of deer slugs beside it. Walker patted each pocket of the coats and pants, looked inside the shoes, then knelt and was checking whether anything was taped to the bottom of each shelf when Stillman appeared in the doorway.

"Find anything?"

"A shotgun up on that shelf, and a pistol in a compartment in the headboard of the bed."

"No paper, huh?" said Stillman. "We'd better go."

Walker got to his feet and walked to the stairs with him. "What about you?"

"Not a lot of surprises. He had quite a bit of money. You can see that from the furniture, the way his house has been remodeled. Damned if I know where a dime of it is, though. He didn't leave anything that we could use to find it. His little den has a desk in it, but he seems to have used the place mostly to read magazines, watch TV, and talk on the phone."

"You mean there's no paper around at all?"

"Sure there is. Birth certificate, deed to the house, pink slip for his car, bills—water, power, heating-oil company, credit cards. That was a disappointment, because he hasn't been using them on his travels. He's got another set somewhere besides the one he had on him in Florida. The phone bills don't have any long-distance calls on them. I don't think I missed much. I even found his spare set of keys."

They were at the cellar stairs. Stillman started down, but Walker said, "We can't give up like this."

"We're not. I plugged bugs into the phone jacks upstairs and down. And, of course, I took the keys," said Stillman. "I'm looking forward to the luxury of opening a lock with the actual key."

"But we can't come back. Pretty soon the cops in Miami or the FBI will identify him and announce it. His buddies will come and clean this place out."

"Then we'll pick it up on the bugs. That's another luxury I'm look-ing forward to," Stillman said. "The minute they get started I pick up the phone and call the cops to come get them. And you know what? Whoever comes in to look for incriminating evidence about them-selves will experience a moment of intense pleasure just before they hear the sirens. Because this guy didn't have any."

29

Walker could already see his shadow on the pavement, a fantastic elongation of his silhouette that stretched across the road, stepping into the shadow of the Explorer that was nearly a square. He started the engine as soon as he could get inside.

Stillman said, "Very slowly, just the way we came."

Walker eased the transmission into gear and rolled off the shoulder to get the Explorer moving, then very gradually accelerated in the direction it had been aimed when he had parked. He concentrated on keeping the engine running just above idle and the speed low enough so he could coast to a stop at each corner.

Stillman said, "Go down this street, turn onto Main just before the river, then head for the highway. I think we'll have breakfast in that last town we went through on the way."

"South Haverley? Why South Haverley?"

"It looked a little bigger and livelier than Coulter, even an hour ago. I'd rather not hang around here doing nothing while we wait for something to open up."

Walker turned onto Main and headed out of town. This time, when he came to an intersection, he stopped only long enough to be sure he wouldn't be accused of running the stop sign. Now there were lights on in a few of the houses, and twice he saw police cars. One was cruising along a parallel street in the same direction he was going, and the other had stationed itself on a quiet block just off Main, in the time-honored way of traffic cops waiting for speeders.

When he had crossed the bridge across the river and was driving between the open fields again, he kept staring into his rearview mirror.

"What are you looking for?" asked Stillman. "Cops?"

Walker glanced at him. "It's not entirely out of the question, is it? We did just pull off one of our many unsuccessful burglaries."

"Relax," said Stillman. "I saw two patrol cars on the way out, and if anybody had reported anything, they would have collared us then. And it wasn't entirely unsuccessful."

"No?"

"No. We know James Scully was one of them, and we know he wasn't the one who's been moving all those insurance claims from your company."

"You could tell that?"

"I told you he wasn't in the habit of making long-distance phone calls—none at all last month, when there might have been a lot of conversation with people who were getting started on scams in Pasadena, Miami, and God knows where else. After seeing his place, we know he had plenty of spending money, but it was the sort of money that a guy who does high-risk work might get as pay. And he didn't have the kinds of things that the money guy will have."

"What kinds of things?"

"Office supplies. Pens, calculators, computers, airline timetables, maps. His friends might have gotten in and out already and removed incriminating paper. They would have no reason to get rid of paper clips. The magazines I found all had subscriber's address labels, so they were his—all guns and naked women." Stillman paused. "I'd say that Scully was pretty much what he seemed to be the night we met him: the sort of guy you tell, 'Go get Walker and Stillman,' and he goes out to get Walker and Stillman."

"So now we're stuck again."

"Temporarily becalmed," said Stillman. "If the other guy in Florida was a sort of relative, it's possible he lived nearby—maybe in Coulter, or in one of these other little towns around here." He let his eyes rest on Walker for only a half-second before he said, "Let's find some breakfast."

Walker began to breathe more evenly as soon as he was back on the Old Concord Road. There were other cars on the highway now, and the bright summer sunlight seemed to lend not exactly benevolence, but at least reality to the world. What he could see now included long views of trees and fields and hills, not just a section of pavement lit by the funnel-shaped beams of his headlights surrounded by vague shapes and shadows. There were flowers growing in patches here and there, and being able to see the detail and complexity of their forms made him less uneasy. Approaching traffic now resolved itself into sequences of cars, and not just the glare of headlights brightening and then disappearing. It even made him feel better that two of the first six cars had out-of-state license plates. This was tourist season, and the uncomfortable feeling he'd had that he and Stillman were the only strangers disappeared.

They found a restaurant just outside South Haverley that had been built to look like an enlarged farmhouse. A few of the dozen cars in the parking lot had plates from Massachusetts, New York, or Vermont. When he pulled into a space and got out of the Explorer, he noticed that the muscles of his shoulders and neck were stiff from the tension of the night and morning, then remembered that he had been awake for twenty-four hours.

They sat beside a window that looked out on the highway, ordered steak and eggs for breakfast, and then watched the traffic continue to build while they ate. When Stillman was signing the charge slip, Walker let himself return to thoughts of the immediate future. They got back into the Explorer and Walker started the engine, moved to the edge of the highway, and signaled for a left turn while he waited for an opening in the traffic.

"You know where we're going?" Stillman asked.

"What choice do we have?" said Walker. "The case is in Coulter."

They drove back to the sign that said COULTER and made the turn. There were two cars ahead of them on the road that sliced between the hills and onto the flat plain beyond, and as each turned to the right, Walker stared at the occupants. The first car held a couple in late middle age and the second a younger couple with children in the back seat.

Walker drove more confidently over the covered bridge this time, and across the fields to the town. Coulter looked different in full daylight. There were people on the street, cars parked in front of the old-fashioned commercial buildings. The public library was not open yet, but there were lights on inside, and two little girls were on the front steps with stacks of books beside them, watching two slightly older boys playing catch with a baseball on the lawn.

They went on past the old church, and Walker could see the blue sign ahead that said POLICE.

Stillman seemed to read his mind. "Keep going. I want to see it."

It was a wide, single-story modern building made of tan bricks that didn't match the reddish color of the older buildings in the area. Walker's second glance made it look even better. The town was about half the size of Wallerton, the little place in Illinois where Ellen Snyder had been murdered. There, the police station had been about half as big, and much older.

"Pull around the corner, and we'll park on the side street," said Stillman. When they got out and walked back toward Main, Stillman nudged Walker. "Look at the parking lot."

Walker looked at the row of police cars. "Looks like sixteen," he said.

"I guess we didn't have to worry about car thieves," said Stillman. "Let's go for a walk."

Walker's impression of the place began to grow more specific now that his slower pace let him see details. The town had been laid out in the eighteenth century, when there had been a hope that cities designed on a rational plan would stay that way, and this one had. The streets were on a regular grid. Main Street ran down the middle of town from the bridge, with two parallel streets on each side of it: Federal and New Hampshire on the left, and Constitution and Coulter on the right. The cross streets began with Washington, set right above the river on the first high ground. Then came Adams, Jefferson, Franklin, and Grant. Walker suspected that Grant Street had been changed from something else, because all the houses on the street seemed to be older than the Civil War. It had probably been a tree, because this was where the names of trees began: Sycamore, Oak, Maple, Birch, Hemlock, and Cherry. The streets all ended in fences that separated the town from old pastures.

The houses were nearly all of the older varieties—wooden ones that seemed to belong in the late eighteenth century, and brick ones with Victorian-style porches and elaborate wooden trim. A few were nearly new, but they were built to the scale of older times, when a family might include eight children and a couple of maiden aunts. As they walked up another street, and another, Walker's impression was confirmed. "It's a pretty prosperous place."

"Yeah," said Stillman. "I suppose the houses don't tell the whole story. Most of them are a few generations old, when the money could have come from something we can't see anymore because they sold it—lumber, or granite, maybe. Real estate has got to be cheap around here."

"They take care of the place, though," said Walker. "About a third of these houses look as though they've just been painted." They walked back the way they had come.

A few minutes later, at the next intersection, Walker noticed something at the end of Grant Street that looked different. It was a long, one-story building that appeared to be the work of the same architect who had built the police station. It was plain, tan brick with only tiny windows at the top, just below the roof. The parking lot beside it seemed to be full.

Stillman noticed it too. "I wonder what that is."

They walked down the street toward the building, until Walker could make out the stainless-steel letters attached to the brick facade. " 'New Mill Systems,' " he read.

"Just some kind of business," said Stillman. "Let's go back."

They returned to Main Street. The town didn't look any different from the other small, old places in the area. The single church had a stone set at the corner of it with the date 1787. The library had opened now, and Walker could see through the glass doors that the girls had already made their way past the librarian's desk to an alcove full of tall, brightly colored books that had to be the children's section. The boys had disappeared. As he passed, a pretty young woman with serious-looking glasses came from behind a counter and knelt on the floor beside one of the girls.

People passed by or went into the twenty-five or thirty buildings on Main, and Walker could see that they had little curiosity about a pair of tourists. But when they went into a coffee shop, the elderly man who waited on them said, "You haven't been in before, have you?" He was staring at Walker.

"No," said Stillman. He pointed to his Danish pastry. "If this is any good, you might see more of us."

The old man looked at Walker. "You," he said.

Walker froze.

"You look a lot like the Ellisons. I'll bet you're here to visit."

"Do I?" said Walker. "No relation that I know of. We're just here exploring."

Stillman seemed eager to keep the old man talking. "How about you? Have you lived in town long?"

"Long? I was born here."

"Really," said Stillman. "That reminds me. I was going to ask somebody, so I'll ask you. I didn't notice a hospital."

The old man shook his head. "Never had one. In the old days, the doctor would come out to your house. I was born a couple of blocks from here. No more, though. Now, if your wife is due, you drive her to Keene."

"The world's a different place," said Stillman regretfully.

"You can miss those days if you want," said the old man. "I sure don't. I got a pacemaker." He pointed to his chest. He noticed that a young man and woman had stood up from their table and were bringing their bill to the counter. He stepped around the other side to meet them.

Stillman spent the next few minutes eating his pastry and looking around him. Walker could tell he was trying to make eye contact with the people nearby. There were three well-dressed women in their thirties who looked like lawyers, a pair of boys in their late teens who were drinking some kind of whipped fruit concoction, and a pair of men about Stillman's age who seemed to be sitting together to share a newspaper. Stillman seemed to have no luck, so he stood up and gave the old man his bill and some money.

As he pocketed his change, he said, "I was wondering. The place a couple of blocks over—New Mill Systems. What do they do there?"

"Do?" The old man looked confused, then a little embarrassed. "Oh, some high-tech stuff. It's way beyond me. I can't program my VCR." His eyes seemed to stray from Stillman's face and dart over his shoulder.

When Walker turned, he couldn't pick out anyone who was paying attention. The three women were leaning forward talking and laughing, the two middle-aged men were still engrossed in their newspaper, and the boys were just standing up to come toward the counter too. Maybe that had been what had distracted the old man, Walker decided. Teenaged boys were always closely watched.

He followed Stillman into a drugstore and watched him go up the aisles picking out a small bottle of sunscreen and a pack of chewing gum. The only employee in the store was a man in a white coat who was at least as old as the man in the coffee shop, sweeping the floor. He put aside his broom, went behind the counter, and took Stillman's money.

Stillman smiled and said, "Is this the only drugstore in town?"

"Yes," said the man. "Got a big drug habit?"

"No," said Stillman happily. "I was looking for those Dr. Scholl's pads for inside your shoes, and I didn't see any."

The man pointed, his hand shaking a little. "Over there. That aisle."

Stillman followed his gesture, then came back with a flat package that he tossed on the counter. "Thanks," he said. Then he added, "I wonder if you could give me directions to New Mill Systems?"

The man's brow furrowed a little and he looked up in the air for a second, as though he were trying to place the name. Then he said, "That way up Main, turn left at Grant, and you'll already be there. You a salesman or something?"

"Sore feet gave me away, huh?" said Stillman. "Maybe you can help me. What is it they make?"

The old man shook his head. "Something to do with computers. I hear it's mostly government contracts, though, so they may not even let you in." He went back to his broom.

Later, at the end of a side street, they found another large, modern building; this one had COULTER SCHOOL emblazoned on a sign. It was summer, so Walker wasn't surprised to see that the building was deserted and the windows dark. He could see that it must have been built to accommodate all of the town's children. One side of the building had a small playground with swing sets and monkey bars and slides, but at the other end there were full-scale athletic fields.

There seemed to be only one real restaurant in town. It was in a big turn-of-the-century brick building across the bridge on the other side of the river, and the sign on the door said simply FINE DINING. There were about forty tables, twenty of them set with crisp white linen, and three waiters who hurried back and forth carrying trays and folding stands to set them on.

Walker studied the old photographs on the wall above their table. There were men in high collars, pinch-shouldered, rumpled suits, and derby hats standing beside a horse and wagon, a gathering of women in full skirts, wasp-waisted and wearing feathered hats, in some garden. There was one that had men standing in the street outside a building he had seen on Main that still bore the sign BANK OF COULTER, but the street in the picture was cobblestones. There was another picture that seemed to be the building they were in.

Stillman asked their waiter, "What was this building originally—a mill?"

"Yes, sir," answered the waiter. "People call it the Old Mill. But that was a hundred years ago."

"That explains that place we saw before. New Mill Systems. You happen to know what they sell?"

"Electronics. Something to do with communications."

When they had finished their lunch, they walked back along the river to the other side of Main, and made their way up the side streets there. As they reached Maple Street, Stillman looked at his watch. "It's after two-thirty. Let's get back to Keene. We can stop at Foley's and get your new glasses, then go to the hotel and get some sleep. When I wake up, I'll call you."

30

Walker awoke in the dark, already looking at the telephone. He wondered if that was what had awakened him, but he waited for a few seconds and it didn't ring. He looked at the digital clock beside the bed. It was already ten-fifteen.

He considered calling Stillman, but he remembered that Stillman had definitely said he would do the calling. He went to his suitcase, opened it, and laid out fresh clothes, then went into the bathroom for a shower. He left the door open so he could hear the telephone.

He dressed quickly, then left the room and counted the doors as he walked down the hall to the exit. When he reached the parking lot, he counted the windows from the end of the building to find Stillman's room. The light was on.

He went inside and knocked on Stillman's door. He heard Stillman say, "Just a minute," and the door swung open. Stillman walked back to his desk and picked up the phone that had been lying there off the hook. "It's just Walker," he said into it. "He and I have got to talk. I'll call again when I can." He hung up and turned his attention to Walker.

"I thought you were going to sleep," said Walker.

"I did. When you get to a certain age, you don't need as much. When was the last time you talked to Serena?"

"Just before we went to Coulter. It was . . . what? Three-thirty A.M."

"Nothing since then?"

"No. Why? Is something wrong?"

"She left. I just talked to Gochay, and he said she quit. She picked up her belongings and walked out on him."

Walker said, "Just like that? She didn't say anything like that to me." He felt a sudden emptiness, a sense of loss so deep it surprised him. He had never gotten an address and telephone number for her except Gochay's. She had never offered one.

Stillman intruded on his thoughts, as though he could read them. "She's perfectly capable of finding you anytime she wants." He lifted the telephone again and punched in a number, then punched two more digits, listened in silence for a few seconds, then hung up. "Uh-uh."

"What was that?"

"My bug in Jim Scully's house. It's plugged into the phone jack, and whatever it hears is recorded on a little sound-actuated recorder. It doesn't ring, just plays back what it's heard. It hasn't heard anything. Forget Serena for a minute. We've got to figure out how to get from Scully to the other dead guy—this cousin of his."

Walker sighed and forced himself to think. "You made some acquaintances—the waiter, the druggist, the old guy in the coffee shop. In a town that size, I'm sure one of them must have known Scully."

"It takes time to get people to talk. We're liable to be asking about him an hour before or after the FBI announces he's been killed by two guys who can only be us."

"The Coulter police, then?"

"I've been thinking about it. They probably know what we need to know. Guys who grow up to carry guns for a living usually get noticed long before they turn pro. Say we take the direct approach. We go to the station, identify ourselves, and tell them what we want—a short list of Scully's friends and relatives. There's no rational reason for the police to give it to us. If they do, what's our next move? We can't go to their houses, break in, and look around. In fact, if the police know Scully's house has been broken into, we'd be confessing to that."

Walker was frowning as he stared at the wall.

"What is it?" asked Stillman.

"That town. I guess I wasn't sleeping very deeply, because when I woke up, I was already running the statistics."

"The statistics?"

"Well, think about it. Coulter has four hundred and twenty-eight people in it. From looking at it, I'd say there are about a hundred and sixty-five houses: eleven purely residential streets with around fifteen houses each. That's roughly two point six people per dwelling. The average family in the country has two point six four people, so that works out about right. About a third are kids under eighteen, so you figure a hundred and forty-three of those, and two hundred eighty-five adults."

"The school looks about right for that. Maybe a bit on the roomy side," said Stillman. "But there might be farm kids bused in."

"Yeah, it's okay," said Walker. "Even without them. There's obviously money in town for public works, so you'd expect it to be better than minimum. But there are sixteen cars in the lot of the police station."

"Seemed a little high, didn't it? I've been wondering about that too."

"It was two-thirty in the afternoon when I looked for the last time. You have to figure some of the cars were out, don't you? Looking for speeders, or something?"

"There were," said Stillman. "We saw two out in the morning."

"That's right. Let's be conservative and say we saw all the police cars in town. Eighteen. Suppose only half are ever manned, so each of the three shifts has nine cops. If there's no chief, dispatcher, watch officer, or anybody but those nine cops, you still come up with twenty-seven cops. That would mean roughly one in ten adults in Coulter is a police officer."

"It's a lot of cops," Stillman mused. "I can see we're lucky we didn't get our asses tossed in jail for burglary. What do you think is going on?"

"I don't know," said Walker. "The place seems to have a lot of money. Maybe they're using it to keep people employed."

"That's a possibility," said Stillman. "At least they're not suspects. You know, maybe in a town this size that's the way to narrow down the field. If a person has a job, he's not running around Florida killing people. Where else do people work?"

"How about New Mill Systems?"

"How many people do you figure work there?" asked Stillman.

"We saw at least thirty cars in the lot. Since there's nobody in town who doesn't live within easy walking distance of the place in good summer weather, figure that's half the work force. That would be at least sixty people. If you figure two hundred and eighty-five adults, you've got about a hundred and forty-five women and a hundred and forty men. Sixty percent of all women over eighteen work outside their homes. That's . . . what? Eighty-seven women. Of all men over eighteen, seventy-five percent are employed outside. That's a hundred and five. The work force is a hundred and ninety-two. Twenty-seven are cops. That leaves a hundred and sixty-five. If sixty of them work for New Mill Systems, that's one in every three working adults. If another third live by selling goods and services to the company and its employees, it's two-thirds of the economy."

"Interesting," said Stillman. "Nobody seems to know what they do in that building. One says computers, one says communications, and one says high tech, which means nothing."

"It could be all three," Walker said. "It doesn't matter. If we want to use it to eliminate people who work there, we need to know who they are."

"I know one way that might do it," said Stillman. "Another burglary."

"On what?"

"The pharmacy. The old guy said it was the only drugstore in town. That makes it the only place you can fill a prescription. There are federal record-keeping requirements. Paper, not computers. Over the years, just about everybody needs a prescription once."

"So our guy would be in the records. How do we know which he is?"

"Same way: the process of elimination. Some are women. The ones who work for New Mill Systems will all have the same health insurance. The ones who work for the city will have another. Some would be paid by Medicare, and that would mean they're over sixty-five." Stillman paused. "There may be other things that I haven't thought of yet that will eliminate others. I'll let you think of those."

Walker glared at Stillman for a moment. "It's a lousy idea. Let's go do it."

Stillman immediately began packing his lock picks and video camera and flashlights into his leather bag. "Get that jacket I bought you in Nashua, the navy blue one. And put on a different shirt. Green would be good. And dark shoes. I'll meet you in the car."

When they were on the road again, Stillman stopped sorting his equipment. "You didn't happen to look closely at the door locks in that place, did you?"

"I don't remember very clearly," said Walker. "The ones on the front door were old brass. There was a long handle with a thumb latch." He squinted. "I think there was a dead bolt above it."

"What did the keyhole look like—the regular kind, or a weird shape, like a circle?"

"Regular, I think," Walker answered. "Why this uncharacteristic concern?"

"I told you about security systems," said Stillman. "Some are simple and easy."

"I take it this won't be one of them."

"I doubt it. Even in small towns, the drugstores are full of drugs. In some circles, money is a second choice. Having cash just puts a middle man between them and what they really want. We might run into some features we can't easily defeat."

"If we can't get in, what are we doing?"

"Oh, we can get in," said Stillman. "The only thing that's at issue is how we get out."

When they reached the COULTER sign, Walker made the turn. He was getting comfortable with the road now, and soon they were in the open between the two fields. Stillman said, "Slow down and watch this side."

"For what?"

"There's a dirt road up here. There . . . stop."

Walker stopped, and Stillman got out. He lifted a section of fence rail that served as a gate and walked with it, then waved Walker in. Walker drove off the road and found himself on a dirt surface. Stillman closed the gate and got in again.

"Turn off your lights."

Walker obeyed. He looked at Stillman, who was watching him impatiently. "It's a dirt road," said Stillman. "Follow it."

Walker sighed. "I think the term 'dirt' is accurate. I'd hardly call this a road." He cautiously moved forward.

"Keep going. I have a theory I want to check."

"Does your theory tow stuck cars?"

"Just do it."

Walker bumped along over the rutted, uneven ground, and then the ride became smoother. The road was so narrow that at times he could tell both front tires were passing over grass at once.

"See the barn ahead?" asked Stillman.

"Yeah." In the dark field, it was a high rectangle of deeper darkness. Walker drove on slowly. He found that he could see much better than he had expected, and soon he was approaching the black shadow of the barn.

"I got this idea when you said there were no cows," said Stillman. "Stop." He got out and ran ahead. In a few seconds, Walker saw his flashlight go on, then sweep the floor of the barn, then go out. When he returned, he said, "It's empty. Pull inside, and turn around so you're facing out. Then kill the engine."

When Walker had done it, he joined Stillman. They began to walk across the field. After a few minutes, Stillman spoke again. "Here's how we do it: we go up the back of Main Street. There's a passage. I don't know if it counts as an alley, because it's empty ground and unpaved. But it runs behind the row of businesses. Anyway, we walk it without going up Main."

"Okay," said Walker.

"When we get to the drugstore, we take a few minutes to see what we're up against. If we can't get in, we'll leave. If we do get in, we'll do just what we did before. We'll videotape the records."

They crossed the second bridge into town and hurried off Main

Street before they reached the first street lamp. They made their way up the passage behind the long row of buildings. When they reached the back of the drugstore, Stillman stopped. He examined the windows, and Walker's heart sank. They all had bars on them.

He saw Stillman's flashlight go on, then saw the beam of light inside the glass. It moved slowly, then went out. A moment later, it went on again at the next window. Walker went to join Stillman at the back door.

"What do you think?" he whispered.

"It's a dummy."

"What?"

"The alarm. It's not turned on. Maybe it's not even hooked up. Anyway, there's no power going to the panel. The indicator light's not on." He quickly picked the lock and opened the door. "Come on in."

Walker stepped inside and closed the door, then ducked low and began to search the back counter. He flicked his flashlight on to confirm his impression, then let it play along each of the walls slowly. He stood up. "It's not a pharmacy. It's just a storeroom. There aren't any prescription drugs."

"Yeah," said Stillman. "I've been trying to remember that conversation since I looked in the window. I asked the old boy if it was the only drugstore in town. He said yes."

"There's nothing here but over-the-counter stuff. There's not even a locked cabinet."

"He said drugstore. He didn't say there was a licensed pharmacist around who could fill prescriptions. People must do that in Keene." He touched Walker's arm. "Let's go."

They made their way back to the barn, then drove out to the highway. The silence seemed to have settled on Stillman, and he didn't speak again until they were back in Keene. "I'm going to try working with the phone book. Go think about this some more. If you come up with another way of finding out who the cousin was, I'll be in my room."

When Walker opened the door to his room, he looked inside.

There, asleep on the bed, was Serena. She heard him, opened her eyes, and said, "Boy, I'm glad that's only you."

"So am I," he said.

"I mean I'm glad you're alone."

"Yeah. That's what I meant too."

31

Walker awoke, not remembering when he had fallen into a dreamless sleep. He had somehow drifted off with Mary Catherine Casey in his arms, and now she had wriggled out, leaving him feeling cold and alone. He opened his eyes and lifted his head to see her sitting cross-legged beside him, still naked, staring down at him with unblinking catlike patience. He rolled toward her, but she remained motionless, so he propped himself on his elbow. "What?" he said. "Was I snoring or something?"

"I was wondering about you," she said, "so I decided to see if I could read your mind. Don't worry: I couldn't."

"Want to try again?" he asked.

She gauged the angle of his eyes. "Not necessary."

"Why are you here?"

"Because when I give somebody my word, I do whatever is necessary to keep it." Her green eyes remained on his with unwavering intensity.

"Who did you give your word to?"

"You," she said in mild surprise. "I told you yesterday I was going to drop everything I was doing to find out what you needed to know."

He frowned. "Look, I'm glad to see you—"

"I noticed that," she said.

He persisted. "But it never occurred to me that you were going to quit your job."

She gave a deprecatory toss of her head so slight that Walker saw it as a dismissal. "It wasn't really a job," she said. "It was just an arrangement."

"What kind of arrangement?"

She sighed, as though it were all such old history that he should already have known it. "Constantine's not IBM. He's like a pirate ship. You sign on as long as the take is good and you feel like staying aboard. You get a cut of the money. If you stop in a port you want to visit, you get off and Constantine sails on."

He stared into her eyes for a moment, then decided to ask. "How did you get involved in that, anyway?"

"You don't approve," she said. "Tough."

"You're not going to tell me?"

She shrugged. "I'm a bad girl."

"Maybe I'm asking why you're a bad girl."

She looked at him as though appraising him, then sighed. "I'm acceptable looking, and I'm very smart. People always noticed the one, but they never noticed the other. They also had all kinds of rules for how I was supposed to behave, and the rules didn't seem to give me any benefit."

"I'm not sure I understand," he said.

"I went to college in engineering. The same men who hit on me—complete with assurances of their love and respect—also assumed that the reason I was getting good grades was that I was sleeping with professors. Since I didn't sleep with professors, the ones who would have liked me to were resentful. The professors who didn't like the field filling up with women weren't glad to see me sitting in the front row. The others just treated everybody equally, which was lousy." She looked at him closely. "You see? No advantage."

"You seem to have learned a lot about computers."

"I liked them. When I got a diploma, I went to work for a company in Irvine that sells computer security. I bumped into Constantine."

"Did he work there too?"

"Hardly. I was always hearing about the enemy: people who spent their time moving in and out of systems they had no business knowing about. Most of them are kids. It's always been a cheap thrill for teenaged boys killing time, waiting for their skin to clear up so they can get laid. They don't want anything, so it's actually no big deal, although nobody admits it. Sometimes companies even hire a few to test the locks and barriers. But everybody talks about the other ones, who aren't kids. They're theoretical, mostly: James Bond villains who want to launch a missile, or crash a plane, or shut down regional power grids and all that. Or robbers who are going to divert billions of dollars from banks. I heard stories, and went hunting. One night after a few months, I trapped Constantine Gochay."

"What do you mean, 'trapped' him?"

"What he was doing was pretty harmless. He was reading bank statements in a big system in New York. The bank was one of our customers, so I was in there snooping, and noticed. I traced him backward and found out where he was. I went to see him."

Walker frowned. "Why? Why would you do that?"

"Huh?" Her brows knitted.

He tried again. "Why didn't you just call the authorities and get him arrested?"

She smiled. "Selfishness."

"I don't understand," said Walker. "What did you want?"

"Reverse it," she said. "What would I get by turning him in? He wasn't in there stealing money. He was snooping, just as I was. He was probably just three boys from the chess team at Antelope Valley High School. But he was in a place that was very, very difficult to get into. I wanted to know what he knew that I didn't."

"You just went to that house and rang the doorbell?"

"Well, no," she said. "I sent him a snappy message that appeared on his screen to tell him when I was coming. I figured that would make these three boys' little hearts go pitty-pat. Then I drove up there. We talked."

"What did he say?"

She looked at the pillow critically. "It was better than I expected. He had discovered a few technical things I didn't know. Everything

comes out fast—programs, chips, hardware. Often even the manufac-
turer doesn't know all the capabilities or the vulnerabilities or the implications of something that's on the market until it's been used for a
couple of years. He had all the technology, and all the techniques. But
what he had that was most useful wasn't machinery."

"What was it?"

"Sneakiness. A lot of the useful stuff—how money moves through
banks and credit companies, reservations for planes and hotels, personal customer profiles, personnel files—is in the big proprietary
systems that are operated by giant corporations. They're heavily protected. You can't get in by brute force. Code breaking is not easy,
and failing is dangerous. So what would Gochay do? He knows that
these same giant corporations are heartless about layoffs. When two
giant banks merge, and ten thousand people are dumped, how closely
is the new management looking at each of them? Gochay would
cruise the Internet looking for people posting their résumés. Once in a
while he would find somebody fired from a big company who knew
something—passwords, systems weaknesses—and had just been convinced for all time that his loyalty to the company was a joke. So he'd
pay them."

"And that's all?"

"Sometimes. Sometimes they didn't know much, but just getting
something like the name of the systems controller was enough. Gochay
had programs for that. They would generate every variant of their
names, the birth dates of all members of their families, house numbers,
phone numbers, and so on, and try them all as passwords in a milli-
second. That kind of thing."

"Did he hire you—make an arrangement with you—because of the
company you left?"

She shook her head indulgently. "No. I knew some things that he
didn't, but the company didn't know them either. And I wasn't a dis-
gruntled employee. I was doing fine."

"Then why did you do it?"

"Why did I start a life of crime? You had to be there. At six one
evening, I walked out of this absolutely sterile building filled with people just like the ones in engineering school. An hour and a half later, I

was in that weird house, talking to this huge, bizarre man with wild black hair and crazy black eyes. He was doing something exciting and dangerous, and he wasn't interested in me at all."

"He wasn't interested in you?"

"He was interested in money."

"Let me get this straight," said Walker. "Are these the reasons why you shouldn't have done it, or why you did it?"

"I was twenty-two. I'd finally gotten out of school, and was going to have the great American adventure of going off to work, independent and free. After two months at it, I could see the future: all of it, from then until I turned sixty-five. It wasn't that nothing exciting had happened yet, but that it could never happen."

"So Gochay was an adventure."

"Part of what an adventure is, is throwing in your cards for a reshuffle. It wasn't that I wanted to stay with Gochay forever, but that if I was there, anything could happen. As for him, he had much more work than he could do. He didn't think he could turn his best customers down. So he offered me a deal. I would pick the jobs I wanted to do. I would get seventy-five percent of the pay. He would get twenty-five to cover all of the overhead and his risk. I thought about it for a week, and then gave two weeks' notice. I dreamed up the name Serena because it seemed to fit. You weren't surprised that Constantine Gochay would have a girl around named Serena, were you?"

"No," he said. "I guess not." He thought for a moment.

"It was fun. Being in a school and then a job with mostly men was a lot of trouble. When I'd walk into a room, I'd feel stares like laser beams moving across various body parts. I guess in my own small way, I'm kind of an exhibitionist—but I like a limited audience. Working with Constantine, I wasn't a girl, I was a revenue center. I could be anybody at all, and when I wanted to, I was anybody I felt like being."

"Why did you terminate your agreement with him?"

She looked down at him, and he could see amusement in her eyes. "You want me to say it's because I've changed my ways, my heart is in your hands, and I would crawl across the continent to nuzzle up to you in a cheap hotel, don't you?"

Walker knitted his brows and made a thoughtful face, as though he were having trouble deciding. "It's not so cheap."

"Admit it."

"Well, yes. I was hoping it was something like that," he said. "It would be a sound basis for a relationship, certainly."

"Did I say I wanted one?"

"Don't you?"

She said carefully, "I left the company—decided to be a bad girl—because I never got to decide before. It felt good. When I met you that night, I thought, 'Why not? What's stopping me?' and decided that whatever had stopped me before, I shouldn't let it. That turned out to be a good idea, because it felt even better. Yesterday I left Gochay because what you're doing seemed to be the most interesting thing that was going on."

"But what you're interested in isn't really me?"

She shrugged. "You're a man. What you do is look at somebody you find attractive, somebody you don't know at all, and decide you'd like to have sex with her. You aren't deciding you're in love with her. You're not thinking that far ahead, and you don't feel guilty about it. You did that when you met me. Why can't I do that with you?"

He said, "I guess I can't think of a logical reason."

"Well, if I had stopped being interested in you, I wouldn't have come," she said. "What I know so far, I like. I haven't thought about more than that. I'm enjoying doing as I please."

She flopped backward on the bed and lay still, staring at the ceiling. He crawled over and looked down at her, but she shut her eyes.

Walker said, "Well, that's fun. But let's get back to this nuzzling business. I liked talking about that." He lowered himself and began to brush her neck with his lips.

She shivered and pushed him away. "That tickles."

"I'm not sure, but I think that's part of the point of it. Not much after your crawl across the continent, but—"

"I didn't say that was true," she interrupted. "I said it was what you would like to believe." She sat up and pulled the covers up to her neck. "Actually, I took a plane, and the rest of the nuzzling can wait . . . for now." She couldn't keep the corners of her lips from turning upward a bit, but she said, "I have something to tell you. I've been trying to find out who James Scully was, and who his distant cousin was."

"How are you doing that?"

"I figured that the FBI is doing all of the routine, likely, logical things. So I have to do something else. The lab report I intercepted made me think of genealogy."

"You mean you're doing his family tree?"

"It had to be something I could do on a laptop and a phone in an airplane. Genealogy is America's second-biggest obsession, after their lawns. So there's plenty of information available. You always start with the Mormons."

"You do?"

She sighed. "Yes. It's an article of the Mormon faith to try to find out who their ancestors were, and baptize them retroactively to get them into heaven. They've been at it for a long time, and they share. So you start with the Family History Library in Salt Lake City. They also have the International Genealogy Index, the Social Security Death Index, and the Military Index."

"Those guys didn't seem religious, foreign, or retired, and if they'd been in the military, wouldn't their fingerprints have—"

"It's not for them," she said. "Their common ancestor is at least a generation back. So I tried the Library of Congress Local History and Genealogy Index."

"Did any of this get you anywhere?"

"Everywhere, and that's not where I need to go. It got me quite a few Scullys, and if you add in their cousins, it's an astronomical number. It hasn't gotten me a sure way to know which one is yours."

Walker lay back on the bed and stared at the ceiling. "Another dead end."

"It isn't," she said. "I just need a shortcut. I've got thousands of Scullys: maybe a hundred families in New Hampshire, and an unknown number of others on the list whose recent locations aren't given. By 'recent' I mean this century."

"What's the shortcut?"

"Coming here. I think your James Scully didn't move to a rural village in New Hampshire from Chicago or New York."

"Why not?"

"It doesn't feel right," she said. "If you want to be invisible, small towns are poison. If he was some kind of nut—say, an extreme survivalist–racist–mad bomber type—he probably wouldn't pick Coulter. Those guys move to the south or west, where there's more real estate that's really empty and less concern about gun laws. I suspect that he felt safe here because he was born around here. That would mean his relative probably was too."

"And coming here is the only way to find out?"

"What I want isn't available any other way. The Health and Welfare Building in Concord has a Bureau of Vital Records. They've kept track of every marriage, birth, and death in the state since 1640, and every divorce since 1808. If you give me the right lead, I can find not only James, but any relative who was born here—meaning the other dead guy."

"It sounds as though it could take months."

"It could," said Mary. "If you go into those places acting like a skip-tracer—or an insurance investigator—it would. You just have to endear yourself to somebody who knows the system and get them interested in helping. I've already started being endearing, and it's gotten me my first introduction." She squinted at the clock, then looked a second time. "I'd better get going."

Walker sat on the bed and watched her with the same sense of bereavement that he had felt while he'd watched her prepare to leave his hotel room in Los Angeles. Seeing her pull clothes over that smooth, white body was like watching the moon being obscured by dark clouds.

She said, "Don't sit there ogling. Get up and get dressed so you can buy me breakfast."

When they left the hotel room they walked past Stillman's door. It opened and he emerged. He nodded to them without a change of expression and said, "Morning, Serena."

She answered in the same tone, "Always a pleasure, Max." She was Serena again.

He walked with them to the restaurant, then selected a booth along the far wall. As soon as they had menus in their hands, he looked over the top of his and stared at Serena. "Did you bring something to the party?"

She said, "I'm trying to find out who the cousin was, so you can see what's in his house. Is that what you want?"

"That's what we want," said Stillman.

"I've made a contact, and that should speed things up."

His eyebrows bumped up, then down again. "A contact?"

"Yes," she said. "I called the Bureau of Vital Records and talked to a lady. She knows another lady who lives on a farm outside Jaffrey. She's an amateur historian who knows about the families and the little towns around here. I called her, and I'm going to see her this morning."

Stillman said, "Take your boyfriend with you."

She smiled and glanced at Walker, then back at Stillman. "I don't think so. Night with the girls, day with the boys."

"Take him," said Stillman. "He has his limitations, but he's big and strong, and if anything's after you, he'll throw himself in front of it."

Walker glared at Stillman, then looked at Serena to find that she was studying him speculatively. She made a decision. "All right. Just let me do most of the talking."

32

The farm had not seen a plow in at least a generation. The fields surrounding the small rise where the old white house had been built had settled into a man-smoothed, grassy expanse of lawn. A long fieldstone fence had been laid along the edge of the farm beside the road. Walker imagined the first farmer stopping his horse each time his plow turned up a stone, then prying it up with a pole and staggering with it to the edge of the field to add to the fence. Here and there big, stubborn rocks had been left in place, undefeated by the farmers, and now a few trees had grown tall in the middle of the field.

There was no gate anymore, just a gap in the fence and a concrete driveway that extended only twenty feet in, then changed to a gravel strip leading up to a small barn that had been converted to a garage.

Walker turned Mary's rental car into the driveway and then let it crawl onto the gravel and up to the house. As soon as it reached the wider turnaround near the barn, he parked.

"Silvertop alert," muttered Mary. "Smile a lot. It may not be enough, but it will be something."

He could see that she was already working her face into a demure smile that went with the modest blue summer dress she was wearing. He glanced toward the house, and he saw that the front door was open. A woman appeared in the shade behind the screen door. She was wearing a dark suit and a white blouse, as though she were on her way to work at a bank. Her hair was white, like spun floss, and she was staring at them expectantly.

Walker got out and opened Mary's door. As she got out, she whispered, "How gallant."

"I'm just afraid to go first," he whispered back. "Kick your way in, grab the tea, and run."

They approached the door along a flagstone walk between rows of tall purple irises that all seemed to Walker to be full of bees buzzing ominously. The woman pushed the screen open a little, and Mary said, "Mrs. Thwaite?"

"Who else?" called the woman. "Come in." Her voice was a resonant soprano that sounded as though she might have once been a singer. She swung the door wide as they reached the porch, and they stepped over the threshold.

Mary was already busy impersonating herself. "I'm Mary Catherine Casey, and this is John Walker." As she fell into character, her smile warmed.

Mrs. Thwaite shook Mary's hand and then Walker's. "I'm delighted to meet you both," she said. "We'll have tea in the sun room." She led them through a parlor. The ornate wallpaper was obscured by heavy antique furniture, and gilded frames with big paintings of dark mountains under brooding cumulonimbus clouds, then under an arch into a white sun porch with walls that were rows of windowpanes looking out on a rose garden. In the middle was a table set with teacups and silverware.

Walker waited through the elaborate, leisurely tea ritual. Mrs. Thwaite was not inclined to abbreviate it, or to forgo any of the antiquated formalities. Mary Casey seemed to have prepared herself for this. She sat with a perfectly straight spine that never touched the back of her chair and responded with fierce, immovable correctness. She saw everything Mrs. Thwaite did, and heard whatever was behind the voice, things not said but simply understood by women of a certain sort. Mary was helpful without actually doing much helping, because only certain motions could be performed without presuming upon the prerogatives of the hostess, who must do the steeping, pouring, and serving. She moved delicate china objects into her reach, but never too soon or too late, then made them glide to their proper places. Always, she kept up a fluttery patter about the garden outside the windows, the china, the tea, the tablecloth and napkins, and even the angle of the sun, as though Mrs. Thwaite had cunningly contrived to plant the giant oak two hundred years ago to shade the windows today.

When the tea and cookies and pastries had been distributed and all formulaic utterances exchanged, Mrs. Thwaite's face assumed the contented softness that indicated her gods had been appeased. She said, "How do you know Myra Sanderidge?"

"I don't, really," said Mary. "I was just doing a little research and I talked to her on the telephone. She said that if I wanted to know anything about this part of the state, I should ask you."

Walker surmised that this Myra person must be the one at the state archives. How could Mary know her? He couldn't imagine that this had been anything but a purely formal trap—an opportunity for Mary to claim a false legitimacy, but Mary had effortlessly converted it into a compliment.

"Well, you should know Myra," pronounced Mrs. Thwaite. "I like her, and you would too." Walker could tell that this was her announcment that Mary was one of *us,* not one of *them.*

Mary gathered in her winnings gracefully. "I'm hoping to meet her in a day or two. I'm driving to Concord to do a little research. Mrs. Thwaite, I was—"

"Ivy," interrupted Mrs. Thwaite. "Call me Ivy. Now, what are you doing research for?"

Mary's smile grew to a grin. "I suppose it's because that's what I do best, so I always fall back on it when I'm in a new situation. John was already here on a trip with a business friend. He liked it, and I had nothing to do, so he talked me into joining them for a few days. I couldn't do much reading at the last minute, so I used my computer on the plane to see what I could find out, and now I'm hooked."

Ivy's eyes strayed to Walker. "What did you like about it?"

Walker began to sweat. "Well, I . . . the country, mostly. I came into Keene, and I liked the look of it. Then Mary told me she'd found interesting facts about the area—scenic routes, history—and so my friend and I drove around a bit to look at some of the small towns around here. We went up the Old Concord Road through East Sullivan, Munsonville, South Stoddard, a few other places."

Mary prompted, "But the place you liked best was Coulter, wasn't it?"

"Oh?" said Ivy. "You were in Coulter?"

Walker struggled to make as many of the lies coincide with the truth as he could. "It seemed like such a peaceful little place. I was curious about it because it seemed kind of remote, so far off the highway. Then, when we got there, it seemed active, friendly, and—"

"Wealthy?"

Walker smiled. "Well, yes. It seemed to me that all the houses were pretty nice. I wondered about the people who live there."

Ivy looked at Mary, and some understanding passed between them. It was only a second before Mary revealed what it was. "It sounded like a nice place for children."

Ivy's face looked thoughtful. "It's an interesting place. It always has been."

"It has?"

"I gather that Myra told you local history is my weakness. I was a history teacher in Jaffrey for thirty-two years. But I didn't start out to be that. I met my husband in Manhattan, only it was Manhattan, Kansas. I was fresh out of KSU, and he was a young second lieutenant stationed at Fort Riley. You know how those things go."

Walker caught himself nodding in exactly the same rhythm as Mary. "Was this where he was from?"

"Yes," she said. She looked wistful at the memory of it. "When he told me about this place, I secretly thought he must be some kind of aristocrat. His family came to this part of New Hampshire with William Pynchon in 1636. They ended up precisely here a little later. After they'd sold off the trees for lumber, they became farmers, probably by default. They stayed put a long time, but the Thwaites were never rich."

"Did any of them settle in Coulter?" asked Mary.

"Never," said Ivy quickly. "Never in Coulter."

Walker was surprised by the certainty, the finality. He ventured, "It seemed like a pleasant place, but so is this."

"Yes, Coulter probably always was pleasant. But it had an odd reputation. After Randolph and I had been married for a short time, I began to hear a peculiar tone when it was mentioned." She put her hand on Mary's forearm and said, "I'm just like you. I hear something, and I want to know all about it." She withdrew her hand and looked at them knowingly over her teacup. "Well, people implied that it had sort of a racy reputation."

"Racy?" Mary raised her eyebrows. "That would get my attention."

"Me too. I was a Kansas girl, from the rough-and-ready West, and I'd been to college. When I heard that, I thought it must be houses of ill repute, at least. I wasn't used to the New England sensibility yet. I was from a place where you talked with your mouth wide open, and used your finger to point at what you saw. When I couldn't get anything much out of anybody, I went to look for myself."

"You went there alone?" asked Mary.

"Sure," said Ivy. "What I saw was . . ." She smiled and paused for suspense. "Pretty much what you saw." Her smile turned into a laugh. "I was so disappointed, all that morning. I walked up and down staring at people, looking into their eyes for signs that they had hidden depths. Nothing. Of course, in those days, it wasn't as well populated as it is now, or as well-heeled."

Walker said, "It wasn't? The houses all looked as though they had been there for a hundred years or more. There were a few new ones, but they all seemed to be in the middle of old blocks, where there would have been something else before."

Ivy's eyes sharpened. "You're a good observer. And you're right. In those days, all the houses were big and fancy and old. Most of them were run-down, and quite a few looked as though they hadn't been occupied for years."

"Odd. I wonder why."

"So did I. All the little towns around here have a few big houses like the ones in Coulter. At one time there was lots of industry— pottery works, glass factories, furniture factories, textile mills, shoe factories, granite quarries. A lot of people made fortunes, and built houses to let passersby know it, right up until 1900 or so. But those were business owners. There were a lot more laborers than owners. I didn't see any tenements or workers' cottages in Coulter. I was trying to get a sense of this area, and Coulter was just part of that. I remembered, when I was asking questions of people, to ask about Coulter too."

Walker said casually, "Did you find out anything about the people that built the houses? Family names or anything?"

"I was an outsider asking prying questions, and people around here didn't always take that well. Finally, one of my students took me to meet her great-grandfather. His name was Jonathan Tooker. She said he had lots of interesting stories about things, and that I was the one to hear them. The old gentleman was—I think—ninety-eight at the time, and that was fifty years ago."

She stared out at the garden as she spoke. "Jonathan said the people there grew rich as what used to be called 'Yankee traders' when that was not necessarily taken as a compliment. They were itinerants, tinkers who fixed, sold, and traded things. But they were crooks. They sold cheap goods disguised and labeled as first-rate. They traded for old machinery, shined it up, and sold it as new. Jonathan said that while they were on the road, they bought stolen goods, and even sometimes stole it themselves. He said that if they got their hands on something that really was first-class, they would use it as bait: they'd take cash deposits on orders and never deliver, or just use it to get into houses."

"I don't understand," said Mary.

"Well, there were certain items that were the genuine article, superior goods. An example would be the McCormick reaper. There were dozens of kinds of reapers, but now nobody can name one, because the McCormick was best. They would have one on a wagon when they came to a town. It made them seem like respectable merchants. People would trust them, invite them into their houses. While one man was making a sales pitch or luring the farmer outside to watch a demonstration, another would be pocketing the silverware or jewelry. Jonathan said there were all kinds of schemes and tricks. He said that later they traveled by rail, and that let them extend their range to Ohio and Indiana, Michigan and Illinois, but the pattern was about the same. They'd come home at the end of summer and spend the fall and winter working to make old things look new, cheap goods look expensive, and disguising stolen items for resale. Did you see the mill while you were there?"

"The old mill?" said Walker. "It's been made into a restaurant."

"That's where all that tinkering went on."

"A textile mill?"

"It wasn't that. People used 'mill' in the British sense, to mean factory. But it worked the same. It was on a stream because water power could be used to turn a lathe or a wheel to grind or polish. And they could take base-metal cutlery or vessels, silver-plate them, and dump the chemicals in the stream. After I heard it from Jonathan, I went and looked at the place. I didn't see any reason to believe he was wrong, but of course, the evidence was long gone."

Mary said, "I suppose it must have been. And you said there weren't as many people?"

"Jonathan's theory was that Coulter's whole repertoire of tricks and swindles required farmers with money to spend. When hard times hit in the 1920s, the victims didn't have enough money to keep Coulter in business. Jonathan was a great admirer of simple explanations, but maybe it's true."

Walker said, "And the people moved away?"

She nodded. "Looking back on it, I guess you could say the town pretty much died. When I was there fifty years ago, I'll bet two-thirds of those big houses were empty. I don't know where the people went." She brightened, as though a new idea had amused her. "I suppose they went out West with new swindles."

"Then you believe what Mr. Tooker told you?" asked Mary.

"I've come to. Over the years, I heard bits and pieces of it again. A painter from Stoddard I hired about twenty-five years ago had the worst old truck I ever saw, and he was always grumbling about it. He said that when he bought it, he'd been 'Coultered.' I perked up my ears, and he told me some of the same things Jonathan had. It seems that around here at one time, people would call anyone who was a cheat or swindler a 'Coulter.' I was thinking of doing an article on the place at one time, but I never got around to it."

Walker said, "Did you ever make any notes, or anything?"

She stared out the windows at the garden, "Well, yes, I did. I remember writing things down when I was in Concord, looking up the names of early settlers . . ." She stopped. "But that's all gone now. My investigation never turned up any primary sources on the swindling. It was all just old stories. I didn't keep the notes."

"Do you remember any of the names?" asked Mary. She turned to Walker. "What was that one you wondered about?"

"Scully," said Walker. "There was a distant relative on my mother's side who lived in New Hampshire, and I wondered . . ."

Ivy thought for a moment, then shook her head. "No. It was so long ago."

Walker tried another strategy. "I wonder if the survivors just multiplied. Forty years is enough time."

"Oh," said Ivy. "But those are all new people. A few years ago, when that new research place was built, people started moving in. All those big old houses that got built with ill-gotten gains were being rehabilitated, restored, and painted when I last saw the place. I wouldn't be at all surprised if someday the whole town was made into an official historic district. And not one person in it will have any idea what sort of place it was."

Walker waited through the rest of the visit, letting Mary guide him through the ritual. She led the conversation away from Coulter and on to ever-widening generalities about the district, and he could tell that she was giving Ivy Thwaite a chance to remember something else. Then Mary announced that they were overstaying their invitation. There was another exchange of extravagant mutual praise and thanks, a lot of solicitous, superfluous help with the clearing of china and linens from the table. As they were making their way to the car, Ivy Thwaite opened her screen door again and said, "I'm going to call Myra Sanderidge right now and tell her to expect you soon. Let me know if you learn anything interesting."

"I will," said Mary. "And I'll tell her I already have."

Walker drove carefully out toward the road, and Mary looked at him. "Well?" she asked. "What did you think?"

"I think you've seduced old ladies before," he said. "It's a whole side of you that I never saw before. I kind of liked it."

"Don't get too used to it," she said. "Just because I know how decent people behave doesn't mean I want to be one of them."

He shrugged. "I'll keep a lot of bail money on hand."

"Save it for my expenses," said Mary. "She gave me an idea of how I should go about this, and if she really does call Myra Sanderidge, it will go ten times as quickly—a few days, not a few weeks. As soon as I can drop you off at your hotel, I'm going to Concord."

33

Walker stood on the corner of West Street and Main and watched Mary's car until it had slipped into the rest of the traffic and moved out of sight. He had insisted that she not drop him at his hotel, where anyone watching him would see them together. She had laughed at him, but she had complied.

As he walked to the corner of Keys Street, he wished he had gone with her. He still had not been able to figure out exactly what their relationship was, or what it should be, and she was no help. If he had asked her she would have come back with "Who said this was a relationship?" The one thing he had decided on his own was that every time she left, he hated to see her go. As he passed the familiar shops and restaurants, he consoled himself. It was likely that whatever Stillman would decide to do next would be dangerous, and it would almost certainly be unpleasant and illegal. He would feel better if she was away for a few days in some big public building surrounded by musty old papers.

Spending the morning in a glass room surrounded by thick, gnarled old rosebushes with cabbage-sized roses had not made him forget. The people he and Stillman had been searching for were killers. When the sidewalk brought him past the last high building, he could see Stillman's rented Explorer in the parking lot beside the hotel.

He stepped in through the side entrance, came up the hallway, and knocked on Stillman's door. Stillman opened it with the telephone receiver at his ear, and Walker stepped inside. Stillman was standing at the desk with an open telephone book in front of him. He nodded at Walker and said, "Mr. Fisher? How are you today. My name is Eric Campbell, and I'm calling to let you know that Golden Future Funds has some information that could be of great interest to you. Are you of retirement age, sir?" He listened for a moment, making a note on a sheet of paper in front of him. "Is anyone in the household under sixty-five? No? Then I'm afraid I've wasted your time. Thank you for your patience."

He hung up and dialed another number. "Hello, is this Mrs. Gilman?" He listened. "Miss Gilman. I'm sorry. This is Calvin Arnott calling from Kirby Travel in Manchester. We're trying to give away a vacation for two in Antigua, and I said *give* away. It's a promotion from Delta Airlines." He listened for a moment. "Well, sure. Can you give me your boyfriend's name?" Stillman wrote furiously. "His age? Good. The drawing is on the first of the month, and we'll call you that day if you win. Good luck."

He hung up the telephone and glanced at Walker, then looked down at his list and put his finger on the next line. "Welcome home. Get anything?"

"Misplaced hopes," said Walker. "I was hoping she would know people in Coulter. I'd sip my tea and she would say, 'Scully? Sure, I know the family. All nice people except Jimmy and his cousin Billy. They hung out with those awful Johnson brothers.'"

"I take it she didn't have much for us."

"I know more than I want to about the town, but it doesn't put us any closer to finding out who the second guy was."

Stillman looked at him impassively. "What about the town?"

"Why all the houses were fancy. The place was founded by what she calls 'tinkers.' They arrived when the Industrial Revolution hit New England and traveled around selling tools and machinery, mostly to farmers in the fringe settlements as the frontier moved west. They had a reputation for cheating and swindling their customers."

"A fine old American tradition," said Stillman. "Everybody who got rich did it by cheating somebody." His voice trailed off as he returned to his papers. "Well, nice try, anyway. Where's Serena?"

"She's on her way to Concord to check the birth and death records." Walker sighed. "Another waste of time."

Stillman didn't contradict him. He dialed another number. "Hello. My name is Mike Metzger, and I'm calling for Mr. Philips. Yes. The Internal Revenue Service. You're Mrs. Philips? Oh, then maybe you can help me. No, you're not being audited, we're doing a projection. If you could give me the names of the dependents you'll be declaring on your Form 1040 next year, and their ages." He wrote as he listened. "I see. Very good. Thank you for your time." His finger moved down his list.

Walker turned and stepped toward the door, but Stillman said, "I've just got a couple more calls, and then I thought maybe we could get lunch. Why don't you go change into tourist clothes?"

"Good idea," said Walker. "Where do you want to go?"

"The Old Mill in Coulter." He didn't wait for Walker's response, but dialed the next number. "Hello. My name is Art Miller. I'm calling from MCI-WorldCom. What I'd like to offer is six hours of free long-distance calling for each member of your household just for trying our service. How many people would that be? Can you give me their names and ages?"

Walker muttered, "I'll be right back," and went to his room to change.

When he returned, Stillman was saying, "We're not sure yet when the estate-planning seminar will be held. In small-town areas we like to be sure which date people prefer, so we'll have the best attendance. Which date during the first week of September would be best for you? Good. Now that I've got your personal profile, we'll be able to tailor our advice to your needs. We'll call. Thanks." He hung up, then stood and stared at his sheaf of papers.

Walker said, "What was that all about?"

"I'm making a list of men between twenty and fifty, with special attention to men who can't be reached by telephone—meaning they could be the one who departed for the great area code in the sky with James Scully."

"Why all the different impersonations?"

Stillman said, "You design it for the person you're talking to. You hear an old codger's voice, you want a list of his heirs. You hear a young woman, you want the men in her life. Simple."

To Walker it wasn't simple. It meant that each time Stillman heard a voice, he had to be ready to become the right caller, with the right lie. "How's it going?"

"About as well as can be expected. I've called all the listed numbers, and picked the names that are possibles and those that aren't home. That's a lot better than we started with, but it's not a small enough number to do anything with."

"Have any idea how the FBI is doing?"

"Yeah. McClaren says they're doing lousy. No names yet. Let's go to Coulter."

This time, when they drove into Coulter, Walker tried looking at the town through Ivy Thwaite's eyes. Now the proportions made sense to him. The big buildings on Main Street had been built to accommodate people who had brought ready money in from elsewhere. The ground floors of the ornate buildings had probably always been occupied by rows of small shops, just as they were now. They had sold clothes and personal accoutrements to men whose livelihood as swindlers depended on good costuming, and to their women, whose major compensation for being isolated in a remote village would have been a high standard of living.

Now, through one of those meaningless coincidences that history always seemed to produce, the town had been reborn in the same form. A cadre of young engineers or computer geeks or science nerds with an idea to sell had eschewed the high prices and congestion of Boston and built their own version of Coulter.

Stillman parked on Main near Grant Street. As they strolled down Main Street, Walker noticed that today, too, the town had attracted a few tourists. When he and Stillman crossed the bridge over the river to the Old Mill, they had to wait inside the door while the waiter con-

ducted a family to a table, and Walker picked up a strong southern accent in the children's chatter. There were several cars in the nearby lot
that had out-of-state license plates.

Other waiters had appeared at the far end of the big dining room,
and they were setting tables in an area cordoned off by a white rope
strung between brass stanchions. Walker counted ten tables.

When they had been seated and the waiter was taking their order,
Stillman acknowledged Walker's distraction. "What's going on over
there?" he asked the waiter.

The waiter half-turned, as though he had not noticed it before.
"The tables? I guess they're getting ready for a private party. I just
came on."

While they ate, Walker noticed Stillman occasionally watching
the preparations without letting himself appear to. He spoke little,
and Walker knew it was because he was listening to conversations
around him, probably trying to distinguish the natives from the
tourists, and the old-time residents from the newcomers who had mi-
grated here to work at New Mill Systems.

Walker occupied himself by looking at the wall above him, where
another part of the restaurant's collection of old photographs was
hung.

When they were outside, Stillman said, "Interesting, wasn't it?
Waiters don't usually come on at one-thirty. Either they work lunch or
they work dinner. On a big day, they work both."

"Maybe they brought him in to help get ready for the party."

"Mysterious that he didn't know what it was."

"I think Ivy Thwaite was right about this place."

"Oh?" said Stillman. "You mean the waiter is secretive because it's
a congenital condition he inherited?"

"Sorry. I wasn't thinking about him. I was looking at the pictures
on the wall. I noticed some new things. The place had electricity. It
was all wired up before the turn of the century. Most towns like this
still had gas lamps for years. Everybody on the street was all dressed
up and riding around in a fancy buggy."

"You have to remember they were getting their picture taken,"
said Stillman absently. "That was probably a big deal at one time—an

occasion—so they didn't get their pictures taken in old boots covered with cow shit."

"There was nobody on the whole street like that."

"Then probably it was Sunday."

Walker sighed in frustration and looked back at the Old Mill. "I could see that building in the picture. You know what? It didn't have a sign."

"A sign of what?"

"A sign. A sign that said what it was. Did you ever see a business— I mean one that has customers who are strangers and isn't illegal—that didn't have a sign on it?"

Stillman walked beside him for a few steps. "You've got me. I don't mean you're right. I just don't know. If I did see one, it didn't have a sign on it, and I didn't know it was a business."

Walker took in a breath, preparing to explain, but then he let it out. "You're right."

"Then can we talk about the present?"

"Sure."

"Between last night and this afternoon, I managed to make a list of the grown men in this town. It came to a hundred and forty-three, pretty close to your guess."

"Damned close," said Walker.

"All right," Stillman conceded. "Damned close. Of course, if I missed a few, then it would just be pretty close." He turned onto Main Street. "On the phone, I managed to eliminate all but thirty-eight of them."

"How did you do that?"

"By talking to them, mostly," said Stillman. "Our boy is dead, re-member?"

"Yeah."

"Some of them had wives who said their husbands were at work and could I call back at five-thirty or something. A lot of them gave me phone numbers I could call to reach the old man right away. Those I eliminated too. A few I didn't talk to turned out to be too old for our purposes. Anyway, we've got thirty-eight left that weren't answering last night or today, or whose relatives said they were out of town."

"That was pretty good," said Walker.

"But not good enough."

"What if we limit it to the phones that nobody at all answers?" asked Walker. "He's dead, after all."

"You mean we can assume that if a woman answered and she wasn't crying, then the man in her life isn't lying on a slab in Florida? You're forgetting that the FBI hasn't identified either man yet. This guy's next of kin hasn't been notified yet, so we can't be sure they know he's dead. And if you were a man who committed felonies professionally, it would be pretty hard to keep the little woman in the dark about it. If she knows what you do for a living, she knows how to cover. Even if you were good enough to deceive her, you would still have to feed her a bullshit story, so she could tell people why you weren't out front mowing the lawn this week. And these guys seem to travel a lot. Most likely their relatives are used to them not showing up on time."

"I suppose so," said Walker. "Forget that idea. What about making a list of people who have no visible means of support?"

"You mean like the idea I had about checking their health insurance in the drugstore?"

"It's not as elegant, but we only need to eliminate thirty-seven now. We go in every door on Main. Write down the men who work as waiters or store clerks or cops: anybody who has a name tag, or anybody whose name is on an office directory. That should eliminate a few of the ones you couldn't reach by telephone. They were out working when you called." He squinted. "A big step would be to somehow get a list of employees at New Mill Systems."

"I tried New Mill this morning. I called and asked for the personnel manager. Some guy came on, so I said I was from the New Hampshire Equal Employment Opportunity Commission. I asked for a list of employees broken down by age, sex, and race."

"Race?" said Walker. "I haven't seen a pair of brown eyes since I got here, let alone brown skin."

"What do you want from me? I asked the guy what he expected to hear. No dice. He said the company employs fewer than a hundred people, and has been certified exempt from reporting requirements."

"Is that true?" asked Walker. "Are companies like that exempt from discrimination laws?"

"How the hell do I know what the law is in New Hampshire? It doesn't matter anyway. I'm not going to take him to court. The list I wanted would have been of people who didn't do anything wrong."

Walker's eyes settled on the sidewalk as he contemplated the problem. "Thirty-eight men . . ."

"We've been in New Hampshire for three days, and none of the devious ways has worked. What I think we've got to do is start taking some chances."

"Start?"

"Yeah. Risk drawing attention to ourselves. Ask direct questions of anybody who will talk to us. 'Do you know James Scully? Who does he hang out with?' "

"I think you're right," said Walker. "It would probably go faster if we split up and talked to as many—"

"Maybe not," said Stillman.

Walker looked up and stared at him. His eyes were squinting ahead. "But you just said—"

"Look," said Stillman.

Walker turned his eyes to follow Stillman's gaze. Far up the street, two men were getting out of a car parked along Main Street across from the coffee shop. Walker studied them, not quite daring to make a decision yet, straining his eyes and waiting for them to turn their heads so he could see their faces.

Stillman tugged his arm lightly to divert him into an alcove that shaded the entrance to a clothing store, and the movement of Walker's body made him come to his senses. Waiting in plain sight for them to turn around would be insane. What they appeared to be were the two men who had pretended to be cops in the alley in Pasadena, but he wasn't sure. He was positive he knew their faces, their postures, and their walks. In his shock and alarm he had studied them, imprinted them on his memory that night.

"Your eyes are better than mine," Stillman said. "Stand here." Stillman nudged him near the corner of the display window where he could look up the street through both panes of glass. "You won't stand out between those mannequins. Steady. Don't move, just look."

Walker obeyed. He stood absolutely still, staring, holding his breath. One of the men had moved out of sight along the side of the car, toward the front. The other was at the trunk. He leaned over, opened the trunk, and bent down to get something out. Then he stood erect again, slammed the lid, and turned. Walker could see the movement of the shoulders, then the dark hair. The man looked up the street to check for traffic before he stepped away from the car. Then he looked down toward Walker, and Walker saw the bushy mustache. The two men trotted across the street. Walker stepped back.

"It's them," said Walker. "They're here."

34

Stillman's eyes were gleaming. "Well, now that is a real gift from above," he murmured.

"Should we follow them?" asked Walker.

"I think we'd better concentrate on making sure we don't bump into them. We have to assume their memory for faces is as good as ours."

Stillman stepped to the edge of the alcove where Walker had stood, then slowly moved his body to the right to see more and more of the sidewalk along the row of old buildings. When he had one eye beyond the corner of the display window, he said, "They went into the coffee shop," and stepped out.

They turned away from the place where they had seen the two men and strode briskly toward the end of the row of buildings. Stillman said, "Let's get across the street down there by the bridge, then head along the river to the next street."

Walker led the way to Washington Street, where Main narrowed to funnel traffic onto the bridge, then glanced back toward the coffee shop before he ventured across. He and Stillman reached the other side quickly, and it took them only a few more steps to reach the curb, cross the sidewalk, and slip out of sight behind the bulk of the big building on the corner. He waited for Stillman to catch up. "What are we doing—getting the car?"

"It's parked on Main, remember? We can't get to it without putting ourselves in sight of the coffee shop," Stillman said. "But I guess I'm finally going to get to say something that you'll be happy to hear. Those two, thanks to us, are already wanted for questioning in connection with a homicide investigation. Also for assault. We're going to the police station to get their asses thrown in jail."

Walker noticed that his heart must have been beating hard since he had seen the two men. It was beating hard now, and it didn't slow, but it wasn't preparing him to contend for his life. "I can hardly believe it," he said.

"It's almost over," said Stillman. "Once we get the police to put down their coffee cups, our whole reason for being here is going to begin to fade. About all we're going to have to do is say, 'Yep, those are the ones.' We'll find out some real names, the cops here will hold them, and the authorities all over the place will have time to start dreaming up the charges that mean something."

Walker was frowning. "Why do you suppose they're here at all?"

"I'm not sure," said Stillman. "If I needed a theory to keep me warm, I would guess it's for the same reason we're here. They want to get a good look at Jimmy Scully's house, to see if he left anything lying around that leads to them." They reached the corner of the first street parallel with Main, which was called Constitution Avenue. As they turned and started up the street, he said, "Come to think of it, I was forgetting about the other guy, the one who had similar DNA to Scully. There's his house, too. We still don't know who he was, but they do. We were under the impression that he might have lived around here, and it could be we were right."

Walker touched Stillman's arm. "Wait. What if they leave before we get to the station? We should go back to Main and get the license number of their car."

"New Hampshire plate, NXV-76989."

"Pretty good," said Walker.

"Presence of mind," said Stillman. "Work on it. In this business, you can't get by on afterthought."

"Good thing I'm not in this business." Walker held Stillman in the corner of his eye, but his reaction was invisible.

They walked with the same quick, long strides up Constitution Avenue, under old maple and oak trees that merged above the road to form a canopy over the pavement and kept them in uninterrupted shade until they came to a cross street, then closed over them again until the next one. Walker noted their progress impatiently as they crossed Adams, Jefferson, Franklin, Grant, then the streets named after trees: Sycamore, Oak, Maple, Birch, Hemlock. The houses along Constitution were nearly all from a period that had been referred to loosely in Ohio as colonial—mostly white, with two rows of shuttered windows, a center entrance with a pedimented doorway, and chimneys at both ends. It was a strange place to be doing what he was doing now: rushing to the police station to get some murderers arrested.

He could see that he and Stillmen were coming to the side street where they had parked yesterday to look at the police station. He said, "Is there anything I should know before we tell them? Anything I should keep to myself?"

Stillman answered, "I'll do the lying, and you swear to it. While we were in Miami, we got an anonymous tip that one of these guys lived around Keene. We haven't done any investigating since we got here— just looked around in these little towns to get our bearings—and we just happened to see those two."

"The cops are going to buy that?"

"We've only been in Keene two nights, and we can prove it. No cop is going to think that's a long time not to accomplish anything."

They headed for the back doors that opened onto the parking lot. Stillman nodded toward the row of shiny patrol cars. "Fifteen today. Ought to be enough for our purposes."

The doors opened onto a short, bare white hallway with doors on either side. To the right, Walker could see that one of the doors was steel, and had an impressive electronic lock with a numbered keypad. He supposed that it led to a cellblock, and this must be the entrance the police used to bring a suspect in from a patrol car. It would preserve the tranquillity of upper Main Street. In a short time, he thought, those two men would be taking a trip through that doorway.

The corridor opened onto a large reception area, with a low

wooden counter along the whole left side, and several plain, un-marked doors along the walls behind it. On the right side of the room were squat, heavy wooden benches that were bolted to the floor.

Two uniformed policemen were sitting at desks behind the counter. One of them was in his late thirties with blond hair that was cut too short on the sides, revealing the ridges and bumps of his skull. The other was shorter and had a dark mustache waxed at the ends to turn upward and small, close-set blue eyes. Walker was pleased with them: they were just frightening enough to inspire confidence.

Stillman walked up to the counter, and they both stood up. The smaller one hung back and leaned against a desk, watchful, while the tall one stepped forward. Stillman said, "Good afternoon, officers." His voice was loud and his words clearly enunciated.

The policeman at the counter said, "Yes, sir," and the other folded his arms and waited.

"My name is Max Stillman, and this is John Walker. We're here investigating a fraud case for McClaren Life and Casualty." As he spoke he was producing one of his business cards. He handed it to the cop, who studied it as though it actually said something.

"What can we do for you?" asked the tall man.

"A few minutes ago, we happened to recognize two men on Main Street. They're wanted by police in Pasadena, California, and Wallerton, Illinois, in connection with a kidnapping, murder, and assorted other charges."

The policemen looked at each other without speaking, but an understanding passed between them. The shorter one went through one of the doorways behind him, while the other reached under the counter and produced a piece of paper that looked to Walker like some kind of report form and a pen.

"Can you give me their names?"

"I'm afraid I can't," said Stillman.

"Did you bring a warrant for them?"

"No, we didn't," said Stillman. "If you need it, the Illinois State Police can wire you one. The main points are that you've got two men in the coffee shop down the street from here who are wanted, dangerous, and probably armed. They're driving a new blue Chevrolet with New Hampshire plate number NXV-76989."

"Description?"

"One of them is six feet tall, one seventy-five with light brown hair, wearing blue jeans and a tan shirt with a military cut and button breast pockets. The other is six-one, about two hundred, dark hair and mustache, wearing a blue oxford shirt, blue jeans, and a dark green nylon windbreaker. That one is carrying a briefcase."

The shorter cop reappeared with a gray-haired man about Stillman's age. His face was thin, with a strong chin and defined cheekbones, and eyebrows that seemed habitually stuck in a look of determination. He wore a tie and a short-sleeved white shirt with a gold badge pinned to the pocket, but as he walked in, he was putting on a summer-weight sport coat that covered his shoulder holster. Walker was even more pleased with this man. Walker had spent enough time in police stations lately to know this was the boss.

The tall cop stopped scribbling, looked up from his paper at Stillman, saw where his eyes had focused, and turned. "This is Chief Raines. Chief, these fellows say they just identified two men who were—"

"I heard that part," the chief interrupted. "You gentlemen positively identified both suspects yourselves?"

"Yes, sir," said Stillman. "They were going into the coffee shop down Main Street, and we came directly here."

"You've seen them before? Not just a picture on a circular?"

"Yes," Stillman answered.

"Both of you?"

"Yes," said Walker. "We've seen them at close range. We're absolutely sure they're the right ones."

The chief turned to the taller cop. "You've already got full descriptions of them and gotten all the information?"

"Not quite, Chief." The tall cop turned back to Stillman with his pen held ready. "What was that place in Illinois?"

"Wallerton," said Stillman. "But it might be quicker to call the state police in Springfield."

"And what murder are we talking about?"

"The victim's name is Ellen Snyder. You already have our names."

"Right." The tall cop turned around to look at his boss expectantly, holding the paper in both big hands.

Chief Raines said, "Elton, get the state police in Springfield and have them verify, fax a description and a warrant." The tall cop walked through another of the doors behind the counter. Raines said to the shorter cop, "Carlyle, let's get some officers down there to see what we've got."

The orders were coming quickly, but they seemed to be contradictory. Walker wasn't sure whether he should be pleased or not. He looked at Stillman, who had slipped into his expression of quiescent inscrutability. He was looking down, ostensibly at the counter in front of him, but Walker could see that his left arm was bent across his belly. He was looking at his watch.

Chief Raines said, "I want you to get officers into position on the streets near the coffee shop. No black-and-whites in sight, and no uniforms where the suspects might see them. Nobody moves in until I give you the word on frequency two. Just keep the coffee shop covered, front and back, and stand by." Carlyle nodded and headed for the door behind the counter.

Stillman seemed to awaken. "Chief Raines, if I may—"

"No, you may not," said the chief, evenly. "Here's how it is. Maybe some big-city police forces will burst into a coffee shop any old afternoon and arrest whoever you say, just because it was you that said it. Around here, we need to have more to go on. If what you said is true, then it won't take but a few minutes to get confirmation."

"Of course," said Stillman in the same cool, even tone. "I don't blame you."

"Good," said the chief with finality. He began to turn toward the doorway where Carlyle had disappeared.

"But," said Stillman. The chief stopped in mid-turn. "It's just that I happened to notice that there seemed to be only one road out of town."

Chief Raines cocked his head. "Yeah. We have noticed that too. Sit tight and I'll let you know as soon as we've gotten through to Spring-field." He walked off to the complex of inner offices.

Stillman turned, walked across the open floor, and sat down on one of the benches. Walker hesitated, then went to join him. Stillman was hunched over, his elbows on his knees, his eyes on the floor.

Walker whispered, "Is this the way you expected it to go?"

Stillman pursed his lips as though deciding not what the answer was, but whether he was going to answer. "I was hoping they'd haul them in and take care of the formalities at their leisure. But he's doing pretty much what he's supposed to do, given all considerations."

"What considerations?"

"He doesn't work for us. He works for the town of Coulter. The voters don't mind if he locks up a couple of out-of-town murderers, but there's not much thanks in it. He's not going to take on any foolish risks to do it."

"What do we do?"

"We already did it. Now we wait."

Walker looked at his watch. It was two thirty-five. He sat back on the hard wooden bench and stared at the front of the wooden counter across the big room. He stared until he got to know every line of the wood grain, then stared at the smooth floor until he began to alternate the patterns in the dark granite squares and the white marble squares, first seeing them as a white floor with black on it, then as a black floor with white on it.

He heard a door swing open on the back hallway, and stood up to walk to the center of the floor. He counted six policemen striding out the rear entrance to the parking lot. He saw Stillman's eyes on him and nodded. Stillman's shoulders lowered, as though the muscles had re-laxed, and he leaned his back on the bench. When the sounds of en-gines starting and cars in motion reached him, Stillman looked at his watch again. Walker didn't have to. Twenty-five minutes had elapsed.

Chief Raines emerged from the door beyond the counter and beck-oned to them once. When they had moved close enough so he didn't need to raise his voice, he said, "Okay. You're for real, and the mur-der is real. We ought to have them before long."

"Thanks, Chief," said Stillman. He turned to go back to his bench.

"Before they get in here, you and I had better have a talk," said the chief. He stepped to the side and lifted a hinged section of the counter-top to make an opening.

Walker and Stillman followed him into a large office in the corner of the building. Walker had started anticipating the questions. He had been in three police stations in a month, and he was beginning to feel expert. Raines had the manner of a man who had a great penchant for getting straight to the part of a story that mattered, but whose position made everybody he ever listened to give him obfuscation, evasion, and misdirection. He sat down behind his desk, leaving Walker and Stillman to decide whether they wanted to sit, and which of the four chairs in the room they would do it in.

"What are these two suspects from Illinois doing in Coulter, New Hampshire? What do they want here?"

Stillman said, "We can't say for sure, of course. What we think is that they're here because they had a friend—a confederate in the fraud case, anyway—who lived here. He was killed in Florida, and they'll want to be sure he didn't leave anything that will get them into trouble."

"Who killed him?"

Stillman answered, "Strictly speaking, it was my friend Walker, here." Walker's jaw tightened, and Stillman hastened to add, "Purely in self-defense."

"And he lived in Coulter, you say? What was his name?"

"Scully. James Scully. He lived over on Birch Street."

Raines grunted, but Walker couldn't tell whether it was puzzlement or a confirmation of a long-held expectation. He looked at Walker. "Has it crossed your mind that they might be here looking for you?"

"Sure," said Stillman.

Walker nodded, hiding his surprise. He had never thought of the possibility, and Stillman had never mentioned it. Walker felt foolish. He had allowed the enemy to become a group of nonhuman abstractions, beings who acted only out of logic and efficiency. He had imagined them simply trying to steal the most money and gain the most anonymity because that made simple sense. Motives like hatred and revenge had dropped out of his cogitations. He had fallen into a trap that he had never known existed, and it could have killed him.

The chief persisted with his questions, but Walker's tension was not the fear of incrimination that he had felt when he had been interrogated in other places. He was acutely aware that time was passing. He told himself that the chief's glacial pace meant nothing had gone wrong, but behind the voice he kept straining his ears for gunshots. The distance couldn't be more than half a mile, he estimated. The chief had by now perceived that there was no question he could ask that Stillman could not answer instantly and flawlessly but to little purpose, so he directed one now and then to Walker. It was always one that Walker had anticipated, because he had become adept at picking out which parts of Stillman's answers the chief would want to rephrase and repeat to Walker to detect a contradiction. When the questions came, he was not alarmed. It was what cops did.

When he heard footsteps outside the door, Walker stiffened. The door swung open and the tall cop stood in the doorway without stepping inside. Raines slipped outside and closed the door behind him. Walker strained his ears, but he could not hear the voices, and Stillman had settled again into his barely animate stolidity, his eyes focused on the wall as though he were unaware of Walker's impatience. After a minute or two, Raines returned. His expression was weary and irritated.

"When you recognized those suspects, they must have recognized you too," he said. "They weren't in the coffee shop. Officers have been checking other shops and restaurants for over an hour, but they haven't turned up." He walked to his desk, took a roll of Life Savers out of the top drawer and put them in his pocket, then walked back to the door. "I've just sent one team to Scully's house to watch that. But it's not looking real good. There aren't a lot of places in this town where two strangers could hide." He opened the door and walked out.

35

For a minute after Chief Raines disappeared, Stillman sat in his state of immobility, staring at the carpet. Then he stood abruptly. "You heard the man. We're waiting around for nothing." Walker noticed that when Stillman stepped to the door, he opened it only a crack, then listened before he swung it wide. They stepped quickly through the hinged opening in the counter, then out the rear entrance to the parking lot. Stillman set a quick pace until they had returned to Constitution Avenue. Then he slowed a bit, as though he was forcing his body to convey a kind of leisure.

Walker said, "If leaving was the right thing to do, why did you peek out the door to be sure nobody was looking?"

"Because I didn't want somebody to give me a competing opinion that I had to listen to."

"Are we going back to Keene?"

"Afraid not," said Stillman.

"Is there something I'm missing?"

"It took us about five minutes of fast walking from the time we saw those guys on Main Street until we got to the police station. We didn't even stop to get the car, because it would have cost us extra time to circle around those guys and back to Main to get it. So why did they leave?"

"Maybe the chief was right. We saw them, and they saw us."

Stillman's eyes were narrow and intense. "Suppose he is right. What would those two guys do?"

"Beats me. Get in their car and leave, I guess. If the car wasn't there when the police arrived, I'd say it's settled."

"Right. But they're playing the same game we are. They didn't come here because they needed a break from stealing money. They want to get into Scully's house, just as we did, and the cousin's house."

Walker held Stillman in the corner of his eye. "How do you know they haven't already done it?"

"Because if we had gotten it done, we wouldn't go down the street and stop for espresso and a Danish afterward. We'd get the hell out of here. They're here in daylight, casing the town, just the way we did. They're playing a game with rules that we know. They've stolen a lot of money, and they think there's probably something in a house in this town that implicates them. If they get to it before anybody else does, they win. If we get to it first, they lose. You have to look at the situation and say, 'What would we do?' "

"What would we do?"

"Same thing they did. We'd get in our car and drive off. But this isn't just a question of fraudulent insurance claims, it's murder with special circumstances. Death penalty. If that were you, would you leave evidence here?"

"I don't suppose I would," said Walker. "But if they saw us here, wouldn't they think that we must have come to search Scully's house and his cousin's too?"

"Sure," said Stillman.

"And we were here first, so wouldn't they think it's too late?"

"Just the opposite. If they had what they came for, they wouldn't be hanging around the coffee shop. If we had what we came for, we wouldn't be loitering around on Main Street either. We'd be gone. If they saw us, then what they saw was proof that it's not too late, but that they've got to make a move very soon. Tonight, after dark."

Walker was skeptical. "Tonight? Not tomorrow night?"

"If they saw us, they know how close we are to getting there first. After dark tonight is the first time we could pull a break-in. They'll try to beat us to it."

"With all those police around?"

"They don't know about the police."

"How the hell can you know that?"

Stillman spoke quietly and patiently. "Think about what happened. We were walking up Main Street when we saw them getting out of their car. Then what?"

"We went straight up Constitution Avenue to the police station."

"Right. It took about five or six minutes to walk up there, and another twenty-five for the chief to tell his men to move in. When they did, they didn't see our two guys. They had their descriptions, the make, year, and license number of the car. Besides that, there can't be more than twenty-five people in this town today that the cops haven't seen twice a week since they were born. But the cops didn't see our two guys. I'd say that means our guys were gone before the police got there, wouldn't you?"

"I guess so," Walker admitted. "What do you suppose they're doing now?"

Stillman walked on, staring into the distance. "They're changing clothes, getting a different car, and waiting for dark."

Walker dreaded the answer to the next question. "And what are we going to do?"

"Pretty much the same thing: wait for dark."

Walker put his hands in his pockets and kept going in silence. Stillman looked at him and a small smile came to his lips. "Don't worry," he said. "If we're right about this, there are two addresses they'll have to hit in order to win. If they decide to go to Scully's first, the cops will move in and snap them up."

"That's not what you're hoping for, is it?" said Walker.

Stillman shook his head. "No."

"You're hoping they'll pick the other place," Walker said. "What you want to do is spot them somehow, and let them lead us to the other dead man's house."

Stillman beamed and patted Walker on the shoulder. "It's not something to be glum about. If they actually get into the house and start searching, all we have to do is call the cops. Even if every single thing went wrong, and we couldn't get the cops, we could sit and wait.

As soon as they finish that house, they'll still have to go to Scully's. The cops will put them in a bag."

For the next few minutes, Walker's mind kept producing questions, then answering them for itself. What if the chief was wrong, and the two men had not recognized him and Stillman? Then they would break into the houses as planned, and probably be less cautious about it. What if they had come to Coulter for some other purpose that he and Stillman had not thought of? Then they would proceed with it—whatever it was—and Walker and Stillman might catch them at it. What if the two men had seen not only Stillman and Walker but also the police? Then they would either risk an attempt to hit the houses anyway, or they would stay away. No matter which choice they made, nothing would be lost if Walker and Stillman waited.

At Oak Street, Walker turned toward Main, but Stillman said, "Keep going this way."

"The car is up the other way."

"Yeah," said Stillman. "I don't want to move the car just yet. It's been there long enough so people will be used to it, and moving it attracts attention."

"Attention?" Walker's eyes narrowed as he looked at Stillman. "Are you trying to keep those two guys from seeing us—or the police?"

"By now the chief might have noticed that we're gone," said Stillman. "He might say, 'Good riddance,' or he might want to keep us where he can reach us so we can identify those two guys. But if he has us sitting in the station, then the opposition gets what it wants: we're on the sidelines until it's all over. You know what we need?"

"A lawyer?"

"No," said Stillman. "A place where we can be out of sight for a while, and still be able to see what's going on."

"Too bad it's not Sunday," said Walker.

"What do you mean?"

"The church would be open. There used to be a couple of them that looked like that where I grew up. They usually have a way up into the steeple."

Stillman said nothing, but Walker saw that his eyes rose and he craned his neck to see the church steeple through the treetops, and when he reached the next corner, he turned his steps toward Main Street. He kept going until he was at the rear of the church. There was a small door up a pair of stone slabs that served as steps, but when he tried to turn the handle, it didn't budge. He muttered, "That's not what I was hoping for. I thought the damned things were always unlocked."

"I don't think anybody rushes in to ask for sanctuary anymore," said Walker. "I'll go around and check the front."

He stepped to the corner of the building, looked up and down for police cars, then ventured the few steps to the front door. He tested the big brass handle and found it unlocked. As he turned to go back for Stillman, he saw that Stillman was already at the corner of the building. Stillman stepped across the lawn, and they were in.

Walker quietly closed the door. They stood motionless in the small foyer and listened. There was a hollowness in the old wooden building that was audible, as though the air in the big empty spaces had a sound of its own. Walker could hear muffled noises from outside—cars passing on Main Street once a minute—but he heard no sound from within.

He took a step and heard the wooden floor creak, then waited without moving for a response, but none came. He took three more steps and was under the wide portal into the sanctuary. The style of the place seemed to him to proclaim its age. The plain, dark, close-grained wood of the pews seemed to have been made of boards two feet wide. There was a pulpit raised slightly on a wooden platform, and beside it on the wall of the plain, shallow nave were two huge high-backed chairs, but there was little adornment. He turned and looked up. There was a balcony at the rear of the sanctuary, probably for a choir. He looked for stained-glass pictures on the windows, but the panes were simply divided into lozenge-shaped patterns of stained glass on the lower half, with thick, clear glass at the tops to let in light.

He returned to the entry to find Stillman looking at him inquiringly. "Nobody's here," Walker whispered, then wondered why he needed to.

Stillman spoke only a bit more loudly. "I found the way up. It's in the cloak room." He led Walker into a tiny room at the side with only one small window. Above the coat racks rose a series of varnished wooden slats attached to the wall. Walker's eyes followed them to the ceiling, where there was a recessed square that had to be an access hatch.

Walker stared at it skeptically. "This was my idea, wasn't it?" He sighed. "Maybe you'd better stay down here and try to break my fall if it gives way."

"Deal," said Stillman.

Walker climbed the first few feet easily, but as he rose higher, the reasons why this was not a practical idea began to enter his mind insistently. Climbing the bell tower of somebody else's church seemed to him to go beyond the level of merely presumptuous tourist behavior. It had the feeling of blasphemous intrusion. But climbing the first few rungs of a ladder in front of Stillman had a quality of irreversibility. Without some compelling reason, it was difficult to simply stop and begin feeling for lower rungs with his toes. He kept his eyes on the ceiling and climbed.

When he came to the top, he pushed up on the wooden hatch cover, half-hoping the compelling reason would come in the form of a cover nailed in place. But the cover rose smoothly. He lifted it aside and stuck his head through the opening. The atmosphere smelled of years of dust. It was dim, but not completely dark, so he could make out some shapes. The floor on this level was the same plain hardwood as the floor below, but it had been left rough-cut, not sanded or varnished. The walls were bare wood with studs and crosspieces showing. As his eyes adjusted, he saw that there was another set of rungs nailed between two studs, leading upward. He pulled himself up onto the floor, looked down, and beckoned to Stillman.

He waited until he saw Stillman's face and shoulders ascending toward him, then stepped out of the way. Stillman had to shrug to squeeze his shoulders through the opening, then raised his arms and lifted himself the rest of the way. Walker set the hatch cover back over the opening.

Stillman looked around until he saw the ladder, then said, "Going up?"

Walker repeated his climb to the next level. There was no hatch covering the opening above him, and he could see that the hatchway and a small hole near it were the source of the light. The walls above seemed to be golden with glowing horizontal stripes. When his head rose through the opening, he understood. The top level was the belfry. In the center was a heavy, tarnished brass bell suspended from a steel rod. The small speck of light he had seen from below was the hole for the bellpull. He could not recall seeing a hole in the ceiling in the foyer of the church, but he supposed there must have once been one.

The four walls of the belfry had panels of louvers, probably to keep the bell's peal from being muffled. Most of the light was coming from the louvered opening on the western side, where the late-afternoon sun was moving lower. The louvers were an arrangement he liked instantly: the level he had just left had been oppressively hot, but up here he could feel a cool, steady breeze. He moved close to the south wall to peer down through the louvers, and found that the church roof blocked the foreground but he could see the streets beyond.

"This is perfect." It was Stillman's voice behind him. Stillman pulled himself up and stood on the east side of the belfry, raising and lowering his head to look between different slats of the louver. "You can see most of the town from here." He turned to look at Walker. "Whatever you do, don't bump into that bell."

Walker bent and looked upward under the rim of the bell. "The clapper's gone. They must have taken it out when they stopped using it."

Stillman sidestepped from one panel to the next, moving around the belfry, peering out at the sights below. When he stopped, he said urgently, "There!"

Walker stepped away from the bell and moved his face to the opening. He could see the flat squares that were roofs of the old buildings along Main Street, the tops of big trees just below the belfry. Beyond were the pitched roofs of houses in neat rows on either side of each gray strip of concrete. To the west he could see the winding course of the tan riverbed, with the black ribbon of water in the middle. "What is it I'm looking at?"

"They're on this side now," said Stillman.

Walker moved to the next panel, where Stillman was. He could see the tops of black-and-white police cars. There were four of them, slowly scuttling along the grooves below the treetops that were the streets west of the police station. When a car reached the end of a residential street at New Hampshire, it would turn west for a block and go up the next one until it reached Coulter, then turn west and go down another block. "At least they're not giving up," said Walker.

Stillman was already shading his eyes with both hands and staring into the distance to the west. "Damn. You can't see the old covered bridge from here, because the woods are in the way. Probably too far anyway. If they had only gone down there and blocked it off when I told them to, this would already be over."

"Why do you suppose they didn't?" asked Walker.

"Inconvenience. That's what it always is."

"It doesn't look that hard."

"Not to do it," Stillman said. "To take the heat for having done it. People who want to drive to the next town to rent a movie have to wait an extra minute while a cop stares into their back seat."

Walker watched him for a moment as he stepped from that panel to the next, always looking down. "Is that what made you quit the police force—local politics?"

"What makes anybody not quit?" said Stillman. "The job stinks. Low pay, long hours, and now and then you get to have a wrestling match with a mean drunk."

"Did something happen?"

Stillman glanced at him. "Yeah, a lot happened. What did you have in mind?"

"The captain in Miami seemed to think maybe there was something you did that didn't get made public."

Stillman shook his head. "No, there wasn't anything like that. It was wrong for my temperament, so I made a career change."

"Not much of one."

Stillman shrugged. "I was thirty years old. What I had learned was how to fire a sidearm, come out of a street fight better off than the other guy, and drive a car fast. What was I going to be—secretary of state? I had a little practical experience in tickling the law-enforcement establishment to get them to do what I wanted, and had made a few acquaintances who had other useful skills."

"What's the difference? Is it just money?"

Stillman shook his head. "No. The difference is, if the phone rings and somebody wants me to do something, I can say no and hang up." He stared at Walker for a moment. "And if somebody asks a question I don't want to answer, I don't." He turned away again and looked out between the slats.

Walker moved away from him to the northwest corner. He shaded his eyes and squinted to the west along Main Street, past the river and across the open fields to the woods that hid the covered bridge, and to the row of hills beyond. The sun was low now and had a blinding glare, like a fire that burned brightest yellow just as it was consuming the last of its fuel. That was the direction where the two men had almost certainly gone, and was probably the direction from which they would return. But after a time, the low angle of the sun made it too painful to look to the west, and he turned to the north.

He stared down at the quiet residential streets on the other side of Main. He picked out Birch Street, where James Scully had lived, then the block, and, finally, from his memory of the morning when he had searched for it, the very house. The old trees threw long shadows and made the green of the lawns deep and soothing to his eyes, so he devoted himself to Birch Street, staring closely into each of the yards, trying to detect the policemen who had been assigned to watch Scully's house. He moved on, but kept returning to that block during the next hours. He did not see any uniformed men crouching there, or any movement or change that would have signaled their presence. He looked at the plain rectangular box of New Mill Systems, and tried to pick out each car in the lot on the unlikely chance that the two men had parked their rental car among the herd and gone to wait in the woods.

Stillman had lapsed into a long silence, still moving from panel to panel according to an unpredictable schedule. He would spend fifteen minutes at one, then just a minute at another. When he spoke, his voice was calm and quiet. "What do you see?"

"Not a whole lot," Walker answered. "There doesn't seem to be much going on anymore. How about you?"

"They did a pretty good sweep for an hour or so after we got up here. Since then, it's been a lot more subtle. They've got three patrol cars on the road instead of the usual two, but there seem to be a few cops walking around in plain clothes trying to look inconspicuous." He pointed at the louvered panel in front of him. "See? There's one."

Walker moved to the panel and looked down, standing tall to achieve the proper angle. There was a man in a sport coat walking along Main. He turned into the drugstore. "He's a cop?"

Stillman said, "Either he's checking in with a radio or he's making calls on a cell phone every five minutes that last three seconds each."

They kept watching as the sun sank below the three hills and the steady breeze began to turn cool. The foot traffic on Main Street thinned, and Walker saw some of the shop proprietors come out, close their doors and lock them, then walk up Main and turn onto the residential streets on both sides.

At eight the street lamps flickered once or twice, then came on steadily. By then, the windows of the businesses that sold food or drinks were the only ones that had not gone dark. The belfry was high above any source of artificial light, and it had fallen into deeper darkness than the rest of the town. After some time, Stillman held his wrist close to his face, leaned toward the louvered panel, and stared at his watch. "Time to go. Watch your step on the way down. It's hard to see."

They climbed down the ladder to the second level, where there was no opening and the darkness seemed nearly total. Walker had to feel around the floor to find the hatch cover. When he had, he lifted it up carefully and listened for a few seconds before he whispered to Stillman, "You first."

Walker heard rustling sounds while Stillman was going down through the opening, then the soft shuffle of his feet on the rungs. When Walker heard Stillman's shoes creaking the floorboards of the cloak room, he started down after him. The moment his head had cleared the opening he began to feel a bit better. The air was cooler, and there was a dim glow through the open doorway of the cloak room, the faint filtered light from the sanctuary windows reflected off the white walls. He carefully replaced the hatch cover and descended to Stillman's side.

They did not speak again until they were outside the building, moving in the shadow of the wall toward Constitution Avenue. Stillman said, "If those guys go to Scully's first, we're out of luck. The cops will get them. We have to hope they go to the other house first. We'll wait down by the river, near the entrance to town, where we can see them coming and follow on foot."

They turned at Constitution Avenue and walked purposefully toward the river. They would slow down as they came to each intersection, then turn so they could cross the street in the middle of the block, where the street lamps could not reveal them. When they reached Franklin Street they could see the bright lights in the windows of the Old Mill Restaurant reflected on the black surface of the river.

When they were on Washington, nearly to the spot where Main Street narrowed to cross the short bridge, Stillman tapped Walker's arm and they scrambled down the steep bank to the edge of the water, where they were in deep shadow again. Walker found a broad, flat rock on the dry riverbed. When he sat down, Stillman came to sit beside him, facing the town. Walker said, "Why are you sitting like that?"

"Because I have full confidence that you're capable of seeing a car coming toward you with its headlights on. This way I can see what's coming up behind us."

While they waited, Walker watched each car that came into town. He would see the glow of headlights appear beyond the fields, bright dots that flickered now and then as they passed behind the trunks of trees. He would stare behind the lights, trying to discern the shape of the vehicle in profile before it reached the bend in the road and the headlights turned to aim at him as it crossed the unused farmland. When it came closer, he would duck down so the light skin of his face would not make him visible, and he would listen to the deepening pitch of the engine noise until he heard a bump. That was the front tires hitting the slight seam where the road met the bridge. From then on, the car's headlights were aimed above him and to his right, and for two seconds he could see the car and its occupants clearly illuminated by the street lamps of Main Street.

In the first hour, he estimated that he had seen a dozen cars arriving. Some of the cars had women and children, some solitary men, but each face had presented itself to him as the cars crossed the bridge. It was nearly ten-thirty now, and the numbers had tapered off. He began to sense that the road would soon be deserted until the two men arrived to commit their burglaries.

Then he saw a car that seemed different. It had come out of the woods that hid the covered bridge like the others, then made the turn toward town. It was going across the fields past the two barns when he put his head down to protect his invisibility. He identified the difference by sound. This one was not traveling at the usual constant speed. It would accelerate briefly, then coast until it had slowed considerably, not quite stopping, then accelerate again.

He nudged Stillman without raising his head. "This car is different. It keeps slowing down."

Stillman turned and watched the headlights, then ducked down too. "He's looking for something. Get ready."

They both turned their bodies away from the bridge. The car grew louder and the headlights brighter. Walker heard the bump, looked over his shoulder to stare through the car's windshield, and stood up quickly. The driver was Mary Catherine Casey.

36

Walker was up out of the riverbed and dashing across Washington Street before he had acknowledged the need to make a decision. He sprinted to the corner of Main, trying to reach it in time to see where the car was going. He forced his legs to slow his pace to a fast walk as soon as he was in the pool of light cast by the street lamp at the corner. He stared up Main, and saw the pair of red taillights moving away. Mary was going at a tantalizingly slow speed, but she was pulling farther and farther away every second.

He was almost sure he knew where Mary was going to stop. She would come to the spot on Main where Stillman had parked the Explorer, and recognize it. She would park there and then begin to search for Walker and Stillman. He turned up Constitution, where there was less chance he would be seen, and ran after her. As he ran, he wondered what she was doing here. He had expected her to be in Concord for at least a couple of days. She must have returned to Keene, not seen the Explorer in the hotel lot, and come looking.

He turned up Grant Street, then turned again onto Main and saw her. She was wearing jeans, a red short-sleeved top, and sneakers. At first she seemed not to recognize him. Her body turned to the side with the knees slightly bent and her weight on her toes, as though she was deciding whether to run back to her car. Then she visibly relaxed. He saw her take a deep breath and blow it out, then step off and trot toward him.

When they came together, he put his arms around her, but she pushed him away impatiently. "Where's Stillman?"

"Back there by the bridge. Why?"

She glanced toward the Explorer. "Please tell me you've got the keys to this thing."

"I don't. Stillman drove."

"Then come on." She took a step toward the driver's side of her car, then stopped and held out the keys. "Drive to where he is."

Walker took the keys, started the car, and headed up the street to the next corner and turned right. "What's wrong?" he asked.

"I'm not sure it's anything serious, now that I've found you," she said. "But there's potential."

"Why? What happened?"

"When I got back from Concord, I went to my hotel, changed, and called you. You didn't answer, so I walked over to your hotel and sneaked into your room, just like before." She looked at him, and her eyes were wide. "Somebody else has been in your room."

"How do you know?"

"It's a mess. The bed is all torn up, the suitcase dumped on the floor, and all the pockets of your clothes turned out. I went to Stillman's room, and his is worse. Somebody knows you're here, and they know where you're staying."

"Is there any chance that they saw you?"

"It's possible, but if they did, they don't know I've got anything to do with you. I went in through the restaurant. On the way out, I was spooked, so I made some very strange detours. I even took a quick stroll through the Colony Mill Mall to be sure nobody could follow me."

He looked at her, concerned. "Would you be able to tell?"

"Of course I would," she said. "I was a southern California mall rat. What do you think teenaged girls are doing in those places? They're trying to get somebody to follow them."

Walker drove down Washington and parked in a spot far from the street lamps.

Mary jerked her head one way, then the other, her eyes impatient and troubled. "Where is he?"

"He's down there in the riverbed. We were waiting for those two guys to show up when you came along."

"What two—" She stopped herself. "No. Don't answer now. Let's just go get him." She slipped out of the seat and hurried around the back of the car. As she stepped into the street, he was surprised to feel her small, thin fingers around his. She tugged his hand and hurried him across the pavement and down the rocky bank until they were on the dry, pebbly ground beside the water. Then her fingers slipped from his and she surged ahead, nearly lost to sight in the shadowy darkness beside the high bank, where the lights of the town did not reach her.

Walker followed, planting his feet carefully while he watched the distant spot beyond the fields where the headlights always appeared first. Every few seconds he would turn his eyes away from it to the right, to check the end of Washington Street and the short slice of Main Street that he could see from here.

In a moment, Mary had found Stillman. They were crouched low beside the big rock where Walker had been sitting, and Mary was whispering with animated gestures. Walker came close and knelt on the pebbles beside Mary.

Stillman turned his head toward Walker. "Did you hear those guys found our hotel?"

"Yes," said Walker. "I don't know how they did it."

"It's the biggest hotel in the biggest town around here," said Stillman. "It's where I'd look first. It's a good thing we didn't move before Serena left for Concord. This gives us a little edge we didn't have before."

"Edge?" said Mary. "What edge?"

"If they've looked at everything in our rooms, they know we haven't found a damned thing yet."

Mary blew out a breath and shook her head. "If that's your idea of an edge, it's pitiful."

"It will have to do," said Stillman. "The fact that we've got nothing will convince them that pulling the break-ins won't be a waste of time. Whether they knew it at the time or not, searching our rooms means they can't change their minds. They've made it pretty hard for us not to know they're around. If they're going to do it, tonight's the night."

Mary said, "Is that what you're sitting in this ditch for? You're waiting for some men to come here and pull a burglary?"

"Actually," said Walker quietly, "it's two."

"Men or burglaries?"

"Both."

"How does that help you?"

"The houses they're going to break into belong to James Scully and the other man who was with him in Florida. When they go there, we'll know who he was."

"Terrific," said Mary. "Then we can get out of here now."

"You found him?" asked Stillman. "You know who the second man was?"

"Why do you think I came back from Concord?" she said. "I found what I wanted to know. Come on. I'll tell you about it while we're driving back to Keene." She popped up and took a step, but Stillman's hand shot out and grabbed her arm.

"Wait," he said. "Tell us now."

She reached across her chest and plucked his hand from her arm. "Myra Sanderidge helped me make a family tree for James Scully. His father was Thomas Scully, and his mother was Mary Holbrooke. Thomas had two siblings and Mary had eight siblings, but they don't matter, because the connection has to be two generations back—the grandparents. Like everybody else, James Scully had four of them. His paternal grandmother and maternal grandfather were only children. His maternal grandmother had two brothers. One was killed in an accident without getting married, and the other had two daughters. One died at sixteen, and the other lived eighty-two years without getting married. So it's his paternal grandfather that's the connection. He had a sister named Amanda Scully, whose married name was Bowles. She had two daughters, both of whom had girls, and one son, whose name was Philip. And Philip has one son named Gerald."

Stillman leaned toward Walker. "Did you follow any of that?"

"I'm afraid not," Walker admitted apologetically. His eyes were on Mary.

She sighed, giving out a quick, angry huff of air. "The only near male relative who is not a first cousin or closer, and who was born thirty-some years ago, was Gerald Bowles."

Stillman stood and began patting his pockets. "He's on the list."

"What list?" asked Mary.

Walker said, "He made a list of adult males in Coulter, and whittled it down to the possibles—not accounted for, not answering their phones, and so on—and—"

Stillman said, "Can't see in this light," and climbed along the edge of the riverbed. He stepped quickly across Washington Street and stopped to unfold a sheaf of papers. He stared at one sheet, then moved to the second. He leaned to catch a bit of the light from the street lamp, then folded the papers again. "It's 302 Maple Street."

Mary moved toward her car. "Either drive or hand over the keys."

Walker held out her car keys. "We'll meet you at your hotel as soon as this is over. I can't leave him to do this alone."

"What are you talking about?" she asked. "I was just offering to drive to Maple Street."

Stillman said to Mary, "Serena, I don't want you here."

"You don't have a way to get rid of me without attracting attention."

Stillman stared at her intently for a moment, then sighed. "If you're coming, then come." As he took his first step, he said, "Leave the car. If things go wrong, we'll all know where it is." He set off up Washington Street.

He passed Constitution and kept going until he reached Federal, then turned east on a course parallel with Main. Walker studied the houses along Federal. They were about the same as the ones on Constitution, mostly center-entrance colonials that had been heavily refurbished and remodeled, but a few were nineteenth-century red-brick houses that probably had been replacements for vanished originals. At each step, he looked for heads in windows, lights that illuminated too much of the sidewalk, or pedestrians. But everyone seemed to have gone indoors hours ago, and many of them were probably asleep.

At Grant Street, Stillman stopped and whispered, "Here's how we do it. Serena, you find yourself a spot on Maple Street that's out of sight a block or so down from 302 on the Main Street side. If you see a car come along with two men in it, or you see two men on foot, you signal Walker with this." He took a small flashlight from his pocket and placed it in her hand. "Once you signal him, slip away, get back to your car. If we're not there in ten minutes, head for Keene."

She looked at him suspiciously. "Is this just a way to get rid of me?"

"No," he said. "It's a way to make you useful. The police are looking for strange men prowling around town, and you're the only one who doesn't fit the description."

He turned to Walker. "You find a spot right near the front door where you can see it if she turns on the flashlight. Keep an eye on her hiding place. If you see the light, come get me."

"What are you going to be doing?" asked Serena.

"I'll just be taking a look around in the house," said Stillman. "Let's go."

"But that's . . ." She let her voice trail off as she followed Stillman up the street.

Stillman didn't speak again until they reached Maple. He stopped at the corner and stared along the quiet, tree-lined street for several seconds, then turned. "Okay. It's down there about half a block. No mistakes, and no delays. We know those guys are on their way. Serena, go."

Walker felt there was something terribly wrong as he watched Mary's small, thin shape moving off down the sidewalk alone. Stillman seemed to read his thoughts. "She's going to be safer than you are. She's not pulling a burglary."

They set off when Mary was a hundred yards ahead. Walker kept his eyes on her until she seemed to be no more than a small variation in the shadows, and he would lose her occasionally, then find her again just because he knew how much space she would have traversed in

that time. Then Walker caught a glimpse of her gliding up the front
lawn of a house with dark windows. When she reached a thick, flow-
ering bush, she was gone.

He turned his attention to Stillman, who was walking along beside
him, studying each house they passed. When he spotted the right one
ahead, Walker saw him slow down and study it as he came closer.
Number 302 was a narrow Civil War–era brick rectangle with three
stories that stood out a bit from the older ones near it. The house reminded Walker a little of a New York brownstone. He moved cautiously to a place near the front steps where he could see Mary's hiding
place, then crouched lower to lose himself among the shrubs along the
front wall. Stillman nodded and moved silently along the side of the
building.

Walker had seen Stillman work often enough that he could imagine exactly what he was doing: he would move along the side, stopping to examine each window, then continue to the back of the house,
looking for a door lock he could pick or a window he could jimmy.

As time passed and Walker began to feel himself alone on the dark,
silent street, his senses seemed to magnify each sight and amplify each
sound. His eyes passed across the front door, where there was an old
handle that had tarnished and darkened, and a shiny new brass key re-
ceptacle for a dead bolt. He wondered if Stillman had seen it and admitted defeat, or had simply not wanted to fiddle with a lock where he
was visible from the street. He sighted along the foundation of the
building looking for basement windows, but he saw none. He heard a
noise. It was sharp and metallic, like the snapping of a latch. It took
him a second to realize that it had come from above. He quickly
moved around the corner of the house, pressed his belly against the
smooth, old-fashioned bricks, leaned to bring one eye back to the corner, and craned his neck to look up.

This time there was a quiet scraping noise. A window was opening. Could Stillman have gotten up there so quickly? There was a long
silence. Walker held his breath and stayed motionless. He saw a man's
head slowly emerge from the open window, facing down at the spot
by the steps where he had been crouching. It wasn't Stillman. Walker
pulled back, then forced himself to look again. The head came out a

bit farther, so the shoulders were visible. There was a movement, and the right arm swung down, holding a long, dark club-shaped object— a flashlight. The bright beam came on, made a few jerky movements on the shrubs by the steps, and Walker pulled his head back from the corner. He saw the beam go past the front of the building to his left, then retreat. Walker looked again in time to see the man withdrawing his torso into the house. As the arm bent to bring the flashlight inside, the hand turned it off, but not before Walker had seen the dark blue shirt and the glint of the badge. The window slid shut.

Walker whirled and hurried along the side of the building as quickly as he could. He stepped around the corner at the back of the house and saw Stillman kneeling at a kitchen door, his face close to the lock. When Walker took his second step, Stillman popped up and faced him.

"What's up?" he whispered. "Did she signal?"

"I just saw a man in the second-floor window. He was a cop."

"Damn," whispered Stillman. "They're staking this place out too."

"Yeah," Walker hissed. "But how? We didn't know who the second man was. We never told them there was a second man."

Even in the dim light, Walker could see Stillman's eyes narrow. "Get Serena to her car. It's time to get out."

37

Walker made his way across the yard behind Gerald Bowles's house, staying close to the rear wall so that a policeman at an upper window would have to lean out in order to see him.

He did not hear a window opening, so he moved to the next yard. It was a colonial house, but the back had been opened up a bit to accommodate a pair of French doors leading onto the patio. He could see into a dining room that had been decorated in an eighteenth-century style, with bright red walls and framed pictures in rows that went from just below the fourteen-foot ceiling nearly to knee level, a table with gracefully curved legs, and a huge sideboard. At the far end of the room he could see a narrow doorway that led down a corridor into the kitchen. There was a young woman in a green sweater, her shining blond hair pulled tight into a short ponytail. She turned to a counter, lowered her eyes, and poured two cans of cola into glasses. Walker slipped across the French doors and into the darkness beyond.

The next three houses had lighted windows too, but they were all smaller and higher, so he was able to crouch and move under them without slowing his pace. The fifth house was dark, so he turned and trotted down its driveway to Maple Street. He glanced back up toward Gerald Bowles's house, but he could see no sign of the policemen inside, and the angle had become oblique enough so that the upper windows were less threatening. He hurried to a spot where the shadows on the pavement were deep, and rushed across to the other side.

He moved to the bush where he had last seen Mary, but she was not there. He whirled, staring frantically to all sides, then heard a low, breathy whistle, and followed it to the next house. She was up on the front porch, crouching behind the balustrade. He moved toward her, and she came down to meet him. He took her arm and hurried her toward the far side of the house, leaning close to whisper, "There are cops inside the house."

She whispered back, "That's a relief. I saw Stillman come out of a yard a block away and leave, and I didn't know what to do."

Walker kept scanning the street, now and then glancing back at the Bowles house to reassure himself that he was not taking Mary into a spot that was easily visible from the upper windows. When they had gone around the house to the back yard, he stopped and pointed. "The next street this way is Constitution. We've been up and down it a couple of times without seeing anybody."

Mary moved across the next few back yards with him until they emerged beside one that faced Constitution Avenue. Walker stepped out onto the driveway and stood still for a moment, staring up the street toward the police station, then down toward the river. There seemed to be no cars out this late on the residential streets, and it had been at least two hours since he had seen his last pedestrian. He beckoned to Mary, then waited for her on the sidewalk.

When they had walked in silence for a block, he said quietly, "We don't know what's going on. We knew the police were putting a team at Scully's house, but not this one."

Mary looked at him in amazement. "You talked to the police, and then decided to pull a burglary?"

"It's not what we had planned," said Walker. "I guess that's what's been wrong since the beginning. We don't have a strategy. We just react. Something bad happens, and we fall all over ourselves to get into the middle of it as fast as we can."

He walked on a few paces. "We saw two men here, going into the coffee shop on Main. They were the same two who cornered us in an alley in Pasadena. We figured—or Stillman did—that they must be here for the same reason we were: to look for evidence that would connect them to Scully and the other dead man, who turned out to be Bowles. So we tried to get the police to arrest them. When the cops tried and the two men didn't turn up right away, Stillman mentioned that they were here to break into Scully's house. The police chief said he'd put cops there to catch them at it."

"It seems as though you don't have much to complain about," she said. "They're doing more than you asked them to."

"That's the problem," Walker said. "We didn't know about Bowles until you told us. How did they?"

They were coming up to Grant Street. Walker moved ahead, looked to the left, then the right, and froze. A man was turning off Main Street onto the sidewalk on Grant. As he moved away from the bright lights, he broke into a run. He was coming toward them.

Walker said quietly, "Try to look normal. If he's okay, he'll go past us on Grant. If he's not, run for your car."

He stepped off the curb to cross the street, his arm around Mary's waist as though they were simply a couple out walking on a summer night, but Walker kept the man in the corner of his eye.

Mary said, "If I run, what are you going to do?"

Walker didn't answer. He took a couple of deep breaths and looked at the next hundred feet of Constitution Avenue to pick the best spot to turn and fight, then looked back at Grant Street.

The man passed under the street lamp at the intersection, and Mary said, "Stillman."

They stopped and Stillman trotted up to them, breathing heavily. "Glad I caught up with you," he said. "The Explorer's gone."

"Gone? How can it be?" said Mary. "It was there when I drove into town. That can't have been a half hour ago."

Stillman's breathing was already slowing. "Well, it's sure as hell gone now. This would have been a hard place to steal a car today, so I'd say it's been towed. I'd call the cops and ask, but my cell phone was locked in the glove compartment."

"I don't remember any 'No Parking' signs," said Mary. "I remember looking, because I was going to—"

"It doesn't matter," Stillman interrupted. "We'll just use your car

and get out of here." But Walker could tell that Stillman had concluded that it did matter.

They walked more quickly for the next block. Stillman was silent,
but he seemed to be much more cautious than he had been earlier, and
his face was grim. He would halt the others long before each intersection, then slowly move ahead while they waited. When he was still
partially hidden by the corner house or its hedges, he would survey the
cross street, peer up it toward Main, and then hurry across, not paus-
ing to let Walker and Mary catch up until he was on the next dim
stretch of sidewalk.

The second time he did it, Mary said to him, "When you went to
the police station, whom did you talk to?"

"There were two rank-and-file cops and the chief of police," said
Stillman. "Look, don't let your imagination run away with you. The
cops in a town this size could hardly not know a guy like Scully, and
probably anybody who would hang out with him. If they heard he was
killed, they would naturally look for the other guy."

"So why didn't they tell us?" asked Walker.

"Why should they?" said Stillman.

Mary said, "Did you pick up any of their names?"

"Who?"

"The cops."

Stillman was distracted, concentrating on the sights around him
and the sounds on Main Street. "Uh . . . Raines. That was the chief."

Walker said, "Another one was called Elton. And Carlyle. I remember hearing the name and wondering if he was related to the people who own the clothing store on Main."

"Great," Mary whispered to herself. "Just great."

"What?" asked Walker.

She shook her head. "It's nothing. This place is just giving me the
creeps."

Stillman turned to look into her eyes. "Anything I don't know
about?"

"It's probably just me," she said. "I spent a whole day in Concord
reading old records and having Jonathan Tooker's tall tales rattling
around in my brain." She walked on. "When I was doing Scully's

family tree, Myra kept bringing me all the papers she could find that came from Coulter. About twenty names kept popping up over and over. Coulter was a family name. And there were Scully, Holbrooke, Bowles, Ames, Derby, Perkins, Griggs, Starke, Fairweather, Gates . . ." Her voice subsided.

"And?"

"Elton, Carlyle, and Raines," she said reluctantly. "They're all related to each other in six or seven ways by now. For all I know, if we did a blood test on the police chief, his DNA would be closer to Scully's than Bowles's is."

"Let's not scare ourselves," said Stillman. "You could probably say the same in any small town east of the Appalachians. And in small towns, the police know who a man's friends are. That's probably the reason they knew enough to check Bowles's house. Anyway, they're doing it, so there's nothing more we can do here except get into trouble."

They were all silent as they reached Adams Street. Walker noticed that Stillman was making his precautions even more elaborate now. He did not cross Adams until he had stood and watched for at least thirty seconds.

When they caught up with him again, he was waiting beside a tree on the lawn of a dark house. Walker whispered, "Did you see something?"

"Not see," said Stillman. "Feel. Maybe it's just listening to Serena. What do you say we cut through a couple of back yards and pop out beside the car?"

"Sounds good to me," said Walker. They moved to the space between two houses and turned to go across the back. The houses closer to the river seemed to be older, and the spaces between them larger. They moved through the next three yards; then Walker caught a glimpse of the street and recognized the spot. He said, "I've got the keys. Wait for me. When you hear the car engine start, you'll know it's okay."

He slipped silently along the grassy side of the house. He could see a few of the lights in the windows of the Old Mill Restaurant across the river, and now he picked up faint voices floating across from its parking lot. It seemed terribly distant and unreachable, like a place in a painting. He moved closer to Washington Street, and now he could tell that the voices weren't coming from the restaurant. They seemed nearer. He reached the corner of the last house, bent low, and moved forward to get a view of Washington Street. Mary's car was gone.

38

Stillman and Mary followed Walker along the side of the house toward the front and looked out onto Washington Street. They could see the lighted windows of the Old Mill Restaurant across the river. Stillman slowly, cautiously sidestepped farther out, his back still to the clapboard siding, and peered up the street and along the banks of the river to the south.

Mary moved up beside Walker. "Why would they tow my car?"

But Stillman said, "Look at that." He pointed and they looked to see the men walking along the riverbed. "Five lights," he said. There were two wide-beamed spotlights that shone ahead of the men on the pebbly shoreline, two that played along the opposite bank, and one that swept methodically back and forth on the surface of the water. The lights on the ground ahead made the men's dark silhouettes stand out clearly. There were six walking abreast, and each carried what appeared to be a short-barreled pump shotgun like the ones police used.

Stillman leaned out farther and craned his neck, then pulled back to let the others see. There were lights from a second group of men about the same size moving away from them in the opposite direction. Stillman stepped back along the side of the house a few feet and leaned close to whisper.

"That's probably why they towed the car," he said. "They seem to think those fellows are hiding along the river. They may even think it's their car. It's possible somebody saw the two of us down there and called the cops."

"Wait," said Walker. He was staring over Stillman's shoulder at the Old Mill Restaurant. A dark blue van had pulled over the bridge and into the parking lot. Two uniformed policemen climbed out and walked into the restaurant.

Behind the windows, they could see that there was some kind of commotion going on. People were standing up from their tables. Others passed quickly across a window, as though they were getting out of the way. A police patrol car crossed the bridge and parked at an angle by the van, and two more cops hurried inside.

After a few minutes, the door of the restaurant swung open, and people began to appear. There were a pair of policemen, then a waiter, who pushed through the door and held it open. The two cops went to the van. One slid the side door open while the other climbed up into the driver's seat.

The next one out was a man in a plaid short-sleeved shirt wearing handcuffs that kept his arms behind him and made walking awkward. Behind him was a policeman gripping his biceps. Walker said, "He's not one of them. They got the wrong guy. He's just a tourist. I saw him at lunch today with his wife and kids."

The next one out was the wife, and she was handcuffed too. Walker waited in dread. When he had seen them earlier, they'd had two children with them. But none of the next three prisoners were children. There was an elderly couple, and a man who had a fishing hat that looked as though it had been placed on his head by somebody else.

Walker waited for the two children to appear, but the waiter who had been holding the door open went back into the restaurant and swung it shut behind him. Walker didn't quite dare feel relief. The five prisoners were moving their heads and opening their mouths as though they were talking loudly, but Walker could not hear what they were saying. The young mother appeared to be the most angry. As the policemen pushed the others into the van, she pivoted to face one of the cops. She stood straight with her shoulders back, and Walker could see from the way she held her head up to look down her nose at the cop that what she was saying was not calculated to make him happy.

The cop finished guiding the older man into the opening of the van, then turned to reach for the woman's arm, as he had done with the others. She twisted her body angrily to pull the arm out of his reach, but the cop seemed to have been waiting for this. He extended his reach, spun her body around, and gripped her hair from behind. He jerked her head back and dragged her to the van. Instead of stopping at the side door as he had done before, he stepped up into the van without letting her go. Walker could see her legs working quickly to keep up with him, then to push herself up into the van to stop the pain. The feet slid inward on the floor, and one of the cops from the patrol car pushed the door shut and banged the side of the van twice before he went back to join his partner.

The van pulled forward, swung around in a wide circle and out of the parking lot, crossed the bridge onto Main Street with the patrol car behind it, then was lost to sight behind the buildings.

Walker whispered, "They're tourists. How can the police think they have anything to do with this?"

Mary said softly, "What if they're looking for us?"

"We're just witnesses. I don't think they'd look this hard for witnesses," Stillman said. "Besides, they've seen us. Two of us, anyway. They know what we look like. Nobody's going to mistake that girl down there for Max Stillman."

"Then what are they doing?" asked Mary.

"Probably something happened in the restaurant," said Stillman. "A fight in the bar or something. If you're looking for two men, you don't arrest four and throw in a girl for equal-opportunity purposes."

"You mind if we get away from the river?" said Walker. "Everything seems to be going on down here."

"Hold on a little longer," Stillman said. "If you're not where everything's going on, you won't know what it is."

They crouched between the two houses, watching. After the disturbance at the Old Mill, the night subsided into quiet again. Walker could hear frogs peeping somewhere in the shallows on the other side of the river. The men who had been walking the banks with flashlights had long ago moved beyond his sight, and had not returned. Time passed, and its passage was soothing, making the shock and alarm of the scene outside the restaurant slowly diminish. He sat down beside Mary near the back of the house, and after a time she leaned on his chest and burrowed to place his arm over her shoulder. She whispered, "Walker, are you scared?"

The question should not have surprised him, but it did. It was what he had asked Stillman once. He had no answer at first. The word didn't seem to describe what he felt tonight. He was aware that there was danger out there in the riverbed and maybe even on the streets in this neighborhood, but he had begun to feel that he knew how to stay away from it for the moment. He searched for another term, but each seemed to be unsatisfactory because it complicated the feeling rather than elucidating it.

"I think it's probably not as bad as it feels right now," he said. "Seeing the cop grab that woman by the hair, that was horrible, up-setting. Maybe we'll get to testify for her when she sues the town."

"If they can get a jury around here that isn't related to the cop," said Mary. She sat up in sudden frustration and looked toward the front of the house. "What's keeping him?" Her body became very still, and she slowly rose to her feet, not taking her eyes away from the slice of clear space between the houses. As she took a step forward, Walker heard her mutter to herself, "What now?"

Walker was on his feet, moving past her to Stillman's side at the front of the house. Beyond the river and the Old Mill, far across the open fields where the road cut between the hills, there were headlights. He saw lights moving into the woods where the loop in the river brought it back and the covered bridge crossed it. The lights came out of the woods toward the empty fields, past the two old barns. He counted eight sets of lights, then ten, then fourteen. The first of them made the final turn and the headlights swung and settled, aiming along the straight stretch so the brightness seemed to build and the glow cast shadows of trees on the walls of the old buildings on this side of the river.

"Have you figured out what it is?" asked Walker.

"It's not our two burglars," Stillman answered. He pointed at the parking lot beside the Old Mill. "They seem to be expected."

There were police cars in the lot again, this time four of them. There were a couple of policemen out of their cars and standing by the entrance to the lot. When the headlights of the first car to arrive shone on them, the cops waved the driver into the lot, and kept waving. As each car after it came within range, the cops waved it in toward the row of parking spaces at the wall of the building near the front door. "It looks to me like the party of forty they were getting ready for this afternoon has arrived," said Stillman.

As each car parked, the occupants opened their doors and got out. They all seemed to be men, most of them in pairs, but some in threes or fours. There were cops near the door of the restaurant who moved along the row of cars, shaking hands with the newcomers, talking, gesturing. A few of the men went into the restaurant, but most of them walked around in the lot, talking with men from other cars. As more cars arrived, the drivers and passengers gathered into an amorphous crowd.

They did not look to Walker as though they had come for a party—at any rate, not the same party. Some of them wore jeans, some pressed pants and sport coats, and a few wore ties. One of the police cars started and made a wide turn, throwing its headlights on the row of parked cars. "The cars all look new," said Walker.

The police car pulled to one end of the row and stopped, and another pulled up at the other end. Stillman said, "Now, why do you suppose the police would come to the party?"

Something else was going on now. The men were moving, forming themselves into two ragged lines near the two police cars. Policemen opened the trunks of their cars, and the lines began to inch forward. As each man arrived at the back bumper of a police car, the cop leaning into it handed him a short-barreled pump shotgun. The man would move around the car and stop at the hood, where there was a big cardboard carton. He reached in and took a box of shells out of it, stood apart a few yards, filled his pockets with shells, and handed the rest of the box to the man nearest him, who would do the same. Others would stop to push a few shells into their shotguns' magazines before they did anything else.

"Looks like reinforcements," said Walker. "Maybe cops from other towns?"

Mary tapped Stillman and Walker both on their shoulders. "Can we please go now?"

"I'd like to see which direction they're going first," said Stillman. "When you see a man with a shotgun, it's better to be behind him than in front."

Almost all the men were carrying their shotguns differently now, with the muzzle upward, so Walker could tell that they were loaded. The men began climbing back into their cars. There was a discussion between one of the cops and the driver of the lead car, and then they began to move. The first one came up over the bridge, turned right onto Washington Street, and stopped to wait for the others, only fifty or sixty feet from their hiding place.

Stillman said, "Now we can go." He hurried back the way they had come. When he reached Mary, he pulled her along with him. They moved through the yards they had crossed on the way to the river. When they reached the first cross street, Stillman stopped and looked both ways, then ran across, and kept running up the sidewalk on Constitution Avenue. It was several blocks before he decreased his pace.

"What is it?" asked Mary. "What are they doing?"

"They're getting ready to make a sweep," said Stillman. "It's not a good time to be outdoors. We'd better head for the church."

Mary said, "The church?"

But Stillman set off again at a run. Mary let out a sigh and set off after him. Walker kept his eyes on Mary as they ran, but he sensed that she was not having trouble keeping up. He knew that she was frightened and confused, but she seemed to have made a decision to hold those feelings apart for now and concentrate on the need to run. After a few more blocks, Walker could tell that Stillman was beginning to feel the strain of the long hours and the running, but Mary looked like any young woman out for a jog on a summer night. She ran with her fists clenched and her head up, her knees rising high. He found himself wishing she had a dog, or a pair of earphones over her ears, instead of two male companions.

When they reached the back of the church, they stopped in the shadowy space behind the building to let their breathing slow and their hearts stop pounding. Walker said, "I'll go around and see if it's still open."

Mary's hand came up and pressed against his chest. "I'll go. They haven't seen me." She slipped around the building toward the front. Walker and Stillman followed as far as the front corner, staying close to the wall to avoid straying into the lights from Main Street. Walker waited a few seconds, but found waiting unbearable. He stepped around the corner and saw her leaning hard to push open the heavy front door, and hurried across the facade and up the steps with Stillman's breaths huffing in his ear. When they were inside and the big door closed behind them, it was too dark to see anything.

Mary whispered, "I've still got the little flashlight."

"It'll show through the windows," said Stillman. "Let your eyes get used to the dark." His voice told Walker he was slowly edging toward the doorway of the cloak room.

Walker took Mary's hand. "Come away from the entrance." They found the wall and the doorway by touch. When they were in the cloak room, she slipped her hand out of his. "This isn't a great hiding place."

Walker said, "The steeple is above us, and there's a belfry at the top. We've been up there." He lifted her hand and set it on one of the varnished slats attached to the wall. "This is the ladder."

She was silent for a few seconds. "I think I see it. That square way up there?"

Walker asked, "Are you afraid of heights?"

"Of course I'm afraid of heights," she snapped.

"Stillman can go up first, and then you," said Walker. "I'll be under you, and if anything . . . happens, I'll catch you."

Stillman's voice came out of the dark. "He's easily dumb enough to do it, you know." Stillman set his toe on the lowest wooden slat and began to climb.

Mary said to him, "If you fall, don't expect me to catch you."

"I'll use extra caution." He kept climbing, and soon they heard him lift the cover off the hatch. Their eyes had adjusted to the darkness, so they saw his legs grow shorter and disappear into the deeper darkness above.

Walker started to guide Mary to the ladder, but she shrugged his hand off. "I see it," she said. She reached to the highest rung she could and climbed. Walker watched from below, trying to discern the exact position and attitude of her body in the dim light so he could judge her trajectory if she slipped and fell backward. She kept her head up and climbed like a person who hated it and was determined to get it finished before she had time to think. In a minute only her legs were visible. She suddenly rose out of sight as Stillman took her hands and lifted her up.

Walker climbed quickly too, then carefully replaced the hatch cover and looked around him to find the others. The open square on the third level above them seemed brighter than the second level, even at night, but he could see little. He heard a shuffle of feet and moved toward it. He whispered, "I'm up."

Mary said, "Good for you. I'll go first this time, and you can both catch me." She was already climbing. Her body momentarily blocked the light in the opening above, then disappeared again, and Stillman began to climb. Walker waited until he was up before he climbed too.

He reached the upper level to find Stillman standing at the western side of the belfry, staring out between the slats, and Mary, at the eastern side, looking at him. "This isn't as bad as I expected."

"It's not the sort of place where somebody will just happen by and stumble on us," Walker agreed.

Stillman said, "They're moving." Walker and Mary stepped close to Stillman and looked down. The cars had spread out along Washington Street, and now they were taking positions at each of the streets that ran up from the river into the heart of the town. At some signal that Walker could not see, they began to cruise up all of the streets at once. On each street there was a lead car with its high-beam headlights on. Behind it at least a hundred feet was a second car with its headlights off.

Stillman said, "See what they're doing? The first car comes along, trying to light everything up. If it goes by you, and you're an optimist, you think you're in the clear. You break cover and move. Only you're not in the clear because there's another one coming along that you didn't see."

"I hope those two guys are optimists," said Walker.

"Come here," said Stillman. "When the cars coming up Main get right below us and close to the street lamps, see if you can make out a license plate."

Walker knelt on the floor and put his face close to a louvered opening. He could see the two cars coming slowly up the brightly lit commercial street. Both of the cars on Main had their high-beam headlights on. Each time the lead car reached a corner, it would pause briefly while the driver looked up the cross street and the car behind caught up. Then the lead car would move forward again. The lead driver seemed to be trying to stay abreast of the cars on the other streets.

As Walker stared at the white license plate, a suspicion formed in his mind. The print on it seemed to be green. He squinted and leaned forward as the car approached the block where the church was, trying to screen out the glare of the headlights and keep his eyes on the plate. It passed the church and stopped at the corner. As the car behind it came closer, its bright headlights made the reflective surface of the rear license plate glow more and more brightly. "It's not New Hampshire," said Walker. He could see that the green numbers were outlined in orange. "The first plate looks like . . . Florida!"

Stillman nodded. "That's what I was afraid of. When the first one crossed the bridge, I thought that's what the plate looked like. But I figured you had seen a lot more of them lately than I have. It explains why they're all new. They're rental cars."

Walker said, "The second one is something else. Maybe Georgia."

"What does that mean?" asked Mary.

Stillman said quietly, "It means we came to the right place. It looks like everybody involved in those murders is turning up here at once."

"It seems that would make it the wrong place," she said. "I wonder why they're all here now."

Stillman answered, "This afternoon, before we saw those two guys, we were in the Old Mill. Waiters were setting up for a party of thirty or forty. We couldn't figure out why. It must have been for them. They've been away—down in Florida, where the hurricane was—stealing more money. It was going to be a welcome-home party. I guess the two we saw this afternoon were just the first ones to arrive."

"They must all live here," said Walker. "It wasn't just Scully and Bowles."

"So nobody down there is searching for those two killers, right?" said Mary. "They're searching for us."

Stillman nodded. "I think the cops figured that as soon as they told us the two killers were gone, we'd leave. Only when we didn't leave, the plan had to change. They decided to wait until after dark, when these guys got here and they'd have the manpower to find us. By then the rest of the town would be asleep, most of the strangers would be gone—"

"Those tourists," Mary interrupted. "The ones in the restaurant."

Stillman said, "I think they were supposed to be gone, back to wherever they were staying, before those guys got here. They weren't. They couldn't be allowed to see forty men show up, get guns from the police, and search the town. The cops will probably keep them in a holding cell overnight, where they won't see or hear anything. In the morning they'll tell them it was a case of mistaken identity, apologize, and let them go."

Mary was quiet for a few seconds. "How are we going to get out of here?"

Stillman said, "If we look closely enough, we'll see an opportunity."

"To do what—shoot our way out?"

"Those men down there appear to be prepared for that sort of thing," said Stillman. "We, on the other hand, are not."

"We're not?"

"No guns," said Walker.

Her eyes widened. "You came here looking for killers, and you didn't even think to bring a gun?"

"We weren't looking for killers," said Walker. "We were looking for a dead man's house." When she remained rigid, he added, "We were just doing research."

She glared at him, then at Stillman, and folded her arms across her chest. Then she turned to face the slatted panel beside her, clearly only because it was a way to end the conversation. After a moment, her arms unfolded and she grasped one of the louvers as she brought her face close to it. "Uh-oh."

Walker stepped to her side and looked. Some of the cars had reached the spot at the east end of town where the streets ended and a long fence separated the town from a vast, grassy expanse of field. The cars were moving toward Main Street. "They've come to the end," he said. "What's wrong?"

"Not the cars," Mary said. "Down this street. The houses."

Walker bent lower and looked out between the two louvers that were at Mary's eye level. He could see that on Oak Street, something new was going on. There were police cars with their red and blue lights flashing, creeping slowly up the street. There were other cops on foot, walking quickly from house to house, knocking on doors. He raised his head one level to see the block on Oak where the police cars had already been.

Lights shone from all the windows, and the porch lamps and drive-way floods threw broad patches of light on the ground. In the new il-lumination, he could see people. There were pedestrians coming out into the middle of the quiet block, walking in small groups. Sometimes there were pairs or small knots of people, but all walked toward Main Street. They looked like victims of some disaster streaming out of a city.

He moved his vantage again. The police cars had left the block where he had first seen them. Lights were turning on there, too. Doors were opening, and people were coming outside. As they reached Main they passed under the bright street lamps, and he could see them better. There were men and women, and some who appeared to be teenagers. A pair of men who passed directly under the steeple before they crossed the street had white hair. Every person he saw was carry-ing a gun.

39

From the church steeple, Walker watched people stream up the side streets toward the far end of Main. "There must be two hundred people," he said. "I can't believe it. Maybe the police just told everybody that there were two killers hiding in the town. That might get them all out of their houses."

Stillman squinted as he gazed down at the people in the street. "If they did, I think we can be pretty sure the description they gave doesn't fit the two guys we saw in the coffee shop." He was quiet for a moment. "I'm having trouble believing this too. I'm developing unsightly bruises from pinching myself."

Mary sat on the floor and muttered, "Keep doing it. Maybe you'll find a gun in your pocket."

"I don't think firearms would do us much good. If I could just walk up to all of those people and shoot each one in the head, it would still take more ammunition than I can carry."

She looked up at Walker. "What are they doing now?"

"I'm not sure, exactly," said Walker. "See if you can figure it out."

She stood and looked toward the east end of Main Street. There were men in police uniforms running up and down Cherry, the last cross street at the edge of town. They were waving their arms, moving people into a single line, with about six feet between them and their backs to the chain-link fence that separated the town from the empty fields. Mary moved to the next panel, and she could see that the line of citizens continued to the north end of town. When she turned and stepped to the south panel, the roof of the church below her blocked some of her view.

She stood beside Walker. From here she could see the foot of Main Street, where the bridge crossed the river, and the parking lot of the Old Mill Restaurant. That end of town seemed deserted except for the four police cars parked in the lot.

Stillman called them to the eastern side. "The cars are starting to move again."

Walker and Mary watched as headlights advanced slowly along the line of people. The cars that had been searching side streets moved back to their places and began to creep slowly down in the direction of the river. Then, on some order that could not be heard from here, the long line of people stepped forward.

The people walked straight ahead, across the street, up the lawns on Cherry, along sidewalks and driveways. Doors of houses opened, and the lights came on in the darkened windows, first on ground floors, then on upper floors. From here, people could be seen entering, then moving across lighted windows. Then back doors opened and people streamed out. Garage doors were slid upward, flashlights shone into the interiors, and then the searchers moved on. Others whose courses took them down open streets stopped and shone lights into parked cars and under them, looked up on porches, and searched the shrubbery in front yards. All along the line, the searchers moved forward at about the same pace, the line wavering a bit, but not breaking.

Fifty feet behind the line of citizens, there were men about twenty paces apart with rifles held at the ready across their chests. Occasionally one of them would point or wave an arm, as though he was directing the people in the line ahead to straighten their alignment, or exhorting them not to overlook some possible hiding place.

"It's a tiger hunt," said Stillman. "The people in that line are the beaters. The ones behind with the rifles are there in case we bust through the line." He moved to the panel of louvers on the western side. "They'll have something big waiting for the tiger at the other end. Let's see what it is."

Walker and Mary stood at his shoulders. Far down Main Street they could see the Old Mill, the river, and the opposite bank. The four police cars were still parked by the restaurant, but the activity there seemed to have ceased.

"They don't have the bridge blocked," said Mary.

"Looks a bit too inviting, doesn't it?" said Stillman. "If we wanted to drive out, that would be the way. If we wanted to go on foot, we'd still have to cross the river."

They watched for several minutes, but the sight did not change. The lights of the Old Mill Restaurant looked bright and warm and welcoming from up here.

Walker moved to the north side, where he could look down below the front of the church onto Main Street. The row of people had reached Oak Street now, and he could sight along the wavering line as it passed. To his right, all the houses glowed with light. Every window was illuminated, every outdoor flood was shining down to cast a circle of white on an area of pavement or turn a lawn day-green.

The lights on the streets to his left began to go on, one by one. "What I'm wondering is what happens when they get to the city limits and haven't found us," Walker said.

"We'll see," said Stillman. "I'm hoping they'll figure we got out on foot, and send everybody home to bed." He had not moved from the west side. His eyes were still on the river.

"Could that happen?" asked Walker.

"I don't know why not. We reported seeing two murder suspects in town, and the police made a huge effort to organize a manhunt. If we've got a complaint, it's our word against everybody else's. Our interpretation of events would sound a bit eccentric, to say the least."

Stillman suddenly bobbed up on his toes to peer out above a higher louver, then settled for a lower one. "Come here," he said. The others moved in beside him to look to the west. The cars that had been prowling the streets a block in advance of the line of citizens had reached Washington Avenue. The cars all turned onto Washington, and now they were pulling over to park by the curb.

In the riverbed, there seemed to be sudden activity. Flashlights were going on at intervals of fifty feet all along the river, as though a signal was being passed. After a moment, men began to step up the banks to join the ones getting out of cars on Washington.

"That answers my question," said Stillman. "That's what the beaters were trying to herd us into. They wanted us to try to cross the river."

The line of townspeople reached the last row of houses on the near side of Washington Street. The lights in the windows went on. Porch lights threw a glow over the stream of people moving through the yards between the houses and spilling in from Main Street, Constitution, Coulter, Federal, and New Hampshire. They all came together to mill about in Washington Street and along the banks of the river. The long line had now dissolved, and the people looked like the crowd at a carnival.

A police car turned its flashing red and blue lights on and drove slowly along Washington. Walker could hear a faint, echoing amplified voice from a bullhorn, but he could not pick up a word. Men and women who had been in small knots talking turned and stepped aside to let the patrol car pass. Others stepped back onto the sidewalks on either side of the street. The car's progress was extremely slow, but at last it emerged from the crowd and reached Main. It turned to head away from the river.

Behind the police car, the crowd closed, already beginning to move after it. In a moment, the fast walkers were turning to follow the police car up Main. They streamed up from the direction of the river, some on the sidewalks, others in the middle of Main Street. They walked in pairs or small groups, talking as they went.

Walker put his arm around Mary and watched the people coming up the street. He waited, hoping that some of them would go into houses on Washington and turn off the lights. He held his breath as the central mass of people moved beyond Adams, Jefferson, Franklin. The compact crowd was now stretched out into a long stream, but Walker could tell that nobody was going home.

Mary said quietly, "Not so tight," and Walker realized that his arm had become tense. He pulled it away from her.

Far below them, there was the creak of a heavy door opening, and then voices. At first Walker tried to convince himself that the sounds were coming from Main Street, but then there was an unmistakable echo, the voices bouncing off the bare walls of an enclosed space. The people were gathering in the church.

40

Without having made a decision or spoken a word, they found themselves crouching, listening as the townspeople began to crowd into the church below them. The three were absolutely still, barely breathing, but huddled close as though that provided some measure of safety. After a long time, Walker slowly, cautiously, raised himself a bit and peered out onto Main Street, then turned and looked to the west. He eased himself back down with Stillman and Mary.

"The streets are empty," he whispered. "There are just the four police cars on the other side of the river by the restaurant, and a couple more cruising up and down. Everybody seems to be here."

Stillman said, "It feels to me as though it might be time to make a move."

Mary's eyes widened. "You mean go down there?"

"I don't see how that does us any good," said Walker.

Stillman said, "Remember when we were in Scully's house? I took his keys." He took them out of his pocket and held them up where they caught a bit of the filtered glow from the sky. "There's a car key." He looked at them thoughtfully. "None of the rest of them drove to Florida. They flew down, and rented cars to come back. No reason to think he and Bowles did any different."

Mary said, "Wait. Didn't you say the cops were going to put men in Scully's house, just like they did in Bowles's house?"

Stillman said, "Sure, but I don't know any reason to believe what the cops told us, do you?"

Walker said, "We were up here watching all afternoon, and I tried to see if I could spot policemen at Scully's house, but I couldn't."

Stillman said, "They've just walked through and turned on every light bulb in town, including the ones at Scully's. There may have been cops there, and there may still be. But our chances of seeing them with the lights on are pretty fair, and we haven't. The whole town seems to be in the church under our feet right now, so if we could get past them, we'd have a chance."

"If they went to bed, we'd have a better chance," Mary said skeptically.

Stillman said, "Any minute now, the decision could get made for us." He paused. "So what's it going to be?"

"I don't think we'll get a better chance at a car," said Walker.

Mary took a deep breath, but she didn't let it out. "Okay," she said. The breath still seemed trapped in her chest.

Walker looked out the four panels again. He picked out Scully's house. "I still don't see anybody at Scully's. There's nobody on Birch Street at all."

Stillman said, "We'd better get started." He crawled to the opening that led down into the darker second level. "One last thing. These people aren't just going to let us out of town. If they get their hands on us, they'll kill us."

Mary said, "Do you think you're making it easier to climb down there?"

"I'm just telling you that we have to think differently tonight," said Stillman. "If somebody points a gun at you, putting your hands in the air won't keep him from pulling the trigger."

"I figured that out a while ago," she said.

Stillman descended until he was lost in the gloom. Walker listened, but he heard no footfall. Then Mary sat on the floor, put her legs into the opening, found an unseen rung of the ladder with her foot, and began to descend too. Walker took one final look out between the louvers in the belfry, but he could see nothing that had changed. He moved to the ladder.

When Walker reached the lower level, he eased his foot down slowly to avoid making a noise. He had become so used to the almost imperceptible sounds of the others' breathing and movements, the heights and shapes of their bodies, that he had developed a sensitivity to where they were in the dark. He lowered himself to his knees and felt for the hatch cover. Stillman knelt beside him as he lifted the hatch a quarter inch and peered down at the cloak room below.

The light seemed impossibly, frighteningly bright in the first seconds, but after a moment his pupils had contracted enough to let him judge that the cloak room was dimmer than the foyer. The light that had seemed so bright was coming from the hanging fixture there. He could see that the hardwood floor below him was bare. He moved to the left, lifted the hatch cover a bit more, lay on his belly, and looked again. He could not see the whole foyer from this height, but the part that he could see was clear.

He lifted the cover off and began to descend into the cloak room. He could hear somebody speaking in the church. It was a man's voice. Walker kept going, trying to keep his footsteps silent.

"Sure it's trouble," said the voice. "It's not anything we can't handle if we all pay attention to what we're doing. It just takes patience."

A higher-register voice—a woman—replaced the male voice. Walker could tell she must be sitting in a pew facing the front of the sanctuary, because her voice was muffled. She reached the end of her brief statement, and there were other voices, making what sounded to Walker like murmurs of assent.

Walker had reached the floor now. He moved to the wall beside the doorway, cautiously tilting his head to search the foyer for people. Then he looked up to see that Mary was halfway down.

As the murmurs subsided, the man's voice rose above them. "You have to understand," said the voice, and Walker realized it was familiar. "These two aren't exactly the FBI SWAT commandos from hell." A wave of laughter washed over Walker, and as it did the voice paused, then continued. "They're bureaucrats—investigators from an insurance company. They make their living finding people's lost silverware, and taking videos of disability cases on the golf course." This time, Walker recognized the voice: Chief Raines.

Walker felt a hand touch his shoulder, and he whirled to see Mary behind him. He looked above her and saw that Stillman had cleared the ceiling and was using the sound of the laughter to cover the noise of pulling the lid over the hatch. Stillman began to climb down quickly. When the laughter turned ragged and people were beginning to quiet down again, he slowed his pace.

Chief Raines said, "I think all that happened was that they found a hiding place we missed. What I'd like to suggest is that when we're through here, we all go back to our own houses—nobody alone, but in groups of four at least—and search. Look in every closet, every corner of the basement, every inch of the attic. If you see anything, there will be cars patrolling every street, and help is as close as that. When you're positive the house is clear, lock it up tight. Keep all the outdoor lights on, but turn off the inside ones. Put at least one person downstairs and one upstairs, looking out the windows all the time."

The chief was interrupted by another voice from the floor that Walker couldn't understand. The chief answered, "Now that everybody's back from Florida, we've got more than enough people, and we'll be raiding places we haven't hit. Even if we don't corner them, they'll be on the move. They don't want to stay here, they want to get out of town. If everybody is looking, somebody will see them."

Walker felt Mary tugging on his arm. He turned and saw that the cloak-room window was open and Stillman was just easing himself out to the ground. Walker lifted Mary up into the space, and she slithered through and out. Walker climbed out after her, turned at the sill, and dropped to the grass, then carefully pulled the sash down.

When he turned around, Stillman and Mary had already moved off toward Constitution. Stillman seemed to be carrying something. At the corner, they began to run, and he sprinted to catch up. They kept up their desperate pace until they reached Birch Street, then turned onto it and moved toward Main.

Stillman stopped. He handed Walker and Mary light summer jackets. "I borrowed these from the cloak room," he said. "Maybe they'll help us get across the street." Walker slipped his on, watched Mary put hers on, then moved forward, but Stillman held his arm.

"Not yet," he said. "It's not enough."

"We're not going?"

"No," said Stillman. "We've got to wait."

"But they could be out here any second."

"That's the idea. Look around. We're the only ones out on foot. It's like everybody died. When that meeting is over, the streets are going to be full of people. None of them will be as far east as Birch Street, but we'll still look as though we came from the meeting."

Mary turned her eyes to Stillman but said nothing.

Walker said reluctantly, "All right."

"Give me a minute," said Stillman. "I'll get as close to the corner of Main as I can. The second the doors open up, I'll move. The two of you walk across together. Hold hands or something, and walk at the same speed as everybody else. I'll cross alone from here, and we'll meet on the other side."

He stepped off alone. Mary and Walker stood on the sidewalk and waited. She said quietly, "Did you hear what that man was saying in there?"

He nodded. "That man was the chief of police."

"But the whole town was in there listening, agreeing. It's not just one or two cops fooling people. It's everybody. They're all in on it."

"Let's just hope everybody came to the meeting," said Walker. Then he froze. "Kids. When we were here before, we saw kids. There must be people in some of the houses watching them."

"We should warn Stillman."

They saw Stillman wave his arm and set off across Main Street. "Too late," said Walker. He put his arm around her waist, tightened it once in a quick squeeze, then let it rest there. "We've got to go. Just keep your face turned away from the windows."

They walked to the corner and stepped into the street. Walker looked past Mary toward the church. The doors had opened and people were walking down the steps, across the sidewalk, and into Main Street. He adjusted his pace to theirs. Before he and Mary had stepped across the double line in the center of the pavement, he could see that the street to the west was already clogged.

Some of the townspeople were moving along the sidewalks on

Main Street away from the church, and others came east and then crossed the street as Walker and Mary were doing. Walker kept his steps even and unhurried, expecting at any second to hear running footsteps behind them.

Then they were stepping up over the curb, and after a few more steps they were on Birch, moving away from Main. Birch Street was still much brighter than it had been when Walker and Stillman had been to Scully's house the first time. Walker had to force himself to keep from running to get to the house before the first of the residents returned to see them. When he and Mary were almost there, he could see Stillman waiting at the corner of the house.

"The garage is wide open, and his car is inside," said Stillman. "It's a Chevy Blazer."

Walker said, "Want to try for the gun in the bedroom?"

Stillman shook his head. "No. Nothing has changed. If we shoot off a gun, there will be eighty people on us in a second. If we don't need to fire it, what's it for?" To foreclose the argument, he moved up the driveway and into the garage.

When they were all inside, Stillman handed Mary the keys. "You drive. You're the only one they haven't seen."

Stillman climbed into the back seat, while Walker got into the front. Stillman tapped him. "Duck down."

Mary started the engine, and backed down the driveway into the street. Walker crouched on the floor and felt the vehicle lurch forward. She announced, "We're still ahead of the crowd. I'm going to turn left and go down the next street toward the river." She made the turn.

"I see lights ahead," she said. "It looks like a cop car."

"It doesn't matter whose car it is, he's nobody we want to get close to," said Stillman. "Can you turn anywhere without looking as though you're avoiding him?"

"I'll make the next turn and go toward Main again." She made the turn slowly, then sighed. "There are people in the street. I can get through them, but if they know the car, they can hardly imagine I'm James Scully."

"See if you can turn at the next corner and get near the river that way," said Stillman.

They felt the car's speed decrease, and then felt it coast. "There are two more cars on that street with their headlights pointed this way." She accelerated again. "I'm going on to Main Street."

She reached Main, then stopped. "This is not good," she said. "I can see more cars up ahead before the bridge. Two of them are cop cars."

Stillman said, "Turn toward them so your headlights are what they see."

She turned the car, then turned again at the first corner. "They're not following," she said. "It looks like they're just waiting for us to go toward the bridge. Maybe I can come up Washington behind them."

"Then turn right again at the next corner," he said.

"Okay." Walker felt the car tilt as she turned.

"What's ahead of you?"

"Not much. There's a driveway at the end of the street. A big building. The sign says New Mill Systems."

"Good," said Stillman. "Drive until you're almost there, and pull over."

In a moment, the car stopped at the curb. "I'm parked. What do you recommend now?"

"Can anybody see us if we sit up?"

"Nobody's back in these houses yet, but I just saw a couple pass the corner on Main, so it won't be long."

Stillman and Walker sat up. On either side, the street was brightly lighted from the windows of the houses and the floodlights on eaves and above porches. Directly ahead was the dim parking lot of New Mill Systems. Walker could see the usual thirty or forty cars in the lot, and beside the lot, the boxlike brick building with its small, high windows lit like all the others.

Stillman said, "Pull into the lot."

"It's not closed," said Mary. "The lot is full of cars."

"That's right," Stillman said. "We won't stand out as much if we're one of thirty cars."

Mary pulled ahead into the parking lot, turned off the headlights, and headed for the darkest corner.

"Not there," said Stillman. "Find an empty space in the middle someplace."

Mary parked in the third row and turned off the engine. "Well, here we are. Why are we?"

Walker said, "It doesn't seem as though we're analyzing the problem right. We need to think."

"While you're thinking, come with me for a minute," said Stillman. "Serena, stay put. Keep the key in the ignition and watch for trouble. If it comes, pull out fast and pick us up."

Walker got out and waited while Stillman joined him. Walker gazed away from the building at the fields beyond. "Do you think we could make it that way?"

"I did until I saw those rifles come out this evening. A weapon like that isn't much use in a town where everybody's related to you. It'll go through the wall of a house and come across the living room still dangerous. And you don't need a big scope to hit anything half a block away. I think they're hoping we'll get sick of hiding and try running. As soon as we're in ankle-high grass with nothing on any side of us for a hundred yards that's bigger than a daisy, they'll take us."

"Then what are we doing?"

"This whole town seems to be armed. If one person in this lot got distracted when he parked here, he may have left something that I can use."

"What are the chances of that?"

"Better than if we don't look," said Stillman. "You take a close look at this building. See if there's a way in."

Walker stepped toward the New Mill Systems building, then stopped between two cars and pretended to tie his shoe. He used the time to study the structure from below. He searched the eaves for cameras and floodlights, but he didn't see any.

He went toward the rear of the building. There had to be something back there besides these featureless brick walls with their tiny windows. He turned the corner. There was nothing but a concrete walkway directly beside the building, a treeless lawn, and a high chain-link fence like the one at the east end of town. He kept going. He turned the next corner. There was a big Dumpster placed close to the wall. He looked at it closely. There was a padlock on it, so he couldn't even open it to see whether it would be a good place to hide.

From here he could see the parking lot. With difficulty, he picked out Scully's red Blazer in the third line of cars, but he couldn't see Mary. He scanned the lot for Stillman. He didn't see him at first, but then he detected a shadowy shape drifting from car to car, hunched low to peer in the windows.

Walker took a step toward the lot, then stopped and looked at the position of the Dumpster. Quickly, he put his hands on the lid, pushed down, and raised himself to the top. He brought his feet up and knelt there for a moment, then carefully placed his feet near the rim so his weight wouldn't cause the lid to bend and make a booming noise. He stood, shakily, and looked through the small window.

He was disappointed. There was a big room that looked like the inside of just about any other business. It wasn't so different from the open bay on the seventh floor of the McClaren Building. There were desks with computer terminals, filing cabinets along the walls, and bulletin boards with maps and papers pinned to them. The night shift was in: a few people were at desks working, a few walking around carrying papers or coffee cups. Then he began to notice small, unexpected things.

He craned his neck to see the map above the desk closest to him. It was Florida. At the far end of the room was a big console that had a lot of electronic equipment on it, small modules with dials and speakers. There was a woman wearing earphones sitting in front of it, fiddling with some knobs.

Walker put his hands on the wall of the building and leaned closer so he could look down at the woman sitting at the desk to the left, below the window. She was staring at a computer screen, typing. Walker kept his face to the right side of the window and tried to see her screen, but he could not. He leaned farther, saw her open the top drawer of her desk, take out a piece of chewing gum, and start to unwrap it. Inside the drawer, beside the gum, was a pistol.

His eye caught movement to his right and he instinctively ducked close to the wall, prepared to jump. Then he picked a shape out of the shadows and recognized Mary, making her way toward him, and in a moment he could make out the bigger shape of Stillman, hurrying along behind.

"This isn't a good place to be," he whispered. "This is it—the place where they run everything. It's like a command center."

"Maybe that's good," Mary replied. "Maybe they won't look here while we call."

"Call?"

Stillman held up his hand and Walker could see a small black object in it. "I found one that was open. No guns, no keys, but there was a cell phone in it."

"What are you waiting for?" said Walker.

"I didn't come back here to ask what you wanted on your pizza," said Stillman. "I wanted to get out of sight." He stepped around the corner into the shelter of the building and in a moment Walker could hear the beeps as he began to punch numbers on the phone. Walker felt his heart beating faster. The waiting seemed impossible to bear.

Stillman said, "This is an emergency. I'd like to be connected with the Federal Bureau of Investigation. Yes, the FBI. The closest one to Coulter, New Hampshire." He paused. "Okay, just give me the number and I'll dial it."

Walker's eyes moved to the window as he tried to calm his nerves. The woman across the room looked different this time. She had the earphones clamped on her head, and she was moving the dials on her console with intense concentration. Walker heard the beep as Stillman terminated his connection.

The woman was standing now. She half-lifted the earphones from her ears as she raised her head and called out. Two men and another woman left their desks and hurried to lean over the console.

Walker said, "I don't like—"

"Sshh!" Stillman was dialing again.

"This is an emergency. My name is Max Stillman. I'm in the town of Coulter—"

The woman at the console flipped a switch. Stillman stopped talking and flinched. Even from atop the Dumpster, Walker could hear the whistling, crackling noise coming from the cell phone.

"They're jamming your call," said Walker. "Turn it off."

The noise stopped, but Walker could see that the people inside the building were suddenly animated. The woman at the console was saying something. Others were gathering near her. Walker watched in horror as the lady just to the left of the window opened the desk drawer and took out the gun. It looked huge in her small, manicured hand. Three men came in from another room carrying shotguns, on their way to the door.

"They know we're here!" he said, and jumped from the Dumpster.

They ran along the side of the building, with Stillman in the lead. At the corner he did not stop with his customary caution to look, just kept running for the line of parked cars. He moved between two of them in the first row, then to the next row, and the third, with Mary behind him and Walker last. When Stillman was beyond the third row, he turned up the aisle and dashed toward the Blazer.

Walker heard a metal door swing open and bang against a wall. There was a sound Walker had not heard since he was fourteen, but it was so distinctive that he identified it instantly: the click as the shotgun foregrip was pushed forward an inch, followed by the quick *snick-chuck* as the slide moved back, then forward to pump a shell into the chamber.

The roar tore the air, and the rear window of the car beside him was swept away, blown backward in a shower of shattered glass. There was another roar, and the car ahead of him shuddered and listed a bit to the side as its left front tire was ripped apart and the car dropped to its rim.

Stillman plucked the keys out of Mary's hand, pushed her into the back seat, and climbed in behind the wheel. As he started the car, Walker flopped inside beside Mary and slammed the door.

The car's tires squealed and Stillman backed through a gap in the next row to put more cars between him and the men in front of the building, then stomped on the accelerator and sped across the lot to the street. There was another loud report, but Walker could not detect any damage to the windows.

"You can sit up now," Stillman said, then made the first turn to the right.

"Do you think you got through to them?" asked Mary.

"The FBI?" said Stillman. "They picked up the phone, but I didn't get to tell them what was on my mind. I think that was our chance to yell for help, and nobody heard us."

41

Stillman drove up New Hampshire Street, keeping the Blazer at a speed that would not attract attention. "In some circumstances, I might consider driving one of these things down the bank of a stream somewhere and hoping the water's not deep enough to swamp it. But the reason they built a mill and a bridge along this stretch is that this is the narrows. The river is deeper and faster by the town, and the banks are steep."

"I have another idea," said Walker. "It's not a great one."

"Tell us, and we'll insult it ourselves," said Mary.

"When we first saw the police station, there were sixteen cars in the lot, remember?"

"Sure," said Stillman.

"Well, there don't seem to be anything like that number on the streets tonight."

Stillman's expression seemed to intensify. He turned at the next corner and turned again to go east. "You're absolutely right. There are definitely going to be a few in the lot. At least one might have the keys in it. If not, I can probably—"

Mary said doubtfully, "You want to go to the police station to steal a police car? Why is that better than this thing?"

Stillman spoke quietly, as though trying not to alarm her. "Because this one has been seen, and we're going to have to try to run the bridge."

Stillman accelerated as he went up each block, then slowed at each corner to look both ways before he accelerated again. Suddenly, he swerved to the right. Ahead of them was a police car, parked a yard from the curb on the right. A policeman was out of it at the front door of one of the houses. The door opened and he stepped inside the house. The second cop was getting out of the car on the driver's side. He saw the Blazer's headlights coming toward him, so he stood and waited.

Walker and Mary ducked down as Stillman passed him. Stillman said, "This one's going to cross the street on foot. Looks like they're going house to house. There he goes. Hold on tight."

Walker tried to articulate what he was thinking, but Stillman acted too quickly for him to speak. Stillman stopped the Blazer, then threw it into reverse. He turned in his seat to stare out the rear window, backing up fast. There was a loud, sickening thud, and Walker sat up and watched in horror as the man flew ten feet back, hit the pavement, and rolled.

Stillman stopped, flung his door open, and jumped out, bathing the interior of the Blazer in light. Mary and Walker got out too, as Stillman ran to the injured man. He knelt, then stood up, carrying the man's sidearm in one hand and his keys in the other. He dashed to the police car and got in. When the others were beside him, he accelerated down the street.

"Do you think he's dead?" asked Mary.

"No, but he thinks he is, and he'll probably stick to that opinion until they get him to a hospital." Stillman drove hard for a block, then said, "Serena, honey, crawl over into the back seat. Put your lap belt on, but lie down low. There's not enough room up here."

Mary turned and climbed to the back. Stillman slapped the policeman's pistol against Walker's chest. "You take this." He let go.

Walker caught the gun before it could fall into his lap. Stillman said, "That's got a police-only fourteen-round magazine. In a minute, I'm going to have to drive down Main Street with my head held high, so I can see where we're going. When we get near the bridge, there will be a lot of people waiting with guns. At that point, I would appreciate it if you would use that pistol. If all you do is kick up some dust and get them to duck instead of taking a calm and steady-handed aim at my forehead, I'm going to be pleased. If you also happened to hit somebody, it would improve our chances of causing hesitation and uncertainty."

Walker said nothing. He examined the pistol to be sure he knew where the safety was, adjusted his hand on the pistol grip, and tested the weight, then turned to look over the seat at Mary.

Mary put her hand on Walker's shoulder. Her face was ashen.

Stillman was now nearly to the corner of Sycamore Street. He braked gently as he went into the turn. "All right, ladies and gentlemen. I think this has to be our street. We've got to have room to build up a little speed before we hit the bridge."

Walker and Mary touched hands over the back of Walker's seat, and then Mary put her head down in the back. "I'm ready," she said.

Walker turned to face the windshield and gripped the pistol. "Me too."

Stillman glided to the corner, stopped to look both ways, then drifted ahead slowly and turned west onto Main. He accelerated smoothly until the car was going about forty miles an hour, then held it there. Walker saw Grant Street go by, and looked at the speedometer, but Stillman's speed was constant.

Walker saw that a few pedestrians were still out on the sidewalks, making their way home, but most of them had already gone inside, presumably to complete the thorough search that the chief had suggested.

As they passed Grant Street, he had a glimpse of another police car with its lights flashing, moving fast along New Hampshire in the direction of New Mill Systems, or possibly toward the place where Stillman had hit the cop.

He looked out the rear window and saw another police car followed by three of the newly arrived rental cars making a quick turn off Main at about Birch Street. He began to feel a small, tentative hope that stealing the police car had been the best thing to do. As they passed pedestrians, he saw each of them look up to see the patrol car moving past, but then some looked away to talk to their companions, and some half-turned to look back at the other cars coming down Main toward them.

Stillman's eyes kept flicking up to the rearview mirror. He reached to the console and turned on the radio. There was buzzing and squawking, so he turned the channel knob twice and heard a female voice. "Officer down. Repeat, officer down. Location the three hundred block of Maple. Suspects have been spotted at New Mill Systems. All prowl units respond. Repeat—"

Stillman switched it off. "They got the order mixed up," he said. "That's why they're all going the wrong way." When Walker said nothing, he glanced at him, and looked alarmed. "You've got to be up to this. They're doing their absolute best to kill us right now."

Walker said, "I know. I'm not forgetting."

Stillman's eyes snapped ahead again. He took a deep breath and his face set in a look of stony concentration.

Franklin Street flashed past, and Walker could feel that Stillman was accelerating again. He saw the speedometer nudge up to fifty. Far ahead, there were two police cars parked at oblique angles on the bridge, with their front bumpers nearly touching. Walker saw that Stillman was not slowing down. He was going to try to punch through between them.

Walker turned on the radio, plucked the microphone off its hook, and pressed the thumb switch. He gave his voice a laconic radio monotone. "Can you get those two units off the bridge, please? We got an injured man in the back."

He could see that one of the men standing on the bridge had heard. He got inside one of the cars, and Walker saw him turn his head to stare up the street at the approaching police car.

Stillman flipped another switch on the dashboard, and Walker saw the black hood beyond the windshield reflect blue, then red, then blue again as Stillman sped on.

"Looks as though they're buying it," said Stillman.

But the radio buzzed with sudden life. "Give identity of the victim. Repeat, identity of the victim," pleaded the female voice. Another voice, a male, broke in. "I'm Code Six at the scene, and the victim is still here. He's Darryl Potts and he's not in the back of any car yet." "First caller, give your code and location." "I see him. He's on Main, heading for the bridge," said a new voice.

Walker pressed the talk switch again. "I see him too. He's trying to clear the way to get Darryl to the hospital. Move those units now!"

The dispatcher cut through the growing cacophony, her voice artificially calm. "Cancel the last request. Close the bridge. Repeat, close the bridge and stop all traffic."

Stillman's foot stomped on the accelerator, and Walker felt his head snap back against the headrest. The wind rushing in the window tousled his hair and flapped his shirt sleeve. Walker dropped the microphone and used his thumb to slip off the safety of the pistol. He stared out the windshield. There were more men at the bridge now, a few climbing up from the riverbed and the others trotting from the Old Mill parking lot.

Walker put his right arm out the window, raised the pistol, and aimed at a group of them standing in front of the cars. He fought the wind to hold his aim steady, squeezed off the first shot, and saw a man jerk and fall. The others scattered, some jumping aside, some running toward the backs of the cars.

Walker fired at them, not aiming along the sights anymore but pointing the gun as though he were pointing a finger, pulling the trigger, then fighting the recoil and lowering the muzzle in time to fire again. His shots hit the ground in front of the cars, throwing gravel and bits of pulverized asphalt into the air, punched holes in car doors, smashed windows and windshields, spraying glass.

As they came closer, he leaned out a bit farther, brought his arm in front of the windshield, and fired over the hood at the car to his left, then aimed again at the car to his right, trying to scatter his fire as widely as possible. Each time he saw any movement or caught a partial glimpse of a man beside, above, or below a car, he fired at it. Usually, a head or leg quickly jerked out of sight in a reflex of alarm, but there were a couple of shots when he felt an intuitive sensation between hand and eye that told him he may have hit something.

He sat back in his seat but kept pulling the trigger until the second before Stillman plowed into the space between the two cars. There was a sudden, jarring jolt that slapped his seat belt against his hips and his chest, a bang of metal, then a scraping and buckling punctuated with the crack and shiver of glass. There was a feeling that everything in his body that could move had been tugged, strained, and shaken—his bones, his internal organs, his brain. He had blinked at the last second, and opening his eyes seemed to do no good.

His mind began to clear, and he noticed that the car was still moving. It was dark because both headlights were broken. He spun in his seat to look behind. One of the cars had gone through the fragile railing of the bridge and was toppling into the water. There were men around it, some beginning to struggle up the bank to get out of the way, but one of them was lying in the water.

Two men stepped toward the road and fired guns, so Walker put the pistol into his left hand and aimed a couple of shots in their direction. The men only went to their knees and fired more shots. A round hit the rear window, and glass exploded into the car, stinging Walker's face. He turned to the front and saw that the shot had left the car through the upper part of the windshield between his head and Stillman's. Stillman switched off the flashing lights and kept driving on into the dark.

Stillman found a silver handle beside him, manipulated it, and a spotlight went on. "Here. See if you can aim this at the road."

Walker reached across Stillman, took the handle, then pushed and pulled it until the beam threw a faint glow on the road ahead. Stillman accelerated into it. "You can let go now." The car sounded as though the engine was laboring, and there was a scraping noise that seemed to rise in pitch as the car went faster.

Mary's voice came from a space just behind Walker's shoulder. "Do you think there's any chance they haven't blocked the other bridge—the one with the roof on it?"

"None," said Stillman. "I'm just trying to make it to the woods." He looked into the rearview mirror. "Shit."

Walker looked back. The scene at the bridge was still chaotic, but the four police cars from the Old Mill parking lot were pulling onto the road now, following.

"Got any ammunition left?" asked Stillman.

"I don't know," said Walker. "How do I tell?"

"Let's forget it and hope you do. This long straight stretch is where they'll try to catch us. I'll keep the ride as smooth as I can for the next ten seconds. If you could put a bullet anywhere on the front car, it would dampen their enthusiasm a bit."

Walker said, "Wait until I'm in the back seat. I can't hit anything with my left hand." He unfastened his belt and slipped over the seat, then turned and pulled his legs over after him. Mary crouched in the corner of the seat to give him room. He rolled down the side window behind Stillman, but it only went down halfway. He stuck his arm out over it and said, "Ready."

Stillman steered the car, keeping it as steady as he could. Walker detected the sensation that it was not going as fast as it had been, but the wind blew at him from the back, pushing his hair forward and making it flutter at his forehead. He aimed the gun carefully between the two headlights and squeezed.

The headlights swerved suddenly, then swerved back and forth a couple of times as though the driver were struggling for control, then straightened. Walker could tell that the car was farther behind now. He leveled the pistol again, but when he pulled the trigger, the gun gave a feeble click.

"Good enough," said Stillman. "That should do it. Sit back and hold on." He switched off the spotlight, and the road ahead disappeared. He drove on for ten seconds, twenty seconds, then wrenched the steering wheel to the right. They went across the shoulder, bumped hard over a ditch, the car losing its reassuring contact with the earth, then came down and bounced violently.

Stillman drove across the grassy field, bumping and bouncing as they hit small rises and ruts, but after a moment he was accelerating again. Walker raised his head to stare forward over Stillman's shoulder, and saw that the fields weren't quite invisible. Ahead he recognized the deeper darkness of one of the old barns, and beyond it, the black line of trees at the edge of the woods.

Stillman drove around the barn, then turned to glide into the dark enclosure. He stopped. "Time to put this car out of our misery."

Mary tried to open her door, but couldn't. "I forgot it was a police car." She crawled over the seat to the front, and got out. Mary stretched, then bent to test her back for injury.

As Walker emerged from the car, he said, "Are you all right?"

"It's all going as I'd planned," she said. "Except that I always hoped I'd get to die in my prom dress."

"You still might," said Stillman. "But first we have to get through the hard part." He walked toward the front of the barn, looked out at the road, flung the car keys into the field, and began to run.

42

They ran across a broad field that afforded no cover, not even variation. The ground had been tilled and plowed and leveled two centuries ago, and now it was covered with clover and grass that could not have been taller than four inches. Directly ahead of them the sky ended in a dark smear of thick foliage, and below it, the shadowy trunks of trees began to emerge from the darkness.

Stillman was a generation older than the others, but as he ran, Walker watched the broad back straighten, the thick, heavily muscled arms pumping, the legs pounding the ground like pistons. It was hard to imagine him moving any faster. Mary ran with her teeth clenched in a hot, ferocious determination, as though she were not merely straining to use the little time that was left to get herself out of the sight of enemies but trampling them, trying to get each foot to hit as many times as she could. Walker gradually built his speed as he ran with her, trying to keep himself a half step ahead to make her run faster. The strategy seemed to nettle her, and she responded as he had hoped, stretching her strides to make her small, light frame come abreast of him, her feet seeming barely to touch the ground until she and Walker caught up with Stillman, then split apart on either side of him, dashing into the woods.

They did not stop until they reached a low thicket that impeded their forward motion and made them pause to search for an opening.

In a moment, Mary had found a way around it, and Walker and Still-man followed her into a small, weedy clearing. They crouched to keep their heads below the top of the thicket and looked back through the upper branches.

Walker had expected to see the headlights of police cars bouncing along across the field toward them, or at least spotlights like the one mounted on the car they'd stolen, sweeping back and forth to light up the three running figures for the rifles. There was nothing. The cars had vanished. "Where are they?"

Stillman said, "Looks like they went ahead to wait for us. What do you suppose we ought to know that we don't?"

Mary said, "Everything. They've been living here for two hundred years. They probably know what we're going to do before we think of it."

"I think we have to assume that's close enough to the truth," said Stillman. "Let's try to do something irrational, that doesn't fit."

"Like what?"

"I don't know. . . . They must know we turned off on this side of the road. Maybe we could get on the other side of it and swim the river on the upstream side of the bridge."

Walker said, "That's irrational, all right. We just went to a lot of trouble to make it to the woods, where they couldn't see us. That would put us in plain sight for forty feet."

"Only if they're looking at the road. They're all in the woods, and probably on the downstream side of the bridge, watching for us to try to cross here."

Stillman stared into Walker's eyes for a moment, his face close in the darkness as though he were trying to read something behind them. "What do you think, Serena?"

"I think . . . I think it will kill me to go across that open road."

Walker said, "Well, then—"

"But," she added quickly, "I think they'll know that. They'll take one look, and think no sane person would do anything but get into the deepest part of the woods and crawl until he reached the river. I think we should do it."

Stillman subjected her face to the same scrutiny he had turned on

Walker. Then his eyes squinted. "You know, this could be the last time the three of us get to talk like this—maybe the last time any of us gets to talk to anybody—so we'd better agree on how this is going to work."

"Okay," said Walker.

"I go first, then Serena, then you, single file along the edge of the woods"—he pointed—"that way. I'll stop for a bit to be sure my theory doesn't have any obvious holes in it, then cross. If no guns go off when I do, you cross. When we get far enough from the bridge, we'll cut into the woods toward the river. If anything goes wrong—"

"We run into the woods," said Mary.

"Right," said Stillman. He began to turn toward the road, then stopped. "If we get separated, forget the other two and concentrate on getting yourself out. That's our only hope: that one of us gets out. You're not abandoning us, you're saving us."

He looked at the others, waiting for a word that never came. Reluctantly, Walker nodded, then Mary.

"All right," he said. "Let's get started before they have time to get comfortable."

He set off, moving toward the road at a fast walk, still just inside the edge of the woods, where their silhouettes would be lost among the dark shapes of the trees. When he was close to the road, he stopped and waited for the others to catch up. They squatted and remained still, listening. In the distance they could hear the chirping of frogs along the river, but it did not escape Walker that there should have been some much closer: the frogs were silent because there were men along the river near the bridge.

Stillman slipped off without warning. Walker could not tell whether it was because he was satisfied that no one was near or he was responding to some sense that the moment was right. Walker strained to hear, but there were no new sounds as Stillman drifted silently across the road. He listened for ten breaths, then patted Mary's shoulder, and she hurried across too. Walker waited again, but he began to have the uneasy feeling that his chance was about to pass. He crossed as quietly and quickly as he could, not stopping until he found the others in a set of low bushes just inside the woods a hundred feet beyond the road.

Stillman instantly stood and moved off, still keeping them under the trees. They continued toward the south for at least ten minutes. Now and then Walker would fall behind and look back, letting the others move ahead so he could be sure that any sound he heard would not be theirs. When he was satisfied, he would turn again and let his longer strides bring him up within a few feet of Mary's back. As they went, he began to lose the uneasy feeling that they were being watched. The noise of the frogs had been constant for a long time now, and he had seen nothing in the woods to indicate that anyone had come this way recently.

Stillman made the turn toward the river. When Walker reached the place where he had turned, he saw what Stillman must have been waiting for. There was a path. It seemed to be an old one, because there were sparse tufts of weed growing in it. Most of the bare spots were hard, with the tops of big rocks just at the surface. The path was deep, but it was narrow, only a foot wide at its extreme. He bent low to study it, trying to make his eyes discern what they could in the dark. He wasn't sure it was even a path. It could have been the bed of a small stream that emptied into the river during heavy rains, because its incline seemed relentlessly efficient, diverging only to go around the small rises and then straightening again toward the river.

He remembered paths like this from when he was a boy in Ohio. He and his friends had come across them frequently when they were in the woods, making their way to the remote fishing spots that were reputed to be the best. The boys had never been able to agree on what the paths meant or how they had gotten there. Walker had always argued that they were deer runs, on the grounds that if he had antlers he wouldn't want to get them caught crashing his way through bramble bushes and thickets. His real reason was that he had wanted to believe that he was penetrating forests that were still wild and alive.

Walker stopped again beside a big tree to watch and listen. He heard nothing, and silently ratified Stillman's judgment. He had probably chosen this path because there was nothing on it: no dry leaves to crackle, no twigs to snap under their feet. As he moved forward again, a cloud of mosquitoes began to whine around his ears and bounce against his face. He felt the irritated, panicky sensation they always provoked, but he resisted the urge to swat them. He gently waved them out of his eyes, zipped his stolen jacket to the neck, and kept going. The mosquitoes meant they were getting close to water, probably a low, swampy area where there were standing pools.

He could see that Stillman and Mary were under attack too, because they were moving faster, occasionally fanning their hands near their faces. They kept going, and then they abruptly stopped. Beyond the trees just ahead there was the silvery glow of moonlight on water.

Walker cautiously came up to them, and they all crouched beside the path to watch and listen. The night was still and hot, the air barely moving the upper leaves of the trees along the other side. The river here was wider than it had been in town, maybe fifty feet across, and it looked slower. The bed of the river was wider too, with weed-tufted banks about three feet high and then about ten feet of muddy flats that must have been covered after a rain.

There was no need for speech. If there was such a thing as safety tonight, a chance to see the sun again, it lay on the other side of that wide, sluggish stream of water.

Stillman moved forward two paces, sat on the grassy spot above the mudflat, turned his head to look up and down the river, and remained still for thirty seconds. Then he slipped off the edge and walked across the mudflat, his feet sinking in and making soft sucking noises when he pulled them out, leaving deep tracks. He walked until the water was at his thighs, then lowered himself into it, giving a little shiver. He pushed forward, half-swimming, half-walking, until he was in the middle of the channel. Walker could tell when the bottom fell off below his feet and he began to swim, because the current had been deceptive. Stillman was still moving toward the far bank, but the water was pushing him along with it to the right, in the direction of the covered bridge.

It was Mary's turn. Walker turned to look for her, but she was invisible. He was leaning forward to be sure she had not somehow gone already when he heard a swishing, rustling sound behind him and to his right. The sound made him cringe—she was making so much noise. But he saw that it was a shape bursting through the thick brush, and somewhere in the sight he caught a glint of dark metal. He dodged to the side.

The man seemed not to emerge from the bushes but to form out of shapes that Walker had already looked at and failed to put together. The man had stepped into the path, but Walker saw that the attitude of his silhouette was wrong: he was facing away, looking at the river, where Stillman was swimming.

The man made a hasty, jerky move to raise the shotgun to his shoulder. Mary came out of the bushes behind the man already running, and threw herself into the small of the man's back, bending his body like a bow. The shotgun pointed straight into the air, and for an instant, the man was looking at the sky.

He pivoted, trying to bring the butt of the shotgun down on Mary, but Walker pushed off on the balls of his feet with his head down. He caught the man in the stomach, felt the air huff out of him as they left the edge of the bank and, for an instant, flew.

They came down together, then slapped into the mud at the edge of the river, so that the man's head and shoulders made a splash but his back and legs were in the mud. Walker was aware that the shotgun had not come with them, but he could not free himself to find it. The man swung at him, and Walker's vision was jolted as the half-clenched fist knocked the side of his head. Walker endured a jab in the stomach, then brought his elbow and forearm down into the man's face, throwing the weight of his upper body into it.

The man's legs were working as he struggled to flip over, then straining to bend enough to bring a knee up to Walker's groin as he flailed at Walker's head with his arms. As both men grappled and sought to plant their feet, they moved deeper into the water, where Walker's weight was not enough to hold the man down.

The man rolled in the water; Walker brought his arm around the man's neck from behind, and sensed with revulsion what he could do, and realized that it was what he must do. He tightened his arm muscles, climbed higher up the man's back to get his knee onto the man's spine, and pushed him under.

The man fought, bucked, tried to roll again, but his efforts took him down into deeper water. The muddy bottom gave him no solid place to plant his feet, and Walker kept the pressure on him so the head never came to the surface. There were bubbles, great wrenching movements. Walker felt horror and shame as he clung to the man, sensing by touch the desperation and fear in every movement.

The man stopped. His body went limp. Walker clung to him. There was one final fit of kicking, twisting, bucking, and then the man's body did what Walker had known it would do, and gasped in an irresistible reflex to get air. The lungs filled with water, and the man lost consciousness. Walker waited, counting the seconds, until thirty had gone by and it was impossible that the man was alive. Then he let go and raised himself in the water.

Mary was at his shoulder. She hugged him, and he could see that her eyes were clenched shut and tears were coming, but they were not tears of relief. She was filled with regret, mourning with him for the horror and shame of what he had just done. Then she pulled away and walked with difficulty through the mud to the bank, bent over, lifted the shotgun out of the grass, and held it out to him with both hands.

Walker took it, and they moved together into the river. They kept going, leaning to the left against the steady weight of the current, and then they were waterborne. Mary swam with an awkward breaststroke, the clothes and shoes making her movements slow. Walker imitated her, holding the shotgun above the water with his right hand and stroking with the left. He was tired, and his arms were heavy, but he kept himself moving by telling himself lies about resting as soon as he made it to the other side.

His toe hit mud and he kicked again, and this time it held. He reached out for Mary, grasped her wrist, and pulled her toward the bank until he could tell that her feet were on the bottom too. Together they began to walk toward the bank. There was an eye-searing flash of light from his left as a flashlight beam passed over them, then a glare as it came back and held on them.

Mary ducked under the water, and a gun went off across the river. The splash of the bullet rose in a thin vertical column four feet up, and before it came down, Walker felt Stillman snatch the shotgun out of his hand. Stillman aimed quickly and fired, a report that slapped Walker's eardrums and made his diaphragm vibrate in his rib cage. The flashlight fell to the ground, bounced, and lay in the grass, its beam on the twitching hand and wrist of the man who had been holding it.

The silence returned, a much deeper quiet than there had been before. The frogs' chirping had been replaced by the silence of many beings stopping in place and listening. It lasted for five seconds, and then the woods seemed to erupt with sound. There were shouts, branches breaking, heavy footsteps. Beams from flashlights appeared and swept back and forth, then danced crazily on bushes and trees as men ran with them.

Stillman and Walker both turned at once. Mary was already sixty feet downriver from them. She waved to beckon them toward her. It was not a strategy, just the simple need to go in the direction the sounds weren't coming from, and to move away from lights into darkness. Both men went after her, trying to reach the bend in the river, the next spot where there might be something to hide them.

Mary disappeared beyond the turn, then Stillman. When Walker was about to slip past the end of the curve, he took a last look. The lights were converging. He could see a few of them playing about the mudflats, then finding something and staying on it. They had found the body of the man he had drowned. In a moment their eyes would pass across the deep footprints in the mud, and follow them into the river.

43

When Walker swam around the curve, Stillman and Mary were still ahead of him, floating downstream. Looming above them was the dark rectangle of the covered bridge. Mary was the first to be swept under it. She grasped one of the bridge's new concrete supports and held on. Walker took a couple of strokes to bring himself into line with it and stopped himself beside her. He looked around for Stillman and saw him clinging to the one beside theirs. Stillman pushed off, holding the shotgun above the water, caught their support, clung to it with one hand, carefully set the shotgun on top of the block of concrete, and lowered himself deeper into the water.

The tumult was growing. There was the sharp, hollow sound of men running across the bridge above their heads, shouts and footsteps from around the bend where the bodies had been found. From somewhere above them, they could hear a police radio. The female dispatcher's voice was unperturbed and unchanging. "Unit Ten, please proceed to Main and Washington to assist in clearing the bridge. Unit Three and Unit Six, please return to the station . . ." The answers were gruff and so muffled as to be incomprehensible from here.

Stillman moved closer to the others and whispered, "They're all going upstream to the bodies."

Mary said, "We left tracks in the mud. They'll know we're here."

"By the time they see tracks we can't be here," said Stillman. "Give the rest of them a couple of minutes to reach the bodies, and then we'll go up by the bridge."

Walker looked in the direction Stillman was indicating, and saw that the spot where the bridge rested on solid ground formed a wedge-shaped space that was protected a bit on each side by the steel girders that lay under the original structure. "All right," said Walker. "This time I'll go first. I'll try to get a car. Then you come behind me with the shotgun in case—"

"I know," Stillman interrupted.

Mary said, "We'll all go at once. It's harder to shoot three people before one of them gets to you."

Walker hesitated, but she said, "You know I'm right."

"Move into the shallows now and up onto dry land," said Stillman. "We've got to get some of the water out of our clothes, because the dripping makes noise."

The three drifted quietly to the shore under the bridge, then crawled higher into the low space at the end. The water ran off them, and Walker noticed that Stillman had been right about the noise. While they were lying on the ground the water streamed off them in small rivulets and soaked in without a sound. The night air felt cool on their wet bodies.

Walker waited for a shiver to pass, then pointed upward, and the others nodded. Walker turned and slowly, quietly made his way out along the bank until he could stand, then climbed the bank to the grassy, level space beside the outer wall of the covered bridge, and stopped to listen. The shouts of the searchers were rarer and farther off now, and the flashlights threw a dim glow in the trees beyond the bend in the river.

Walker stepped around the wall and looked into the bridge. There was a police car parked in the middle of the bridge facing the town. There was a man behind the wheel with the door beside him open.

Walker went down on his hands and knees and began to crawl toward the rear of the car, trying to stay in the blind spot to the right along the wall. The dispatcher's cool voice said, "The Main Street bridge is now clear. Units Five, Four, Twelve, Nine, and One, please proceed to New Mill Systems. All other units please stand by at your present locations and wait for instructions. We are now in a Code One Hundred situation. I repeat. Code One Hundred is now in effect."

The driver of the car seemed to be affected by the news. He straightened in his seat and flicked a switch on the dashboard as Walker reached the rear bumper of the car. The siren made a loud, shrill scream, then went lower and up again.

Walker rose to a crouch, dashed around the car to the door, and reached inside. He hooked his arm around the man's neck and dragged him from the seat onto the rough wooden planks of the bridge. The man groped at his side for his pistol, but Stillman came from behind, grabbed it out of its holster, and held it to the man's forehead, where he could see it.

Stillman held the shotgun out to Walker, and Walker released the man and took it. He peered into the interior of the car, then stood. "The key's in it."

Mary slipped by him, sat in the driver's seat, and started the engine, but there were other sounds now. Men were calling to one another in the woods. "Come on," she said. "That siren was to call them in."

Stillman dragged the man to the opening at the side of the bridge, the gun still at his head. He growled, "One chance. Jump or I kill you."

The man rolled over the sill of the opening and disappeared into the darkness, and a second later there was a splash. Walker got inside with Mary and rolled down the window. Stillman got into the back seat and said, "Go!"

Mary had backed up almost to the end of the covered bridge when Walker said, "Wait." She stopped.

They looked out through the opening at the far end of the bridge. Across the field, there were lights. The whole stretch of highway from the woods to the Main Street bridge and beyond looked like a river of white headlights, coming their way.

Mary said, "Maybe we can outrun them," but there was no conviction in her voice.

"We've got to do something to the bridge," said Stillman. "Give me the keys."

She handed them to him. He ran to the back of the car, opened the trunk, and stared inside. There were three kinds of fire extinguishers, a first-aid kit, a road-emergency kit. He opened them all as Walker came up beside him.

Stillman took a pair of scissors from the first-aid kit, then cut the hose from one of the fire extinguishers and stepped to the side of the car and handed the hose to Walker. "Siphon some gasoline onto the bridge."

Walker stuck the end of the hose down into the gas tank, sucked hard on it until he tasted the gasoline coming into his mouth, then lowered the hose as far as he could and tried to spit the poisonous taste out. There was a clear, steady stream of gasoline dribbling out and soaking into the boards of the bridge.

Stillman appeared at his side holding a highway flare. "That's enough gas. Get in."

As Walker got inside, Stillman yanked out the hose, capped the tank, and said to Mary, "Back out of here at least fifty feet, turn the car around, and wait."

Mary backed out across the clear approach to the bridge, turned and backed into the brush, then swung forward to aim the car at the highway. Walker spun in his seat, looked out the rear window, and watched Stillman.

Stillman stepped out of the covered bridge, bent double, and scraped the flare on the pavement to light the match on the end of it. There was a sputter of sparks, then a brilliant red glow like a slow-motion explosion. Stillman backed away a few steps, tossed the flare in a high arc, whirled, and ran.

The flare spun crazily in the air. Walker could see Stillman's broad body like a black void in the middle of the rosy glow, sprinting toward the police car. The flare reached apogee and started its descent, but before it could hit the boards of the bridge, it ceased to exist. There was the flash of the gasoline fumes trapped in the enclosed space igniting, and there were bright orange flames billowing out the entrance over Stillman's head like a hand reaching out to snatch him, then receding into the interior.

The dry, seasoned boards of the bridge's sides caught instantly, and the faint breeze that Walker had barely been able to detect a short time ago was now funneled into the tubular bridge as though the fire was sucking it inward. The superheated air had no place to escape, so it spread, rippling along the ridge beam to the other end in seconds. The boards of the roof began to issue whitish smoke, and in a moment it suddenly ignited, like the smoke above a candle.

Across the bridge, Walker watched the first of the cars pull up a short way off and stop. A figure got out on the driver's side, and Walker leveled the shotgun on it, then held his fire. Other doors opened, passengers scrambled out to stand on the road and watch. As they gathered together to gape at the tall, snapping flames that were engulfing the bridge, Walker gaped at them. The first figure that had exited was the young woman Walker had seen hours ago in her kitchen. He recognized the shining blond hair pulled tight on her head, and the dark green sweater. She held her arms out from her sides, and the two children came close to her, letting her hold them.

Stillman threw himself into the back seat and the car began to move. Walker could not take his eyes from the rear window. He stared past the woman at the road that was now lit up by the burning bridge. Other cars had been blocked, and drivers and passengers were getting out and walking ahead to stare at the fire. Walker said, "They weren't coming after us. They were trying to get out."

Mary was steering the car with the intense attentiveness of a person driving through a blizzard. "What do you mean?"

"It's families. Women, kids. They're evacuating the town."

Stillman had been peering out the back window too, the policeman's pistol in his hand. "He's right. It can't be anything else. When they found the guy in the water, they must have thought we'd already gotten out."

As the road came out of the woods and curved to head into the cleft between the two hills, Walker felt the car jerk to a stop. As he whirled to face the front, he saw the dark shapes of vehicles blocking the road, and then he was blinded by bright lights. The shapes of armed men seemed to emerge from the darkness on all sides at once. A man's voice came out of a speaker. It was loud and disembodied, but was not strained or tense. "Drop your weapons, and step away from the car with your hands in the air," it said calmly.

Stillman snapped, "Do it," and got out. Walker and Mary each took one step forward, and then Walker lost his bearings. What felt like a dozen hands threw him to the pavement on his belly, patted him down, took his wallet, wrenched his arms behind him, and snapped handcuffs on his wrists. He was aware of several pairs of men's feet striding back and forth near his head, and low voices conferring. A female voice said sharply, "Max Stillman."

Stillman's voice came from nearby, but Walker could not see him from here, because the three had been placed in a triangle with their feet toward one another. "I'm Stillman."

Walker could hear shuffling as men raised Stillman to his feet.

The woman said, "Special Agent Nancy Atkins, FBI. We've got two agents in that town, and all I want to hear from you right now is exactly where they are."

"I think they're in jail," said Stillman. "Before they started hunting us tonight, the cops rounded all the strangers up and took them to the police station."

Walker heard a murmur of muffled instructions, the sounds of running feet, men talking into radios, car engines. A minute later, he heard the deepening growl of helicopters as they swooped in overhead.

It was already afternoon when Stillman, Walker, and Mary walked down the road along the line of empty cars. The cars had been pushed to the side of the road, searched, and left with doors and trunks open. Federal officers were slowly, methodically taking fingerprints and making lists of the items they were finding, removing, and putting into large plastic bags with labels. Far down the line behind them, a second team was coming along more slowly. This group had toolboxes and a variety of electronic devices. They would come to a car and begin dismantling it: taking door panels off, probing the padding of seats, opening hoods, and peering up under the dashboards with gooseneck flashlights.

A convoy of four big panel trucks came up the road, slowly wobbled over the prefabricated surface that had been laid over the skeleton of the bridge, then accelerated toward them. They stepped off the road onto the shoulder to let the trucks pass, and Walker felt the hot, dusty wind from their passing. He stared after them.

Stillman said, "Damned convenient of the people of Coulter to load all their valuables into cars for us."

They walked toward the town. "All I want right now is to claim my rental car," Mary said. "Then I'm going to drive it to my hotel and take a bath."

Stillman said, "If they give you yours first, don't leave before you talk to me."

"Why not?"

"I want to see the notes you left in the car—the ones you took when you were in the public records office in Concord."

Walker turned to look at him. "You're staying here? What are you doing?"

"I want to hang around the FBI people and see if I can get a copy of their list of all the people in the town."

"But we made one when we were looking for Scully's cousin."

"Of course we did," said Stillman. "But I'm waiting for the official, revised edition. Between the car registrations and house deeds and fingerprints, they'll probably come up with a good list by the end of the day."

"Why are you doing all this?" asked Mary. "They're all in jail already."

"I don't work for the FBI. What I'm getting paid for is finding out what made these people pick McClaren Life and Casualty."

"I'm not sure how my notes are going to tell you that," said Mary.

Stillman shrugged. "We'll see."

When the three reached the police station, the FBI agents who had set up a temporary headquarters there released the cars to them. Mary Casey's rental car and Stillman's vehicle were both in the police lot with their doors open. Mary took her keys out of her pocket, opened the trunk of her car, looked inside, and muttered something under her breath.

"Something wrong?" asked Stillman.

"My notes were in my laptop. It looks like the Coulter police noticed it after they towed the car. Want to see it?"

Stillman and Walker looked in the open trunk. The computer looked as though it had been broken up with a sledgehammer, then run over by a car.

"I don't see the hard drive," said Walker.

"We never will," said Mary. "That's just the mess they made getting to it." Then she slammed the trunk, got into the driver's seat, and started the engine.

Stillman nudged him. "Go ahead," he muttered. "She'll look once, and if you're not on your way, she's gone."

Walker watched Mary turn and glance over the seat at him, then begin to back up. She swung the car around, then pulled forward so it was headed out toward Main Street, stopped, and slid over to sit in the passenger seat, looking straight ahead through the windshield.

Stillman stared at her thoughtfully, shrugged, and said, "See you later." He watched while Walker got in behind the wheel, made the corner, and headed down the quiet street toward the temporary bridge out of town.

It was nine hours before Stillman turned up at Mary's hotel room. He knocked loudly, and when Walker came to the door in a hotel bathrobe, he handed him several sheets of paper stapled at the corner. Walker stared at each page, looking at the long column of family names and addresses. When he had finished, he looked at Stillman. "Does this do anything for you?"

Stillman shook his head. "I faxed the list to McClaren's. It doesn't do anything for the personnel office, either. None of the surnames from Coulter match an employee. If there is an inside person, we can't get him the easy way."

Walker frowned. "But if there is, it's got to be possible to find out who it is. They registered everything with the state: births, deaths, marriages, divorces." He glanced over at Mary. "If there is an inside person, he's got to be a relative."

Mary propped herself up on an elbow on the bed and said, "Families do have two sides. The person wouldn't necessarily have the same surname. It wouldn't take much to trace the genealogies back one more generation and see if there are any cousins Walker knows." She gave a half-smile. "You have to buy me a new laptop anyway, Max. I'm willing to get it in Concord and spend a few days on this."

An hour later they were on the road to Concord. By late afternoon, Walker, Stillman, and Casey were sitting at a long wooden table in the Health and Welfare Building on Hazen Drive, staring at the first set of names that their search of the New Hampshire archives had produced. They worked for two days after that, looking at birth records, digging up marriage certificates, and constructing family trees. At the end of the third day, Walker raised his eyes from the latest list of names and said quietly, "I know who it is."

Walker was at his desk in the cubicle when he heard the elevator's doors hum and slide open. He listened to the *pock-pock-pock* of high heels coming down the open aisle of the bay, then saw Maureen Cardarelli in a gray business suit with a short skirt move past the entrance to his cubicle. Her eyes slid in his direction, then forward, then did an exaggerated double take. She stopped and walked to the doorway warily. "Walker?"

"Accept no substitutes," he said.

"You're here?"

"I think we just said that," he said. "How have you been?"

She ignored his question. "I . . . can't believe it. You're still in analysis?"

He knitted his brows and shrugged.

"You're supposed to be . . . we heard you were out of here," she said. "You were going to be one of the myriad vice presidents that nobody ever sees, who fly around the world writing policies for sultans' jewelry collections and things." Walker could hear a tiny tinge of malice in her voice, a small but growing hope that what she said was not true.

Walker shrugged again. "I just got back, and you're the first one I've seen."

Her face seemed to flatten. "Well, I hope I haven't ruined a surprise or something." Now she was afraid it was true.

Walker said, "I doubt it, but if you did, I'll act surprised and cover for you."

She looked uncomfortable. He had never seen her at a loss for words before. She shuffled her feet as though they were trying to step off without her. "Well, welcome home," she said. "I'd better go check my voice mail." She gave him a warm, studied smile that she sensed was so good that it almost rescued her from embarrassment, then turned and disappeared. He heard the *pock-pock-pock* receding down the aisle.

The next one was Kennedy. His head appeared in the doorway, and Walker sensed that Cardarelli must have told him. "Hey!" he said in surprise. "You're back."

"I guess so," said Walker.

"Boy, you really missed a lot around here," said Kennedy.

"Not as much as you did."

"Really?" His eyes shifted to look up the aisle, then down it. He seemed to see something that troubled him. "Got to hear all about it, but we'll have to talk later. I've got a pile of stuff on my—"

Walker interrupted. "We're not going to be able to talk later, so I've got to ask you this now. Why Ellen Snyder?"

Kennedy stood absolutely still, his eyes on Walker. "I don't understand."

"I mean, the rest of it makes sense. I've thought about it so much that it's not even surprising anymore. It was your family, your town. You probably grew up knowing you were going to get inside some company and do something like this. But you knew Ellen. She liked you, was nice to you. Why not somebody you'd never met, never seen, in some other part of the company?"

Kennedy's eyes were bright and intense, never moving from Walker's. His mouth slowly curled up in a hint of amusement. He seemed to lean forward slightly, coming closer. His lips began to move in an almost unvoiced whisper, so Walker had to read them. "That's . . . how . . . it's . . . done."

For this moment, it seemed to Walker that the rest of the world had been cleared of people, that he and Kennedy were the only ones. The look on Kennedy's face was unspeakable, not the look of conscious evil, but a look of something that wasn't exactly human. The eyes were watching him, not with cruelty but with an undistracted interest that was completely devoid of empathy, like an animal looking at something that was part of its diet.

Walker was jolted out of his paralysis by sudden, quick footsteps, so near that he knew what the noise had to be. The voice belonged to Special Agent Nancy Atkins. "William Kennedy." Walker couldn't see her from his desk, but from the angle of Kennedy's eyes, he knew she was flashing a badge, or something. Kennedy's head turned back toward Walker. He stood absolutely still and stared into Walker's eyes as Nancy Atkins said, "You have the right to remain silent. Anything you say can and will be used against you in a court of law." Kennedy kept staring at Walker while his hands were being tugged around behind him by the other agents and the handcuffs put on. "You have the right to have an attorney present during questioning."

Walker closed his eyes, not wanting even to hear, but her voice reached back to him all the way from the elevator. "If you cannot afford an attorney . . ." He heard the *ding,* then the doors opening. After a few seconds, they closed.

Walker opened his desk drawer. The report he had written a month ago was here, a copy that Joyce must have left when it was distributed. He set it on his desk and stood up.

Stillman's shape blocked the doorway for a second, then moved aside. As Walker stepped out, Mary stood before him with her arms folded. "Who's the babe, Walker?"

"Babe?" He hesitated and looked around. "Oh. Maureen Cardarelli. She works in another section."

"She seems to be working your section. Tell me about her."

Walker considered for a moment. "She's a woman who . . . a woman who, if she thought I was in danger, would probably get into her car. She wouldn't necessarily drive toward me."

Stillman said to Mary, "He means he's yours to torment at your leisure as you see fit."

"Oh?" said Mary. "You know these things?"

Walker shrugged. "Kind of unlikely, I know, but he does."

Stillman put one hand on Walker's shoulder and the other on

Mary's and they set off down the aisle of the bay. "I heard Cardarelli blowing the surprise McClaren had planned for you. Too bad."

Mary's eyes widened. "You mean that stuff about sultans? That was for real?"

"No, that part was a load of crap," said Stillman. "Walker couldn't sell life insurance to a man being eaten by a crocodile. But they'll take care of him." Stillman looked at Walker. "What do you think? Want to go up to the twelfth floor right now?"

"No," said Walker. "I want to go to Joyce Hazelton's office and pick up the paychecks that have been piling up for me. Then, I think the three of us should take a cab to the Clift Hotel."

"What for?"

"It's my turn to buy lunch. And drinks. The big old-fashioned kind. We'll need you to search the memories of your youth and draw a blueprint for the bartender. Then you get another cab."

"Then what?"

"You'll have to search the memories of your youth for that, too," Mary snapped.

"I didn't mean that," said Stillman. "I meant after that. After your two paychecks are spent."

"Then I'll decide what to do next." He saw Stillman studying him. "Don't you remember? You set me free."

Walker was moving toward Joyce Hazelton's office, but Stillman hit the button for the elevator. "Joyce isn't in there. She's waiting for me in my car." The doors opened and he stepped into the elevator. "We'll have to start with the drinks. It's not lunchtime yet."

ABOUT THE AUTHOR

THOMAS PERRY won an Edgar for *The Butcher's Boy,* and *Metzger's Dog* was a *New York Times* Notable Book of the Year. His other books include *The Face-Changers, Shadow Woman, Dance for the Dead,* and *Vanishing Act,* chosen as one of the 100 Favorite Mysteries of the Century by the Independent Mystery Booksellers Association. He lives in Southern California with his wife and their two daughters.